Reviews of
Little Dove, Lakota Ancestor

"It's really very exciting writing! I'm impressed."
- Heather Harder, Author and U.S. Presidential Candidate 1996 and 2000. Crown Point, Indiana

"The chapters about Greece are absolutely riveting!"
- Angel Chakaris, Entrepreneur, Telluride, Colorado.

"You come away with a deep feeling of the Native American spirit and view of life and the world. Well worth reading just for that."
- Eric Tischler, writer, Nevada

"This book is fabulous! There is so much information in it and so much history, yet it is easy to read."
- Judy Howe, Teacher, Macungie, Pennsylvania

"I loved your book! Of all the books I've ever read, yours is one of my top three or four favorites."
- Cristina, Teacher, Sacramento, California

"This book could be a best seller!"
Director, Aspen Writers Foundation,
Aspen, Colorado

Little Dove, Lakota Ancestor

Inspired by a True Story

Sakina Blue-Star

This Docu-novel is part
accurate family history and part
imagination. You get to decide
which is which.

Dedication

I would like to dedicate this book to my ancestors, who are watching over me -- especially to Little Dove and her husband, with thanks for their guidance and sharing of their Lakota Sioux and Choctaw-Cherokee wisdom. I also dedicate it to my descendants: my sons and daughters and their children and all of those who are yet to come.

To those who also have been deprived of their Native Indian heritage: I hope it will be helpful to find out about how I discovered mine. Many people know they had an Indian Gramparent, but were told little about them. ASK! Your ancestors are happy to help, if you ask. They can guide you to answers.

We all have many earth-walks. It is the nature of karma (i.e., what goes around, comes around) to walk sometimes in boots, sometimes in moccasins, to see what that is like. Some people who killed off Indians in a previous life come back to experience the result of the result of their actions; to feel the hopelessness of having lost everything they hold dear, being alienated from society, or the despair of living on bleak reservations.

On the other hand, many of those who were Native Americans before have come back in pale bodies. But they bring with them a love of Mother Earth, and all her children. It was prophesied: the Ancestors said they would play a trick on the Red Man; they would come back in White bodies!

We live in a time of change. There has been a wondrous resurgence of Native American spirituality in recent years. Enlightened beings such as Dhyani Ywahoo, Jamie Sams and her grandmother Twylah, Sun Bear, Wallace Black Elk and others have shared their wisdom with us, and we are grateful.

To all of the children Of the Sky Father and the Earth Mother, I lovingly dedicate this story.

Many Blessings,

Sakina

The Gillespie Plantation

"I grew up on a plantation in Mississippi, but we freed the slaves long before the Civil War," Sara told her grand-children. "And we didn't call them Servants. We called them, "the Help".

Contents

Foreword

I was not told about my Native American heritage when I was growing up. A lot of other people also had that same dark secret locked securely
in the family closet -- but are now interested in bringing it out. After all,
it was said, Indians were 'savages'! It was dangerous to admit that ancestry
-- they might be killed off, carted off, or re-programmed: denied their culture. This book tells about how I found out about my Native heritage. Much
of this family memoir is true; other parts have come through inspiration,
and might not be.

In other words, it's kind of "Hit or Myth."

It's hard for those of the younger generation to understand the depth
and intensity of the prejudice that existed towards people of Color (Blacks,
Indians, etc.) until quite recently, especially in the Deep South, and thus
the reason for hiding such ethnic origins. An 8th Black blood made you
Negro, and you could be bought and sold, violated, beaten and worked to
death in the 1800s. As late as the 1960's, Black People were not shown on
TV, except occasionally as maids or Minstrels.

In Germany of the 1930's, some people who thought they were Ger-
mans were shocked to find out that they had a Jewish Gramparent they had
not been told about, in order to protect them from prejudice. But the Nazis
were thorough in their genetic research, and so those of 'tainted blood'
were slated to be exterminated, along with other non-Aryans. American
Indians, or mixed-bloods, often suffered a similar fate.

In the 1950s, Hollywood showed us what Indians were like. They rode
around circling the wagons of innocent pioneers who wanted to "tame the
land"; they said "Ugh!" a lot, yelled war whoops, and liked to scalp people.
In John Ford's film 'The Searchers', John Wayne played a man who was out

taming the West when his niece, played by Natalie Wood, was captured by Comanches. Wayne tried to find her for years, and when he finally found her, he discovered that she was living with her Indian husband. Wayne said, "She's been with a buck", and after that he was chasing her around trying to kill her. Back then, that was the attitude most white people had.

The message was plain! Better dead than bed a Red.

Columbus Day is nothing to celebrate for Native Americans. When Christopher arrived, he was greeted by the Taino tribe, who welcomed him by saying, "Taino Teh!" – "Take my Heart!" The Discoverers took not only their hearts, but the rest of them as well, killing off thousands of these gentle Caribbean people. There are few survivors left.

I am a descendant of holocaust survivors.

At the 50th Anniversary Commemoration Ceremony of the Nazi holocaust horror, Jewish survivors of that appalling episode in history spoke eloquently in Washington, D.C. One survivor told about his escape from a concentration camp, and his subsequent flight to this country.

"In conclusion," he said, "I thank God that I live in the United States of America, a free country, where there has never been a tyrant, and there has never been genocide."

Tell that to the Native Americans, I thought!

It is the other holocaust that I speak of, the one perpetrated by said United States of America, whose official policy toward the indigenous population of this land in the 1800s was one of extermination, and later, relocation of the remnant, to bleak reservations. "Kill the Indians, by whatever means necessary," was a typical Cavalry Officer command at that time. The other alternative was assimilation, after a suitable period of re-programming (education), to turn the 'little savages' into 'civilized human beings'.

Scholars have said recently that there were from 65 to 90 million Native Americans a few centuries ago -- and now there are officially three million. Is that not genocide?

In Nazi Germany, millions of 'undesirables' were herded into boxcars and exterminated in gas chambers. In the 'Land of the Free' (and once home of the braves), getting rid of the indigenous people was done by warfare, sometimes slaughtering whole villages, like Little Dove's (my great-grandmother); by introducing disease or alcohol, or by forced relocation.

Hitler got his ideas for concentration camps from what he read about the treatment of Indians in Western novels. The Cherokee were first penned up in camps, where they often died of the imported diseases of their captors, to which they had no immunity -- and then taken on their 'Trail of Tears', a 900-mile death march from their mountain-forest homes in the south-east to bleak reservations in Oklahoma. On the trail, over 4,000 of them perished, due to ill treatment, exhaustion, or exposure to blizzards and freezing weather.

My ancestors were survivors of this American holocaust. They chose the alternative of assimilation, after their people were killed off or 'removed' to what was thought to be worthless land. This is their story.

"Where shall we hide the children?" the Assiniboine Grandmothers asked. "We'll hide them among the enemy!" it was decided. This was the reason for so many mixed marriages, and adoptions. They wanted the genetic memory, the DNA that came from the Star People, the SPIRIT of the Native Americans to survive. Grandfather Long Bow was Choctaw-Cherokee, and the Cherokee say they came from the stars -- the Pleiades. They did not want the Star-Knowledge to die out.

So we became mixed-bloods, Metis, and the blood-line continued. And even though we were not told who we were, some of the old abilities of the Seers in the family remained and resurfaced; and I, for example, became a Spirit-Speaker, with my ancestors being able to speak through me.

This is the story of Little Dove, my maternal great-grandmother, and other relatives. Her Lakota Sioux village, her family and friends were annihilated, but she managed to escape. As a young girl, she was adopted into a Wasichu (White) family; she adapted, she survived.

I cannot prove my Native American heritage. They didn't take a census before the Cavalry killed off Little Dove's entire village; and as we 'passed for White,' to prevent us from being taken on the Trail of Tears, I am not on Cherokee rolls, though our blood-type is different from others.

My sister Mallory, however, did find some family records that seem to corroborate our Scottish-Cherokee ancestry: "Four Gillespie brothers came over from Scotland and settled in Georgia (in Cherokee country), and established the Black Hawk Trading Post there. Three of these Scots-Irish brothers eventually went north, and the other moved to Mississippi." That's where my grand-mother Sara Gillespie (Little Dove's daughter) grew up. Mallory said we also have a strong connection to the Keetoowah band of the Cherokee Nation, who are currently attempting to get back to their ancestral lands in Arkansas.

The film 'Dances with Wolves' showed how we lived, but it was the movie 'Little Big Man' that showed how we died. "My God!" I thought when I saw it. "They finally told it the way it really was!" That was in the Cavalry slaughter scene where no-one survived but Little Big Man (Dustin Hoffman) and Grandfather (Chief Dan George), who thought he was invisible.

On the Cherokee side, we were able to 'fake it' -- to pass for White – partly because of a Scots-Irish grandfather way back.

I thanked my seer friend Sandy for enlightening me about my ancestors. "Well, your grandmother came into the room," she said. "She wanted you to know!"

In February of 1996 I went down to Mexico and rented a little cottage by the sea, so that I could get away from the constant interruptions and distractions of my busy life in Sedona, Arizona, and WRITE. And so I did.

I intended to tell a different story: About the amazing people and the extraordinary events that had filled my life since moving to Sedona in 1983. I wrote about that for a while. Then one day I thought, 'I'll write a little story about how I found out about my American Indian heritage - and then I'll get back to writing the book.' I thought it was going to be a short story about my ancestry. But once I got started, it just kept flowing. I was receiving information from the spirits of my forebears.

My ancestors wanted their story to be told!

Happily, the tide has turned, and many people these days are interested in the wisdom and ways, the beauty and the spirituality, of Native Americans; and of the Star People from whom they descended and with whom some of them are still in touch. That is the purpose of this book, to share the knowledge I have learned from my friends of many tribes, and that I have received from my ancestors. It is time to release the pain, and get on with the HARMONY and UNCONDITIONAL LOVE. After all, we have each walked in many moccasins, many shoes. Each earth-walk is a lesson, for the experience, for the understanding, in order to become a completed entity.

Soon Planet Earth, and the pure-hearted ones, will shift into a higher realm, into the 5th dimension, I believe that most of this story is true, although much of it has come from the realm of spirit. It is a combination family memoir and information received through inspiration. Some things have checked out to be accurate, and some have not. It is hard even for me to delineate just where the fine line is between fact and fantasy. Perhaps some of it is how it might have been. But some persons who have checked out certain chapters for accuracy have received many of those `shivers' that tell that a truth has been told.

In any case -- it is my story! I hope you enjoy it.

Sakina Blue-Star, Sedona, Arizona * June 1997

In the Sacred canyons of Sedona, Arizona, Sakina became a voice for her ancestors Little Dove of the Lakota Sioux, her Choctaw-Cherokee husband, and their daughter Sara.

This is the story of how they survived the Native American holocaust byadapting to the White world.

Explanation and Appreciation

Explanation

Some of the words or phrases in this book are not grammatically correct, but they're the way Native People talk. They say 'I was gifted a canupa' (pronounced chanupa) – a Ceremonial Pipe -- instead of "I was given a pipe." They speak of 'fringed regalia,' not 'a dress'. Black People in the deep South in the 1800's spoke with an African accent; I have attempted to re-create their speech, as well as that of my Scots ancestors. I capitalize some words to emphasize their importance, or some syllables for purposes of pronunciation. Anglos say Pow-hattan; Cherokee medicine man Rolling Thunder's daughter White Fawn said, "We say 'PO-ha-tahn." The Great Spirit may be called Ton-KA-shi-la; Grandfather.

Appreciation

I would like to give my heartfelt thanks to the wonderful people who have helped me put this project together.

My gratitude goes to Satara, who patiently typed up page after page in Mexico (I wrote it by hand), and checked out each chapter for mistakes.

John-Aaron Bauman was truly helpful when he was staying at my house in 2008 and I was re-typing and editing my book. When my computer would give me a hard time at 2 A.M., he would patiently come in from the next room when he heard me say, "Aaah!" and help me through the latest crisis. Thank you, friend.

Genii Townsend, a Puppeteer, and her partner Charles Betterton were delighted with my little mini-museum, part of my vast collection of artifacts and dolls of all Nations, honoring all Peoples. Genii wrote a book about a Crystal City manifesting in Sedona, and was intrigued to read an article about me telling of Sedona being called "The Crystal City of Light" in ancient Lemurian times. Charles said he could help me get my book out, with the intention of generating income for my planned 'Inter-Cultural Museum and Learning Center', in conjunction with Rev. Mary-Margareht Rose's nonprofit church and Earth Mother Father Foundation - Healing and Learning Center. I spent a year working on getting the book in shape, going through a couple of computers. Charles lent me his when mine died. But then he went off to California, and I gave up again.

In 2010 Glenn Molinari came along. He liked my story about Little Dove, my Lakota ancestor. He went through the process of getting it properly copyrighted. He re-formatted it on his computer and added the artwork and photographs. Glenn came over to my house many times to help me with my computer - it's not my language!

My friend, the late Rev. Mary-Margareht, a spiritual teacher and healer, said she would help through the Earth Mother Father Foundation, a non-profit spiritual and healing Center. Proceeds from the book are to go to a Learning Center and Inter-cultural Museum.

Eric Tischler worked with us at a distance, devoting a great deal of time to format it as an e-book and then re-formatting it for this print edition, and created a new web site for it at http://www.littledovelakotaancestor.net. Bless you, Eric!

I would also like to give my thanks to my many friends and teachers, some of whom have taken me into their family, who have shared their wisdom teachings with me: Cherokees Willie Whitefeather, Dhyani Ywahoo, and Grandmother Golden Eagle; Apache healer Billie Topa Ta-tay (Four Winds); Lakota Wallace Black Elk and his cousin Grandmother Eloise, who gifted me with the name Blue-Star; Assiniboine Georgia White and her daughter Morgenstarr; Pima elder Pete Jackson; the Dineh (Navaho) Benally family; and the Hopi: Elders Grandfather David Monongye & Grandfather Martin, and youngers, Roanna and Lewis and their wonderful family. And most especially, thanks to my dear friend Thundercloud.

As to my beloved soul-mate, Sundance – he will be the subject of another book, 'Many Lives, One Love'

This is a very different world, than the one in the 1990s when I wrote about my Ancestors, my Family. I hope that Little Dove still soars!

Sometimes the story flows,
and sparkles in the sun…
And then around another bend,
it slows.
But curving once again,
and rippling in the wind,
In night's dark beauty
Star-shine glows.

—Sakina Blue-Star

Sakina went up onto a high ridge, by the Kachina Mama, raised her climbing staff to the sky and made a dedication: "Use me! As long as it is in the Light, and to help!" As she spoke, hundreds of birds flew around over head.

Chapter 1

Looking Back Through Time

Sedona, Arizona is a magical place! Native Americans have long come to these Sacred Mountains and Canyons on pilgrimages to seek their vision – to know what the Great Spirit wanted for their lives. As in the Bermuda Triangle, where remnants of Atlantis are said to be, this Arizona Mecca, this vortex-energy area can easily propel receptive ones into other dimensions.

In this town full of psychics, Sandra Bowen is one of the best. Co-author of 'Mysteries of the Crystal Skulls Revealed', she knows how to listen, telepathically, to these members of the crystal kingdom.

When I visited her in January of 1995, I was wondering what was coming up next.

"Hold this crystal," she said to me, handing me a small, palm-size quartz point. Then she took it and held it, closing her eyes and focusing with her inner vision. She told me about several possibilities that might be coming up, and also about some past-life connections I knew to be accurate.

"Thank you!" I said, feeling that the message was complete. Then, as an afterthought, I asked:

"Oh. Do I have any Native American heritage I'm not already aware of?" I knew I was related to Chief PO-ha-tahn (as he is called by his tribe), and his daughter Pocahontas, but that was back a ways.

"Yes," she said, focusing. "Your great-grandmother."

I was startled! My great-grandmother? Why was I never told? "On which side? My mother's, or my father's?"

"Your mother's side!"

I was amazed! My grandmother had grown up on a plantation in the Mississippi Delta; my mother had always emphasized the importance of proper Southern lady-like behavior.

"What tribe?" I asked. Pause.

"Sioux."

"Her name was Sue? Oh...." I laughed. "Lakota. Of course."

How exciting! That would explain so many things! Such as why I was so obsessed with all things Native American. It was in the blood.

Elated, I went home and told my friend Jackie Matrunick, who was staying with me at the time, about my discovery.

Jackie shared my excitement. She, too, was of mixed-blood, and her Cherokee heritage had also been hidden in her family in order to survive.

The Cherokee people were taken from their homes in the Smoky Mountain area in a forced removal called 'The Trail of Tears', in the early 1800s, in which more than 4,000 of them died on the way to Oklahoma.

I knew about Jackie's Native American heritage, but until my reading with Sandra Bowen in 1995, I did not know about my own -- except for being related to Pocahontas, but that was way back. And, on the East Coast, I was adopted into the Wampanoag family and tribe of the elder, Princess Evening Star, as they called her; sister of Chief Wild Horse.

I knew that the Spirits of the Ancients would speak through me, but I did not know why. I only knew that they would speak, or sing, or dance, through me; ever since I had gone up onto a Sacred Mountain near Sedona many years ago, raised my climbing staff to the skies, and made a dedication to the Great Spirit:

"Eh-YO! Use me! As long as it is in the Light, and to help!", I cried out -- but in an ancient language that I had not learned in this lifetime.

Jackie was staying with me in Sedona in January of 1995, and her husband Stan came up from Phoenix to do some of the portraits of the Spirit Guides that he is famous for. He toured cross-country for some 40 years, often appearing on TV, in newspapers and in magazines. In his traveling ministry, Rev. Stanley Matrunick did over a quarter-of-a-million Spirit portraits, along with messages from guides, guardians, teachers and Masters in spirit.

He taught me how to do Spirit portraits, shortly after I had moved to Sedona in 1983, and I have been doing them ever since. But besides his ability to do pastel portraits of what some might call guardian angels, he can draw recognizable portraits of loved-ones-on-the-'other side'.

"Let's ask Stan to do a portrait of your great-grandmother!" said Jackie. "But we won't tell him anything about her ahead of time." Like her husband, Jackie is an inter-denominational minister, as am I.

I was excited and anxious to have my session with Stan. I asked for my maternal great-grandmother.

He turned on the tape recorder, said a prayer asking for truth and what would be helpful, and began drawing on his lush velvety-velour colored paper with rapid strokes.

"She was an Indian woman," he began.

More quick strokes. "Do you know what tribe?" I asked; I was looking for a confirmation.

"Was she Cherokee?" he asked.

Oh. "I was told Sioux," I replied.

"Well, I feel Cherokee around her. I see her along the Mississippi River... and the Missouri. That's where she met her husband. He was a trapper, or a scout."

I looked at the map later and noticed that the Missouri River went up into Sioux country, the Dakotas; as well as flowing into the Mississippi, which went down South to where my grandmother grew up.

The portrait was wonderful! "She liked red," Stan remarked, as we observed her high-necked red dress. On it she wore five strands of beads; on one of them there was a bone pendant with an eagle on it, flying over a mountain.

"I have one like that!" I said excitedly. I later realized why it had such significance for me. In that other lifetime, I had given it to her. She always wore it.

The portrait revealed a handsome woman, strong but kind, with black eyes, and black hair parted in the middle and pulled around back to be wrapped in a bun -- the way my grandmother always wore her long hair, though hers was grey or white when I knew her. (You can see this picture in Chapter 9.)

It came back to me that soon after I had taken the six-hour course in spirit-guide portraiture from Stan, while I was practicing drawing, to see which spirit was with me at the time -- my maternal grandmother, Sara (we called her Amam), turned up! I was surprised that she was still around me. She had been much closer to my older sister, Mallory.

I was thrilled with Stan's portrait of my great-grandmother, and with the information that was coming through. But I wanted more confirmation. Rather than go seek out psychics, I thought: why not seek my own vision? I do this for others, why not do it for myself?

I sat quietly and took a few deep breaths to relax. I gave thanks to the Creator, and love to the Creation; surrounded myself with a protective blue light; and asked for whatever was of truth, and which would be helpful at this time, to come through.

What came to mind was something that had happened a dozen years before. Frank Baronowski, a radio and TV personality from Phoenix, had come to town. He would demonstrate his ability to take someone back into other lifetimes through hypnotic regression. If the person in the hypnotic state remembered being in the Civil War, or World War II, for instance, Frank would find the official records afterward that would prove that he or she had, indeed, been in that regiment, or unit.

I had participated in a large group session with Frank at a church -- but he came back to do another session at someone's home, with about a dozen people gathered. He chose me as a subject.

I was asked to relax, in a reclining chair; the back was down, feet raised.

"You are going deep, deep, into a state of total relaxation," the voice droned. "You are going back, back, back into the past....

"Okay. Now you are going forward. You are in your 15th summer.

"What do you see?"

"I see tipis."

"What else do you see?"

"Women scraping hides, drying meat on racks, men coming back from the hunt. There's a stream on the right, and a forest on the left."

"What are you called?" he asked.

"I am called 'Girl Who Loves the Forest'. I love to go into the forest, and talk to the birds, the rabbits, the raccoons, and the deer. Sometimes we have to kill the deer, but always we say 'I know that your life is just as important as mine; but if you will feed us now, then we will feed your children

4

when we go back to the earth. And every time I pass this way, I will honor your spirit!' In this way there was balance."

"Okay," said Frank. "Now advance five years. Where are you now?"

"Inside a tipi."

"Who else is there?"

"My husband, and our little son. I love my husband very much -- he is strong and brave, and he is a good hunter. He loves me too; but he does not say so, because he is a man!"

"Okay. Now go ahead to the end of that lifetime."

I gasped! "Oh, NO! I can't!" I felt horror at the scene I was seeing. "The Long Knives got me! I fell on top of my daughter; I was trying to protect her...."

I saw clearly the vast plains I had been running through after all of the people of our village had been slaughtered by the U.S. Army, and the two cavalry-men galloping along. One of them skewered me by thrusting his sword through my back, jerking it out, and riding on. I saw my body, which covered that of my daughter, getting smaller and smaller on the empty plains, as my Spirit rose high above....

"It's okay, it's okay," said Frank quickly; "Now go forward three days. Is anybody there now?"

"Yes. My brother."

"Is your daughter still alive?"

"Yes, just barely."

"How did your brother know where to find her?"

"My Spirit went and told him."

"All right. Come back to the present now. One, two, three. You're back."

Wow! What an experience!

Eloise Halsey was a Lakota Sioux woman of great wisdom. She is now in spirit, but she was my dearest friend for many years. Eloise, or Shining Blue Star, grew up on the Rosebud Sioux reservation in South Dakota, where she was very close to her cousin, Traditional Lakota Sioux spokesman Wallace Black Elk.

Wallace was her protector, her best friend, when they were growing up. But when she grew up, she married Henry and moved to Phoenix where he worked at the Indian School for 40 years. My husband Sundance and I drove down from Sedona to visit her one day.

As we sat there, she said, "Oh, Sakina, you'd be surprised at what's on your lap!"

I looked down, surprised all right. All I saw was lap.

"It's a turtle! It's dancing around in a circle, kicking up its little arms and legs. You were called Turtle Woman, when you were a Sioux Medicine Woman."

'Wonderful!' I thought. It felt right.

She turned to Sundance. "And you had a bear," she told him. "You raised him from when he was a cub."

"I remember," he replied. "I've always loved bears." Sundance had a teddy-bear I had given him, which he called 'Grrr.' It reminded him of the one he had cherished as a child, which had been his only friend.

Grrr is a very special bear, a Medicine Bear. He wears a small child's leather vest with fringe, which I had found at a thrift-shop and brought home to Sundance, thinking that he could use the leather for a medicine pouch or something.

"Oh, no!" he exclaimed. "That's for Grrr!"

Grrr Bear was later gifted with a Taos drum, a Hopi rattle, a Lakota beaded rosette necklace, and a deerskin fringed pouch for his crystals and other things that Medicine Bears use. He has traveled all over Turtle Island, Mexico, and Canada with me -- he is my protector -- and he emits great love and healing energy wherever he goes.

"His name is really Chief Grrr," Sundance said of this inter-tribal bear. "And he has a Russian cousin, named Grrr-ba-chief." He has participated in many ceremonies with me, at medicine wheels out in the sacred canyons.

Meditating on these things, going back in time, I remembered being Turtle Woman, in that Lakota (Sioux) lifetime. I called my daughter Little Dove in that earth-walk, and I had given her the bone pendant with a fly-ing eagle on it that she always wore. No wonder it had seemed so special when I found one in recent times!

It was interesting to realize that my grandmother in this lifetime would have been my granddaughter in that other time. The Hopi believe that we come back in the same family, as a grandchild, niece or nephew; and the Lakota (before the White Man), believed in many earth-walks also.

My vision continued: I was seeing my brother disposing of my body, and doing an honoring ceremony; then taking my Little Dove, who was 9 years old at the time, to a safe place high in the inaccessible reaches of the Teton mountain range. There he gave her into the keeping of a Medicine Woman elder, who lived in a cave, and who taught her the ways of healing, with herbs, crystals, and with guidance from TonKAshila, the Great Spirit.

As she ascended the mountain, she turned to watch a pair of eagles soar around a lake far below her, and settle into the tall trees. A good sign! A dove also appeared, and circled her three times. It was her special totem creature, the winged one who had come to welcome her at her birth; the first thing I, her mother, had seen then: symbol of Peace, and Spiritual Purity.

Her other teacher (besides the creature-beings, rocks and trees themselves) was an ancient man, well over 100 years old, who had also sought the caves for refuge. He taught her the history and the Sacred ways of the Lakota people, and of the one-ness of all beings. "Mitakuye oyasin," he would say. "We are all One; we are all related. We are all children of the Sky Father and the Earth Mother. Our ancestors came from the stars. One day we will return."

Little Dove spent four years in the mountains with the ones she called Oldest Grandmother and Oldest Grandfather. 'Grandfather' was a term of respect among The People; they respected their elders for their wisdom. The Great Mystery, the Creator, was also referred to as Grandfather, Tonkashila.

There came a time when Oldest Grandmother had already 'dropped her robe' (passed on), and Grandfather knew that he would follow soon to the 'Happy Hunting Ground'; where trees and grass and water and animals were plentiful, and all lived in harmony. He had been there many times in vision, but soon, he knew, he would not return from that place of great joy.

He told Little Dove that it was time for her to go down off the mountain.

"You will be captured by the Wasichu," he said, "But you must allow it to happen. Their ways are very different from ours. Sometimes someone from another tribe would capture one of our women, or we would take one of theirs; but after a time they would learn each other's language and customs, which were not so different from their own, and they would become part of a family, infusing new blood into the tribe -- and perhaps helping to create an alliance.

"But these Pale Ones who came across the Great Waters, the sunrise ocean, they do not honor all life, as we do; often these white-eyes do not even honor each other. They break their own laws, as well as the treaties they made with us. They think that we are somehow less than they are, and that it is all right to take over our traditional hunting grounds and kill off our people.

"And yet there must be some good in them, for they too are children of the Sky Father and the Earth Mother, as are all beings on this earth. So you must observe them carefully, as you have observed all those in the natural world; you must learn their ways and become one with them, that the blood of The People, the heart, the Spirit of the Lakota People will continue; because one day, the child of your child's child will return to share our wisdom and ways with people of all tribes and Nations. And she will be called Blue Star."

As he spoke, what looked like a bright comet with a bluish cast to it streaked across the clear night sky, trailing a sparkling tail behind it. "A message from the Old Ones, Grandfather," said Little Dove, with a smile. "Our Star Brothers give us a sign."

Chapter 2

Captured!

My spirit would come to Little Dove from time to time. In the early days we knew that the spirits of our ancestors were watching over us, and we could see into other dimensions.

Many Native Americans can still see Spirit; others have been told it's just their imagination, that they didn't really see what they saw -- so they stopped seeing it.

The ability to see Spirit was passed down, through his genes, to my younger son. Several times, just after we moved into an old sea-captain's house on Cape Cod, Massachusetts, he saw the spirits of people who had lived there before. When my sister Mallory visited us there from Spain, she had a vision in which she saw the two brothers who had built the original part of the antique Cape Cod house in the 1700s, and the Wampanoag Indians who had befriended them before the house was built. Her Indian name is Turtle Dove.

Chip, my older son, built a sweat-lodge by the water, when we lived on a lake. In a vision, he has seen himself sitting by a campfire, when he was known as the powerful Chief Black-Hawk; and he still carries some of the anger from that time, at being forced to move west of the Mississippi, to leave the ancestral lands of his people, and at having to watch them being killed off when they tried to protect their homeland.

My daughters also have been in contact with those on the other side, through different means -- automatic writing, though they don't speak of it anymore. My offspring have also known of the Star People, through U.F.O. sightings.

When Little Dove came of age -- when she came to her first moon-time -- my spirit came to her. Oldest Grandfather said this was something he could not teach her about, and Oldest Grandmother had gone on.

"If we were still living in our village," I (as the spirit of Turtle Woman) told her, "there would be a very special ceremony at this time of your changing from being a girl into a woman. You would have been taken to the Moon-lodge, with the other women on their moon, this time of greatest power for a woman. You would have been instructed in the responsibilities and ways of woman, of wife, of mother.

"I would have made a soft, brain-tanned doe-skin dress for you, with long fringe, for you to wear as you danced in the Coming-of-age Ceremony, glowing from your inner beauty. The young men would of course take notice of both your inner and outer beauty. My heart is sad that this will not be for you.

"Yet because I am in the Spirit World, I can see beyond the seasons that are to come – and I know that although there will be some pain and sorrow, some obstacles in your path, there will also be joy and contentment: you will have a strong husband and bear fine sons and daughters. Teach them well, the wisdom ways of our people."

After Oldest Grandfather crossed over into the Spirit World, Little Dove sang him over to join the ancestors and, reluctantly, she came down off the mountain. The animals and birds were her friends, but she hadn't seen any people except for the two Elders for years, and she was somewhat apprehensive about what was to come. She knew she was to be captured by the feared enemy, the Wasichu.

She prayed to the Great Spirit for courage. It was not our way to show weakness, or fear, in the presence of the enemy.

One beautiful fall day, Little Dove went down by a stream to drink of the cold, clear water that bubbled along. The rays of Grandfather Sun were giving it a last golden glow, as the creatures of the forest drank along its banks.

Little Dove laughed as she watched three frisky little squirrels chasing each other around in circles, then up a tree, out on a branch, hopping to another branch, and down again, to repeat the cycle.

Suddenly she felt herself imprisoned by the strong arms of someone who had come silently up behind her! She had been caught off-guard, and her heart beat wildly: 'This is how an animal fees when it is trapped,' she thought. 'This is it! What was predicted -- but I must show no fear.'

Her captor turned her around to face him, holding her tightly by the shoulders.

"Purty lil' thing!", he said, with a grin whose meaning she did not care to interpret. Her people honored each other and all beings, and did not violate. But she knew these Wasichu were different.

"A young'un, this is; bet she ain't been broke in yet. Well, got to get back to the fort before dark; I can wait. I'll take 'er to my quarters. Bet she can cook, too, or I'll learn 'er how."

The soldier observed that she was docile, but didn't want to take any chances on losing this prize -- so he tied her hands in front of her and led her to his horse.

I, Turtle Woman, appeared to her at that point, reassuring her that it would be all right. She knew that with her mother walking beside her she was protected. He thought she was too stupid to be afraid.

It was dark when they arrived at the fort. After he went inside the big log gate, the soldier helped her to dismount from in back of his saddle. What a stroke of luck! He was very pleased with himself.

He led her across the courtyard, as they called the dusty open area inside the stockade walls with officers' quarters and enlisted men's barracks along the sides; it was dimly lit by gas lamps. The door of the commanding officer's house opened, and Captain Gray's wife stepped out onto her little porch, holding up a lantern to see who had come into the fort after dark; which was against the rules, unless they had specific orders or permission.

The soldier froze in his tracks, and saluted. 'Damn!' he thought. 'She caught me!'

"Evenin', ma'am," he said politely, hoping that somehow his little Indian captive had become invisible.

"Is that you, Sergeant?" she asked. "What have you got there?" As she approached them, her lantern clearly showed the Indian girl, eyes cast downward, wrists securely bound.

"Why, she's just a child!" Mrs. Gray exclaimed. Little Dove was 12 then, but she had not yet attained her growth. Sensing kindness in the woman's voice, she looked up at her, her large, luminous black eyes shining like polished obsidian in the lantern's glow. She reminded the woman of a captured fawn. Her heart went out to this wild young thing.

"Where do you think you were going with this girl, Sergeant? And why do you have her tied up like an animal?"

The sergeant looked down at his boots, kicked a pebble, and stroked his scruffy beard.

"Well, she is a wild thing, ma'am; she's just a savage. I reckoned I could tame 'er some, give 'er some civilizin'. My quarters could use some cleanin' up, an I could use some good cookin', could I learn her how to do it. An' if she don't take to good Christian ways, as some of 'em don't -- I could turn 'er loose again."

He gave it his best shot. It didn't work, and he knew it. Damn! But the Post Commander's word was law; so was his wife's. 'I shoulda took 'er before I came back to the fort,' he thought.

"She may be just a little heathen," said Mrs. Gray, "but she's one of God's creatures. I know what you men do with these Native girls, and I'll not have it. Maybe her soul can be saved."

She took the rope away from the sergeant, who shuffled off grumbling to his quarters. Being a non-commissioned officer, he had his own room instead of bunking in with the soldiers in the barracks. He'd thought he could sneak her in, in the dark – but the forces of fate intervened. Double damn!

Mrs. Gray led Little Dove inside her small log house, sat down, and untied her wrists.

Rubbing her sore wrists, the maiden stood quietly, looking downward.

"Well, now! What are we to do with you, my girl? I'll get you cleaned up tomorrow. I can teach you how to clean, and cook, and sew. Might be right useful around here; I thank the Good Lord for bringin' you."

The Captain's Lady indicated that Little Dove should climb the ladder and sleep in the loft, and she was happy to do so. There was a blanket there, and an old quilt -- she saw that she would be sleeping on long, flat, thin sticks cut from the trees, instead of on the soft body of Mother Earth, where The People in the lodges would be renewed each night by the nourishing energies of the Mother. In the morning, one gave thanks to Grandfather Sun for the new day.

From her 'eagle's perch', she could observe her new surroundings, and the woman who was her rescuer. Hair pulled back and knotted at the back of her neck; dress tight around the middle (making it hard to breathe, she thought), and then very full below the waist -- no fringe, for the snakes to strike at if one forgot to warn them by a song that one was coming. It was practical: Brother snake would strike at movement, and sink his fangs into the fringe instead of one's leg. And the fringe, like the feathers of a bird, helped the water drip off a person's garment after the rain, instead of staying soggily in the buckskin.

The White Woman did not sit on the earth, Little Dove noticed, but on a knee-high plank of sticks, with a back-rest covered with some soft fabric. In front of her was something tall and round, covered by a cloth... A drum, perhaps? And on that, a round thing most magical: Round like a ball, it (the lamp) contained a tiny fire inside, that shown through the little globe; translucent, like mica, the globe had flowers painted on it. Next to this was a black object with a small gold symbol on it: The mark of the Dawn Star, the great healer-teacher and prophet who had come to The People long ago to show them how to live in harmony. The symbol was a stick going up-and-down; and another going across it, near the top. Perhaps these people also knew of the Holy One, Dawn Star!

Mrs. Gray turned over the top of the black thing, which had thin, white leaves inside of it that had lots of tiny marks on them and some pictures. Little Dove had seen many pictures on tipis, and on cave walls, left by the Old Ones. She could tell by the careful, reverent way the woman held this strange object that it must be very sacred, some sort of Medicine Piece.

The door opened, and Captain Gray entered. Mrs. Gray explained to her husband what had taken place.

"You did WHAT?" he yelled, his voice filled with anger, like that of a warrior hearing of some terrible deed of an enemy. He looked up at the "little savage" (after all, he was an Indian fighter), and she withdrew back into the shadows.

"Calm down, dear; she's just a child, and I'm sure she'll be a great help to me."

The Captain was an imposing man, in his blue uniform; crossed-swords on his brimmed hat; brass insignia on his epaulettes, to match the shiny buttons; and a tasseled-sash and sword at his left hip. He always wore

14

it; he felt it demonstrated his authority. The fitted pants went down into high boots he tried in vain to keep polished.

"Well, I guess it'll be all right," he said. "Might be nice for you to have a little female companionship. Hope it won't be a problem for the men... You'll have to keep an eye on 'er.'" There were only two other women on the post, and they were officer's wives. 'Course the men went to town, now and then, to visit the bawdy house.

It would be nice to have a servant again, thought Mrs. Gray; she missed some of the amenities she had enjoyed when she had lived in Philadelphia -- before her husband had been posted to this wild frontier, to make their country safe for civilization.

Next morning, Little Dove came down the ladder, and Mrs. Gray showed her the out-house. Strange custom! By the smell of it, these people used the same place every time -- instead of spreading it around, to fertilize the earth, and covering it up. Even the animals knew to do that. And where was the stream? Didn't they bathe every morning in the waters, after welcoming Grandfather Sun?

She was given unfamiliar food for breakfast; she took a morsel of each kind of food and put it aside, as an offering, for the spirits.

"What are you doing, dear?" she was admonished. "Put your food back on your plate -- and don't use your fingers; use a fork." She was shown how to do it.

Mrs. Gray handed her a broom. What on earth was it, she wondered? She turned it upside-down. A staff, perhaps. Straw attached to the staff, instead of an eagle feather on a coup-stick. Another Medicine Piece.

"Oh, for pity's sake, she doesn't even know how to use a broom!" Strange sounds, strange language... She did not know the words, but she understood the tones. She had not heard impatience often, but she did recognize it.

Mrs. Gray showed her how to sweep the dust out the door.

In a tipi, the dirt is packed down, not swept away. Well, she would keep watching; she would learn.

Little Dove spoke very little in the first few weeks, though she would occasionally attempt a sound now and then when Mrs. Gray patiently repeated words. "Broom," she said. "Broo-oo-m. Ta-ble. Chair." Okay, she'd give it a try. "Tay-buh," she said. It was a start.

"Suh-nuh…moo-nuh." Sun, moon. "Sank yu," she practiced. For thank-you in Lakota, one said "I honor your spirit."

A few weeks later it was decided that it was time to go into town. "We've got to get you some decent clothes, my girl!" she was told. "I'll get some gingham, and make you a nice frock."

Town was a half-day's wagon ride away. They went to the General Store, to stock up on provisions for the fort, and Emma Gray picked out some blue-checkered gingham for her young charge. Little Dove looked around at all the merchandise; many new wonders here!

A man came in and, tipping his hat, said, "Howdy, ma'am," to Mrs. Gray. 'Ah! This is the greeting of these people!' thought Little Dove. 'It is not too unlike the greeting of the plains tribes; 'Hau,' we say, with palm upraised; 'Peace!'

She decided to practice this new phrase on the next person that walked in. That happened to be an old miner.

"Hau, de-mom," she said, making the motion of tipping a hat.

Two men were playing checkers on a checkerboard atop a barrel, in front of a pot-bellied stove, and they had been watching this Indian girl.

"Did you hear what that lil' savage said?"

"Lord a mercy, I believe I did! 'How-dy, ma-am!' -- to a man!" -- and they both burst out laughing. It was a real knee-slapper.

Little Dove knew they were mimicking her, making fun of her. She did not know their words, but she could feel their energy, and it was not good. Well, that wouldn't happen again! It was almost a year before she spoke again, and that was because they heard her talking to the animals, when she thought she was alone.

The Grays had been worried that something had happened to her voice, and that she couldn't speak any more. They were delighted to know at last that she could not only talk, but knew English quite well. She had listened carefully and had been practicing at night, while they slept.

After she made the girl her first gingham dress, Mrs. Gray threw away her deerskin dress into the trash. Little Dove was horrified! Surreptitiously, she retrieved it; rolled it carefully into a bundle, tied sage around it so the mice would not chew on it, and tucked it away in a secret place under the eaves. Someday, she hoped, she would be able to wear her regalia again. It was sacred to her.

Being a keen observer Little Dove made rapid progress, learning the ways of these strange people.

One day Mrs. Gray was sitting at her window sewing, behind the lace curtains that she had brought from the East, and she overheard two soldiers talking in the courtyard.

"Look at that dirty lil' heathen," said one, as he watched Little Dove fill a bucket with water at the pump. Silence.

"Oh, I don't know 'bout that," the other voice said. "She don't look dirty to me. All spiffed up in 'er purty new dress, hair's neat; face clean. Looks cleaner 'n a lot o' civilized folks I know. Like the one standin' here beside me."

"Humph!" he reacted. "All the same, jes' cause she ain't wearin' animal hide no more, don't mean she ain't a little heathen."

Mrs. Gray decided it was time to do something about that. She began reading the Bible to Little Dove aloud each night. When her husband was there, he would listen too. He was a God-fearing Christian.

Little Dove noticed that their god was a warrior-god, who advised his people, the Is-ra-lites, to kill off whole tribes, leaving not one male alive. No wonder their warriors -- their soldiers -- killed off whole villages of her people! They were more fierce than the Ab-SA-ro-keh (some called them Crow), traditional enemies of the Lakota, and of just about everybody else; but they were admired for their courage and skill.

That was what warfare was about among the plains tribes: demonstrating one's bravery, one's skill. To count coups -- to get close enough to an enemy to kill him, but simply touch him instead -- that was the object of the battle. To capture something important to him: A prize might be his coup-stick, with his hard-won eagle feathers attached to it; or some other special object, like his medicine pouch. Only the weak ones were killed, and that kept the tribe strong.

This Wasichu god was not like Tonka-shila, Creator, whose gentle spirit was in all things: The mountains, the trees, the waters, the earth. And in all of the creature-beings, including the two-leggeds. But she noticed that no one wanted to hear about her beliefs, so she just listened.

She was, after all, a captive. Well, she had been taught, the enemy can capture you and make you work for them; but they cannot enslave your spirit -- not unless you allow it.

Little Dove, Lakota Ancestor

Mrs. Gray noticed that her young charge took a keen interest in her 'understanding the marks on the paper', as she read from the Bible. So the next time they went to town, she went to the schoolmarm and obtained a discarded primer, and taught the girl how to read.

One day Little Dove heard the other officer's wives talking about giving a party for Emma Gray. They would be honoring her, on her special day -- her birth-day, they called it -- and there would be feasting, and gifts. A give-away ceremony! There was hope for these people, after all.

Little Dove wanted to make something special for her benefactor, who had shown her many kindnesses in a hostile world, and had been patient with her when she made mistakes. She would have to get the materials to create something with. Mrs. Gray had shown her how to crochet; she would make her a pretty shawl, of her favorite colors -- violet, with blue -- to keep her warm. She would know that she was wrapped in Little Dove's love.

But how to get the yarn? She would go down by the river, and gather willow branches to make a basket to trade at the trading post in town. She looked forward to the next full moon, when she would go to the river. Two or three miles was an easy jog for her.

The hardest thing about this new life for Little Dove had been having to live in a box (a house). How strange to dwell in this square place, shut off from fresh air and sunshine, when all the plains people knew that the world was round; the horizon was round; the stars traced a great circular arch across the night sky, reminding The People of their true home. The tipis, sensibly camped by a stream, were round; the seasons were arranged in cycles; and the Councils were in circles, showing that no one was any greater than any other, and all had their sacred point of view.

She missed listening to the voice of the wind; the breezes caressing her face; speaking to the spirits of the animals, the trees, the Ancestors. My spirit came to her now and then, and I told her I would always be there if she called upon me. This was a difficult apprenticeship, we knew, but necessary for her mission: to be a way-shower, a rainbow bridge between peoples.

Little Dove rarely went out of the house; 13 now, and very beautiful, she did not like the way the men looked at her. On the weekly excursion into town, their wagon had an escort of two soldiers; sometimes the Sergeant pulled this duty, but he never looked at her. When they were shopping at the General Store, he went to the other end of town, where the painted ladies in frilly dresses sat on their balconies.

When Grandmother Moon was at her fullest beauty, Little Dove had a secret rendezvous with the Spirits of the Ancient Ones. She would get her doe-skin dress out from its hiding place, put on the dress and her moccasins, and tie an eagle feather into her hair. (So much more comfortable than the pinafore dress and high, tight shoes!) Slipping quietly out when the household was sleeping, she would silently climb the ladder, when the soldier on guard was at the other end of the high catwalk, loop a rope around one of the pointed posts that formed the outside wall of the fort, and lower herself down on the outside.

She was not allowed to go outside the fort (except to go into town with Mrs. Gray): It was too dangerous! Danger from what, she thought? The Indians? The danger for her was here inside the walls. The thing that pained her most was hearing the soldiers talk about "those damn Savages", "Those dirty little heathens," -- or worse yet, the common epithet "The only good Injun is a dead Injun!"

But outside of the walls -- Freedom! Little Dove walked or loped down to her special sacred spot beside the "Crooked River," as the Wasichu called it, or "Waters that Bend like a Snake," to her Nation. There among the willows and the great cottonwoods, she would do her graceful dance, honoring the Spirit Keepers of the Four Directions; Grandmother Moon and the Great Star Nation; Mother Earth; the Standing People (the trees) and the green (growing things); those that walked or crawled or swam, or flew through the air. She prayed to Tonka-shila to watch over her Red Brothers and Sisters, and to bring understanding to them; for she knew that there must be a reason for what was taking place in their lives....

It was a beautiful ceremony, and she was joined by a whole tribe of spirit Ancestors who came to watch my precious Little Dove sing her heart-song and dance her dream. I, of course, was always among them, and it was a joyful time.

On the occasion when she gathered the supple willow branches for basket-making, she also gathered flowers that grew along the banks. If she put them into water, they would last until birthday time. She bound the

Little Dove, Lakota Ancestor

Down by the river at the Full Moon, Little Dove did her Ceremony honoring the Ancestor Spirits, Creator, Mother Earth, Star Nation, and all the Creature Beings.

Sakina Blue-Star is representing Little Dove in the picture above.

willow strands into a bundle and tied it onto her back, to leave her hands free for climbing the rope back up the wall into the fort.

She made the baskets quickly and well, in her hideaway up in the loft. She dyed some of the strands with beet juice, and wove a pretty pattern into each basket with them.

Little Dove managed to smuggle one of the baskets under her cloak into the wagon for the day-long journey into town and back. At the store she waited until Mrs. Gray went out to talk to the preacher's wife. "How nice that there's a little church in town now!" Mrs. Gray exclaimed. While they talked, Little Dove made her trade. The storekeeper threw in some sewing things, too, and a tiny pair of scissors, shaped like a crane.

Little Dove was adjusting to her new circumstance. Sometimes the Spirits of the Ancestors would come to her in Dream-time. She tried not to think about the fact that she was living in the home of the one who was responsible for killing off her parents, her grandparents, her sisters and brothers – and everybody she knew.

LITTLE
DOVE

Sakina
2 . 95

Chapter 3

Birthday Party

The special day arrived; the two officers' wives came with gifts and food -- and surprise! They had also invited the schoolteacher and the minister's wife, who had driven out from town together.

The gifts were brought out. The teacher gave Mrs. Gray a book. "It's about Benjamin Franklin. It mentions a time when he and President Jefferson went to a Tribal Council meeting with some Indians -- Mohawk, I believe, or Iroquois -- and got some ideas for the Constitution. Living here on the frontier, I thought it might interest you."

"Why, thank you, my dear! How thoughtful of you! I'm sure it will."

Little Dove rarely showed emotion in what she still considered her captivity, but this time she could not repress a smile. She hoped she would be allowed to read this book. Mrs. Gray had showed her how to read, and she had become quite good at it.

Lt. Graves' wife Tabitha presented her with a portrait of the Captain. It had been painted by an itinerant painter who had passed through town, and kept as a surprise.

"This is a present from all of the men in the company," Tabitha said.

Emma Gray was thrilled! "How grand he looks, with his sword at his side, and his beard neatly trimmed," she said. It had an elaborate gold filigree frame around it.

The preacher's wife gave her a Bible, and she was pleased. "The old family Bible has seen so much use," she said; "It's quite worn and frayed. This gift is very welcome."

Sarah, Lt. Carlin's wife, was from a well-to-do family in the East; from the whaling community of Nantucket Island. Life at the fort was difficult for her, but she had high hopes for her husband's advancement.

Emma opened the satin box from Sarah carefully. In it was a set of lustrous pearls, the necklace beautifully contrasted against blue velvet.

"Oh! My dear! How extraordinary! I am overwhelmed!"

"My father brought the pearls back to Nantucket on his clipper ship, from the South Seas," Sarah explained.

After the ladies had finished exclaiming over the necklace, the preacher's wife, Mrs. Tate, turned to Little Dove. Mrs. Gray called her Dawn, because of her custom of going to the fort's east wall each morning at first light, climbing the ladder, and watching the sunrise. She also watched it set in the west. She always said a silent prayer: "Thank you, Grandfather Sun, for your light this day, and your warmth."

"And what did you get for Mrs. Gray, dear?" Mrs. Tate asked the girl. There was an awkward moment for the lieutenants' wives. Being new in the area, Mrs. Tate did not realize that this was a little heathen in their midst. Little Dove looked as though she might have Spanish or Italian Background, and as Mrs. Gray had black hair also, one might well think the girl was a relative, rather than a servant. Since there was no separate dining room out here, she ate with the family.

"Perhaps she didn't get her anything," said Tabitha. "I don't believe she has any money."

"Oh, but I do have something!" Little Dove spoke up. "But it is very humble, not grand like these other gifts." She went over to a corner, and brought out her offering. She had made two baskets; one to trade and one to contain the shawl.

She presented the basket, with a curtsy, as she had been taught. It had pretty patterns woven into it, and flowers tied to the handle.

Mrs. Gray took the basket, and pulled the shawl out of it. It had fringe carefully tied around the edge, in a special way learned when the girl was small.

"Why this is lovely, dear!" exclaimed the one-who-was-being-honored. "Where did you get this?"

"I made it!"

"It must have taken many hours. But where did you get the materials?"

"I traded for what I needed."

Mrs. Gray was moved, almost to tears. What a sweet thing for her to do -- this quiet girl who always did as she was asked, and who never complained, even though she had been roughly taken away from her family and the life she had known.

"Where did you get the flowers?" she asked. "They don't grow around here." The river was several miles away.

Little Dove did not answer; she would not lie, but sometimes she found it wise to withhold some of the truth. She just smiled, and looked down at her shoes.

Mrs. Gray chose not to make an issue of it. "What a lovely shawl," she said, trying it on. "My favorite colors!"

It was time for the visitors from town to leave. "Do bring the young lady to church with you, Mrs. Gray," said Mrs. Tate. "And I do hope you'll all come soon."

The lieutenants' wives left shortly after.

"Where do you suppose she got those flowers?" one asked of the other. "Do you suppose there's something going on between one of the soldiers and that little squaw?"

"Oh, my! I wonder who?"

It caused considerable talk around the fort. After that people looked at her in a different way, and Little Dove did not know why.

Mrs. Gray made a decision. The next time the Captain returned from one of his forays "to see what those redskins are up to," she told him about it.

"I have decided that it is time to have our young lady, Dawn, baptized," she said. "She reads the Good Book a lot, and she's turning into a fine Christian girl. I do not feel that she is a servant anymore. As you know, I have always wished for a daughter -- and I wish to adopt her. I have made up my mind."

Her husband studied her for a few moments.

"Well, Mrs. Gray, I have never known a woman to be more stubborn than you be, once you made up your mind. I suppose you know what you're doin'."

Actually, it was not too unusual for people to adopt young heathens, and Christianize them. Saving their souls was popular.

I've got somethin' to tell you, too, woman," he said, sitting down beside her. "They're closin' up the fort here; don't seem to need it anymore.

Things are quietin' down in this area. We'll be movin' into a town over in the Dakotas, near the Missouri River. We'll have a nice house in town."

"Oh, Captain Gray, I'm delighted! Back to civilization! And our daughter (might as well get him used to her being called that) will be able to go to school."

In their new town Little Dove was baptized, and given the name Emma Grace -- after her new 'mother', and because it was by the grace of God that she came into their lives, she was told at the time of her official adoption.

Mother Emma told Grace about her ancestors. "You'll have my heritage now, my family history and stories, since you don't have any of your own."

How wrong she was on that! thought Little Dove, now called Grace. But she would save her stories for her own children.

"My ancestors were French," Mrs. Gray told her. "Huguenots. There was a great religious persecution, and my family was lucky to escape with their lives -- for many did not. They took our lands, our liberty and our lives, because we did not believe as they did. We suffered greatly."

Little Dove, as she still thought of herself, could relate to that.

"Their name was Pochet (Poe-shay), and it was changed to Pochey when they went to England, where they lived for several generations. Then, still seeking freedom – to believe as they chose -- they came to America, where they are called Posey. Here they can worship in their own way, without fear of persecution."

"Do you think that I will ever be able to worship in my way?" the Indian girl asked quietly.

"But your way is pagan, dear. You worship trees."

"We honor life in all things. We worship Creator."

"Huguenots were Christians -- but they were Protestants. They were persecuted because they were not Catholics, like the French rulers of that time."

There was such a difference, really. She hoped the girl could understand that.

Eventually she got used to being called Grace. It was a sacred name, after all; and people of her tribe often went through name-changes as new circumstances warranted them. And she loved school -- at last she had something else to read besides the Bible, and she was always hungry for knowledge.

Grace was 16 when she and her family were invited to the Jamboree. The dance was to be held in the stable, down by the Missouri River, as that was the only place big enough for a lot of people to get together and kick up their heels. There was to be a picnic beforehand.

She had become a good cook, and she brought a basket of roasted chicken, corn and other vegetables from the garden, and pie she had made with blueberries picked that morning.

She had many friends now, and they enjoyed exchanging food and gossip.

"Who is that tall man over there, who looks like a wild man, just out of the woods? I haven't seen him around here before," said her friend Rebecca. "Yes, look at him! All lanky, leather, leggings and fringe," Celia observed. They laughed.

"Might be an Indian."

"He's got blue eyes, though, and a reddish tint to his hair when the sun shines on it."

"Maybe he's a half-breed," said Rebecca.

Grace studied him carefully. Those words, "Might be an Indian," made her heart beat faster! She remembered seeing him back at the fort. He would bring them game sometimes, that he had hunted or trapped along the streams. Sometimes he had been asked to scout out a new territory, or show them where the hunting was good, to supply fresh meat for the soldiers.

He had always caught her attention. Though not Lakota, he looked more like her people than anyone else she had seen in the White world. His otter-fur hat still had the head and tail intact; and he wore a buckskin shirt or jacket and pants well-fringed, over soft moccasins. He had a large hunting knife at his belt, with his powder-horn strap crossing his chest. A long-rifle, a strong bow and quiver of arrows, traps and pelts or game would be slung over the rump of his appaloosa stallion. The pony wore a colorful blanket, but no saddle.

Little Dove was remembering this when he felt her gaze, and turned to look at her. Embarrassed, she turned away, got up, and went inside the barn. The fiddlers had begun to play.

The musicians were on a platform on the far side, and bales of hay had been placed around the edge for people to sit on.

A few of the couples had begun to dance. They were playing a lively Irish tune; Emma Grace wished she knew how to do their dances, but they were so different from her own, guided as they were by Spirit.

In any case, she had never felt comfortable with men, white men, since her first unfortunate encounter with the one who had captured her. She had often been warned to "stay away from the soldiers!", and she had never told her new mother about how her real mother had been killed by the cavalrymen who had destroyed her whole village and all of her loved ones.

As she reminisced about these things, a sadness crept over her. Though she learned their language and their customs, she would never really be a part of these people. They were still Wasichu.

Mrs. Gray had tried to comb the girl's hair into seven long 'sausage curls', like the other young ladies wore, but her hair didn't take to it. For this festive event, however, she had made her daughter a pretty calico dress, with a long ruffled skirt, and bought her graceful dancing shoes to wear instead of the uncomfortable high, stiff every-day shoes. She pulled some of the girl's dark hair from the sides of her head around to the back, tying it with a ribbon and letting it hang down on top of the rest of her hair, which was loose instead of in its usual one long braid.

Little Dove/Grace was suddenly aware of someone standing in front of her. It was the tall man in buckskin.

"May I have this dance, Ma'am?" he asked politely, with a little bow.

"Oh!" she said; he had caught her by surprise -- and she was unaccustomed to being slightly flustered. "I regret that I do not know these dances."

"Nor do I, Ma'am." She was also unaccustomed to being called "Ma'am". "But I brought you some cider. Perhaps we could go outside and talk some, or walk down by the river. "

"That would be pleasing to me," she said. She felt unaccountably comfortable with this man. He did not seem like a stranger.

They walked down by the river, and watched a stern-wheeler coming up-river against the current, with smoke billowing out of the tall stacks. She had never seen one before; this was something new -- and it was a marvel! Passengers, some coming up the Missouri from Westport Landing or

St. Louis, lined the railing: Elegant ladies in large hats and capes over their long dresses, and gentleman in top-hats, frock coats, and trousers, which not so long before had replaced knee-britches and hose.

"I am called Long Bow," said the tall man walking beside Little Dove, "because I prefer to hunt quietly. I save the powder for bear."

Bear, she thought. Walking on two legs, he is sacred to my people. But sometimes he would offer his robe to The People, that they might be warm and fed. She no longer spoke of these things, however.

They sat beneath a willow tree and watched the paddle-wheeler churn the waters before it rounded the bend and went out of sight.

He picked some flowers for her. "Pretty posies for a pretty lady," he said. He smiled. She had never been given a gift before (except for the dresses Mrs. Gray had given her), since leaving her people.

"I thank you," she said with a smile.

Long Bow had gathered some willow fronds and went down to the riverside, wet them, and began to weave them into a circle. She recognized the beginning of a basket.

"Where did you learn that?" inquired the 'pretty lady'.

"My mother taught me. Comes in handy for carryin' berries and such. You put me in mind of her... you favor her a lot; same long black hair. Same deep black eyes that sparkle like the distant stars in a midnight sky."

They were both surprised at this poetic turn of his. Although in his mid-twenties, he had not had much contact with young ladies; he found them frivolous. He preferred to be in the forest, with the animals. He hunted in the old way, the way of the Native people; apologizing for taking the animal's life, only killing when necessary for food, and only trapping to exchange for what he needed.

"Tell me about your mother," she said.

"I'll start with my father, and my grandfather -- who was a Scotsman. There were clan wars, between my ancestors, the mountain Highlanders, and the Lowlanders, who raised the longhaired cattle. But when the English soldiers came -- they were truly brutal! They took over our lands, and they violated our women. When we protested, they killed off our men, and burnt whole villages."

Little Dove knew about that.

"My grandfather Gillespie and his brothers worked their way across the ocean on a clipper ship, from Scotland to America, in search of freedom. It was shortly after our war of independence from England, our Revolution. They landed in New Orleans, long before it became the Louisiana Territory.

"New Orleans was full of pirates, ruffians and thieves at the time, and the slave-trade was flourishing -- something offensive to my grandfather, who did not believe that one person could own another. The brothers established the Black Hawk Trading Post in Georgia, in Cherokee country, and Grandpa later moved to Mississippi, where he homesteaded some land.

"Along the way he visited in villages of the local people: the Natchez, the Choctaw, the Creeks, the Cherokee. Some of them were what they call the 'five civilized tribes'; highly intelligent people who live in harmony with the natural world. The Cherokee would 'sing up Grandfather Sun' every morning, helping him to rise until the White People laughed at them, and they stopped doing it. Now they greet the Sun quietly, those that still do."

Little Dove's eyes grew wide, as she listened to these words. She did not know of these people he spoke of, but some of their ways were akin to her own.

Long Bow paused, amazed at himself. He was not accustomed to speaking more than a few sentences at a time, and he often spent months in the forest or on the plains talking to no-one but the animals, the birds, the trees. But it seemed important for him to tell her his story.

"Grandfather preferred the company of these people to the ones from Europe, where there had been powerful lairds, serfs, and not much in between, save the tradesmen.

"Many of the folk who came to this country were those who were released from prisons across the sea. That way the gentry could get rid of the 'undesirables', the criminals; and get them to do the hard work of building a new land. But the ruffians brought their evil ways with them.

"Instead of learning from those gentle souls who dwelt here already, at peace with their world, they killed off anyone who got in the way of their greed for gold or for land. The Native people of the South of Turtle Island are being moved forcibly from their sacred lands, such as the Great Smokey Mountains, and others, to a barren place called Oklahoma. It is thought to be worthless land.

"This removal has turned into a death-march. The People are calling it the Trail of Tears. Thousands have died along the way. The Seminoles, led by Chief Osceola, have fled East to hide in the alligator swamps of the Everglades, where the white soldiers cannot get them. They would rather die than surrender."

These words were a source of wonder to Little Dove. She had not realized that there was a choice, a way to survive the onslaught of these ones who swarmed over the land with their fire-sticks and their cannon which could blow to small pieces a village and its inhabitants; these invaders who would take whatever they wanted.

"My grandfather Gillespie married a Cherokee woman. Some of the Tsa-LA-gi, as they called themselves, had lived in log houses for decades, and they showed him how to build one. They helped him plant corn, cotton, beans, watermelon and other things that grew abundantly there in the rich soil beside the rivers in Mississippi, on land that he cleared. He raised a family, and they thrived.

"My father married a Choctaw-Cherokee girl. I have four brothers and two sisters. My father, half-Scottish, insisted that I learn the ways of the White Man -- it was important for survival, he said, to know how to deal with them. So I studied at their school. But my mother taught me the most important things: How to bring the rain, or send it away. To see the Light in all beings, knowing that we are all One. How to listen to the Ancestors, and to speak to the Star Nation."

A shiver ran through Little Dove's body, as this man who sat beside her quietly spoke these words that touched a chord deep within her. The drum-beat of her heart changed to a faster pace, as it began a sacred dance. She knew that there was something very special about this man, this meeting. A quiet joy filled her heart.

"Look deep into my eyes," said Long Bow, "and tell me what you see." He turned to her and took both her hands into his. Again, a shiver shot through her.

She hesitated. She knew that the light of a person's soul could shine through his eyes, and it could be too strong. A person could be controlled in this way.

Still -- she looked. They stared deep into each other's souls, beyond the beyond. She saw them journeying together; higher, higher, back to the beginning of time. She saw them both on a star-ship, looking down upon the globe of earth; seas rose; and islands, continents, disappeared, re-appeared in different form, and then were gone again.

Now Turtle Island formed; Florida forming one leg, Baja California another, its tail going down south into the land of the Olmec, the Toltec and the Maya, its arms reaching northward. They stood on the ship, with the Wise Ones in council, and agreed to come back in human form to help to heal the rifts that were forming on Turtle's back.

Their reverie was shattered by a harsh voice calling out, an angry voice.

"EMMA GRACE!" they heard. "You come here this instant! I've been looking all over for you: I thought you'd fallen into the river and drowned!"

Grace was startled. She jumped away from her companion as they sat on the grass. It was dusk; perhaps Mrs. Gray had not noticed their hands had been touching.

She was not accustomed to being reprimanded. She had never done anything to call for it,

"I will marry you if you'll have me," said Long Bow in a low tone, as Little Dove got up and walked away from him. She hoped that this had not been overheard.

"Forgive me, Ma'am," she said with dignity. "We were watching the boat with the big wheel, and the gentleman was telling me his ancestor-story; about his grandfather who came from a place called Scot-land."

"He's not a gentleman, dear; he's a woodsman. And there were several gentlemen who were asking after you -- even officers! -- with you looking so lovely in your long dress, and your ribboned hair. But you were nowhere to be found! Land sake!"

Emma had high hopes for her daughter. The girl was 16, but that was certainly marriageable age on the frontier. Native people, in tune with natural cycles, would have paired off even earlier,

"One gentleman was particularly dashing," said Mrs., Gray. "A Cavalry Officer. I told him that our ancestry was French, and was Spanish on your father's side -- that my husband was descended from a Spanish Conquistador."

Grace was surprised. Christian teachings emphasized truth, though she noticed that it somehow didn't seem to apply with 'savages'.

"Well, I could hardly tell him you were an Indian," said Emma.

Weeks went by, and there was no word of Long Bow, whose promise, and shared vision, stayed always on her mind.

One day, when Grace and her mother were walking along the new plank sidewalk in town -- Mrs. Gray stopped, excited, and pointed out the 'dashing Cavalry Officer' on the porch in front of the saloon across the way.

"Oh! There's that nice officer who was showing interest in you at the jamboree! What a catch he would be -- although I hear he's quite a ladies' man. But he's had a lot of field experience, and I understand he's due for a promotion soon."

Little Dove studied his face, as he turned towards them. He looked somewhat familiar... and suddenly it came to her in a flash! She gasped!

"Why, what's the matter, dear? Do you know him?" They sat down on a bench in front of the General Store.

She took a deep breath before replying. "I do. I will never forget that face. Many years before this, when I had completed eight winters, my mother and I were running through the tall grass-lands that stretch to the edge of the world. Our whole village had been destroyed; the lodges of my family and my friends were burnt, often with them inside. If they ran out, they were shot down by the soldiers.

"My mother and I were down at the stream, below the bank -- hiding, and they did not see us. When it got dark, we went across the plains, guided by the half-moon light. 'I will take you to my brother,' she told me; 'he will care for you.'

"The next day we were far from the place of the death of my village, when we heard two pony-soldiers riding up behind us and there was no place to hide. I looked up to see the face -- that face! -- of the 'long-knife', the cavalryman, who plunged his sword into the back of my mother, jerked it out, and then rode on. She fell on top of me; she was trying to protect me."

"Mercy!" Mrs. Gray exclaimed. "What did you do?"

"I had been taught to be brave, but many were the tears that rained upon the earth, and onto the body of my mother. I implored Great Spirit to allow me to follow the spirit path of my mother, Turtle Woman, and of the people of our village. But the spirit of my mother appeared to me, and told me to be strong, to have courage: That one day all would be well, and that I had an important mission in this earth-walk. I was to bring understanding between peoples. To bring love.

"I could not believe she meant that I should go among the feared Wasichu, killers of my people! I did not know then of people like you, who have a tender heart.

"My mother, Turtle Woman, was a Holy Woman of our tribe, a healer, honored and loved by all. She was always praying for The People, doing Blessing Ceremonies."

"But what happened to you?" Mrs. Gray asked.

"After three days, my uncle came and got me. My mother's spirit went to her brother and told him where to find me. He took me to two wise Elders high in the mountains, and they taught me the ways of The People. They told me that I would be captured, but I must allow it -- because the blood, the spirit, of my people must continue. For one day, the child of my child's child would return, to share our teachings of Oneness -- of honoring all life -- with the Rainbow People, the ones of all Nations, all colors, at a time when it would be needed."

Mrs. Gray was without words. It was a lot to take in. Finally she said: "Why have you never told me these things?" She dabbed at her eyes with her embroidered handkerchief.

"I did not think they would interest you. You did not seem to think that what happened to 'pagans' was of importance. And I did not wish to hurt your heart. You have taken me as your own daughter, and you have shown me many kindnesses. I do not forget this, and I am grateful."

"My dear, dear little Grace," Mrs. Gray said. "How strong you were to keep your sorrow to yourself. We have been worlds apart, and you never let me know!"

The Captain's wife gained a great deal in understanding that day.

A month and a half later Captain Gray was sitting at his desk in the parlor looking over some reports when a knock sounded at the door. As the womenfolk were out in the kitchen preparing dinner, he rose to open it.

A tall young man stood before him. He wore a short gray top-hat, a high collar with a wide black bow-tie, a double-breasted coat, and trim grey trousers. He removed his hat.

"Good evening, sir," he said respectfully. "I've come to call on your daughter."

The Captain was surprised.

"I wasn't aware that you knew my daughter!" he replied.

"Yes, sir. We met at a dance."

"Ah -- of course. Do come in."

Little Dove looked up from where she sat at the kitchen table, shelling peas. She could not see who came in -- but she sensed a special energy.

"I wonder who that is," said Mrs. Gray, "and if we need to set an extra place." Grace seemed to have a special glow, she thought; a secret smile. Interesting. Perhaps it was that trapper who came to call. He was the only one she'd shown any interest in. But how would she know it was him?

In the parlor, the Captain was looking him over. "Seems to me we might have met before, but I can't place where?"

"I am George Gillespie, son of Robert, of Clan Gillespie of the North of Scotland. My father owns a plantation down in Mississippi, at the junction of the Yazoo and the Tallahatchie rivers. Many acres planted in cotton, corn, beans, melon... A large house, and many small cabins."

"Slave quarters, I expect."

"For the field-hands, yes."

Mrs. Gray wiped her hands, took off her apron, smoothed her hair, and went into the parlor. Grace followed.

"Why, good evening! And who might this be, Captain?"

"This is Mr. Gillespie, dear. He was just telling me about his plantation, in the state of Mississippi."

"My family's place, sir."

"Indeed. You've a familiar look to you, George; it's haunting me," Captain Gray mused.

Gillespie glanced at Little Dove, who of course knew him immediately. She smiled. 'He certainly doesn't look like an Indian,' she thought! 'But then, neither do I. We're both pretending. We wear masks, like ceremonial dancers.'

"Yes, sir, Captain; we've known each other. I used to hunt, to supply meat for the regiment. And scout some."

"Long Bow! Of course! Didn't know you, all trimmed up and dressed like a gentleman! You kept our company from hunger, many a time, and helped us find our way through the pass when the blizzard came. Saved our hide, you did. The men always spoke highly of you. Honest, quick-witted and dependable, they said. Knew your way around the wilderness."

Well, this was an interesting turn of events! -- thought Mrs. Gray. He looked respectable after all.

"And what brings you here, Mr. Gillespie?" she asked.

"I've come to call on your daughter, Ma'am."

"You'd like to court her?" she said.

"I'd like to marry her. With your permission."

"Oh, dear! My lovely daughter... You wouldn't be taking her away, would you?"

"Not directly, Ma'am. But my plantation is a ways down South."

"Oh, my... Oh, my..." How could she manage without her dear daughter?

"Beggin' your pardon, Ma'am... Captain... I have some gifts for you out in the wagon."

He brought them in. "A dozen beaver pelts, tanned and stretched on a willow frame; popular for top hats, they are; should fetch a good price with the traders from back East." He piled them high in a corner of the dining room.

"For Mrs. Gray, a parasol; it's all the rage with the fine ladies this season. And a fine silk shawl from China, brought back by a Yankee sea captain, and that I come by in New Orleans."

"Oh, my stars! Will you look at that! All those little flowers and birds, embroidered on it... and the feel of it. It's so lovely."

A large, rectangular box was brought in next. "This is for you," he said, handing it to Grace, who had been quietly watching the proceedings. As with the warriors of her tribe, he knew to bring gifts to the father of his chosen maiden, and he brought something for the women too.

She opened the box, which was laid on the dining room table. To the delight of Mother Emma, it was a wedding dress.

"Oh, it's exquisite!" said Emma. A dream come true: She was to be Mother of the Bride. The lace mantilla was from Spain. Grace held it up, and smiled. He had done this for Mother Emma, she knew, and she was pleased.

"How long have you known my daughter?" the Captain asked.

"All my life, it seems. I met her about two months ago."

"And have you spent much time with her?"

"Two hours, perhaps. But it does not take long to recognize true beauty; the beauty of the spirit."

Captain Gray turned to Grace. "And what do you have to say about this, my girl?"

"I knew he would come," she said softly. "It was foretold. When I was a small child, my grandmother told me: 'One day there will come a warrior riding into your life who will be a fine hunter; have great strength but a gentle spirit, and who will walk in balance upon Mother Earth. You will know him by his eyes, the color of the clear mountain skies.' I knew he was the one, when I looked into his eyes.

"I am grateful to Creator, and, All My Relations."

How sweet, thought Emma, thinking that she meant her and her family. Long Bow knew that to the Lakota 'Mita-kuye Oyasin' -- 'All My Relations' -- included the trees, the earth, the creature-beings.

Mrs. Gray sighed. She resigned herself that losing her daughter was indeed, fate; but at least there would be a nice church wedding, and she would gain prestige in the community by having a handsome son-in-law who owned a great plantation. She imagined a large mansion, with Grecian pillars across the front, and a sea of cotton fields with Darkies (as some called Black People then) working in them.

Mother Emma had two weeks to prepare. She and her friends were buzzing around helping Grace collect her trousseau. Bed-linens, petticoats, dresses and aprons; stockings and shoes. Her 'father', the Captain, made a chest out of cedar-wood to put it all in.

From its secret hiding place, Little Dove retrieved her doe-skin dress, with the eagle feather, medicine pouch and moccasins wrapped inside -- and slipped them in between the folds of a petticoat at the bottom of the chest. These were the only things she really cared about.

Above: 1960s, Sakina wears an antique embroidered silk Spanish shawl given to her in Spain by her sister Mallory, similar to the one gifted to Little Dove's adopted mother by Geordie Gillespie.

Chapter 4

Wedding

The wedding took place at the little church in town, with everyone commenting on "what a lovely couple they make!" The preacher went on with the ceremony a lot longer than the pair getting married felt was necessary, but this was, after all, their gift to the family who had taught her so much, and had cared for her.

"Do you, Emma Grace Gray, take this man to be your lawful wedded husband, to love and obey..." the preacher droned. Obey, she thought? But she went along with this strange concept.

"I do," she replied.

"And do you, sir, George Robert Gillespie, take this woman, to have and to hold, in sickness and in health, 'til death do you part?"

"Indeed."

"I do," whispered the preacher.

"Of course."

"You're supposed to say 'I do'!"

"Of course. I do. Indeed!" He got his sense of humor from his Scottish grandfather, who felt that a certain amount of irreverence is imperative in this life.

After greeting friends and family afterward in the rectory garden, Long Bow changed into his buckskins, which were more comfortable for traveling, and Grace changed into a simpler frock and bade farewell to a tearful Emma Gray.

She gave Mrs. Gray the wedding dress, to pass on to the next young lady who might be able to use it. "At least keep the lace mantilla, dear," Mrs. Gray said. "Perhaps one day your own daughter will wear it.

"Do not forget me," she added tearfully.

"I will never forget you. One day you will come and visit us, or I will return to visit you. I am grateful to you."

The wagon was filled with what would be needed for this journey, and a few gifts for their new life. A beautiful black mare pulled the wagon, and Long Bow's spirited Appaloosa trailed behind.

He drove for many miles without speaking; words did not seem necessary between them. As the sun neared the horizon, he stopped at a wooded place near a stream, a secluded place.

"Wash by those rocks over there," he said to his bride, "and prepare us a meal for this special day of our coming together. I will set up camp." He handed her some buffalo meat. "I have prayed over it, thanking the spirit of Tatanka for giving us strength."

Tatanka! It had been a long time since she had tasted of the animal sacred to their people, who provided them with food, shelter, and clothing.

The Wasichu ate the White Man's buffalo, that scrawny creature with no hump. How pitiful -- everyone knew that was where the sweetest meat was.

She went to the wagon and pulled out her doe-skin dress from its box, and, after washing off the trail dust, she put it on -- and felt an exhilarating sense of freedom! She could be Little Dove again!! At last!

She had made the dress big, and long, when she sewed it with sinew at the age of twelve. She knew that it would have to last her for a long time. Now, it fit her perfectly.

Her husband -- what a beautiful thought! -- came to her and took both of her hands in his, and, as they had on the day they met, once again they looked deep into each other's eyes.

"My beautiful Little Dove," he said softly. "They named you well." He kissed her tenderly. It created a fire within her. She trembled; closed her eyes; and took a deep breath.

"I give thanks to you, Wakan Tanka," she said, "Creator of All Things, for this great joy that comes into my heart, and fills me with a love that reaches beyond the stars..." Bright sparks from the cooking-fire danced in her large moist dark eyes, and they were reflected also in the rippling waters of the stream beside them.

Long Bow spoke:

"I also give thanks, Tonka-shila, for the joy that fills my heart. After many years of alone-ness, it is the greatest of gifts to have this maiden of extraordinary beauty, with a radiance from within, to share my lodge, and my life."

This was the real wedding ceremony, for them. After they ate, they would continue it.

"Here is my marriage-ceremony gift for you," he said, handing her a bundle. Carefully, she unrolled it and held it up: a white, soft, brain-tanned doe-skin dress, with long fringe falling from the sleeves and hem.

She caught her breath. "It is the regalia of my vision, when I was small! When I went into the White world, I thought it would remain only a dream!"

She presented him with a gift, also: A fringed buckskin shirt, with a design made from porcupine quills, flattened by her teeth, one at a time, and dyed in various colors from the juice of roots and berries. She had started it even before she knew of his coming, and it had taken her many hours.

"I thank you, Little Dove! I feel your loving vibrations in it and your prayers for me."

He put it on and tied an eagle feather into his hair.

"I go to prepare the Sacred Circle, that we may do our holy dance together," he said as he walked away toward a clearing among the trees.

Little Dove removed her tan dress and put on the white one. It was decorated with a strip of beadwork in blues and black, going down the sleeves and dipping across the front from shoulder to shoulder. The prized brightly colored glass trade-beads, made in Czechoslovakia, had become very popular with Native People of the North.

She joined Long Bow at the circle of stones that he had prepared, praying, with a sprinkle of tobacco, as he placed each stone on the grass. Invoking the Spirits of the place to join them, he called them in, with rattle, drum and song, honoring all the beings in turn.

Little Dove was thrilled to be part of such a traditional ceremony once again! Though her husband's tribe was from the South, he had dwelt among the People of the Plains as well, and he knew their language and their ways.

They entered the circle from the East, where he had placed a yellow stone -- to represent the morning light; beginnings. In the South, a red stone, representing the blood of Mother Earth; growth. The West -- black. Sun-gone-down; a time of vision, dreaming. To the North, the direction presided over by the Sacred White Buffalo, the place of the Elders; wisdom.

On the center stone, the altar, Long Bow had placed his chanupa, his Sacred Pipe. Unassembled, it lay still in its fringed and beaded pipe-bag, with a pocket on the outside for a tobacco pouch, and an antler-tip, to tamp the tobacco down with. Little Dove laid her Medicine Pouch next to it, containing her sacred things: Small bones and feathers from the claw of an eagle; tobacco, for offerings; a crystal given her by Oldest Grandfather, who had taught her how to use it. "You place it inside your head-band," he had said, "in the center of your forehead, when you go into vision -- that you may see more clearly what Spirit is showing you. And it will make stronger the loving thoughts you send out to the children of Mother Earth. It has great power; you must use it with wisdom."

Long Bow lit a bundle of sage and cedar, placed it in a large shell (representing the waters of the Great Mother, from which the world was birthed), and they cleansed themselves with the purifying smoke. He wafted it first toward himself, that he might be pure; then toward her, with strokes of an eagle feather. This would protect them from any malevolent spirits. He then lit a strand of braided sweet-grass, to call in the friendly spirits, for Blessings.

He sat cross-legged upon the ground. Holy Ground, for they had consecrated it. Long Bow took tobacco and put it into the red pipe-stone bowl of the chanupa, which he had carefully fashioned into the head of an eagle. Each carved feather was clearly delineated, and the spirit of the eagle was present.

He gave thanks to the Great Spirit for watching over them; honored the Earth Mother for providing what they needed, and for giving them the sacred tobacco for their prayers. The smoke would carry the prayers to the Sky Father. The bowl, of stone, represented woman, and woman-strength; the stem, of wood, from the Standing People (the tall trees that connected earth and sky), stood for the masculine energies. When these two forces were combined in the sacred manner taught to The People by White Buffalo Calf Woman long ago -- a great synergy was created. Magic happened!

Tatanka, the buffalo, would come thundering across the plains when called in this manner, that the People would not hunger or be cold in the winter nights. For this the Lakota People constantly gave thanks to TonKA-shila (Grandfather).

It was unusual for a man who was not of their tribe to be a pipe-carrier; but, young as he was, the Lakota could see that Long Bow could call in the spirits of the Old Ones, who spoke through him, in vision or in trance. So the Lakota had adopted him into the tribe when he lived among them, and they took him into the Medicine Society.

He had prepared for their wedding, while she was preparing in other ways, by fasting and praying for four days in the Stone Peoples Lodge. He had made many prayer-ties, placing a pinch of tobacco in a small square of cloth as he prayed, and tying them onto a long string of many such ties, to be hung on the low rafters inside the purification-lodge. The lodge was a small dome, built with bent willow limbs and covered with hides. It was the womb of the Mother.

The steam created by pouring water on the rocks in the fire-pit in the center, along with the prayers, would purify a person in body, mind and spirit. Great visions could come, in the lodge, great healings could be accomplished. He had prayed to be worthy, to be of service, to make a good life for his family that was to come.

Long Bow stood up and offered the pipe, with a puff of smoke: To the spirits of the Four Directions, to the Sky Father, to the Earth Mother, and, turning it with a flourish, to the seventh direction, within himself: the connection to Creator. "Mitakuye Oyasin; All My Relations." He then passed it to Little Dove, who repeated the procedure; she watched the smoke take their prayers up to the ear of the Creator, so that He would know their hearts. "Mitakuye Oyasin," she said.

A buffalo skull had also been placed on the altar, and Long Bow now called upon its spirit to return. He had painted the Four Directions (a circle with a cross in the center; black, yellow, white and red) on the center of the skull, and eagle feathers dangled from each of the curved horns.

Lightning flashed, in the clear night sky -- and rolling thunder sounded its powerful drum! Another thundering sound was heard, and the ground trembled, as the spirit of the White Buffalo came into the clearing, snorting and pawing the earth.

Little Dove gave out a cry of delight. "You follow the Medicine Path, my husband!" she exclaimed. "I am pleased!"

All around them the Ancestor Spirits had gathered at their sacred circle. The whole tribe, it seemed, had come to help them celebrate their union. The spirits of those of her village were there, the ones who had been killed by the Long Knives, and many, many others. Standing among them, proudly, she saw me, her mother. (Turtle Woman; Sakina.)

I smiled at her. How thrilled I was! How filled with happiness, on this oh-so-special day!

Little Dove began to dance her joy. Step, dip; step, dip. The dance of the women of the plains, who press love and healing into the body of the Mother, as they walk gently upon her. Twirling, dipping, skipping, she went. The long fringe of her skirt swished like the tall grasses of the plains in a playful wind; when she held her arms out, the fringe became the feathers of a soaring bird. Rising, turning, swooping, gliding on the currents, and alighting once again. Round and round the sacred circle she danced.

High above, the screech of an eagle was heard; they watched it circle, lower and lower, until... Ah-HO! A feather dropped, and drifted down, landing in Long Bow's hands.

"A sign from Tonka-shila; he is giving us his blessing," he smiled. For Eagle, they knew, was the messenger to WakanTanka. Soaring higher than any other creature of the earth, he not only carried the message to Creator -- but would bring a message back to His children, and they were wise to listen.

The feather was pure white, a tail feather of the Whitehead Eagle (Whites called it bald), a precious gift. He presented it to his young bride. "May I always be worthy of this radiant being who stands now at my side."

Lightning flashed once more; the Thunder Beings spoke their approval. The Ancestors, gathered around them, made sounds of approval also, that carried on the wind. They faded out as Grandmother Moon arose in all her fullness and beauty.

"I have sung the song of the Lakota, during the pipe ceremony," said Long Bow. "Now I will sing you a song of my people, the Tsa-LA-gi. (Whites mis-pronounce it Cherokee.) We are a branch of the Ani-yun-wiya, The Principle People. Our ancestors came from the stars -- the Seven Dancers. They are also known as the Pleiades. One day, we will return."

A flash of recognition came upon her: "Oldest Grandfather told me that!" she said with excitement.

They pledged their love to each other "For as long as Sun will shine, Moon will glow, and Stars be in the Heavens."

He began his song, a slow, deep, melodious chant. Again she felt excitement. The words, the language, were unfamiliar to her, but the tune was one she had heard at the church that Emma Gray had taken her to.

"I know that song!" she exclaimed, when he had finished singing. "It was called... Amazing Grace!"

"Yes, my little one; they put their words to our song. And again, you are well-named: for indeed, you are – amazing Grace! A vision of grace and beauty!"

She felt herself begin to tremble, so strong was her love for this man.

"Come. It is time," Long Bow said.

He took her hand and led her out of the circle. The full moon's light showed clearly a little path through the woods. The deer used it to get to the water.

As they came around a bend in the path, she cried out in delight: "Oh! A tipi! The lodge of my people! How good it will be to lie upon Mother Earth again!" He had erected it while she was preparing their meal.

Inside the tipi, they stood facing each other for a moment, and then he took her gently into his arms. He could feel her body trembling. He stepped back, and held her face between his hands, drinking in her exquisite beauty. Being 10 years older than Little Dove, he had had experience of man-woman things, but he knew that she had not; that she had only had years of being repressed, in her time since coming of age. He would be very gentle with her.

Untying the thongs at her shoulders, he slipped her dress down over her arms and let it fall to the ground. She stepped out of it, as he removed his shirt and leggings, but still wearing his breechcloth.

He guided her to a soft pile of furs, and laid down beside her. Gently, his hand caressed the length of her body; he softly kissed her forehead, eyes, cheeks, mouth, throat; then her breasts, her stomach, and down her legs. He kissed her toes before he began his progress back up the length of her trembling body. He suckled her breasts like an infant, and was caressing her hips, which began to writhe involuntarily. Every nerve ending of her body came alive at his touch.

"What is happening?" she cried out. "Why do I shake like this? I do not understand!" Her wanting seemed to have a terrible intensity.

"It's all right, beloved one. It is our time of coming together. Becoming One." He removed his loincloth -- and it seemed that they exploded into each other!

His many years of alone-ness, and hers, were ended.

After the first frightening thrust, their love-making carried her to great heights of ecstasy. The fireworks took them out among the stars -- she was sure she could hear the wings of hummingbirds, eagles, or perhaps angelic beings! They made love again and again, until the golden fingers of dawn's light crept into the opening of the tipi at the top, and under its sides, between the poles.

Little Dove lay spent upon the fur robes; contentment, fulfillment pervading her being.

"I never dreamed that something so wondrous existed on this world! The coupling of a man and a woman -- is this what they kept warning me against?" she asked.

"It needs to be with the right person, to be meaningful," Long Bow replied. "Many men force themselves on a woman, and that can be very painful. There is no honor in it."

"Ah. I understand. One must always honor another."

They spent many days in the secret, idyllic place that he had found for them, tucked away between green hills and lush valleys. The late summer days were filled with making things, hunting, cooking, exchanging stories. Their nights were filled with passion. A little spirit had been waiting to come back to the earth, and slipped into her womb one night. They were to have many children; he would be the first of ten.

"Always remember these special days," Long Bow told his beloved wife one day. "We will become busy with other things, work hard, be separated sometimes. My love for you will always be strong; you are beloved and precious to me, more than life itself. You have my heart's deep love. But I may forget to tell you these things -- so always remember!"

Tears came to her eyes once more.

"What is it, Little Dove? Have I upset you?"

"Oh, no, my husband! But you have given me so much... and I have given so little to you."

He took her hand and put it to his lips, and looked into the windows of her soul.

"You have given me the greatest gift there is," he said. "You are a pure soul, and you have given me your heart's love. It is love that holds the universe together."

There was one more thing he wanted to do before heading south to settle down at the homestead.

"We'll leave the wagon here, and go by pony. There's a special place I want to take you to." He tucked the wagon into a crevice in a mountain, and covered it carefully with branches and leaves. "I'll ride the Appaloosa," he said. "The black mare is yours."

Another splendid gift! Impulsively, she ran to him and held him tight, her ear against his heart.

"My husband," she said. "My precious husband."

It was exhilarating to be wearing buckskins and riding the plains on Indian ponies again.

After a few days of traveling west, things began to look familiar to her. The great plains, the rolling hills, the pine trees dotting the hillsides going down steeply into deep ravines. Pine Ridge, they called this place. Here were the streams her people had camped beside, as they followed the trail of the buffalo, or the seasons.

And then they saw them! The great jagged grey-black mountains rising out of the plains... The Paha Sapa, the Sacred Black Hills of the Lakota people!

Long Bow had wanted her to make one more pilgrimage to this holy place, before moving to the South.

"More treaties are being broken since the miners discovered the yellow-metal-that-makes-White-Men-crazy', as the Lakota call it," he told her. "I wanted to take you here while we still have a chance. But we must be careful; we will need to travel by night for a while.

"Since gold was found here, the soldiers come through even more -- rounding up 'stray Indians' and taking them to reservations. I do not want you to even see these reservations, much less ever be on one. They break the hearts, the spirits, of the People. That is why you were allowed to be captured by these people, to learn to live like one of them -- it is for survival, that the song of the People might live."

46

"Why do they hate us so?" Little Dove asked wistfully.

"They are afraid of our power," said Long Bow. "Our way of living is so different from theirs! They felt that only one of us could survive in this land. And there are so many of them...."

For three days and nights, once again at the time of the full moon, the couple prayed and did their ceremonies honoring the Great Spirit and all beings. Again the spirits of the whole tribe joined them; this time there were even more of the Ancestor Spirits. They had a great pow-wow!

Little Dove was sad about having to leave. She knew that this would be the end of her living in the way of her people. "Why did Wakan-Tanka allow our land to be taken, our people to be killed?" she cried out to the spirit beings.

"Do not be sad, Little Dove," said the spirit of one of the Council Chiefs. "The land was allowed to be taken because our people forgot to be humble. Our warriors took on the ways of tribes being pushed away from the direction of the rising sun; they began more killing, and taking of scalps instead of just coup-sticks, pouches or feathers of an enemy. They still said 'Mitakuye Oyasin', honoring 'all our relations'; but they forgot to live always in peace and harmony, as we were taught by Dawn Star, who came among us long ago."

"Thank you, Grandfather, for giving me your wisdom and understanding," Little Dove said.

"It is a time for all people to share this land -- although there would be a better way to go about it," the spirit Elder said. "And do not forget, my child, as it has been given; that one day the spirit of your mother, Turtle Woman, will return after a time among the stars. And one day she will go up on a Sacred Mountain and call out to us, the Ancestors; and after that we will speak through her, and she will sing our songs and do our dances and our ceremonies, and she will carry our message of living in harmony and balance throughout the Nations of Mother Earth."

Little Dove and Long Bow bade farewell to the Ancestor Spirits, and began their journey back east. Back to the place on the Missouri River where Captain Gray had been transferred to years before from the Wyoming Territory, away from her beloved Teton mountains, another sacred place where she had often been in contact with the Ancient Ones, the wise beings who dwelt within the mountain.

After finding their wagon they headed for the Missouri, where they would put on their 'White clothes' again -- it was safer -- and proceed down-river on a paddle-wheeler steamboat.

That was exciting! Flowing with the swift current, wondering how on earth they would miss that log in the middle of the river, which would somehow manage to slide by, and watching houses and barns, trees and tiny villages pass by. Boys and dogs would run down to the landing before anybody else, where they were going to dock. Down would come the long plank that was raised for traveling, and the stevedores would unload cargo, some of it in large barrels called hogs-heads, before the passengers could disembark.

George and Grace Gillespie, as they were now called, didn't mix with the passengers much, except to smile and nod when passing. They spent most of their time at the railing watching the scene slip by, and enjoying the fresh air.

Long Bow did not want to spend any time in the saloon on board. Men would get offended if they offered a drink and he refused. And he had seen what terrible things 'fire water' had done to his people.

Long Bow had seen villages where White traders had come in with their whiskey. "We come in friendship", they would say; "These are gifts!" The young warriors would drink and whoop it up, and some became euphoric -- they thought this was a short-cut to receiving visions, instead of going the old slow way of many years of praying, fasting and sacrifice.

They would wake up the next day feeling terrible, and everything they had of any value would be gone: Weapons, pelts, blankets, buffalo robes -- and land. "You made your mark on a treaty last night," they would be told. "It's our land now." There was no honor in these people.

"We cannot drink the White Man's whiskey;" said Long Bow. "It is poison to us! It rots our brains," he told his bride. "Too much of it -- of anything -- is bad for anyone, but Natives of this land have a terrible allergy to alcohol, as they do to their diseases. It is only one of the ways unscrupulous ones have used to cheat us, to destroy us." He was pensive.

"Alcohol opens a door to the Spirits -- That's why they call it 'spirits'! -- and they are not necessarily the good ones. Once they take over, it is very, very hard to get rid of them. I have seen this struggle.

48

"Well, we will survive, you and I," Long Bow assured her. "We will have a fine family, a good life. We will teach by example, by living our truth, the truth of the love in our hearts that we share with each other -- and with all beings."

She loved to hear her husband speak. He did not talk often, and when he did, it was worth the listening. How much he knew of the ways of the world and its inhabitants.

They had gone down the Missouri River from the Dakotas, passing through Westport Landing (later called Kansas City) and on to St. Louis, where the river came together with the mighty Mississippi. This they followed on down, twisting and turning in a convoluted pattern along the western boundary of the new state of Mississippi, until they reached New Orleans.

Arriving at their destination in the South, Grace was amazed at all the bustle and activity as they docked.

"The busy seaport of New Orleans, my dear," her husband told her. "From this port, cargo ships and swift clipper-ships sail to distant places all over the world! I know; I have sailed on them."

Little Dove had never been to a city before, and Long Bow wanted to show her the city where he had spent many years in his youth, studying and working at various trades before setting out to see more of the world.

They watched the unloading of their trunks, and later he established her in a little boarding house -- a room in someone's home, really -- while he went to purchase a wagon to replace the one they'd sold before boarding the riverboat.

The lady of the home invited Little Dove / Grace into the parlor for tea.

"Ah unduh-stan you an' yo' huz-bin have jus' cum da-own frum the no'uth," the lady said. Unaccustomed to the Southern cadence of speech, it took a few moments for the words to register in Grace's mind.

Grace smiled. "Yes, ma'am." George had emphasized that they were very polite in the South.

"An' you're new-ly weds! How luv-ly."

"Yes, ma'am."

"He tol' me you cum down from Dakota terri-to-ry. Ah he-ah there's wah-ld Indians up they-ah! Did any of those sa-vages ever at-tack you?"

49

"Oh, no, ma'am." she said, looking down at her teacup.

"Did yuh see many uv 'em?" her hostess persisted.

"Sometimes. At the trading posts..." This was getting to be painful.

"If you'll excuse me," Grace said, "I'll need to be getting some rest. It's been a long journey...."

"Oh, of course, de-ah... puh-haps we'll get a cha-unce to chat la-ter."

I pray not, thought Little Dove.

Grace spoke to her husband about this.

"I'm afraid I cannot always protect you from these things. I know it is difficult; but for the Black People, brought from Africa, it is even worse."

"Why do they bring them from their homeland?"

"They brought the Black People here because they could not make the Red People into slaves," Long Bow said. "If they tried to make us do their hard work, and were cruel to us -- we would just leave, we would go back into the woodlands. Some of our warriors were so angry with these invaders that they would kill them. Then they called us savages, for defending our homes and families -- yet I hear there has been a war of 100 years in Europe, and prisoners are put into dungeons and tormented in terrible ways."

So many things were hard for her to understand.

"Traders in Africa will kidnap people there from their tribes, their villages, and sell them to sea captains from the North," he continued. "They take them to the islands, like Jamaica, and trade them for rum. Then they take the rum back to New England and sell it -- and go back to Africa to buy more slaves. It is called 'The Triangle Trade'.

"In their land, they could run away, but here they do not know the country. And because they look different, they are easy to find. Many people here in the South are very cruel to them.

"Yet perhaps they are not worse off than we are. They are worked hard, from dawn to dusk, in the fields -- but at least they are allowed to live. Our people are killed off, like the ones of your village, or driven to the barren places where we cannot live, where there is nothing to hunt or to gather. Our spirit can easily be broken under such conditions. These places are called reservations.

"But we -- you and I -- we will not be broken. We will play the game, knowing that we are actors, and it is a drama. It is called 'survival'.

"We will go to their schools and their churches, and sing their songs and worship their God. And we will do our own ceremonies in secret, and pass on our ways to our children by right living. We of the Aniyun Wiya, the Principle People, who came from the Stars, will continue to pass on our wisdom-teachings and our spiritual knowledge through our clans, each having the responsibility of sharing certain parts of the ancient teachings.

"And one day -- our prophecies tell us -- we will have the freedom to practice our faith openly once again. There will come a time when all will live as brothers and sisters, in harmony, as One. There will come a time of great change."

Again, her husband's knowledge amazed her. Grace was proud to be his wife. She had learned to pretend before, and was grateful for all the careful schooling in manners and customs she had received from Emma Gray. Emma's heritage would be her heritage. Her grandmother was French, she would say, and George spoke of his Spanish mother. His Choctaw-Cherokee mother had learned to carefully imitate the Spanish ladies from New Orleans, who had been early settlers there.

Little Dove made the transition from her indigenous heritage to the ways of the White world – for survival.

Chapter 5

Homecoming

New Orleans was a wonder of wonders! Grace was astonished at the number of people -- at the hustle and bustle, and the amazing variety of people. She had never seen Black People before, except for a few buffalo-soldiers, as the Lakota called them, because their curly hair looked like buffalo hair. And there were so many of them here! George steered her away from the slave auctions, but took her down to the waterfront and she did glimpse a line of slaves in chains being unloaded off of a boat, with a man cracking a whip over them. George pointed to the other ships, to distract her.

"Some of these sailing ships came from the other side of the world," he told her. "It took many, many weeks or months for them to get here. They bring all kinds of beautiful things from distant lands. I'll show you some, in the shops."

She was enchanted by the houses lining the busy streets, with wrought-iron lace balconies and fountained garden patios that could be glimpsed as one strolled by. The marketplace was crowded with buyers, mostly black women shopping for 'their folks'. Vendors went through the streets calling out their fish and other wares, and elegant ladies with parasols and top-hatted gentlemen drove by in their carriages.

In the French quarter's Louisburg Square, gentlemen wearing white silk ascots and flaring capes, and carrying gold-headed canes, escorted ladies in plumed hats and be-ribboned gowns to their velvet lined coaches. A footman would open the door, a driver would snap a whip above a matched pair of dapple-grays, and off they'd trot. French was heard everywhere, and Grace was pleased to hear that her husband spoke it well. He had a gift for languages.

On a side street, she noticed a Black Man playing a banjo, and another man doing a little jig. Sometimes someone going by would drop a coin in a cup.

George took her to a cove where the pirate Jean Lafitte used to come with his women and his booty, looted on the high seas. He showed her the bayous, where the Creoles lived: People who kept to themselves, who spoke their own brand of French, ate spicy food with an African flavor -- and who had wonderful jamborees when they got together to dance.

The newly-wedded couple bought a few things at shops in New Orleans that George thought they might need. Having inherited some thrifty ways from his Scottish grandfather, he had saved most of what money he'd made scouting, hunting and trapping, for this specific occasion. He had waited many years for just the right person to share his life, and now he was glad of it.

It had been hard to part with his Appaloosa -- a man got bonded to his pony after a time -- but they could not take the horses on the long river trip, and it was a sad but necessary sacrifice. They found another black mare for Little Dove, and George chose a brown horse with black mane and tail. Not gaited, like those of the gentleman who preferred thoroughbreds, but serviceable. A fast runner, could stop in an instant, yet strong enough to do work around the farm, and possessing stamina for long journeys. He called it Swiftwind.

Driving northward, Grace took note of the scenery, which was quite different from the country where she had grown up. There was lush greenery along winding dirt roads in some places, with creeping vines and large green leaves covering the high road-banks and tall tree stumps, making them look like giant Spirit Beings! Protecting, or menacing, depending on your point of view. Sometimes trees lined the road creating a tunnel, a welcome shelter from the Southern sun.

Then there were miles and miles of cotton fields along both sides of the road. Black figures were bending over the white plants, picking the full bolls and filling the long sacks they dragged along with them, trailing behind. Bright kerchiefs made splashes of color in a sea of white.

At the edge of the vast fields were rows of little shacks, some on pilings and some with little porches at the front. "Whole families live in those little one-room cabins," George said, noticing the direction of her gaze. Well, she thought, families of her youth lived in tipis, not any larger -- but it was different. We lived outside mostly, she mused, except for winter story-telling time; but there was grass, and a stream, instead of a sea of dust.

By contrast, up on a hill overlooking the cotton fields, or at the end of a long drive lined with great moss-hung oak trees, there would be an imposing white-pillared house, with green lawns rolling out from the veranda, and tall trees to give shade. The contrast was striking indeed.

Along the way, when nightfall approached, George would drive their wagon through the gates and into the driveway of one of these mansions. When a man-servant came out, he would say "Tell your Master that the son of Robert Gillespie, of Two Worlds, has come to call."

"Yessuh, Massa," a servant would say with a bow. "Ya'll come on up on de veranda an' be comf'table, while I tells de Massa an' de Missus you's heah. Lucius will tend to de hosses. Julius will bring you a julep, to refresh yo'sef."

All the plantation owners knew each other, and this was their custom when traveling. They always had an extra guest room, and the visitors would be invited into the gracious home for a sumptuous meal and a night's rest.

Little Dove said she would have been more comfortable camping out under a tree, but George told her that could be dangerous. She did not ask why.

"So you're Robert Gillespie's boy, eh?" their host would say. "Been away fuh a long tah-m," he would add in his Southern drawl. "An' come back with a purdy lil' bride, ready to settle dah-yun."

The lady of the house would then genteelly grill her about her heritage, and she was thankful that Emma Gray had schooled her carefully in that, saying that this was her heritage now. They were a bit suspicious of Northerners, but she seemed to pass the test. French forebears were acceptable in the South. "Some of the fah-nest fam-ilies came from France," they would say.

Next morning the travelers would be ready to depart, breakfasted and refreshed, their horses fed and watered. "Your hospitality is most welcome, and highly appreciated," George would say to their hosts, giving them a little gift. "Please accept our humble thanks. You know you are always welcome at Two Worlds."

54

"Why, it's been a plea-sure seein' y'all a-gin! An' meetin' yo' luv-ly bride. Y'all come back now, yuh heah?"

One afternoon they came to the gate of a place with a big house that seemed less pretentious than previous classic Grecian pillared plantation homes they had visited. There was a covered porch across the front, for shade from the intense Mississippi sun, but it was not with the tall Doric columns of the neo-classic architecture often featured in many of these gracious dwellings of the region, with their floor-to-ceiling windows and lacy iron balconies at upper windows.

A faded sign, on one of the gateposts, said THE HOMESTEAD. On the other gatepost, even more faded, Grace made out the words, still barely legible, TWIN OAKS. Over the gate was yet another sign, but her attention was distracted by a barking dog before she could read it.

The yellowish hound-dog came running up to them as they drove through the gate, taking very seriously his job as guardian-protector, barking loudly, sending up the alarm.

"Hey, there, Yella-dog," said George. The four-footed one stopped abruptly, approaching cautiously, and George got down out of the wagon to pat him on the head. The hound sniffed thoroughly, and then its tail began to wag so vigorously it seemed as though it might come off! It began jumping up on George and running in circles around him.

"Okay, boy! Calm down! I'm glad to see you, too."

A cousin's place perhaps? He and the dog were obviously old friends.

As they approached the front of the big house, a Black Woman came out to see who it was, shook her head in dis-recognition, and went back in. George stopped the team, looped the reins around a hitching post, and helped Grace to the ground.

Grace stopped to stroke her mare; after so many long days of pulling the wagon, the horse must be tired, she thought. George had gone on into the house.

And suddenly she heard a SCREAM! Pandemonium! People running from every direction, yelling, screaming... a SHOT!! What was happening?

The ponies shied, skittish, pulling at the reins.

Little Dove crouched down behind the wagon: The scene of the attack on her family, her village, flashed through her mind, and it was terrifying! She thought she had left all that behind.

"GEORDIE!" she heard a young woman's voice cry out. "Mama, come quick – Geordie's back!!"

It took a moment to register.

Geordie? Mama?

"Welcome back, Brother!" she heard a man's voice say.

"Mah ba-by boy! What I raised from a chile! Been gone so long; lookin' so fine -- ain' even knowed yuh!" It was the voice of a Black woman. They sounded a little different.

Of course! This was not the alarm at being surprised by an enemy: This was a victory celebration, for a returning warrior after some great deed! Or the return of a beloved brother, after a journey of many, many seasons.

Understanding dawned as she stood up tall, and she slowly ascended the steps to the porch, watching the flurry of activity inside the large foyer of the house. But what of the shot, she wondered?

"Good to see you again, Little Brother!" said a deeper voice. "Sorry my gun went off, hope it didn't frighten y'all. It discharged while I was cleanin' it, I was so startled when Rebecca screamed -- I jumped up too fast!"

Ah! That was it! Little Dove was relieved.

"Hey, Mama," George said, giving a Southern greeting.

"My beloved son! How happy I am that you have returned! You look well!"

"And you, Mama. Osiyo; Doo-heet-soo?" he said, greeting her in Cherokee. (Hello, how are you?)

It was his mother who first noticed Little Dove, standing outside on the porch.

"Come in, child!" she said walking toward Little Dove, hands out-stretched.

"Geordie! You brought a young lady with you!" said Rebecca. "For-give us! We did not mean to be rude! It's just that he's been away so long, and we love our brother dearly!"

Grace smiled. "I understand a loving family. I had one once."

Mrs. Gillespie took Little Dove's hands in hers, and looked into her eyes.

"Why, you're one of us!" she said quietly. A tingle ran through Little Dove, down the length of her body. There was a spark of recognition between them, on some deep level.

"You are welcome here, my dear."

"Thank you, ma'am," she answered, with a smile.

"This is my wife," Geordie said to the assembled family. He put his arm around her waist and said to her, "Welcome home, Little Woya!" (Woya is Cherokee for Dove.)

The sisters observed her. "Oh! She's lovely, isn't she!" "Beautiful!" "Graceful!"

"You've hit on it, Carolyn -- her name is Grace, and she's full of it."

His teen-age brothers snickered, taking a different meaning. Geordie reprimanded them with a look.

"Got a wife, huh?" one of them shot back. "Didn't think you'd ever find a girl who'd have you!"

Geordie laughed; he did not mind being teased. He knew he was home again.

People seemed to come from everywhere; it was the prodigal son returned! From upstairs, from the kitchen, the parlor, the barns and sheds, the cabins and the fields... They came, Black People, Brown, and White People, walking and running, to see what all the commotion was about. "Go get Papa!" someone said, but he was already on his way from the stable, and Gran'pa with him.

They went out back to the garden, in the shade of two tall oak trees, where there was room for all to gather. "This is our Council Circle," Geordie told his bride. Some of the women sat on wicker chairs or settees, with their full skirts spreading out. Men sat on log benches, and the little ones sat on the ground. Servants and field-hands stood respectfully in the background, except for several who came forward to greet them, saying "Welcome back, Massa Geordie, welcome! To you an' the lil' Missus." "Ain't she purdy! Yessum." "She sho-ly is." "We's mighty pleased to have you here, little Missus." And they would bow or curtsy.

"How fortunate that you came back at harvest time, when the whole family is back at the homestead to help out," said sister Carolyn Ann. Her husband James and their children stood by her side.

"We're just about all here except for Gillie and Melissa, and they've been sent for."

"Tell us about your adventures!" said his younger brother William. "You've been gone so long!" chimed in his sister-in-law Lucinda. "How long has it been?"

"Ten years," said a deep voice from the back of the group that was gathered there, and everybody turned to look, stepping aside to make way.

"Ten years now, hasn't it been, Laddie?"

"Papa! Gran'pa!"

"Ten years, indeed, Geordie lad!" said the white-haired man with the thicker brogue.

The men embraced, and Geordie introduced his new wife.

"This is Grace, my Little Dove who flew down from the North. A homing-pigeon, she is! As you see – she's brought me home!"

"So that's the lass that's set your heart a-flutter, is it? And a bonnie lass she is!" His father took her hand, and gallantly raised it to his lips, with a bow. It startled her; she was unfamiliar with this custom.

"She favors your mother a bit, doesn't she?" he added, no longer imitating the Scottish speech of his father, which he enjoyed doing now and then. To remind them of their Scottish heritage. They were all-too-well aware of their Native connection; they were always having to be careful to hide it from outsiders.

"It's good to have you back, son."

"Mercy! Sometimes we thought you were lost to us forever, that you would never return!" said his older sister Rebecca. "And then when you walked in the door without so much as a by-your-leave... and I thought, 'How did he get past the guard-dog, get 'im to stop barkin' so soon?' So I got up an' went to see who it was. Lord-a-mercy, he looks so different! He was just a boy when he left, just sixteen. An' here was this handsome man! He's got a little beard now!

"But then I recognized that smile, an' the twinkle in those blue eyes – an' I let out a scream! I screamed bloody-murder! An' everybody came runnin' to see what had happened."

"An' then my gun went off, while I was cleanin' it, an' I got up so fast to see what happened," said Robert III, who was called Rob.

"Land sakes," said Mama Gillespie, "what a welcome for this poor child!"

"She musta thot she was bein' attacked by a bunch o' wild Indians!" said Carolyn with a grin, and they all laughed -- it was an inside joke.

"Tell us about your adventures, Geordie!" seventeen-year-old brother Peter implored. "What was it like in the South Seas?"

"Ah, you received my packet, then? I never knew if they would reach their destination, as I never settled long enough to have a place at which to receive a reply."

He had sent them a painted picture of the Natives and lush landscape of Tahiti, Bora Bora, and Bali, among other exotic locales, as his ship had reached distant ports years before.

"Tell us about the girls!" said Peter, grinning.

"Hush, now, dear," said his mother. "He can tell you his story later; I'd like to hear something now from our new daughter, Grace! Unless she's too tired, after such a long journey. We might be overwhelming her. Perhaps you'd like to get some rest, my dear?"

"Oh, it's all right, Ma'am," said Little Dove. "It's nice to have a family again," she added wistfully.

Mama Gillespie caught the hint of sadness in her voice, and gazed at her, going into vision: She saw the Lakota village, the tipis, the women busy cooking over little fires, and some scraping hides. Little girls would be helping their mothers, boys were chasing each other, playing games, racing, or practicing shooting at targets with their bows and arrows. Elders were showing little ones how to make things.

Then the men were returning from a successful hunt, carrying a deer over their shoulder, or buffalo hides or meat -- and everyone ran to greet them. The women began a high, trilling sound to indicate their welcome, and their delight.

While the Lakota people were thus preoccupied, she saw the U.S. Cavalry come swooping down into the camp, riding swiftly, swords flashing in the sunlight, shooting anything that moved, torching tipis. The warriors fought as well as they could, but they were afoot, and the soldiers were mounted, much more numerous, well armed with guns, and had the advantage of surprise.

This was not the way of the Plains People, and thus they were completely caught off-guard. One might surprise an enemy, certainly, but warriors went to fight other warriors; they did not attack their families. There was no honor in this.

Mama Gillespie saw Little Dove and her mother crouching under an overhang of the riverbank, listening in horror to the shooting -- and the screams of their people. When the soldiers had gone, Turtle Woman said "You do not need to see this, Little Dove!"

"But Mama, we must pray over our loved ones," she replied, tears streaming down her face. "We must sing them over to the Spirit World, to be with the Ancestors, and with Tonka-shila."

Thus Little Dove's mystic mother-in-law observed them praying over the dying and the dead. "It is a good day to die," said Little Dove's favorite brother as she cradled his head in her lap, and he took his last breath. The Ancestors gathered around to receive the newcomers to the Spirit World. A great wail arose from the woman and her child, as they released the spirits of those they loved.

One more scene was shown: The death of Turtle Woman, and the coming of Little Dove's uncle to get her -- and take her to safety in the mountains.

The rest of the family knew to be silent when their mother was having one of her visions, a spiritual experience. They also knew better than to ask about it. She would share it when, or if, the time was right.

Mama Gillespie went up to her new daughter and embraced her.

"You are safe here," she said simply. "There is much love for you here."

Little Dove felt the familiar tingle that told her a Truth had been spoken.

Rebecca spoke to Geordie.

"We've kept your old room as a spare bedroom for travelers or visiting relatives all these years," she said as they approached the great curving staircase built by an itinerant craftsman generations ago. "Thomas and I and the children are using it now, while we've come to help gather in the crops -- and soon it'll be cotton-pickin' time. But you an' Grace can have it if you like; we're always addin' on rooms here, as the family grows, and one of 'em's almost finished.

"And you must come and see our house, down the road. It's beautiful! You must stay with us for a time."

"I thank you, Rebecca, we'd be delighted. As to where to stay. Is that ol' cabin vacant, that Gran'pa used to live in when he first came here? When the big house still seemed overwhelmin' to him?"

"Why I believe it is. Ol' Tom, the foreman, lived there for many years, but he's just recently gone on to his reward."

"Ol' Uncle Tom!" Geordie said, reminiscing. The phrase had not yet become an insult. "He used to take me fishin' down at our special, secret place near the swimmin' hole. He taught me so many things. An' he used to tell me tales his gran'pa had tol' him, in Africa. Like stories about the critters. Brother Rabbit - he called him Br'er Rabbit – an' Brother Possum and Brother Fox. The Africans believe the animals are our brothers and sisters, like we do, and that they can teach us a lot."

The three of them went out to the cabin, which was bigger than the others built to house the slaves. It was set apart from them, under a tree with moss draped from its branches like a fringed shawl that swayed gently in the breeze. It had two bedrooms, and a large room for cooking and living; and a covered porch across the front. Gran'ma Gillespie, since gone on, preferred it to the big house. It was more like the log cabins of her Cherokee people.

"It hasn't been cleaned since he passed on," said Rebecca, as she opened the door and particles of dust danced in the shaft of sunlight. "But if you'll be comfortable here, I'll have Tabitha clean it out. I believe Ol' Tom's things have been removed already. An' it does have more privacy, set off like it is," she added with a smile.

"What do you think, Grace?" he asked his bride.

"It's perfect!" she told him, delightedly, looking around. A place of their own! She would love fixing it up.

"Well then, I'll have it seen to right away," Rebecca said. "You'll have your own little honeymoon cottage."

Little Dove was gloriously happy! She did not want to leave. But the brass bell's gong sounded on the porch of the Big House, and they heard the words "Supper's ready!" called out, so the family dropped what they were doing and gathered together for the evening meal.

And what a sumptuous meal it was! It took two large tables to ac-commodate them all at harvest time, and these were laden with deep-fried chicken, golden-brown and spicy; mounds of potatoes and boats of gravy, or chicken-and-dumplings if that was your preference; black-eyed peas, yams, hams, and sweet-potato pie. Grits were served at every meal, and biscuits with fresh butter, as well as pitchers of milk and water. Empty dish-es were often replenished by a young Black girl who came and went from the kitchen.

Between the spicy African and the Creole and Cherokee cooking, there were treats for the palate such as Little Dove had never known.

She remarked on it, and glowed under the attention she received as they welcomed her into the family.

After dinner they gathered around in the large front room and im-plored the newcomers to tell them how they had met. "We want romance!" laughed Carolyn.

"We want adventure!" said younger brother Peter.

"I'll tell you a little bit," said Geordie, "and save the rest for other nights, as we'd like to settle in. All right: I met her at a dance, took her down to look at the river, and an hour later I said: 'I will marry you!' And, as you see, I did."

"How romantic!" said Carolyn.

"Could you be leaving anything out?" asked Rebecca. "We want more!"

"And you shall have it. But not tonight." And off they went to the cot-tage.

Geordie went up the steps to the little porch with a wooden railing around it, opened the door, and swept her off her feet.

She was surprised as he scooped her up in his strong arms. She was not familiar with this custom.

"Carrying a bride across the threshold of their new home is a tradi-tion in these parts," he smiled.

The furniture in the Cottage was rustic but comfortable; to her it couldn't have been more perfect -- if one had to live in a house. There was a large comforter and a patch-work quilt (made by loving hands) on the big bed in their bedroom, with the top corner of the fresh sheets carefully turned down on each side. He carried her to the bed and tossed her down on it, threw himself on top of her, removed her clothing and his own -- and made vigorous love to her.

"Welcome home, Mrs. Gillespie," he said, and they both laughed. It was a wonderful way to start off their new life together, and she gave thanks to the Creator.

Little Dove quickly adapted to the life of the family, and was happy to help out however she could. They thought her rather serious until, one day in the kitchen, she told them about her first experience with a broom. The girls laughed hysterically, and the cook and serving girl had a good laugh too. "A Medicine Piece!" said Carolyn. "Did you evah?"

One day she was standing at the window of the Cottage, as they called it, looking out at the row of cabins at the edge of vast fields of cotton, with corn and other crops here and there. Each cabin had their own vegetable garden as well, and the big house had a large one, with herbs also.

Noticing her wistfulness, Geordie spoke to her: "You're wondering about the slaves, aren't you? How Choctaw-Cherokee people can own slaves?"

"It is puzzling to me. It is the White Man's Way, to own land; we feel that no-one owns the land, the air, or the waters of the sea. They belong to the Great Creator. We are only to care for the land, to use what we need, to share. We are to care for each other, as brothers. The winged ones, the four-footed. And, certainly, the two-legged also."

"That is true. But sometimes one tribe would take enemy captives, is that not so?"

"That is so, and they would be worked hard. But if they proved themselves brave, they would be honored; become family. And they were not considered less of a human being than another -- only less fortunate, in that they were captured."

"Exactly! The Black people here have had the misfortune to be captured, or their parents or Gramparents were stolen from their villages and became captives in Africa.

"When my grandfather came to this country from Scotland, he came to escape the system there where the landed gentry, the noblemen, made slaves of the people, the serfs. He married a Cherokee woman, and they worked diligently, and, with his thrifty ways, their hard work, and her knowledge of the land, they prospered. He worked at many trades: blacksmith, tin-smith, wood-carver. And he grew cotton, and showed the womenfolk how to weave fabric like the tartans back home.

"This plantation is one of the oldest ones around this part of the country. When the old man -- the owner -- died, his widow moved into town; to Holly Springs, to live with her daughter. This place got run-down; with no one to oversee the few slaves left, and the house in shambles, the widow wanted to sell it. Her children had taken to town livin', and didn't want to bother with it.

"Gran'pa Gillespie had shod their horses, repaired their carts and carriages, helped build their barns, and supplied them with beautiful materials to make clothing with. He was always on hand to help out if they needed it. So the widow said she'd like for him to have Twin Oaks, as they called it. And she sold it to him for very little, considerin'."

He looked out over the fields. "There were fifty-five acres of good rich bottom-land here in the place where three rivers come together, the junction of the Yazoo, the Tallahatchie and the Yalabusha. And we've added more since. Two of Gran'pa's sons built houses of their own, one on the property and one down the road. One moved away, and my father moved into the Big House, 'cause he had the biggest family.

"For the first couple of years, Gran'pa and Gran'ma and three of their young-uns lived here in this cabin. He said they were never happier."

Little Dove could understand that. She felt the same way.

"Some of those cabins were there when Gran'pa got this plantation. And seven slaves came with the place."

"How many are there here now?" asked Little Dove.

"Probably close to thirty. But you might be interested to know that they're not slaves! They've all been given their freedom."

Little Dove perked up. "That makes my heart happy!" she exclaimed. "Do many people do this thing?"

"No, I'm afraid not. 'Course Gran'pa had to register that they were free, down at the Town Hall, to get the papers. The Registrar thought he was crazy! 'Now what jou wanna go an' do a thing like that fo'?' he asked. 'Weel noo, laddie,' Gran'pa said, 'Did you ever notice that mah field-hands put out more bales o' cotton than any others in the area? The idea of freedom is a power-ful thing; if they think they're free, they work harr-der!

And I benefit! An' I'm not worried about 'em leavin' -- where are they goin' to go? They'd be worse off anywhere else, an' they know it.'

"'Gotta admit you're clever,'" said the Registrar.

'Keep it under your topper, tho', laddie! We wouldn't want too many others gettin' such ideas, now, would we?'

"'Oh, no-suh! That could ruin the economy! We need our slaves.' Gran'pa didn' want other plantation owners gettin' upset with him, an' he didn' want to be incitin' rebellion. There've been a few uprisin's, but sometimes both owners and slaves get killed that way."

Geordie explained that there was a great deal of prejudice in the South, and many White people would get very angry with people who upset the system. A lot of them were kind to their slaves, the house-servants anyway, and would care for them when they were sick. But others were very cruel to them.

The expression 'being sold down the river' could strike terror into the hearts of slaves from other states. It meant being sold to traders who took them down-river to Mississippi, where conditions were worse than anywhere else. Runaways would be hunted down by hound dogs, and severely beaten. Children would be sold away from their mothers.

"In order to thrive here (or even survive), we have to be extremely careful. When gold was found on our land, Cherokee, Choctaw and others were taken to stockades, or Death Camps, to starve, or die of disease, or to perish on the 'Trail of Tears' to Oklahoma. Many thousands of our people have died.

"So we have to be careful. There are laws in this state that say that if you have even an eighth Negro blood, you're Black -- and have no rights. Indians are rounded up and removed to reservations. So we pretend to be White. We say we are Scottish, and Spanish. We do not like to be deceitful -- but the alternative is worse."

Little Dove understood all too well. She had seen the alternative.

"We are always on guard here. The watch-dog sounds the alarm if someone is coming, and we play our roles. When no-one is around, we are more relaxed. But we have called together our Black brothers and sisters and explained to them that we honor them, as we do all things, but due to the circumstances, for their sakes and ours, we must all play our parts in this charade," Geordie continued.

Little Dove, Lakota Ancestor

"They understand; they are grateful, and teach their little ones to be respectful, so they won't get into trouble when they go elsewhere. But they are happy here -- they know that their families won't be separated. And if someone wants to go North, to freedom, they are given a pass to do so. We make it look like they're on some business for the Master. Or one of us may go with them to the North, to make certain of their safety, for there are some unscrupulous slave catchers who do not respect papers, and will sell them off somewhere else.

"They are also given some money, a share of the fruit of their labors -- so that if they or their loved ones wish to go North, they will have something to start off with. Few have gone, for the word has come back that although things are better there in some ways, they are worse in others. There is a coldness there, in the weather and in the hearts of many of the people. And the warmth of a loving family is missing."

"That is the most important thing, I think," said his Little Dove, putting her arms around her husband's waist, as he embraced her and kissed her up-turned face.

The classic book GONE WITH THE WIND, and the film of that name, showed what life was like in the American Deep South during the 1800s. Vivian Leigh portrayed Scarlet O'Hara, Clark Gable was Rhett Butler, Olivia de Havilland played Melanie, and Hattie McDaniel was Mammy. The film had more Oscar wins than any other movie. The above character dolls are from the Blue Star Collection.

Chapter 6

Two Worlds

When Scotsman Grandpa Gillespie and his Cherokee wife moved there, "Two Worlds" seemed an appropriate name for their homestead. Now many Peoples were represented there, living in harmony. There were the European, the Choctaw and Cherokee Nations, the Plains Indian and the African influence as well.

Mama Gillespie was the first one to notice that Little Dove was with child. She was feeling a bit queasy one morning. "Something I ate, perhaps," she said, but her mother-in-law took a look at her -- and saw a little spirit hovering around her, going in and out.

"You must get more rest, dear," she told Little Dove, "and eat well, but not too much. This is the busiest time in a soul's life! This time before they are born. They are always going back and forth, from their wise advisors to your womb, learning how to form little fingers and toes, ears and nose. The spirit doesn't stay in its little body permanently until after the birth, when it draws the first breath."

"Thank you. It is good to have a mother to teach me these things," Little Dove said.

"Well, it seems that I am your third mother!"

"Indeed. I am most fortunate, to have so much wise guidance, and love."

"Sing to the baby. Speak to it, stroke it; tell it you love it. It will thrive."

Geordie showed Little Dove a tucked-away place behind the house, a garden, with oleanders and various tall shrubbery all around it. In the center was a fire-pit; around that a large circle of stones. Outside of that were log benches all around.

"Why, it looks like a Medicine Wheel!" she exclaimed.

"We call it our Council Circle," Geordie answered. "It is a medicine wheel, of course. But Native religions have had to go 'underground' in order to survive. You know how White People are about 'those heathens.'"

"I do indeed. Mother Emma had me baptized. I had to continue my Honoring Ceremonies in secret."

"And so do we. But this is the Ceremonial Circle of my Cherokee grandfather. Before a ceremony, we sprinkle cornmeal on each of the rocks, saying a prayer with each sprinkling. Then we walk around the outside four times, to honor the Four Directions and the races of people. After that we enter through the doorway, an opening in the rocks, in the East, the direction of beginnings. We honor the Sacred Torch -- the fire in the center -- with cornmeal and prayer, and tsalu (tobacco, in Cherokee). We give thanks to the Earth Mother, and the Sky Father, and acknowledge the Star Nation, from which we came. They are watching over us."

Little Dove was excited. She told him about how she used to sneak out of the fort and do her ceremonies at the full of the moon.

"And we shall continue to do them! You are free to do whatever you like here; we honor all paths."

Geordie further explained their tradition. When the people would go inside the circle, they would sit and listen to one of the Elders share the wisdom-teachings.

"When I was a little boy, I loved to listen to my Cherokee grandmother tell about how she lived when she was small. She lived in a village with a large stockade wall around it, to protect them from enemies. They lived in houses that had woven reed mats for walls, on the sides and back, but open at one side and at the top and bottom to let the air move through -- with high peaked roofs to shade them from the summer sun. In winter, they crawled into small round houses, like the igloos of our relatives to the far North, but made of mud and sticks. These would keep them warm on cold winter nights, or during storms."

"That was our time for story telling, in the lodges of the Lakotas," said Little Dove. "On winter nights the Elders would tell us our history. They told about Dawn Star, who came to Turtle Island from the East, at the time of the morning star shining so brightly. His followers came in a giant canoe, they said, with wings like an enormous bird!

"But Dawn Star came walking across the water, with a great light shining forth from him. And that is why my people called him by that name. Our People have two Guidelines: There is One Creator, whose Spirit is in All Things; and Do to your Brother or Sister what you would have them do to You. And to honor All Our Relations."

"Our teaching also, Little Dove." Geordie would call her Grace to outsiders, but Little Dove among themselves. It was acceptable to have 'pet names'.

"Tell me more about how your grandmother lived."

"They made a canoe out of a large log," Geordie continued, "by burning out the insides with coals, and then carving it out with stone tools. There was a stream running through the village, and the women would pick certain reeds or rushes and weave them into baskets by making them soft in the water. The men would shape flints into arrowheads, or spear points. They used a long, thin reed as a blow-gun. The boys played a game with a small net on a stick where they would all try to get a ball through posts at the end of a field. You could do anything but let the ball touch the ground. These games could be very rough! But they taught skill, swiftness and alertness."

"We had such games, too!" she said, excited. "My people loved to play games -- and to gamble. Sometimes they would lose everything in a game, but then they'd come back the next night and win it back. Until the White Men came, the traders. I heard they would go into a village, with their fire-water, teach their games and win at them, and the next day The People would discover that the White Men had gone -- and all of their winnings with them. They play by different rules!"

"I've noticed," Geordie said, shaking his head sadly. He told her about the Cherokee Councils.

"In the center of the village, there was a Council House. It was seven-sided; seven is our sacred number. It is to remind us that we come from the Seven Dancers (Pleiades). You would enter through a low tunnel, bowing low, crawling, to represent humility."

"As we do in the Stone-Peoples lodge!"

"Yes. In the center of the Council House was the Sacred Torch, the fire to remind us of the light that shines within, and of our origins among the stars," Geordie said. "For it was lit from an ember from the eternal flame, brought with us aboard a Star-ship long ago. The Keepers of the Flame never allow that fire to go out. It is in a secret cave, and someone always tends it.

"An ember from it was taken along on the Trail of Tears, to be placed in the new Council House at the end of their journey -- in Oklahoma. On the way, there was a blizzard, and it went out. Runners were sent back to get another ember, and that one arrived safely at its destination," said Geordie.

"Inside the Council House in my grandmother's village, back a few feet from the Sacred Fire, there were seven posts to support the ceiling. Women Elders would be seated in front of these. Women have always had great authority and commanded the utmost respect among the Tsalagi. White People called our Council 'the petticoat government', because women had so much influence in the running of our tribal affairs!"

Little Dove laughed. "Women are respected among my tribe, but the men are more powerful. They are the leaders."

"Behind the pillars of the Cherokee Council House were seven sections of benches, going upward, two or three deep, for the people to sit on," Geordie went on. "All kinds of village matters would be discussed at these meetings. But the say of the Grandmothers, the clan leaders, would be final."

Geordie smiled at Little Dove, and held her hand. "When two people wanted to marry," he said, "the man would bring a blanket and deer meat to the marriage ceremony, to show that he would be a good hunter and provider. The woman would bring a blanket and a basket of corn, indicating that she would grow food, cook, and care for their family. Then the Holy Person would tie a corner of each blanket together, to symbolize their union. It was called 'tying the knot.'"

Little Dove smiled. "Did the knot ever come untied?"

"Well," he replied, "if a woman decided that her husband did not treat her well, or was not a good husband, she could put his blanket and his weapons and personal things outside the door, and he couldn't come back in. The woman owned the house and the things in it. He could go to the Council Grandmothers and ask them to speak to her, to ask her for another chance -- but if she said 'No!' he couldn't go back."

"Among our people," said Little Dove, "a woman would tear their blanket in half, and put the man's things outside the lodge: 'Splitting the

Blanket.' If a man abused a woman, he would be called by the Elders to the Sundance Tree, to pierce; to learn about suffering."

It was a busy time around the homestead at harvest. In the cotton fields, dragging and filling long burlap sacks, those of African heritage were working. Singing made the work go easier, and their voices blended in beautiful harmonies, which wafted across the long rows of fluffy white cotton bolls. Sometimes a leader would sing a line, and the others would join in the chorus. Bright kerchiefs and shirts lent splashes of color to the sea of movement in the snowy-white fields.

Young boys brought water or umbrellas for shade to the workers. Unlike on most of the other plantations, they were able to stop and rest whenever they chose. Still, they worked quickly, making a game out of seeing who could fill up their sacks the fastest.

Members of the Scottish Choctaw-Cherokee Lakota family worked mostly in the large garden among corn, peas, squash, peanuts, beans, yams and other vegetables and herbs -- and tobacco for ceremonial purposes. The Boys and men tended the stock: horses, cows, pigs, and chickens. Girls gathered eggs.

In the evening, after supper, there was music by the cabins. Drums were not allowed by southern plantation owners. They knew that Africans could communicate with each other in this manner over great distances, and that could be dangerous! The Blacks could run away, or they could revolt.

So, like the Native Americans, they had to hide their traditions. But they were allowed to sing the White Man's spiritual songs, and some others considered harmless -- and this they did with fervor. Sometimes they made banjos, an African instrument, out of a large turtle shell with an animal skin stretched over it, like a drum with a handle. The stick, the long wooden handle, would have carved designs making notches for frets, and gut stretched to tuning pegs for strings.

Dancing, singing and laughter would fill the night air! Music and movement were life to the Africans. They sang in the fields, by their cabins, and in the little white-painted churches. Music accompanied all of life's important events for them, including the sending of loved ones to the great beyond. "Swing low, sweet chari-ot, comin' fo' to carry me ho-me..." was a favorite, and "Will the Circle be Unbroken?" was another. "Oh, when the

Saints -- go marchin' in -- Oh, when the Saints -- go mar-chin' in; Lawd, I want to be in that num-ber... when the Saints go marchin' in!" This song would give a departed soul a good send-off, at funeral processions in New Orleans.

Jazz, considered the one real American form of music, is based on rhythms imported from Africa, changed and combined with the instruments they were allowed to use here. The Blues cried out their heart's pain at being wrenched from their homeland, forbidden their traditions (as were American Indians) and often de-humanized by the 'masters' who owned them.

And the truly-American music, of those Native to America, was also suppressed, but would one day enjoy a resurgence -- along with a sense of pride in their heritage -- in Pow-wows all across this great land of Turtle island.

Sunday was the day of rest, but the Gillespie family put on their best Sunday-go-to-Meetin' clothes and went down the road to church in the morning. It was an important part of the drama they were playing. The Choctaw were the original true Mississippians, but those who still followed the old ways were being carted off to reservations, so the Gillespie clan felt that the pretense was necessary.

"Brothahs an' sistahs, let us pray!" the old-time preacher would start the service in a loud, deep voice. "Hear us, Lord! Wash our sins away, with the blood o' JE-sus! May we live in RIGHT-eousness, and steer us away from the hell-fires of damn-NA-tion! DO NOT -- Ah say, do not -- allow Satan to lead us into the ways of wickedness and evil, and steal our SOUL."

What a strange religion, thought Little Dove. So much emphasis on darkness, instead of light. She wondered if the Black preachers learned from these White Baptist ministers, or the other way around. They both sounded very dramatic. Anyway, she liked her benevolent Creator, whose Spirit was in all things, better than their god of hell-fire and brimstone.

"We thank you for our blessings, Lord, for we know that we are your CHO-sen ones!"

"Amen, Lord!" the congregation seconded the emotion. (sic.)

"We thank you for our genteel and prosperous way of living, for our fine gentlemen and gracious ladies, our dashing young men, and our young flowers of Southern womanhood."

"Yes, Lord."

"We are grateful for our good and faithful servants, our Nigras, and we must take care of them, like we do our horses and our cattle. We must see that they are healthy, for we need good breeding stock, to work in the fields and help us preserve our hallowed way of life. We know that they are as children, that their brains are not developed like ours, so it is our responsibility to see that they do their duties. And we must pray to the Lord to save their soul... if indeed they have one." (Sic, sic, sic!)

"Hallelujah!" came the chorus. "Amen."

"Deacon Carter will now pass the collection plate for offerings. I'm sure you will all want to be generous with sharing your bountiful abundance with the Servant of the Lord."

Going to the White People's church was part of the game they played, the charade. It was hard for Little Dove to listen to these rantings, but she enjoyed singing the songs, especially the song, 'Amazing Grace'.

Afterwards, there was tea in the Rectory.

"Wasn't that a lovely sermon!" gushed one of the lady parishioners.

Little Dove felt like she was going to throw up. Perhaps it was morning sickness.

After that there was Sunday Dinner, one of those sumptuous Southern meals flavored with spicy African cookery, and sprinkled with the magic ingredient: Love.

Sometimes people would come to call at Two Worlds on a Sunday afternoon. Or there would be a picnic spread out on blankets down by the river, under the tall oak trees, with their long Spanish moss draperies hanging down. When the azaleas and the gardenias were in bloom, the air would be deliciously scented, and the surroundings colorful. The boys would go out in little flat-bottomed boats to fish, and there would be the pungent smell of a fish fry at sunset.

Sunday evening, when the visitors had gone, the family and their freed slaves would gather at the Council Circle, and they would have their own inter-tribal traditional ceremonies, of the Black, Red (Sioux), and Brown (Cherokee) Peoples. And Grandpa Gillespie would represent the White race, contributing a Scottish prayer.

"A Blessin' be upon ye, mah kith n' kin. May the gud Laird smile upon ye, an' may ye be bonnie an bra-a." Thus he asked the Lord's blessing on his relatives and loved ones, that they might be good and brave.

The Sacred Torch would be lit in the center of the circle, and corn-meal sprinkled into it. The 'Spirit Keepers of the Four Directions' would be acknowledged and honored, thus love for all beings would be going out in all directions. The Principle Ceremonialist, on behalf of all of them, would also send love to the Earth Mother and to the Sky Father, and give a salute -- hand-to-heart, to the Spirit-Eye (mid-forehead), and upward to the sky -- to the Star Nation, acknowledging their origins.

The Africans and their children would express their prayers by singing and dancing their ancient rites, and drums with a soft voice were allowed here, with many bushes to absorb the sound. A guard was always posted at the edge of the property at these times, as well as dogs sensitive to the approach of strangers - and dangers.

After the Cherokee and Choctaw songs and offerings were finished, Little Dove would be asked to do hers. She gave thanks to the Creator, who watched over them, and, stooping down, gave a kiss to the earth, her fingers going from her mouth to the ground. She was sending love to Mother Earth, who nourished them. "I give thanks for the knowledge," she'd say, "that we are that which connects the Sky Father and the Earth Mother. As we ask to be filled with the Light of the Father, and send it forth into the Mother, to spread this light, this love, out in all directions -- and as we say "Thank you, Father; Love, Mother, we thus become a living prayer."

Little Dove would send out blessings to those that walked or crawled or swam or flew. She would do the Woman's Dance, pressing healing into the earth, and then the high-stepping, intricate dance of young maidens. "Looks lak a Hee-land fling, tha-at!" observed Grandpa. She taught the boys how to do the warrior's dance that her brothers had done; the deer dance, the eagle, and the buffalo dance. They would finish their ceremonies with a friendship dance -- all joining hands, with a step, together; step, together; around the circle.

Mama Gillespie always told the stories of the Old Ones and passed on wisdom-teachings at these gatherings. She felt it was very important for her children to know who they really were, and to be proud of it. It was particularly important to offset the kind of thing they heard in sermons at the church, and the prevailing attitudes they echoed.

"Nobody is any better than anybody else, in the sight of the Creator," she taught them, "or any worse." Each earth-walk (lifetime) is another lesson. If you do well with it, you progress; though the challenges may be even greater, at higher levels of learning. Sometimes you fail, and you have to (or rather, choose to) come back and do it over again. And it may be harder the next time.

"So do the best you can with whatever situation you have. And never criticize another until you've walked a thousand miles in their moccasins," she advised.

Little Dove turned seventeen not long before her first child was due. Her mother-in-law was a mid-wife and a healer, and so were several of the Afro-women, so she had plenty of guidance and assistance when her time came.

"The important thing is to be relaxed," Mama Gillespie told her. "You can practice that beforehand. Lie quietly and concentrate on each set of muscles; on totally relaxing the forehead, the cheeks, chin, throat; arms and hands; chest, stomach, and down into your legs and feet.

"What causes pain is when the pushing-out muscles are fighting with the muscles at the opening. If the ones at the opening of the womb tighten up because of fear, instead of relaxing and letting the baby come out, then there can be pain. It can get intense toward the end, but, oh! When that baby comes! It's the most precious, most thrilling thing that could ever happen, when the baby comes out; and all else is forgotten."

Mammy Liza, who had been on the plantation through several generations, told how the process had worked in Africa. "We would hol' onto a pole, in de hut, an' bear down; an' de hepper catch de chile when it come. Dat seem to be de mos' natch-el way of birthin' babies."

"Among my people," said Little Dove, "a girl might go off into the bushes, or down by a stream, when it was her time to bring forth a child. She would have a twisted piece of soft leather to bite down on, but we would make no sound. That could alert an enemy as to our position so they could surprise us, so we were taught to be quiet. And always to show no fear. We ask the Spirits of our Ancestors to help us, and to welcome the child into this earth-walk."

75

When she went into labor, she focused on relaxing, as she had been advised, and although the contractions came and went throughout the day, the powerful ones at the end lasted only a half-hour.

The crowning glory popped out at eight in the evening on a gentle May night. Geordie had sat and held her hand from time to time while she was waiting for the arrival of their firstborn, but men often do not do well watching helplessly while their loved-one is in strenuous discomfort. (Some call it pain.) And they were considered superfluous and in the way at this busy time, when the women took over.

After the head came out, and then, with several more contractions, the body came, it was followed by the announcement: "You got a beautiful little son!" Everyone was all smiles, as Mama G. laid the baby on his mother's stomach, and Little Dove experienced the thrill of the miracle of having brought forth a child. A new life!

Their son was named John Mallory, after the baby's father's best friend. Geordie and he had roamed the seas together, and the forests, in the early years of his adventures.

Mama Gillespie waited for the umbilical cord to stop pulsating, indicating that the blood flow from mother to child had ceased, before cutting the cord. Mammy Liza then wrapped the baby in a soft blanket, and handed him to his mother.

Again the ecstasy of the experience overtook Little Dove, as she cradled the infant in her arms. Geordie and the rest of the family were called in to share her joy.

"Look, darlin', he's openin' up his lil' eyes an' lookin' aroun'!" "He's uncurlin' his lil' fingers!" "Oh, he's so beau-tiful!" were the comments going around.

Mammy Liza took care of the placenta, the after-birth. Her helpers brought fresh linens, and buckets of boiling water from the cook-house to wash the used sheets, after they had been soaked in a tub of cold water to remove blood-stains.

The cook-house was separate from the main house, to keep the latter from being overheated, and was where most of the cooking was done. (There was also a kitchen in the big house for preparing and serving the rest of the food.) Large brick ovens and cooking surfaces turned out mounds of delicious eggs and bacon with biscuits and grits, ham and yams, and chicken and dumplings with black-eyed peas and greens, which were carried to the main house in covered crockery dishes.

A Christening ceremony was held at the church, as a formality; but the real one, as far as the family was concerned, was the Naming Ceremony, conducted at the Council Circle ten days after the child's birth. Here he was given the name Bird-Who-Flies-High. When Little Dove emerged from the cabin on the day of his birth and held the infant up to Creator for a blessing, a red-tailed hawk (a sacred messenger, like the eagle) flew in circles above them, going higher and higher, to the Sky Father. It was a good sign, an omen of good fortune.

Little Dove removed the bone pendant she always wore and placed it for a moment above the heart of her child. On it was painted an eagle, soaring high above the mountains of her Lakota homeland far to the North.

"The blessings of my mother Turtle Woman, and all of our Ancestors, be upon you, my precious Little One!" she said.

Gifts were brought, and each person gave their own special prayer of welcome to the newcomer, with wishes for a good life, and happiness. "May you be strong, brave and wise, and remember the teachings of our Ancestors," he was advised.

Among the Tsa-la-gi, the Aniyun Wiya, it was considered imperative to pass on the knowledge and Wisdom Teachings of the Old Ones, with each clan being responsible for passing on certain of these teachings.

"Usually among the Cherokee the special knowledge is passed down from mother to daughter," said Mama Gillespie, for they were a matrilineal society. "My mother was Choctaw, my father, Tsa-LA-gi. But his mother had only one daughter, and she was taken by White Man's disease, when she was still young. So my mother-in-law passed the teachings of her clan to me. I will share it with your daughters, whichever ones seem appropriate to receive it."

"And the boys?" asked Little Dove.

"Some knowledge is taught to all the children, of course... but the boys are often not so interested in things of a spiritual nature. Except for a Medicine Man, one of the Holy Ones: A Healer, Spiritual Advisor, or Keeper of Records. You will know when such a one arrives. The Medicine Chief of the tribe will know; he will be told by the Spirit of the Old Ones. He will come and do a special blessing on the one who is to continue his work. The

Medicine Chief will simply show up when that one is born, no matter how far he has to travel."

After each one had spoken and given their blessing to the child, there was singing and dancing to celebrate. A favorite spiritual song was sung: "Go tell it on the mountain! Over the plains and ev'ry whe-ere... Go tell it on the mountain, that John Mall'ry is born!" they improvised. Another family favorite, "This little Light of mine! I'm gonna let it shine!" was sung out joyfully. There were Cherokee songs, and Choctaw, and Lakota sacred songs, and some from Africa.

Grandpa Gillespie finished off with a drinking song, 'A Wee Dock in Dorris', suggesting that they have a little drop of the good stuff, to toast, to celebrate.

Geordie hoisted his glass with the rest of them, clicking away; and then, following his own advice, quietly poured it out on the ground. He wondered why Grandpa didn't understand how deadly liquor could be for American Indians -- but then he realized that his grandfather hadn't seen what it had done to the Plains people, when it was used to cheat them out of all they had. The fire-water would leave drunken Indians who had become addicted to whiskey: They often found it the only way to escape, temporarily, the misery their lives had become since their proud and free life had been taken from them.

The plantation was self-sufficient, and was prospering. Three cows provided milk and cheese, and there were a few steers for beef, hogs for bacon and ham, and lots of chickens. The smokehouse was well-stocked with meat, the larder with eggs, butter and cheese, and the hen-house was filled with poultry. Corn, squash, sweet potatoes, collard greens, okra (a favorite with Africans, for gumbo) and other vegetables grew abundantly in the large, well-tended garden.

Popcorn, that gift to the world from the 'Indians', was a great treat for the children. Cotton was processed and woven into clothing. Fish was plentiful from the nearby rivers, supplying a favorite recreation as well as delicious dinners. An herb garden was used for flavoring and healing purposes.

Little Dove sat on her porch rocking the baby in the cradle that had been lovingly made by her husband, who was a Master Craftsman in wood, among other trades. She watched Geordie plowing a field, walking patiently behind a mule, row after row. He was not one to leave all the work to the field-hands.

Her life here seemed to be perfection... and she marveled that this should be so! She was living like the Wasichu, the enemies of her people, and somehow enjoying it. A life beyond the strangest visions she would have imagined when she was a child, as they were moving across the land far to the north. Sometimes they would move their tipis every few days, following the trail of Tatanka, who fed and clothed them. How different her life had turned out to be.

The new mother sang a song to her infant son as he slept. Mammy Liza had taught it to her. "Hush, lil' ba-by, don' say a word; Papa's gonna buy you a mockin' bird!" Mammy said she learned the song in the Islands (of the Caribbean), where she was first sold into slavery.

Baby John stirred, and opened his eyes. Smiling, Little Dove bent down to pick him up and cradle him in her arms. Putting him to the breast, she pondered the miracle of closeness, of joy, that was brought into her life by this child. Did all new mothers feel this way, she wondered? And, oh, my! That first smile! Heaven could not be more glorious.

The words of her own mother came drifting into her memory. "Although there will be pain and sorrow, there will also be joy and contentment. You will have a strong husband and bear fine sons and daughters. Teach them well."

Little Dove remembered her mother taking her to the Naming Ceremony of her cousin. She was about five summers at the time. Her uncle, Jumping Bull, was the boy's father. He and her other uncles, Four Horns, and Hunting-his-Lodge, and her father, Walks-the-Wind, were Sioux chiefs, some in war and some in peace, each with their own function. Her father had 'crossed to the other side of the ridge' (into spirit) when their village was destroyed, but the others continued as respected Tribal Leaders.

Chief Jumping Bull named the boy The Sacred Stand, because of a vision he had when he 'went on the hill' (for a vision). He foresaw his son taking a stand against the invaders, the Wasichu, and protecting their Sacred Black Hills (the Paha Sapa), their lands, and their Sacred way of life. The boy, also called Slow, because of his deliberate way of walking and speaking, would become not only a great warrior but a powerful spiritual leader as well, according to this vision.

When The Sacred Stand went on his own first mystic quest, to see what Wakan Tanka wanted for his life, he too saw that he was destined to be a leader of his people. He saw that he would lead his warriors to great victories, but that there would also be defeats. At fourteen, the boy went on his first war party, and showed his skill and courage by attacking a fleeing Ab-SA-ro-ke (Crow). To honor him for this brave deed, his father gave him his own name, Sitting Bull -- Tatanka Yotanka -- and took the name of Jumping Bull.

Geordie was a loving husband who knew how to keep romance alive. Every full moon, after a ceremony at the Council Circle joined by all on the homestead, he would steal his Little Dove away and take her on a moonlight ride. They would go down to the river, and reminisce about the magical day when they had met, and he had taken her down by the river so far away; and they had looked into each other's eyes and felt the One-ness of all things, remembering their cosmic origins.

"My Little Dove," he said tenderly. "I told you of my family then. I shared the history, and soon you will also know the mystery!" He was referring to sacred mystical teachings of the Tsalagi.

Little Dove smiled. "Beloved husband! Your words call to mind a teaching of the Old Ones, the Masters, who dwell within the Sacred Mountains of the Teton, where I lived with Oldest Grandmother. I will pass on this gift of words to you.

"Yesterday is the history, tomorrow is the mystery. Today is a gift – and that's why they call it the present!" They both laughed, delighted.

"Did they give this to you in English?" asked Geordie, mystified.

"The words came in English, a language that I did not yet understand. The meaning also came in Lakota, but I did not appreciate the poetry of it until the words in English came back, just now, from Spirit."

Geordie -- Long Bow -- watched silver sparkles of moonlight dance on the rippling river, with his arm around his treasured mate. Sometimes they would go on a canoe ride; sometimes he would lay her on a blanket and caress her -- tenderly, then passionately, as they renewed their dedication to each other.

"The night is made for two things," he told her, smiling. "Sleeping -- or making love!"

Above: Sundance and Sakina. In 1985, they lived in a tipi, in the Southern Ute Mountains of Colorado. Sundance and Sakina got together when they went out into one of Sedona, Arizona's magical canyons and had a simultaneous recall of a lifetime when he was a Mountain Man and she was his Arapaho wife. They later remembered other lifetimes together: He had been Walks-the-Wind, and she had been Turtle Woman, the father and mother of Little Dove.

Chapter 7

Lakota Childhood

Little Dove was pleased with her family, and with her life, which seemed to her -- near perfection! With the help of a loving husband, she had another child every year or two. She enjoyed having a large family; they were well provided for, and she had come from a big family herself.

She had grown up in a family of ten, although it was not quite the kind of nuclear family of the White world. She was the youngest child of Turtle Woman and Walks-the-Wind, she had a sister two years older, and a brother, three years ahead of her, named Otter Boy: Like his name-sake, he was very playful.

Otter Boy and Little Dove were very close. They would laugh together, play games and tricks on people, and tag along on the hunting parties, far enough behind that they couldn't be told not to. She was as adept at riding ponies as any of the boys, and intended to be a Woman Chief when she grew up (there were a few of them), for she was also clever and fearless.

Otter Boy would defend her if she had a problem with any other member of the tribe. "Otter Boy is the Protector of Little Dove, in all the seasons of her life. He fears no enemy," he told her solemnly one day, in their own way of speaking. "All the People sing her song, to honor her," he smiled. This was the brother who later died in her arms.

Her grandmother was a seer, a visionary. "In my dreams I see my daughter's child on long trails, living in strange places, crossing the great waters," she told Little Dove when she was small. "Beside her I see a strong husband, and many children living in their large lodge."

Her closest sister was called Buffalo Calf Girl. She was more interested in girl-things. She would help with the cooking, setting up tipis and taking them down when it was time to move on, and gathering berries, roots and other edibles in season. She was good at making baskets to hold them.

Buffalo Calf Girl would ask Little Dove to play with her when the boys were off practicing with their bows and arrows, and she would often do so. They had each constructed a small tipi, about three feet tall, for the doll family they made out of leather, giving them braids made from their own hair. This was how they practiced being mothers. The dolls' outfits were made of soft doeskin, carefully fringed, and miniature baskets and clay cooking pots were replicas of large ones. When the clans moved on, the girls would take down their little lodges and tie the folded tipis to their small lodge-poles, and have them pulled by dogs on their little travois, just like the big ones pulled by the ponies with their pony-drags.

Little Dove had a flair for painting, and would decorate the tiny tipis with special symbols and scenes showing great victories of the little warriors who inhabited them.

Besides this family of three children, Walks-the-Wind had four more by another wife, Pretty Flower. A Chief could have more than one wife, as long as he could provide for his family. He had to be a good hunter. But many people would come to him -- sometimes from afar -- to seek his counsel or his assistance, and the visitors had to be taken care of and fed, their needs attended to. Another wife was helpful in this way. The people who came would also bring gifts to exchange for the help given. Buffalo robes, horses, deer-meat or simply tobacco might be offered, according to the greatness of the service or the smallness of the ability to give something in exchange. But no-one was refused help.

A Medicine Chief, such as Walks-the-Wind (my husband of that time), took care of the spiritual as well as physical well-being of those who came to him. Each Chief had an area of specialty: some were leaders in war, some in peace. At night the Council Fires were often seen long into the night along the riverbanks, as the Elders and other wise ones discussed various topics and situations, each giving their sacred point of view.

Turtle Woman (as I was called in that life) was a noted healer, and did many doctoring ceremonies. It was customary for a Medicine Person to take three days to decide whether or not to take a case. The healer needed to go into meditation to determine the cause of the illness as well as the treatment. If this was a situation which that individual had chosen for some important lesson, such as some obstacle to overcome, or for a karmic pay-back (or because someone else wanted them to get well instead of it being their choice) then the request for healing would be denied, although they would always be prayed for. Sometimes it was time to let go, and that soul's choice had been to be released.

Some of the healing ceremonies would last for many days, and often many nights as well. When Turtle Woman did her doctoring she might request that the entire family participate in the treatment. If one member was out-of-balance, it would bring dis-harmony and illness. Harmony must be restored to all, they reasoned, or the stress which led to the dis-ease would still be there, and a sickness could return.

Pretty Flower cooked and looked after the children, when Turtle Woman, whom she regarded as a sister, was occupied with her healing work. Sometimes finding the right herb for a certain condition would require an extended journey. The Medicine Woman knew how to find the right herbs for specific needs, and she knew how to work with crystals and stones. Many prayer-ties, tobacco offerings, potions and poultices might be needed.

Walks-the-Wind was a Sundance Chief: a spiritual leader who often was 'put on the hill', in Hamblecha, to seek a vision that would be helpful to the people, and was the organizer of the yearly Sundance. The purpose of this often misunderstood ritual was to show one's love for the People; a sundancer was willing to sacrifice himself for them. But his pain could propel him beyond this reality, into spiritual realms -- like people can become unconscious at the time of an accident, and have some wondrous experiences on the other side. As with the Fakirs of the Far East, these rites are about overcoming pain.

The Sundance was a very sacred sacrament, and the Plains Tribes who practiced it were better able than most to understand the God of the Black-Robes (priests), for the Wasichu God was pierced, bled, hung from a Sundance pole, suffered and even died for The People. He then commended himself to the Sky Father.

This God also spoke of a better life on the other side, in the world of Spirit, and the Lakota knew this to be true: The spiritual ones among them had often been to that place of peace and harmony in their visions or meditations. They were thus not afraid of death -- a common cry of a warrior going off to battle was: "It is a good day to die!"

In the winter lodges the story was still told of Dawn Star, the Prophet-Healer who came long ago to teach the Nations of Turtle Island. They were familiar with the stories of the Black Robes, and they had heard of the birth of the Son of the Sky Father. They knew He had arrived on a great round shield that shone at night like the brightest of stars! And the Wise Chiefs from far lands knew of His coming, from their visions. They followed the Star-People by night and the Cloud-People by day to find Him, and held a Give-away Ceremony to honor Him.

Dawn Star taught that all were brothers and sisters, and children of the Sky Father. All beings were related, he told them. And still the Lakota people practice this teaching when they say "Mitakuye Oyasin!", to honor "All my Relations!" The Prophet's sign of greeting was an up-raised hand, with palm forward, accompanied by the word "Hau!" ("Peace!") He told them that as long as they continued to live at peace and in harmony with their world, things would go well for them. But at some point the War Chiefs began to prevail over the Peace Chiefs, and they lost their free and abundant way of life.

'What goes around, comes around' applies to all of us.

The Sundance Ceremony was one form of prayer. It was prepared for by fasting, and going into vision. There would be sessions in the Stone-People-Lodge (also called sweat-lodge), in order to be purified in body, mind and spirit. Little Dove would watch the Holy Man directing the young apprentices building the lodge; it had to be done in a special way, and many prayers would be said. The tunkan tipi would be built with willow branches bent into an arch and covered with hides (later with canvas or blankets), to form a small dome.

A fire-pit was dug in the center of the lodge to receive the stones, which had been heated in a large fire-pit outside of it for several hours, and brought to the lodge when called for by the one conducting the ceremony. The stones were handed in on a large pair of antlers, and received by smaller ones. A dipper-full of water poured on the stones created steam.

The earth that was dug out for the fire-pit in the lodge was put outside of the entrance; this mound became the altar. Here objects would be placed that were to be blessed, such as a canupa (Ceremonial Pipe); or a medicine pouch, or perhaps a buffalo skull to be prayed over. A Medicine Chief could call in the spirit of the buffalo that it had belonged to: It was a most sacred and powerful Medicine Piece. Strings of prayer-ties, small tobacco offerings accompanied by prayers as each one was added, would be hung over the rafters inside the lodge during the inipi ceremony and burned later, the smoke carrying the prayers to TonKA-shila. An eagle feather might also be hung in the purification lodge.

Facing it participants would enter from the left, bending low to crawl through the small entrance in a humble gesture. They would crawl around to the left, then clockwise, until they got as far as possible, the leader of the inipi going in first. He would sit next to the door and receive the stones, pour the water and lead the prayers or songs. When everyone was in place, the door-flap would be closed and the prayers began.

There were four rounds. Each ceremonialist had their own way of doing things. With some, the first round would be to pray for oneself; to be strong, to be worthy, to be helpful to others. The second round would be to pray for relatives and loved ones. After that, they would pray for those who were sick, lonely, or taken prisoner, and finally, for all of the other creature beings. Some Lodge-leaders would have an assistant sing certain songs, and another helper would pour cedar sprinkles onto the rocks as they came in, thanking each stone for giving its life that The People might benefit. Other leaders would have each person have their say, and these would pour out their hearts and souls, and ask Tonka-shila for help.

At the end of each round someone would say "Mi-TA-'kwi-a-sin!", and the door-flap would be raised by the fire-keeper outside, to let in some welcome fresh air and light.

Toxins would come out of the body in the often extremely intense heat created by the steam in the small, tightly enclosed space. But there was spiritual healing that could take place here too, and often events which would seem miraculous to outsiders would take place. The Medicine Man or Woman would call upon their Spirit Helpers, and these would respond. Sometimes the Great Spirit's messenger, Eagle, would come: They would hear, and feel, in the darkness of the inipi lodge, the whirr of its wings! Or they might feel the earth tremble, if Buffalo was called in. And a patient's health would be restored.

When it was over each one would crawl out going the same direction as when they came in, coming out of the healing womb of Mother Earth renewed, for a new beginning. Going outside, they went to the left. One did not cross the line between the fire-pit, the altar, and the entrance to the lodge. Standing around the fire, a canupa (pipe) was smoked, and thanks given. Then wooden bowls would be passed around, with meat (organ), water, berries and green, to honor various elements.

Stone People's Lodge and Vision Quests, sometimes lasting many days, would precede the Sundance. A young warrior might prepare for a Sundance Ceremony by remaining celibate for a year. A tall tree would be selected as the Sundance Lodge pole, and young girls selected for their purity of spirit would dance around the tree for four days asking its permission to be used, and thanking it for giving up its life for the People. They knew that all things have life, and that tree could not just move its spirit into another tree, because the other trees had their own spirit. (The Holy Spirit is every-where, said the Black-Robes, and they understood.)

The Sundance Pole would be placed in the center of the circle, and the dancers would be pierced in the chest by a Sundance Chief, who would put a peg through the cut and attach a line from the top of the pole to the peg. The Sundancers would blow on an eagle-bone whistle with a feather attached, to focus their attention on, and pull away from the pole. The women would pray and sing the Sundance Song, to encourage them to be strong. Attached to the pole, they would dance continuously for three days in the hot sun and through the cold nights, without eating or drinking, until finally they pulled loose, collapsing -- and receiving visions.

They are dancing for The People, showing them that they are willing to suffer for them. And then they go beyond the pain, and have visions which are incredible, enlightening, euphoric! Revelations of the nature of the universe! They may gain insights which can be of help to all of them. And the pain is forgotten; as is the pain that can accompany child-birth, once the miracle has taken place, and the wonder of a new being, new life, has burst forth.

In the time of Walks-the-Wind the Native People could do many wonderful things, for they were in tune with Spirit. They could shape-shift, become an animal or a bird. Part of the training for some Medicine People was to become an eagle, who could soar high above the mountains... and tell the people of the coming of the buffalo, or of an enemy.

At gatherings, a Chief might throw an object to a Medicine Man standing among the assembled circle of dancers -- and the Chief would cause the object to change its trajectory, and curve away from him. The Medicine Man, if his powers were still intact, would cause it to change course again, and catch it. They did these things to entertain the onlookers, to keep their powers strong, and to enhance their prestige. And it was fun!

It was also not unusual to have the spirits of one -- or perhaps even a dozen! -- of the Ancestors appear, actually materialize, in one of the Medicine Lodges, at a Council meeting. These powers and abilities were so alarming to the invading armies of missionaries, settlers, and soldiers, that they were determined to do away with these 'heathen ways'... and Native American religious practices were outlawed, until the Religious Freedom Act was enacted in the 1970's. Wallace Black Elk, Lakota, was one of those who helped to bring this about.

A woman of an Ogallala Sioux clan came to the lodge of Walks-the-Wind one day. "My son Raven Wing goes on a hunting party with his friend," she said, "and while they are busy cutting up the meat from a deer, they are surprised and attacked by a band of Blackfoot. My son is clubbed on the head and left to die, and his friend Sky Bird is injured also. Sky Bird is able to heal his own wounds, using herbs he finds near this place where they are. But my son's wounds are great. Sky Bird finds one of their horses and brings my son home after the sun sleeps many times.

"My son Raven Wing has a large bump on his head, which gives him much pain. He is brave and does not speak of this, but I see beyond his eyes, and I know with a mother's knowing. Words come to me that you are a great healer, and Spirit tells me that you can help my son. If Ton-KA-shi-la wills it, and you are also willing, I would like for you to heal him." She gave him a gift of tobacco, for the Pipe Ceremony. "I have little to offer Walks-the-Wind, but when but when my son grows strong, he comes to you with buffalo robe. This is my word."

"I honor your Spirit," said Walks-the-Wind. "I go to pray on this. I come with answer when it comes to me."

It did not take three days to receive the answer. The swelling on the boy's brain had grown to the size of an egg. He had been a strong warrior, but had become very thin, and it was clear that he could not live much longer.

"The young warrior will be helped. Tonkashila wills it," Walks-the-Wind stated. It was a twelve-day process. The first four days were spent in fasting and prayer. The patient was given teas which would cleanse his system, and a special diet to build his strength. Spirit Helpers were invoked for their assistance, and Medicine Men ancestors for their healing powers. Turtle Woman helped also, making up special brews. She prayed constantly.

The second four days of the healing ceremony were spent in the Stone-Peoples-Lodge, again requesting help from the Spirit World. The Old Ones in the Spirit World heard the drum, and the healing songs, and they came. They ministered to the youth at this time of purification. Any dark spirits hovering around were dispelled.

The third four-day period was spent in recovery, and in giving thanks. Raven Wing began to eat more food, and for the first time in many journeys-of-the-sun from one horizon to the other, he began to smile. His mother's heart was filled with gratitude. "Thank you TonKA-shi-la!" she whispered. "I honor your spirit!" she said to Walks-the-Wind. "Wo-pi-la!" Thank you.

"Wosh-tay," he replied. It is good.

A few days later, after the patient and his mother had returned to their village, Walks-the-Wind arose one morning and said to his wife Turtle Woman: "In the night a dream comes. Raven Wing becomes strong again, he eats, pain goes. Lump on brain is small, like berry. Each day more prayers reach Grandfather-of-All. Soon lump is no more."

As a spiritual leader, he would often 'go on the hill' and 'cry for a vision', fasting and praying and going into trance to seek inspiration and guidance for the People.

Little Dove's family grew again in an unexpected way. Her father Walks-the-Wind's younger brother, Jumps-the-Log, had been on a raiding party, in retaliation for an encroachment into the Sacred Black Hills by a party of miners who had heard there was gold there. There were twenty of them, between prospectors and armed guards, who knew that by treaty they were not supposed to be there. The trespassers were warned by the Lakota warriors that they should leave! But the mining party would not do so -- instead, they fired on the fifteen warriors present, killing three of them.

A large War Party returned and chased the intruders-into-Sacred-Land away, killing several of them. But Jumps-the-Log was one of the three Lakota killed in the first encounter.

A memorial ceremony was held at a sacred, secluded place where no-one went except for such purposes. This was Holy Ground. The slain warrior's body was placed up on a platform high above the earth, symbolizing his return to the Sky Father. Here the Ancestors would receive him. His coup-stick, weapons, eagle feathers and other Medicine Pieces were wrapped in his buffalo-robe with him, and the ceremony began, to release his spirit into the keeping of Wakan Tanka. He had been a brave warrior, the Medicine Chief elder said. He had been a good provider, a loving husband and father. And he'd died nobly, for the People, defending their Sacred Land. But it had been a good day to die, and now he was in a place of peace and harmony, with the Ancestors and with Ton-KA-shi-la.

His young widow stood with the people in a circle next to the arbor on which he lay. His pony stood there also. The widow, whose name was Flowers-Among-Tall-Grasses, had tears streaming down her face. She now began her wail, heart-rending in its intensity, as she cried out her grief, and bade farewell to the man she loved.

The wail went on for quite some time, for she knew that once this ceremony was finished, she would never speak his name again. To do so would be wrong. It would call his spirit back, and she knew that he should be free. He could come back if he chose, of course... (as did the spirit of Little Dove's mother.) But he needed time to adjust to the Spirit World, and she knew that she must let him go.

The responsibility for Flowers-Among-Tall-Grasses and her three children fell to Walks-the-Wind. His two older brothers had gone off and formed bands of their own, and it was the custom of The People for a man to take care of the family of his brother if he died. They did not simply abandon widows and orphans to fend for themselves.

There was seldom jealousy among the women, as in the White world. They did not believe that their man 'belonged' to them, and they were happy to share his attentions. That was one of the reasons that there was such misunderstanding between the two cultures: The repressive morality of the

Victorian era of the 1800's was so different from that of the Native Nations, whose members were appalled at the idea that some women would have a husband and those without one were expected to repress their natural feelings.

Flowers-Among-Tall-Grasses was welcomed into the family. Here was another sister to share the chores, and it made the work go more easily when they could scrape the hides and cook the meals together. When one of them was 'on her moon', at that special time of month when she would go into the separate Moon Lodge to be with others whose flow of blood was being returned to the Giver-of-Life, Mother Earth, then that woman would be relieved of her domestic and child-care duties.

Moon-time was the time of a woman's greatest power. At this time she was an open channel to Spirit, and the objects that she made while in the Moon Lodge were treasured by those who received them. They knew that the moccasins (which wore out every few months), medicine pouches, leggings, or shirts, sometimes decorated intricately with quills, beads, strands of horse-hair, or elk's teeth, had been lovingly prayed over as they were being made.

Because a woman at Moon-time was more open to Beings from the Spirit-World, Lakota men reasoned that the Dark Ones could also come in more easily when a woman was an open channel to Spirit. So the men were careful not to let these women come into their ceremonies at that time, or to be any place where their ceremonial objects were, such as sacred eagle feathers.

Part of their aversion to having women around when they were at this special time of the month might be because, when they were living on the plains, the smell of blood from the moon-lodge could draw animals such as wolves or mountain lions to the village, bringing danger. But a girl's first menstrual period was a cause for celebration, and she would be given a Coming-of-Age ceremony attended by all of the tribe.

The maiden was instructed by the Grandmothers that being on her moon was a holy time, when she was returning nourishment to Mother Earth, who gave the People what they needed. The lining of her womb was sloughing off, to keep it clean and soft for a baby, when a soul chose to return to the earth as New Life. She was no longer a child, but a woman now! It was her time of blossoming from a bud into a beautiful flower.

Each of Walks-the-Wind's wives had their own tipi, near each other, and their husband would share his nights equally among them, his new wife included, after a respectful period of mourning. The lodge of his first wife, Pretty Flower, was larger than the others, and here they would all gather, with the children; on cold winter nights, when visitors came, or just to be together as a family, with ten children now.

The larger lodge is where he kept his weapons and his clothing, rolled neatly into bundles and tucked at the edges of the tipi. His Medicine Pieces, herbs and healing tools, and his ceremonial regalia were in the lodge of Turtle Woman, hanging from the lodge-poles; and his third wife became Keeper of the Chanupa, of the Sacred Pipe bundle. Each dwelling had fur robes of bear or buffalo, to keep the family warm at night in the season of the deep snows, and to provide a soft place for sleeping. The tipis had linings in winter.

It was the men's Job to go on hunting and sometimes war parties, to protect and provide for their families. The women did the work around the camp. They erected the tipis, helping each other out. First, three poles would be lashed together at the top, while laid on the ground, then they would raise them up and add others to this tripod. The hides used for exterior walls would be pulled up by a rope going over the top, like a pulley system. Taking them down, when moving on, was quick and simple.

With the exception of the deep-winter-snow time, life was lived mostly outdoors. The women worked together in co-operation; laughing, singing, relating the latest gossip or stories while scraping and tanning hides, going down to the stream for water, or gathering nuts and berries. Then they'd cook up whatever Mother Nature and the hunters had to offer.

Little Dove was happy with her expanded family. Now she had many brothers and sisters to play with. Her new sister Little Fawn would join with them in 'playing house', as a doll family was made for her too as a "welcome into the family" gift, and they helped her to make a lodge for the wee folks.

With the boys, Little Dove raced, on foot or pony, and sometimes beat them in marksmanship with the bow and arrow, which caused some teasing by the other boys. Sometimes she and her brothers would stay up late and spy on the ceremonies of the Elders. Her new brother, Swift-As-Deer, was so fast that he could run down the deer in the hunt: It seemed that he could become One-with-the-Spirit and fly!

Her favorite time was late summer, when there was a great Gathering of the Tribes, at the sacred mountains of the Teton. It was a time of excitement, with many Nations coming together -- to visit relatives or Clan-kin they had not seen for a long time. There were alliances made, and sometimes dissolution of them, because of some real or imagined affront. There was much trading, and much news to exchange.

And there were the Pow-wows! The singing, the drumming, the dancing, and telling of stories. Hundreds and hundreds of tipis would be set up, and they knew which area to go to by the distinctive way of dressing of each Nation, and the symbols and decorations on the lodges. The flat grass-lands would be filled with circle after circle of cone-shaped lodges, all set near a stream, below the magnificent range of tall, jagged mountains rising toward the sky. As Teton Lakota, Little Dove and her family hosted the many other tribal Nations who came, helping them to get settled and find what they needed.

Pungent smells wafted through the air, as cooking fires sprang up. Shouts and whoops were heard as old friends recognized each other.

"Hau, my Brother! How does it go with you, old friend? Tell me the stories of your bravery and your victories and I will tell you that I don't believe them!" And they would have a good laugh.

A retort: "Tell me the stories of your successes with many women -- and I will say that they are tales to tell children, who will believe anything you tell them!"

The young men would then wrestle each other to the ground. There was much camaraderie at the rendezvous.

And then the Pow-wow would begin! First into the large dance-circle would be the parade of Chiefs and warriors of great accomplishment, their ponies prancing, and carrying their staffs proudly. These tall coup-sticks would be decorated with eagle feathers, perhaps a row of them, and sometimes scalps. (The custom of taking scalps had spread from the east, where bounties were paid for scalps to unscrupulous bounty-hunters who would stir up old tribal enmities in the effort to cut down the Indian population.)

The dancers would follow. War dancers, Eagle dancers, deer dancers, buffalo dancers accompanied by the drummers, who sat around their large drums singing the high-pitched songs of the plains tribes as they beat out the rhythm.

The Host Drum would be of the Teton band, and they would begin, followed perhaps by the Ogallala, the Hunkpapa, the Minneconjou or other Lakota or Dakota branches. A Guest Drum, such as Cheyenne or Arapaho, might also be heard from, if they were having friendly relations at the time.

Little ones had their time, too, to charm the onlookers, and the young girls did a lively dance, intricately choreographed. There would be a regal Head Woman Dancer, with long fringe swinging from her sleeves and skirt, and with a feather fan held in one hand. The women did their earth-healing dance, step-dip, step-dip, heads held high and proud.

Everyone would look up when Eagle flew over the dancing ground, making his great circle overhead. It was a powerful sign: Wakan-Tanka's messenger would carry their prayers to Tonka-shila. He was watching over them!

The sounds and actions of the animals they honored in their dances were imitated; the howl of wolf, the strut of a prairie fowl, the stamp and pawing of the earth made by the buffalo. The Buffalo Nation was represented by warriors wearing shaggy, horned buffalo helmets and robes. The deer-dancers wore the robe of the stag, with head and antlers tied to their heads.

The nights were filled with the joyful sounds of the celebration, the throb of the drums, the flickering fire-light, and with the Spirits of the Ancestors who thronged to join them throughout the long night. After welcoming Grandfather Sun with prayer and thanksgiving for the new day, the revelers would return to their lodges to rest themselves, in preparation for the next day's ceremonies.

They were to gather again at noon, they had been told. Two hours after sun-straight-up, a few stragglers began to come to the ceremonial grounds. An hour or so later, a few more began to assemble. At about four hours after noon, the warriors appeared from behind the many groups of tipis and came racing in on their ponies, going round and round in circles around the dancing grounds, to build up a vortex of energy and get things going. At that point, the rest of the people came. They were on Indian Time, which is: 'Whenever you get there, is the right time.' (My kind of time!)

The Chiefs would hold their councils, speaking on many subjects; and listening to each other's words, on and on, until all had reached agreement. The Medicine People, the Holy Ones, would go high up into the sacred Teton mountains, and also go inside of them, in body or in spirit, and confer with the Old Ones, the great Masters, and the Star People Ancestors who dwelt within them. The Lakota often had contact with the Star Nation, and would see their ships streaking across the clear night sky. Sometimes the Star People would land, and visit.

After many days of trading items and stories, dancing and Counciling, it would be time to gather up their things, take down the tipis, and move on. The area would be left as they found it, for Mother Earth was to be honored. Moving on was the way of life; one did not want to over-use any one area. The seasons and the availability of game dictated the movements of the People.

It was a time of great excitement when the buffalo herds were sighted! Little Dove's brothers looked forward with great anticipation to the time when they were big enough and brave enough to join in the hunt. This was what they had prepared for all their lives.

There would be a Buffalo Dance, with the hunters donning their appropriate buffalo regalia, to make spiritual contact with those being hunted. In this way they would honor the great beasts for giving up their lives for the People.

When the day came, Little Dove, her sisters and her mother rode out to watch from a safe distance as the hunter-warriors urged their ponies on. The hunter would pick out a bison at the edge of the herd, ride along swiftly beside it, and with a well-aimed thrust throw his lance or shoot his arrow into a strategic spot on the shaggy beast. They would take only what was needed, and every part of the animal was used.

More dances were held, this time to celebrate a successful hunt. It was a great blessing for the People.

There was plenty of work for the women to do after that. Cutting up the meat, cooking some of it, and drying some for later use. Scraping and tanning the hides, to make them soft. The fur was left on for bedding, taken off for tipi covering.

Little Dove was pleased with her sisters, and proud of her brothers. Her parents were also a source of great pleasure; they were so highly regarded by everyone, and warm and loving to their children. In the winter they would all gather around the fire, close together, and listen to their father and their mothers tell stories about the history of their proud Nation. There was much love in their lodge.

It was a good life, thought Little Dove. Until that fateful day when the Long Knives came....

Chapter 8

Runaway Slave

Little Dove sat on the porticoed porch watching the river flow beyond the tall trees. They lived in the big house now. Gran'pa Gillespie had moved in with one of his daughters, and Geordie's mother and father had moved into one section of the house while the younger part of the family -- there were six children now -- were absorbed by the rest of the house.

She was rocking her youngest child, Dave. From the beginning, there seemed to be something special about him. Here was a young spiritual warrior, ready to take on the world! She could see great adventure ahead for him.

Little Dove was reflecting upon how different life was here on the plantation, from what she had known as a child. It was so serene! You didn't have to worry about enemy war parties or about the U.S. Cavalry. She had been happy as a child though, until it had all ended in such a terrifying way. It seemed that her children would never know about the horrors of war. They were fortunate.

She was happily unaware of the storm-clouds of war that were blowing up over the horizon. The North was so far away, and she had never heard of Abolitionists.

Little Dove woke up in the middle of the night. Something was wrong! In her dream she saw the face of Mandy, one of the women who cared for her children -- and there was fear and anxiety on her face. The energy of worry was powerful.

She got up, and dressed quietly. Geordie woke up too.

"What's the matter?" he asked.

"Something's happened down at the cabins. I saw Mandy's face in my dream. I must go there." She put on her shawl.

"I'll go with you," he said, putting on his clothes and pulling on his boots. They got a lantern and went down to the row of cabins that lined one side of the cotton fields.

There was a light on in one of the cabins, and although the curtains were drawn, they sensed movement and heard several voices speaking in low, hushed tones.

They knocked gently on the door. The sound of scurrying followed.

The door opened a crack, and Mandy looked out.

"Oh! Lord have mercy! It's y'all, Miz Grace! An' Mastah Geordie! Lordy, but you give us a fright! Come on in!"

There were two other people who worked in the big house, and one of the field hands, standing grouped together in a corner. It looked like they were hiding something.

Mandy walked over to them, and told them to stand aside. There was someone cowering in the corner. It was a young Black girl, and her eyes were wide with terror.

"It's all right, Sugar; these people won't hurt you. They looks like White folks, but they ain't, hardly. They's Injuns. An' they's our frens," Mandy said. "We got us a runaway," she explained to the visiting couple.

Little Dove walked over to the girl, and held out her hands to her. As she slowly stood up, Little Dove put her arms around the trembling young fugitive, who broke down and sobbed. She just held the girl.

"She must be about twelve," said Little Dove. "The same age I was when I was captured by the White People. The enemy, who had killed off my whole family, and all my people." All the black faces in the cabin turned and looked at her amazed! They had never heard her speak of this before.

"How long has she been here?" asked Geordie.

"Two days, Master Geordie. We was tryin' to figure out what to do with her."

"Why didn't you come to us?"

"We didn' want you to fret yo-sefs about it. An' we didn' want you to get yo'sef in trouble! The slave-catchers will be lookin' fo'er. They be boun' to come here some time.

"Her master, he a cruel man. He bin fo'cin hissef on 'er, night after night. He cause 'er a lot o' pain. An' if she cry out -- he beat her somethin' turrible."

Mandy turned the girl around and raised her blouse. She winced. Her back was covered with deep, angry welts.

"Have you put pine-pitch on those wounds?" asked Little Dove.

"No, ma'am. We'll have to go out into de woods an' find us a weepin' pine tree."

Sakina

"I have some up at the house. I always keep some handy for cuts. Pine sap is a great healer. If you mix a little grease with it, it will stay soft."

Zeke volunteered to go and fetch it.

"We couldn' jes turn 'er loose, an' we don' know who to pass 'er on to jes now. To see she get away safe up to de No'th."

"How did she happen to come here?" asked Little Dove.

"Oh, Ma'am, ev'ybody knows you's de kindest people aroun'! We got our grapevine. Ain't nobody else in this part o' Miss'ssippi that done freed they slaves. Gettin' sold down the river - to Miss'ssippi -- is the worst thing that can happen to a slave. They's some powerful mean planters and over-seers down here!

"But you treats us like fam'ly. You gives us money fo' de work we does, an hep us to go up No'th if we wants to. Mos' of us knows we's better off here, so we stays.

"We's got evythin' we needs, right here -- an we got kine-ness. Tha's the mos' impo'tant thing. They's a lot o' luv in yo' fam'ly!"

"Our family," Little Dove corrected her. "We are all children of Cre-ator; all brothers and sisters. We each have our parts to play: We Gillespies act like White People, so they will not take us away, so we will not have to watch our loved ones be hurt or killed. You here pretend to be servants, for the same reason. But we are all family.

"We do not believe that one human being can own another. We do not believe that we own the land, or the waters, or the air! We care for Mother Earth, and she cares for us. We are losing our struggle because those who came here to escape the oppressive ways of their homelands, those who came seeking freedom, deny it to others. They have not learned Creator's great law: 'Do to others as you would have them do to you.' Perhaps we are here to teach them something.

"They are victors because their number is like the grains of sand along the great waters," Little Dove explained. "And they do not honor all beings, as we do."

"Yes Ma'am. You does like de Good Book say: De Golden Rule. You doesn' jes talk about it, like dey does in de White churches. Yessum." Man-dy dabbed at her eyes with her kerchief.

The girl, who was just called Cotton Child, had eyes that were wide with astonishment! She had never heard anyone, White or Colored, say the kind of things she heard tonight.

"I will pray on this," said Little Dove. "We cannot always control what happens, for others have their free-will also -- but if there is a way, and we ask for help, we will be shown. I will seek a vision."

Geordie spoke up. "You can hide her in the attic of our house until we find out how to get her to safety. They won't look there in our house, but they will search here. Have someone stay with her so she won't be fright-ened.

2

"I will lay a false trail. I'll put a strong scent over her old trail, that leads here, to fool the hounds -- and make a new one, that leads away from here and down to the river, far from here, where they'll lose it. I'll need a piece of her clothing, and her shoes. Get her something else to wear."

The Gillespies took the girl and one of the Black women up to the big house. Cotton Child had never been in a 'White house' before, and she timidly looked around as they went into the large foyer, sneaking a peek into the parlor.

"It's all right, Honey Chile," her benefactor told her. "You can go in there. Sit down by the fireplace, I'll bring you some tea."

Cotton Child was overwhelmed! The Missus of the big house had invited her in and was waiting on her. She had never heard the like.

Geordie's woods lore served him well. He sensed that he would have to work quickly, and he was right. Slave-catchers had been sent for, and they came the next day.

"One o' my nigguhs run away," said the angry Master of a neighboring plantation. "Thot she mighta come this way."

"Really, Suh? You're welcome to look aroun'," Geordie said. "There are 12 cabins, down in the quarters; they might know somethin'. Have you checked the woods over yonder?'

"'Bout to," said a surly man who'd brought his blood-hounds along.

The people of African heritage preferred to tell the truth, as did the Native Americans. But sometimes they had to make choices; and it seemed more important -- a higher morality in an immoral world -- to protect their own. So, when questioned, they would simply say "We don' know nuttin', Suh! Nossuh!" Feigning ignorance was survival.

The people in the cabins "didn' know nuttin'."

Little Dove and Geordie Long Bow went to quiet places and sought their vision, reconnecting with their Spirit-Guidance and asking for help. Thus they 'just happened' to run into others who were sympathetic to the plight of the slaves that were being badly abused and sought freedom.

There were still small pockets of Choctaw, Natchez and Creek who were living in isolation in the deep woods, and these would be way-stations, with guides, on the road to freedom. There were a few others of Cherokee or mixed blood like Geordie, and even a few White People, who were willing to help, feeling the wrongness of the system.

Cotton Child was only the first of a group of fugitive slaves who were helped by the 'Underground Railway' that was set up in that area by Geordie and his family. Harriet Tubman, an ex-slave, later became famous for having led many Black People to freedom during that period, but there were also others less well-known.

Geordie heard about an old peg-leg sailor who would walk along a river, to show the runaway slaves where to go to get to the next safe crossing. Every night, he would walk along there, to leave his distinctive footprints as a guide.

"Our Cherokee people sang songs, to help them through their trials along the Trail of Tears," Geordie told his wife. "Black People sing to help the work go more easily, and to express their spiritual joy, their pain and sorrow. We could compose a song that would be a map for them, to find their way North to freedom."

Through this idea the song was born: 'Follow the Drinking Gourd.' The drinking gourd was the big dipper, which pointed the way to the north star -- and the North was where freedom was. The song told them to follow a river -- and then, "Well, the river ends, between two hills, follow the drinking gourd; there's another river on the other side!" Etc. "For the ol' man is a-waitin' fo' to carry you to freedom: Left foot, peg foot, followin' on -- just you follow the drinkin' gourd." (Pete Seeger sang this song in the 1960s.)

Many of the Old Negro Spirituals were songs that were disguised as church songs, which was acceptable. But really what they were singing about was not crossing the Biblical River Jordan, but going North to freedom.

About a century later, I would sing many of these same old 'freedom songs', some with new words, when I marched with Dr. Martin Luther King in Selma, Alabama, to protest injustice. I also listened to him speak of his dream, in Washington, D.C., and was on the platform with him in Boston, Massachusetts. I'd written a song for the occasion, and I sang out about freedom on the Boston Common to thousands of people -- in the rain.

The idyllic life that Little Dove had enjoyed came to a halt in 1861. She had seven children by that time, when talk of Secession, States Rights and impending war began to reach her little world... or rather, her Two Worlds.

"We're gonna whup those Yankees!" "Who do they think they are, tellin' us how to run our lives?" You'd hear talk like that when you went to town to buy supplies or sell crops. And at church, from the pulpit.

"We've got to preserve our genteel Southern way of life," the preacher would tell the congregation. "We need our Nigruhs to work our lands, and we have a responsibility to take care of them, fo' they are an inferior race. They could not just fend fo' themselves, and we bro't them ovah heah. So it is our moral obligation to care fo' them.

"Yankees do not understan' that. They would jus' turn them loose, and then we would have rebellion, chaos, pandemonium! We have seen the few instances when the slaves revolted; they turned on their Masters who had cared for them! They became the savage killers they had been when they lived in the wild, in Africa! That is why we must keep them in line, with methods that may seem harsh to outsiders -- to Northerners, who do not understand about Blacks -- or about that other inferior race: Indians!"

Little Dove winced when she heard the preacher talk this way. They had a Sunday School for the little ones, but they were taught these strange ideas also. She always asked her children afterwards what they had learned, so that she could off-set the negativity with positive concepts of a loving Creator.

"They just don't know about the Higher Truths of right living, in balance and harmony, taught to us by our Elders," she told them. "They think that we are separate from Creator; from each other. They do not know that we are brothers and sisters, and should take care of each other. It is sad."

She still had the habit of taking each child, during the first year of its life, down to the river or to a stream at sunset when the animals came to drink -- and saying, "These are your relatives! You are never alone! You are One with Creator, and you are loved!" This was a custom among her People. As they grew she would teach them that they could send out a beam of light to the creature-beings, from their heart center; that they could speak to the animals and birds in mind-speak, and could also understand them. In her vision, an Ancestor-Chief called White Eagle had taught her this.

The talk of war became more prevalent, and it was everywhere. "We are more powerful than they think, those Yankees, and we will fight to the death -- so that our way of life will live!" It was a matter of economic survival for many, and the young men were confident that they could quickly drive those 'Damn Yankees' out of the South, if they should come there and try to impose their ways upon the Southerners.

"This is another War for Independence! We will be free from foreign domination. We will secede from the Union!" a popular orator declared. This 'freedom', of course, did not include the majority of the population, which was Black. That is why White Southerners were so terrified of having the Blacks 'turned loose' -- in many places they far out-numbered the Whites, who felt they thus needed to control rigidly.

It was often hard to explain to the children why things were the way they were. Cherokee wisdom teachings would be passed on by their grandmother, Geordie's mother: "Nature goes in cycles; we are in winter, nearing the end of a great cycle. If too much damage is done to the Mother Earth, and the hearts of her children -- she will cleanse herself, and this would be the end of this 5th world on this planet. The pure-hearted ones will be protected -- and they will begin a new and more loving world! This will come to pass," she said.

The prospect of war between the North and the South brought some difficult choices for the Gillespie family, as it did for others of Native American blood. Councils were held, to talk over these matters.

Little Dove certainly had no love for the U.S. Army; they had slaughtered her family, broken their treaties, and taken the People's lands by violence, trickery and deceit. On the other hand -- now they were the ones who would be fighting for the freedom of Black People instead of taking it away from the Red People! It was puzzling.

When the War-for-Southern-Independence began, the family came together again in council, to decide what was to be done. Each one around the circle spoke in turn. Women still had the greatest influence among the Cherokee, as they were thought to have greater wisdom, and heart, than the more impetuous men. A man could be ready and eager to go off and fight, but a woman would be much slower to send her loved ones off to battle. She would consider carefully the consequences. So Mama Gillespie presided over the Council.

"Our prophecies have told us of this coming time of death and widespread destruction on Turtle Island," she began. "There will be more deaths in this conflict now upon us than in all other wars of this Country that have been, or will be, until the End-Times of this 5th World. Many of the people

responsible for the deaths and removal of the Choctaw and the Cherokee people from their homeland, and of the Lakota from theirs, will suffer
the loss of limb, land or life. It is the Law of 'What Goes Around, Comes
Around'. Balance. (Karma.)

"The Tsalagi Aniyun Wiya are People of Peace," Mama Gillespie continued. "Yet they have also been warriors, and as long as they were just defending their own, it was acceptable. But our Trail of Tears was allowed to
happen because many of our warriors began adopting the undesirable ways
of some other tribes, such as the taking of scalps (begun by the Whites),
torturing of prisoners, or other practices which were against the teachings
of the Pale One, who came long ago to give us guidelines for Right Living,
in harmony with All-That-Is.

"We are nearing the end of the Fifth World, or civilization, on this
planet. This war, and others to follow, are part of the cleansing. After Mother Earth shakes off the forces that are harming her -- and our Sisters and
Brothers of the Star Nation will assist in this -- there will be a better world!
A time when all will appreciate each other's differences, and see the beauty
in each, and love and harmony will prevail.

"But this is a time of trial," she continued, "and of difficult decisions. I
have called together my sons and the husbands of my daughters so that you
may speak your hearts freely. Each has their sacred point of view. Know
that whatever your choice of path to follow, it will be accepted by the rest of
us," she concluded, and added:

"Follow your heart."

Each position was discussed thoroughly. Two sons-in-law, and Geordie and his brother Robert chose to go with the Confederates -- and defend
what was, after all, their homeland. His other three brothers had already
moved to the North.

"In unity, there is strength," Geordie's brother-in-law Steven pointed
out. "If our Native brothers had worked in co-operation with each other
as the Seven Nations Confederacy of the Iroquois League did, instead of
allowing the foreign invaders to play us off against each other -- we might
have been able to stem the tide, and still live in harmony with the land. So I
will join with those who wish to preserve this land as one Nation."

"And I believe in freedom for all people!" said brother William. "I am
willing to die for this right, for my Black brothers and sisters."

The Black people, sitting in the outer circle, shook their heads in wonderment at such dedication for their sakes. They also smiled. "Bless yo' heart," said Mandy.

"Precious chile!" said Mammy Liza, quietly.

Scottish Gran'pa Gillespie spoke next.

"One Na-tion, under God, with Jus-tice and Li-ber-ty for All," he quoted. "The Constitution of this country was written by wise people. For many people, that is what this war is about: Freedom! That's what brought me here, to America. Ah believe in the United States; a generation ago we fought to create them! An Ah believe in standin' up to oppression. But who is the oppressor here? To the Blacks, it's the South; to the South, it's the North. Some of ye will want to defend your homes, your families. Some will fight for the rights of all people. Go with your heart! Whatever be your choice, Ah sup-port ye in it. Ah give ye my bless-in."

Some made their decision then; others held off a while longer.

Geordie and his three older brothers had gone on a pilgrimage years before, when they were young. Brother William was an infant then, but it was decided that the four brothers should go back to the ancient homeland of their Cherokee forebears, and learn the wisdom and ways of the Tsalagi.

An uncle, Swift Hawk, took them on the journey to the Great Smokey Mountains in Tennessee, so called because of the mist that often hung over them or settled into the valleys below.

This was the home of the Ancestor Spirits, and therefore very sacred to the Aniyun Wiya, the People Who Came from the Stars.

Geordie was 10 years old at the time, Charlie was 12, Andrew 14, and Robbie, 18. Along the way the boys traveled through the forests as much as possible. Each one carried a blanket, a knife, and little else. They slept on Mother Earth, and Swift Hawk told them that if they put their ear to the ground and listened, the Mother would tell them where to find water. Birds would warn them if danger might be ahead. They sang up Father Sun in the morning, and chanted him to sleep in the evening.

The brothers would begin each day by jumping into a stream or pond, if one was nearby, in the early dawn. Swift Hawk showed them how to make fire by striking small pieces of flint stone together, or with two pieces of wood. By twirling a piece of hard wood, sharpened at one end, between the hands against a piece of soft wood on the ground, the rapid motion would create enough friction to cause sparks and then fire.

The uncle taught his nephews how to make strong bows out of seasoned hardwood and sinew, and arrows from strong, slender branches; and how to chip arrow points. He showed them how to track an animal, and what signs to look for that they had been there. "If you see several animals," he said, "don't take the biggest one - take the weakest. That will keep the herd strong." They cooked and ate what they hunted, and gathered nuts, fruits, roots and edible vegetation along the way.

Swift Hawk taught the boys to honor the creature whose life they were taking, and to only take what they needed. Each boy was to hunt his own deer, and they stopped for a while by a stream and he showed them how to brain-tan the hides to make them soft and wearable. They made their own shirts, leggings and moccasins, something usually done by the women, but he felt that the boys should know how to do it. They wore the buckskins from then on, and plantation life seemed far behind.

By the time the Gillespie brothers arrived at the mountain cabin of their Great-Aunt and Uncle (whom they called Grandmother and Grandfather), the boys had become skilled in woods lore. They were now going to learn the spiritual teachings and history of their Cherokee ancestors.

The boys slept in the loft, on pallets covered with skins. In the big room there was a fireplace where the cooking was done in cool weather; otherwise it was done outside. There were benches and tables made from logs in the large room also, and piles of furs that the boys liked to sit on, on the earth floor. 'Grandmother' and 'Grandfather' slept in one bedroom, and the other one had been turned into a place for quiet meditation when their family had grown up and moved out.

Swift Hawk's cabin was nearby, and he and his family were happy to be reunited. He had been gone for most of the summer on this mission to fetch and teach the sons of his brother the old ways. Swift Hawk and his wife had three young children, and now the Gillespie brothers could teach them some of the things they had learned. Sometimes the brothers worked in the family's Black Hawk Trading Post.

The boys grew to love the high, cool mountains and the old way of living. They loved their new grandparents, who still lived in the simple way of their ancestors, following traditions passed down through many generations. With infinite patience they passed them on to their young apprentices.

The four brothers stayed in the Smoky Mountains for two years. Their Choctaw mother missed them, but she knew that this was an important part of their training, and that they were fortunate to be able to participate in a natural Native American life instead of living the life of pretense that was necessary on the plantation in Mississippi. And she still had her girls, and Baby William.

"It's like having the boys away at school," her husband told her. And indeed they were.

They were learning about healing ways, with herbs, sound and color, gemstones, and with prayer. They went into the sanctuary room, the Sacred Space, and offered prayers there. At a little altar, the boys burned pine-sap incense and cedar, filled small clay bowls with cornmeal, tobacco and water, and lit a candle in front of a large crystal in the center of the shrine. They would then sit quietly and still their minds, so that inspirational messages could come to them from the Old Ones in spirit. And they would send out their love to all beings, knowing that the crystal would amplify their thoughts.

Geordie and his brothers were taught the history of their people, and how they had come from the stars. Each clan had the responsibility of passing on certain abilities and wisdom teachings of their ancestors. One day they were taken to a cave high in the mountains. They crawled through a winding tunnel, following their uncle, trusting instinct or Spirit to guide them through the darkness. It was part of their initiation, they knew, to show no fear.

Suddenly they came to a large cavern, and it was light again -- though they saw no tallow lamps or lanterns. The boys were AWESTRUCK! Stalactites hung from the ceiling, the moisture from some of them causing them to glisten as they were reflected in a pool below. Large and small stalagmites rose from the stone floor in amazing sizes and shapes.

In an alcove at the back of the cavern, with a raised rock platform, sat an Ancient One, cross-legged, hands in her lap, eyes closed. Dressed in white doe-skin, with long white hair hanging loose, she sat so serenely and immobile that Geordie thought it might be a statue. Swift Hawk led the four boys toward her, and then indicated that they should stop at a respectful distance and stand before her.

Slowly, the Old One opened her eyes. She looked at each one in turn, deep into their eyes. They knew that she could see into their soul.

She smiled. "You have come," she said simply. "I am pleased that you are here. I knew of your coming; I saw it in the Great Crystal."

"This is my grandmother," said Swift Hawk, "your father's grandmother. White people call her the Queen of the Cherokee, because they know we consider her the most Holy and wise of all of us. We call her Honored Woman."

The boys were pleased and proud to know that their great-grandmother was most respected among their people. Her reputation as a Peacemaker with White People and various tribes was well-known.

The Sacred Woman got up off of the pile of white furs she was sitting on and came down to where the boys were. "Follow me," she said. She led them out of the Great Room and into a smaller cave. The cave was dark when they got there, but Geordie noticed that it got lighter when they went in. He looked around, wondering how that worked.

Honored Woman gave each of the brothers two crystals to hold. "Sit by the wall," she instructed them. "Focus on your crystals. Send forth the Light that you are and know that your crystals will amplify that light."

Geordie, Charlie, Andrew and Robbie did as they were asked. They noticed that the room brightened. "Whe-ew! Amazing!" Geordie whispered.

"Each clan has certain abilities," the Old One said, "and it is important that they pass on these gifts to the generations that follow. It was known by the Cherokee, the Aniyun Wiya, long ago that there would be times of darkness, when Mother Earth would be cleansing herself, and that the Tsalagi (those who lived in the hills) would need to go into the caves for a while. It is the duty of our clan to be Light Bringers. Some of your cousins are in the Great Room, for that reason."

Geordie had observed a few people in the other room at various locations. They did indeed seem to have a bright aura around them.

"We have much to share, Dear Ones," Honored Woman said to her young visitors. One of the things that made her so wise was that she knew that she could always learn from others, as well as teaching what she knew.

"Sit quietly now and withdraw your light," she guided them. The light in the room dimmed. "It is the Light-that-You-Are that was going forth from you. Now go within, and see your light, your spirit, leave your physical vessel and rise above the tree-tops... above the mountains... past the cloud people... up to the Star Nation, and beyond! Explore the Universe, and learn its secrets. When you get high enough - there are no secrets!"

The boys saw themselves as balls of Light, or in their Light-bodies, ascending into the heavens. They passed sky-ships as they hurtled through space, and saw crystal temples and cities. Rainbow colors danced around them, and joyful, harmonious music wafted through the air. Ecstasy!!

It was hard to come back, but they did.

Returning to the large cavern they saw a number of people of all ages doing a graceful dance. Honored Woman explained its meaning, and showed them how to do it.

"You dance to the East, right foot forward, knee bent, arms raised to honor the sun. Left foot arcs to the left; you turn and look back, holding your hands out behind you - to honor the Ancestors, and those who are yet to come." She showed them how to do the same graceful steps to the South, to the West, and to the North. The pattern was repeated, several times. The newcomers caught on after a few tries.

"Some of the dancers are Old Ones," Rob said, surprised.

"Yes, Grandson. Some of your aunts are in their 80s and 90s. But that is what keeps them young and supple. They dance with joy in their hearts!

"I will show you something that is very special, very sacred. You are never to speak of it to anyone," Honored Woman said. The brothers were taken to a sealed chamber; the door opened when the Holy Woman sang certain high notes. Inside - another astonishing surprise! There before them was a large round object, unlike anything they had ever seen before. It was pale silver-grey and metallic-looking.

"Ai-i-ee!" said Charlie. "What is it?"

"Can we go inside?" asked Geordie. Although he did not see a doorway, he thought that there must be a way to get in.

"It is a Sky-Ship," the grandmother said. "This is how our ancestors arrived on this planet, long ago. When the craft malfunctioned, the crew knew they could not get back to their home among the Seven Dancers in the sky. So they shifted into another dimension, dispersing the structure

110

of their molecules so that they could go through solid matter, and landed here."

Geordie didn't know exactly what molecules were, but he got the idea. They were taken inside of the ship. There were big windows in it through which they could see outside, but they had not been able to see in from outside of it. There was a large white screen, some chairs, counters around under the curved windows, and strange markings above them.

"There was much knowledge stored here," the Sacred Woman continued. "Each clan is charged with learning and passing on some of it. No one group has the whole picture of how things are, but when we co-operate and share our pieces of it, the picture becomes more complete, more clear."

The Gillespie brothers had much to think of, much to dream about, after their visit to the great cavern, the secret Holy Place of the Cherokee. Lying on the ground and looking up into the night sky, they thought about their kin who dwelt among the stars. Swift Hawk showed them the small cluster of the Pleiades way up at the top of the sky, which was still the home of their ancestors, their cousins.

There was much excitement at the cabin on this particular evening. Sequoyah was coming, and his friend Chief Zso-lee! (Pronounced as in Zsa-Zsa; he was also sometimes called Jolly.) Sequoyah had invented a written language, with a symbol representing each Cherokee sound, so that the Tsalagi could communicate with each other with 'talking leaves', like the Whites did. This was an extraordinary and unparalleled achievement! In a little over a year's time, the Cherokee had become literate. Some of the symbols were like the ones inside the Star-ship.

After dinner the adults were talking about tribal business. The boys, up in the loft, were quietly listening.

"John Ross wants to use the Cherokee gold to finance his efforts to let us keep our lands here in the East, and to buy more land," said Zso-lee, speaking of their Principle Chief. Though mostly Scottish, John Ross, one-eighth Cherokee, had married the daughter of a powerful chief of the Cherokee Nation, and had great influence among her people as well as having friends among White statesmen, merchants, and authors such as Daniel Webster. Ross and his wife Quatie Ross had a large white mansion with outbuildings and warehouses filled with goods which were brought up the river to their docks. Ross' Landing later became known as Chattanooga, Tennessee.

Some of the Cherokees had moved westward to land allotted to them (taken from the Comanche) in Oklahoma, but most of them did not want to leave their homes in Tennessee, the Carolinas, Georgia and Alabama.

"Georgia annexed Cherokee lands," the boys heard Sequoyah tell Uncle Swift Hawk and his parents. "Ross and some of his people took it to the Supreme Court, and they reversed the decision. Yet I worry about the settlers and their insatiable greed for the land."

"And for gold!" added Zsa-lee. "It makes them crazy. 'The love of money is the root of evil,' their Holy Book says. For us, the gold is to help the people who are in need. We leave it in a box on their doorstep in the middle of the night, so that they will not know who is the keeper of it, or where it has come from. It should be used to help, not to control."

Sequoyah shook his head sadly. "I am afraid that they know now that we have gold, and that creates great danger for us all. I have heard that a little boy was wearing the golden symbol of his grandfather who had gone to Spirit, and that the greedy ones said 'There's GOLD here! We're gonna find it!' I fear that no-one is safe now. I think it is time for us to join the Western Cherokee, in Tahlequah. I hear they are doing well in Oklahoma."

Next morning, Grandmother Waleyla (hummingbird) and Gran'pa Fox thought deeply about the words of their wise guests of the night before. They too had an uneasy feeling, sensing danger.

"Let us go to the Crystal Chamber," she said to the boys, and they went back into the caves.

In the middle of the chamber was a large crystal point, on an altar. Waleyla placed cedar and corn in front of it, and lit a candle. "Spirit of the Great Crystal, speak to us. Show us," she said.

The brothers watched, fascinated, as the foot-and-a half-tall crystal became clearer, and images appeared.

They saw Chief Zsa-lee in his home. Three warriors came up the hill and went in to see him. "Where is the gold?" one of them demanded. "Our chief needs it to fight the White invaders who are taking our land!" he said. "We know that you know where it is." "Take us to it," said another. The third one, a big, angry-looking man, said "Tell us where it is - or we will kill you!"

"I will not tell you. Never. It is to be used only for good purpose, and not for bloodshed. Neither you nor your chief has a good heart. I am not afraid to die."

There was a scuffle. Chief Zsa-lee raised his arm to defend himself; and the big man plunged a knife into his chest.

The boys watched, horrified. But there was more to come.

Returning home, Zsa-lee's young son saw the three men running out of the cabin and down the hill. He cried out when he saw his father lying bleeding on the floor. Cradling his father's head in his lap, the boy said "I will avenge you, Father. I will find these men, and I will kill them!"

"No, my son, you must leave this place, you must live," the dying man struggled to say. "The star-seed must continue. The star-knowledge is in your blood. You must pass it on."

The scene in the crystal shifted. The face of a thin man with a tall shock of white hair appeared in it; angry, yelling:

"They killed Zsa-lee! He was a good man! They're killing their own leaders, are they? The settlers were right; they are savages! Give the order for their removal, to the West."

"Wasn't it a Cherokee, Janaluska, who saved your life at the battle of Horseshoe Bend, President Jackson?" a man asked. He got only a scowl in reply.

"What about the Supreme Court decision, forbidding the taking of Cherokee land in Georgia?" asked another man.

"They made their decision; now let them enforce it!" he replied. "Zsa-lee was one of the best." Much pressure had been put on Andrew Jackson by those who wanted the Cherokee lands, and this gave him an excuse to give in to it.

Now the boys and their family were seeing another scene: Cherokee families being rounded up and taken from their homes at bayonet-point by soldiers and herded into open stockades; many of them dying of cold, hunger, white-man's disease, and heartbreak.

The next scene of this holocaust was some of these gentle people being crammed into wagons, but most of them being marched at gunpoint along the 900 mile trail in 1838.

Many of them, with no shoes or blankets, did not survive the blizzards. Quatie, the wife of Chief John Ross, gave her blanket to a sick child, who survived, but Quatie did not. Some mothers would plead with women along the way who came to watch them pass: "Please! Take my child!" so that the child might live. Over 4,000 Cherokee died along the Trail of Tears.

"Why will our people have to suffer so?" Geordie asked his grandmother.

"We have known this time of trial would come. It is part of a great cycle. But if we can endure, without anger and resentment, we can help to raise the level of spirituality on this planet, and transmute the pain to love. All of the great Masters have suffered for the People. Dawn Star, or Jesus, who is now on Venus, suffered and died for the people."

Pictures of another war, with soldiers in uniforms of blue and gray, now flashed in quick succession across the screen of the crystal. This war would tear apart the whole nation, divide families, leave much of the country devastated. But the Spirit of the Crystal did not dwell on this.

The form of the Crystal Goddess took shape to give another glimpse into the future.

"To you, Geordie, will come a child who will be one of us, the Star People. She will have great power, and knowledge, and will come to spread healing and wisdom on the planet. In the time of Atlantis, and in ancient Greece, she was known as Athena. She will come to you as your youngest child, 10 years after the great war that will divide the nation."

Geordie had not thought that far ahead. He was only 12 years old, himself.

Crystal Goddess continued. "Five years after her birth, it is imperative that you four brothers return here to this place for a reunion. You will be taken up to the Mother Ship for a meeting with the High Council, and given instructions as to how you can best serve the beings on this planet. That is why you are here." The Goddess smiled. "Go well," she said. "I give you the blessings of the Radiant One."

There was one more scene shown in the crystal. A little girl of five years was seen, in a clearing near the mountain home where they now lived. Her long hair had reddish tints to it; some Cherokee had red hair even if they had no Scottish blood in them. The girl held her arms out and twirled in a circle, hair and skirts flying outward. She was joyful!

Lightning flashed in a clear blue sky, and came down to the girl, who shuddered mightily. Then a beam of light descended from a round, metallic disc above her, similar to the sky-ship seen in the cave. The girl was raised up into the ship.

Inside the Star-ship, she was being greeted by a man in a pink helmet and a slender, silver fitted suit. He removed his helmet, and long, honey-blond hair fell to his shoulders.

"I am Ashtar," he said to the girl. "You are my complement, Athena; my twin-soul. I give you greeting and love. You have returned to Terra because you have an important mission on Planet Earth: to help prepare her for the coming times of change. In the name of the Radiant One, Adonai."

The crystal clouded up. The message was complete.

"You have seen what is to come," Grandmother Waleyla said to the four brothers. "This place is no longer safe. We will go into the caverns for a time; but you must decide whether you wish to go to the North for safety, where we have friends who will shelter and teach you, or whether you will return to the place of your Choctaw relations where you grew up – but where there may be danger for the Cherokee people."

Three of the Gillespie brothers decided to go north, in search of freedom and opportunity. Geordie chose to return home to Mississippi, and Swift Hawk would take him there. But they vowed to meet again, fifteen years after the War Between the States.

This portrait of Little Dove as an adult during the Civil War years was drawn by a famous psychic artist, Rev. Stan Matrunick.

Chapter 9

Civil War

The Western Cherokee who had survived the forced removal from their former homelands had settled into Oklahoma, with many of them living much as White People did; feeling that adapting to the reality of the situation helped to insure that they would survive and thrive.

Much of Oklahoma was vast and treeless, but the north-east quadrant had green grass, tall trees, and rivers, in some parts; and this is where they located their tribal capital, Tahlequah. It was here that Albert Pike, a personal representative of Confederate President Jefferson Davis, met with Cherokee leaders and prevailed upon them to sign a treaty pledging their alliance to the South. Many members of the tribe were not in favor of this, however, and left to join the Union forces, in the name of freedom for all peoples.

Geordie heard about a Cherokee regiment, and on further inquiry, discovered that it was being assembled by an old friend from his days as a hunter-scout, along the Mississippi and Missouri rivers. He decided to join up with them. "I've decided to take a Stand," he told his family.

Col. Stand Watie, a Tribal Leader, was a half-blood Cherokee Chief. He was fifty-four years of age when the War-Between-the-States began, and he was noted for being totally fearless in the face of overwhelming odds. An outstanding commander, his regiment played an important part in that War.

Geordie bade farewell to his family, and chose his finest steed on which to ride off to war. "Go well Long Bow, beloved husband," said Little Dove. "You are a brave warrior, and TonKA-shila will watch over you." She gave him her eagle claw, to wear for protection.

"It is a good day to die!" he said... but she knew that he would return.

Geordie signed up with Watie's Second Regiment of Cherokee Mounted Rifles. In March of 1862, Geordie's regiment joined in the Battle of Pea Ridge, near Bentonville, Arkansas. Cannonballs and rifle-fire had the Southerners pinned down; the Union artillery was well concealed; shots were coming thick and fast. They were being opposed by a strong force of cavalry and infantry.

Col. Watie, Geordie, and a few other picked men crept from one tree, hill, or boulder to another, concealing themselves, Indian-style. In the half-light before sunrise, they closed in on a battery of artillery and captured it. The Federals tried repeatedly to re-capture it, but Watie and his greatly outnumbered forces held them off.

By the following day, all of the Confederate troops had been forced to retreat, being pursued by vastly superior numbers... except for Watie's 'Redskin Regiment'. As the Union troops advanced, Col. Watie commanded his soldiers to CHARGE! It was a bloody battle, and the Union Forces won their first victory west of the Mississippi.

Two Confederate generals were killed in that conflict, but very few of the Cherokee were among the nearly 800 dead scattered over the battlefield as the smoke cleared. Their stealthy Indian-style of hiding and fighting from under cover of trees and rocks made them hard to shoot!

As for the attack tactics - Watie had engaged the assistance of War Chiefs of other tribes to help train his men, and they had been joined by some of the other tribesmen who had welcomed the opportunity to be proud warriors once again. Kiowa-Apache instructors taught guerilla warfare; they were accustomed to hiding behind high ridges and watching intruders into their territory come along the trails below, then swooping swiftly down upon them, cutting off any retreat.

Cochise and Geronimo taught their warriors how to become invisible. In the South-west, when being pursued by Army Troops, Apaches would lead them into a tall, secluded box canyon. "Ah HA! We've got 'em now!" their pursuers would say. "There's no way out!" But when they rounded the steep canyon wall - they would be confounded to find no-one there! Their prey had disappeared!

The Apaches would have dug into the desert sand and buried themselves, using a reed to breathe through. The astonished and frustrated soldiers would be right on top of them.

Geordie had also sent word by the Indian grapevine to his old friends among Little Dove's people, the Lakota -- those who had not yet been rounded up. His in-laws were happy to fight without being out-laws, and a good number of Sioux bands sent War Chiefs and warriors to lend their expertise. They also brought along many of their swift war-ponies, which (like the Harlem Globe-Trotters!) could run rings around the larger, less agile Army-issue mounts. And they were happy to fight the U.S. Cavalry!

The proud warriors who had long ruled the plains showed recruits how they attacked. Instead of being in a straight row, they would appear suddenly from behind a hill, with shrill yells and whoops to frighten and discombobulate the enemy. (It worked.) They would dodge this way and that, and slip over on the side of the pony away from the enemy, using its body as a shield, to hide behind -- while shooting (bullet or lance) from underneath its neck, while holding on with the legs and one arm around the horse's neck.

These tactics were extremely effective. The traditional fighting methods of the day were to advance in a straight line, row after row, to shoot at the enemy's straight line, sometimes bringing up a cannon behind them. This was a carry-over from the British way of fighting. These Empire builders and maintainers seemed invincible because of the British Square, with row after row of soldiers advancing relentlessly upon the enemy. When the first row fell, there was another coming: they would alternate; one row knelt while the other shot; kneel, re-load, and fire again.

The first rows were expendable. That little island had too many people anyway. The eldest son inherited the estate, so as not to break it up; the rest, and anybody else wanting adventure, were sent off to India, Africa, Australia -- or to America, before the Americans were revolting. In a manner of speaking.

Although the Cherokee troops were so successful against overwhelming odds, their "unethical tactics" absolutely horrified the White Officers -- of both sides! They were also aghast at the fact that a few of the warriors had taken scalps.

Geordie and the rest of the Cherokee Regiment continued with their guerilla-warfare, making daring raids against Union troops in a continual process of harassment; strike and run; and slipping through enemy lines to steal horses, arms, equipment and supplies. Their success against seemingly impossible odds led to Watie's being commissioned Brigadier General by the Confederate congress early in 1864. In the fall of that year he led two thousand men in an action which captured about 1800 horses and mules, and over two hundred wagons, as well as other strategic material.

A story that my grandmother, Sara Gillespie Borders (Little Dove's daughter), told me when I was a child about that period impressed me greatly.

"It was in the middle of the Civil War," she said. "My oldest brother went to his Commanding Officer and requested permission to go home to his plantation. John said that his baby had just died, and his wife needed him. He requested a twenty-four-hour leave.

"The officer denied permission. 'I can't do that, soldier! We're in the middle of a battle here; you're one of my best soldiers, and I can't spare you! Every man is needed!'

"'I know that, Sir,' John replied. All I'm asking is twenty-four hours. I give you my word that I'll be back by then. My word is sacred."

"The Captain considered his request. 'Where did you say you're from?' he asked.

"'The Mississippi Delta country, Sir, where the Yazoo and Tallahatchie Rivers come together.' The Captain consulted the map.

"'Why, it would take almost that long just to get there and back!' he said.

"'I know that Sir. But I can do it. I just want to bury my baby, and comfort my wife. I will be back by this time tomorrow.'

"The Captain considered. 'All right, soldier... You have 24 hours. If you're not back by then, you'll be hunted down and shot as a deserter.' 'Yes Sir! Thank you Sir. Until tomorrow.' And he set off for home.

"John rode all day without stopping, except occasionally to water his horse. He kept going at a steady gait, rather than galloping and getting his mount over-tired. Now and then he had to dodge an enemy patrol.

"He reached the plantation at night-fall. His wife saw him coming, and ran down the steps to meet him, trying to stifle her sobs. 'Oh, John! I'm so glad you're here!' she said. 'One of the twins just died!'

"'I know. That's why I've come,' he said.

"She was startled. 'How long did it take you to get here?'

"'All day.'

"'But the baby just died an hour ago! How did you know?'

"'I just knew,' he answered. 'I had a vision. Spirit told me.'

"He held her in his arms attempting to console her. 'I have to go right back,' he said, 'but I wanted to be with you at this time of trial. We'll pray together for the spirit of our little one, and commend him to the Light.'

"After the simple service, John rode back, all that night, without resting. His Captain had of course assumed that somebody (rather than some non-body) had told him about his infant's death. He got back just in time, at the end of the twenty-four hours.

"'You've earned a rest, soldier; and you've earned my respect and trust. Get a few hours sleep and then rejoin your outfit in action.'

"After three hours of sleep, he was back on the front lines."

Having grown up with stories like that, it is perhaps not surprising that I am more in tune with Spirit, more receptive to the unusual, than others raised in main-stream America.

John Gillespie was seventeen when he joined the Confederate forces. When assigned to his first post, he requested an audience with the Commanding Officer. This was unusual for a new recruit, but because of his persistence, he was granted a brief meeting. He would not say what it was that he wanted to talk about, saying only that it was 'personal'.

When he was brought into the field-tent which served as temporary headquarters, the Captain was absorbed in looking over maps of the surrounding terrain, planning strategy.

"Well, soldier, what is it?" he asked impatiently, without looking up. "What is so important?"

"It's your name, Captain, Sir."

"My name? What about my name?" He looked up.

"Did you ever know a man named George Gillespie - many years ago? I've heard him speak of you."

"Oh, for God's sake! I've known thousands of people in my time. I don't remember any George..." He stopped to light his pipe. This was getting annoying.

"Perhaps you knew him by Long-Bow, Sir? Or Geordie? He said you used to hunt together."

The captain looked at him anew; his jaw dropped, his pipe fell, and sparks flew.

"Allow me, Sir." John picked up the pipe.

"GEORDIE?" he said. "My old blood-brother Long Bow? Best hunter, guide and scout west of the Mississippi, that one! We used to hunt together. Have adventures. He saved my life a few times... You kin to him?"

"Yes, Sir. I'm his son."

"Well, I'll be horn-swoggled!" he exclaimed, using a term picked up at sea. "Ol' Long Bow's boy! Have a seat, my lad... At ease! Would you like some tea?"

"Thank you, Sir. I don't mean to impose."

"If you're Geordie's boy, then I'm an uncle to you. We were closer than brothers. 'Course you know I can't give you any special privileges, but you're welcome to stop by and chat now and again. So tell me - how is ol' Geordie doin' these days?"

"He's serving with Col. Watie's Cherokee Mounted Rifles, Captain!"

"Ah-ha! Admitting to his Indian heritage now, is he?"

"Yes, Sir! And proud of it."

"Ah, the old days... There were three of us, always off adventuring together. The other was a fellow named Borders. Studied medicine as a young man; we always called him Doc. He'd be Ship's Physician on our sea-voyages; patch people up here and there wherever we'd go, but liked to be on the move, didn't want to settle down. They called us The Three Musketeers, back then! After a while we hooked up with another one; that was D'Artagnon. His name was Gray; Army man; I heard tell he's a Colonel with the Union Forces now. Married a French gal, name of Posey.

"He was a cousin to Doc Borders; I hear Doc's distinguished himself as a Confederate Surgeon. Strange, how friends and kin can end up on different sides like that...There's been so much killin' and pain in this damn war..."

John was pensive. "You mentioned a lady by the name of Posey, who was married to a Col. Gray? Would her name happen to be - Emma?"

The captain choked on his tea, and it sputtered out in front of him.

"You don't mean to tell me you know them too?" he asked, recovering.

"Not directly, Sir. They live in the North, and I've not been there. They're my mother's parents."

A pause, to let that sink in.

"Truly?"

"Yes, Sir."

"I am absolutely amazed! So many coincidences!"

"The Lord works in mysterious ways."

"Indeed He does! ...Well, time to get on with my business here. It's been a real pleasure."

"And for me, Captain!"

"Dismissed... Oh! By the way! What might your name be?"

"Why, Captain John Mallory, Sir... My name is John Mallory Gillespie!"

My grandfather Isaac Borders' brother was named for the same 'best friend': He was John Mallory Borders.

My sister Mallory remembered hearing the following story of the brothers recognizing each other, from our grandmother Sara.

After the fall of Vicksburg and General Lee's retreat from Gettysburg, Virginia, the Cherokee Nation ended their alliance with the South. General Watie's troops were the last of the Confederates to surrender -- over two months after Robert E. Lee had conceded victory to Gen. Grant at Appomattox Courthouse, in Virginia, on April 9, 1865. Geordie and John returned home to their relieved and grateful family that Spring. John had been wounded, but his leg was on the mend.

Geordie, however, had been wounded and captured several months before the end of the war. He had been taken with other prisoners up to Chicago, where he was thrown into a makeshift structure that served as a prison-hospital. Located near the stock-yards, it was stinking and unsanitary. There were abusive guards, few doctors and a great many patients suffering there. It was known as 'The Hell-Hole', because the conditions were so deplorable.

One day the Physician-in-Charge of several hospitals in the area came to make the rounds of the Rebel wounded. In the dank dimness, through his pain, Geordie thought he was hallucinating when he looked up at the doctor who was looking down at him: it was his brother!

Geordie and Robbie did not dare show recognition of each other, for the doctor might be accused of favoritism if he transferred the patient to another hospital (which of course he did) because of a relationship. After all, this was the enemy.

They had not seen each other in many years. In the 1830's, when they saw the Trail of Tears coming, the four Gillespie brothers had been living in Georgia, in their Cherokee grandmother's traditional homeland. To avoid the possibility of the Trail of Tears, three of the brothers had gone north, to Pennsylvania and then elsewhere, and Geordie had returned to his Choctaw mother's homeland, Mississippi. He had more of Gran'pa Gillespie's coloring and could more easily pass for White. The brothers had a reunion 15 years later.

The war was not as hard on the people of Two Worlds as it was on other plantation dwellers in the vicinity. There was devastation all around; the armies of both sides had come through the area several times. But the Gillespie family knew how to survive with nature, and how to get by with very little -- and the others did not.

The family knew how to make bread out of acorns ground into flour, and out of the inside of tree-bark. They knew where to find the berries and roots and wild edible plants; how to hunt, fish, and trap. Their people had lived in the area for centuries; millennia. The nearby forest was their home, their kitchen, and provided what they needed.

They also had the advantage of knowing ahead of time what was going to happen: They would see it in their visions, and be prepared. Some people wondered why the Gillespies seemed to be more unaffected by the ravages of war than the rest of them; some of their neighbors were envious.

Emotions ran high when it came to Yankees, but the people of Two Worlds fed and cared for them too; for anyone who suffered pain or loss could find help or comfort at the home of the Gillespies. It was the way of the Choctaw and the Cherokee. Little Dove was a healer as well.

The Gillespie family knew when the armies were going to come through, and they prepared for them; and also for the wounded and the stragglers. Grander plantation houses would be used as headquarters for the officers of whichever troops were coming through at the time, but Two Worlds had also been commandeered as a place to bivouac the soldiers, when the confederate forces went marching and riding that way; and again by the Union troops when the former were being routed.

Barnyards, smoke-houses, gardens and root-cellars were first to be raided. Prudently the family would have some food and livestock for the soldiers who came, but they would also have stashed some away in secret places for the next group; and for themselves, their friends and their neighbors. They were accustomed to sharing whatever they had; it was traditional among Native Peoples.

When the Southern troops came their way, and said they were going to take the food stores and stock because it was needed by their soldiers, the Gillespies would say: "You are protecting us, and our homes. You are welcome to have whatever you need. You do not have to take it -- it is yours."

When it was the Northern army, they would be told: "You are fighting for the freedom of all people; you are far from home, and you are welcome here. Take whatever we have; it is yours." This attitude was a welcome surprise!

Little Dove insisted on keeping her horse. "I am a healer," she said. "I will need it when I go to doctor the sick and wounded." When he heard that, the Rebel Colonel did not ask what medical school she had attended -- which was unheard of at that time for a woman, anyway -- he just availed himself of her services. She was taken to the battlefield.

The 'Ministering Angel', as they called her, went when and where she was needed. She refused to wear the hoop-skirts then in fashion, and wore the shorter skirts used by young girls, with specially made soft-soled boots (which were more akin to moccasins), and a fitted jacked instead of a shawl. When someone needed her, she needed to be able to move quickly, and be unencumbered, when mounting and riding her steed. She became a familiar figure at these places of conflict.

Her mother, Turtle Woman, and Oldest Grandmother, had taught her much about healing, and she had watched her Medicine Man uncle treat the wounds of warriors. She knew where to find herbs such as bone-set, to mend broken limbs. The bark of red willow could be chewed to kill pain; it is what aspirin is made from. She would heal the wounded, as much as possible, and pray over the dying and the dead.

One time when Little Dove was being taken to a particularly bloody battlefield, she saw Union soldiers riding swiftly over the hill, guns blasting away, swords glinting in the sunlight. She reigned her mare to a sudden stop.

"What's the matter, Doctor Ma'am? What happened?" she was asked. She had been in the midst of war before, and showed no fear.

She could hardly breathe. "I'm sorry, Lieutenant; I can't go any farther. I will have to go back to the clearing by the river. You'll have to bring the wounded to me. I will set up a camp hospital."

"Yes sir, Ma'am," he said, confused. "But what happened?"

Little Dove took a deep breath. "Those soldiers coming over the hill looked just like the Long-Knives, the U.S. Cavalry troops, that killed my parents, my relatives, and all the people of my village when I was a child. I am Lakota."

He didn't know what Lakota was, but he knew pain when he saw it.

"I'll tell them. I'll bring as many of the wounded back as I can, when I get a detail to help me."

When the war was finally over one of Geordie's brothers did not come back. His mother had known at the beginning that one of them would not return... though she did not know which one, and thought that was just as well.

One night early in 1865, she woke up in the middle of the night and saw William, her youngest, standing at the foot of her bed, smiling at her. "Just wanted to say Goodbye, Mama! I'm fine now." And then he just faded out. That's when she knew.

They did a Farewell Ceremony for him the next day, to honor him. The Black part of the family was particularly moved. William was the one who had said he was willing to die for their freedom.

The spirit of William Gillespie returned in the body of the youngest son of Sara Gillespie Borders, his yet-unborn niece at the time of his crossing over. Named after him, William Borders became a warrior, or soldier, also. In World War II, Col. Borders was in the Third Army, on the Staff of General George Patton. He headed the planning of the decisive campaign across Italy, France and Germany that helped sweep the Allies to victory.

The black people on the plantation were also an important reason that Two Worlds did better during the war than others in the area. A few of the Black men went off and joined the Union forces, and one went with

Geordie into the Cherokee Regiment. "We'll make an Indian fighter out of you!" Geordie teased. The Indians called him a Buffalo Soldier.

But most of them stayed put, and they were very protective of 'their People' at Two Worlds. They, too, knew how to 'make do' with very little. They posted guards around the place, and made sure that whoever came along, from the North or the South, knew that these were good people; that they would give whatever they could to help, and that they were to be treated with respect.

Only once did they have Yankee soldiers come along who might have given them trouble: Three stragglers who were far from home, tended to take whatever they could find at gunpoint... and they didn't give a damn. That's when Big Henry come along, rifle in his hand! Even though his hair was beginning to gray, he was a very large man, with a commanding presence. He didn't have to say much -- he'd just look.

"Ah 'spec y'all will be headin' on down the road pretty soon," he said slowly. "If you'se hungry, they's some soup in the cook-house. Ain' nuthin' fuh yuh in de big house." They had some soup, and went on their way.

After the war, Two Worlds was one of the few plantations for a while that could still produce a good cotton crop. At others, the fields had been abandoned: Yankee blockades had kept planters from being able to get the cotton to markets, and many of the slaves had left. Most of the able-bodied men who worked in the fields had gone off to join the Union Army.

Despite the post-war devastation, Geordie still had some connections to foreign merchants from his sea-faring days, and was able, in the war's aftermath, to revive the cotton trade for himself and those others who were able to re-plant.

Except for the young men, most of the Black People stayed on where they were, even though they had been freed: They had no place else to go! They didn't know where to go or how to get there, and had no money to travel with. They were hungry for a while, since the armies had taken just about everything edible -- but then they started planting their gardens again; greens, corn, okra, beans, onions and peanuts. Geordie's family provided a lot of them with seed.

Life was better for some of the former slaves for a while after the war ended. Some Blacks even held office, in the city or county. But then the Northerners lost interest and went back home, except for 'carpet-baggers and scallywags', and it didn't take the Southern land-owners long to figure out how to get things pretty much back the way they had been before. Instead of slaves, they were now called 'share croppers'. "You work for me, and you'll get a share of the crops you raise, as pay. 'Course Ah'll take out some fo' the seed Ah advances to yuh; an' the tools an' equipment; the use o' the mule an' the plow; an' yo' livin' quarters. An' you dasn't run off... 'til you pay me back whut you owes me. If you do, Ah'll set the hounds on yuh. An' y'all 'll end up in ja-yul."

Some of them talked like that.

One night some of the 'good ol' boys' decided to get together with their friends and neighbors and have a Halloween party, out behind Ol' Man Jef'ry's barn.

"Time to do a lil' Hell-raisin', boys!" said Rodney. "An' what better tahm to do it than on the nah-t the damned come out?"

"Well, I'll be damned! You're right!" said Edgar Lee, and they all laughed.

"We'll get dressed up in masks and costumes, an we'll call ourseffs 'The Horribles'!"

"Yeah! We could scare the hell outa some Niggahs!" More laughter.

"But Halloween: This is the time when you honor the souls of the departed, is it not?" said Don Pedro. (Don is a title, like Sir.) He had come from Spain, by way of New Orleans; some of his relatives were the early settlers of that city.

"It is like our 'Dia de los Muertos' -- The Day of the Dead? When we pray for our loved ones who have gone on."

"Oh Ah reckon that's how it stah-ted out," said Edgar Lee. "But it turned into a tah-m fo' whoopin' it up, an' playin' pranks on unsuspectin' folks. An scarin' 'em."

"Whut we gonna do fo' costumes?" asked Billy Bob.

"We all got bed-sheets. We cud be ghosts."

"Ah!" said Don Pedro. "In my little town in Spain, we had a ceremony where we would dress in long white robes, with pointed hats that were also coming down over our faces and heads, with holes to look through. Each year we would have processions through the streets, with candles, to honor our departed ones, our Saints, and our Holy Spirit protector. It is a custom that goes back to the Middle Ages."

128

"Great idea! I'll bring the whiskey, y'all can bring the chickens and yams, an' we'll build a bonfire... an' we'll get rowdy!"

"Yeah! ...an', oh sheet! Don't fo'get the cos-tumes!" That was a real knee-slapper.

They reconvened at sundown, had their cook-out, and got drunk and rowdy. Some of them had followed Don Pedro's guidelines, and had peaked-hat masks made up; some wore different types of masks. Devils were popular, and other scary faces.

The flames of the camp-fire were casting eerie shadows that were dancing on the trees surrounding the clearing. Sparks flew up into the inky sky.

Things were quieting down.

"Let's go spook some spooks!" said Billy Bob. It turned out to be a very popular idea.

The masked-men crept stealthily along the path through the woods toward what used to be called 'slave quarters', and later simply 'the quarters'. When they reached the clearing behind the cabins, they spread out... and crept up, slowly, making spooky sounds; moans, sighs, wails!

The Blacks in or around their cabins looked toward the woods -- to see pale ghostly figures with no faces, in the flickering light of the torches... getting closer and closer... and then these specters let out a blood-curdling SCREAM!

The Black People were terrified! Startled, they jumped, yelled out and ran for cover if they were outside... doors slammed, curtains were drawn; those who had been in the war or had hunting rifles went for their guns. But who was it that was threatening them? You couldn't kill a ghost.

The White-sheet boys were ecstatic! Their scheme had succeeded beyond their wildest expectations.

"We scared the sheet outa' them Darkies!" said Billy Bob.

They were all mighty pleased with themselves. The Blacks did not suspect that it was the plantation owners and their friends, because they always held themselves aloof; being so superior and all.

'White Folks' didn't come down to the quarters unless they wanted something, especially at night... except for a man wanting to bed one of their women.

"Let's go scare some more. This is fun!" Edgar Lee was really getting into it.

They went around to each plantation, repeating the procedure, enjoying the wide-eyed terror they were causing. Billy Bob especially liked to sneak up quietly behind some unsuspecting victim and yell "BOO!"

"Boy, those Dah-kies can sho move fast if they've a mind to," he said. "That Niggah jumped a mile!"

In front of one group of cabins, they built a big bonfire. Someone had the bright idea to lash some logs together into a cross, and erect it behind the crackling fire, and then set it afire also. The flames leapt up into the night; it was quite spectacular. They could feel the fear behind closed doors and windows.

"You know, boys... I think we got somethin' here! A way to scare these people, an' keep 'em in line! Then they'll do whatever we want 'em to, freed or not!"

The idea spread like a wild-fire, started by the bonfire. White Men got together and started clubs; they even made it seem like an altruistic or religious organization, like the Masons, or the Elks. "It is our Christian duty to keep the White Race pure," they said.

"An' to keep the Nigruhs in their place."

Thus the dreaded Ku Klux Klan was born, and the Night-Riders carried their crusade of bigotry, hatred, and White Supremacy across the South-land.

Chapter 10

Grandparents

Grandfather: Rev. Isaac D. Borders,
Baptist preacher from Mississippi

Grandmother Dr. Sara Gillespie
Borders, D.O., M.D.

Returning to the present time-frame: After adding Indian heritage to the knowledge of my Southern roots, I, Sakina, thought a lot about my grandmother, Sara, Little Dove's youngest child -- about what she'd told me about our family history.

It was evident from the beginning of her life that Sara Emma Gillespie Borders was quite an extraordinary person. A tenth child of a tenth child, born ten years after the Civil War, on the tenth day of the tenth month at 10:10pm -- she seemed indeed to have a special destiny. She graduated from the University of Mississippi in 1897 (I still have her diploma), something particularly unusual for a young woman raised in that era on a Southern plantation; where young ladies were supposed to be sweet and genteel, without a brain in their head, and make the man feel that he was the smart one. But she refused to play by their rules.

Sara married a lawyer-turned-Baptist-Preacher named Rev. Isaac Borders; it was a volatile relationship that produced a great deal of conflict, as both of them were brilliant, headstrong, opinionated and outspoken. It also produced five remarkable children, one of whom became my mother.

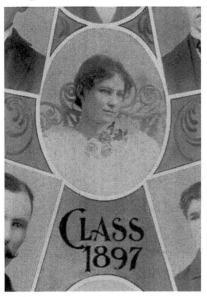

Above: Sara Gillespie at the time of graduation from the University of Mississippi. She was was Secretary and Treasurer of the senior class of 1897 and Senior Essayist.

When her husband was away in France in The Great War (World War I), and her sons and daughters were in school, Sara went to Medical School. She earned both D.O. and M.D. degrees. At that time it took two years to get the M.D., and three years to become an Osteopathic Physician, as the latter would study what the allopathic M.D.s learned, plus the structural, physical therapy.

She had strong, magic hands that could find any kinks in a back; and by kneading and stretching the muscles, fix them.

Some people didn't understand about Osteopathic treatments. Dr. Sara's explanation of the process: "One man said, 'You can't tell me that you can do something up there on my neck -- and my hand will get better!' So I said 'Well, you can't tell me that you can push a button over here on the wall, and a light up there on the ceiling will go on!'"

When it came time for Sara Borders to receive her diploma, some of the medical school staff balked at the idea of having a woman doctor in early 1900s. (They hadn't seen 'Medicine Woman' on TV yet.) She told them that she didn't care about the piece of paper; it was the knowledge she wanted. She just wanted to take care of her family, and her neighbors. Sara was given the diploma.

The greatest plague on earth was the Great Flu epidemic of 1918: 40 million people died! Other doctors lost many of their flu patients, but she incorporated her knowledge of Native medicine, which was contrary to, or went beyond, conventional medical practices of the times; and she lost only one, and that was because he didn't follow her instructions. He kept the windows closed, the blinds drawn, as was customary then. Along with special herbs and healing teas, learned about from her mother, she had her patients open the windows, to let in sunshine and fresh air, instead of closing in the germs.

The diploma reads,

"*University of Mississippi to the Friends of learning everywhere, Greeting. Be it known that Miss Sara E. Gillespie of Leflore County in the State of Mississippi has completed in a satisfactory manner all the requirements in the course of study in this University for a bachelor's degree, attaining an average grade of 88.9 per centum on the course taken. Having shown herself to be in all respects worthy of the degree she is this day by the action of the faculty and of the Board of Trustees declared a Bachelor of Arts of the University of Mississippi and is admitted to all the rights and privileges belonging to this degree. In Testimony Whereof is awarded to her this diploma duly certified by the signatures of the proper officers, and the Seal of the University, affixed this the ninth day of June in the year of our Lord 1897 and the XLIX year of the University.*

FOR THE TRUSTEES, Robert Lowry - PRESIDENT,
Robt B Fulton - CHANCELLOR

My sister Mallory, at the age of six months, gave Sara the name by which she would become known to children, grandchildren, and friends. Baby Mallory was cooing in her grandmother's arms, when she looked up at her and smiled. She began making baby noises: "A-mam-mam-mam-mam," she said.

"Did you hear that?" said the excited new-grandmother to her daughter (my mother), Mary. "She called me AMAM!" And Amam she was, thenceforth, to family and friends.

I loved to go over to her big old Victorian house with the oak-bench swing on the wrap-around front porch. It also had a parlor; a library, overflowing with books; a large foyer with a fireplace; a kitchen; and a big dining room, which, over the years, got filled floor-to-ceiling, wall-to-wall, with papers, magazines and 'periodicals,' as Amam called them.

Upstairs was a round room under a tipi-shaped roof, and other bedrooms with closets under the sloping eaves (lots of eaves-dropping there) that a child could go into, crawl into a low space behind a little door at the back of the closet, crawl through a dark tunnel, and come out in another closet in another room! Great place for hide-and-seek with my sisters.

The attic was fun too. Behind a large wall-panel, there was a secret room, where runaway slaves seeking freedom in the North had been hidden when it was used as an 'underground railway' station during the Civil War. There was enough space for a whole family to hide there.

Down in the backyard, Amam had a grape arbor, and a large vegetable garden to augment the fresh fruits and vegetables that peddler Tony would bring around to the neighborhood in his push-cart. Mmm! Ripe apricots, and juicy blue plums! Many fruits taste like plastic these days by comparison.

Amam knew the names of all the plants, herbs and insects. "Don't ever hurt a preying mantis, or 'walking stick'; they're friendly bugs," she told us. She said that animals, such as cats and dogs, could get along fine if you introduced them properly.

She had a big old gray tiger cat named Aristotle; she loved the Greek classics and was conversant in ancient Greek as well as Latin. Aristotle would pick up wounded birds gently in his mouth and bring them to her, so she could mend their little broken wings.

Amam had lots of interesting stories to tell, about ghosts and spirit-things. Like the time, for instance, when the family was staying in a house in one of the little Mississippi towns where her husband's ministry took them when her children were growing up.

"One night it was hot," she said, "so William (my mother's younger brother) was sleeping on the screen porch at the front of the house. The next morning, he asked me 'Who was that man that came into the house last night, Mother?' and I said 'What man, dear? I didn't hear anyone come in.'

"'Well, everyone was asleep,' he said. 'It was the middle of the night. But I woke up, and saw him coming up the steps; and he came through the screen door onto the porch... but he just walked through it; he didn't open it. Then he went into the house through the open front door, took my Boy Scout hat off the hat-rack and put it on his head, and went on upstairs. A little while later he came back down, put my hat back on the rack, and went on back out through the screen door, down the steps, and was gone.'

"So I asked William, 'What did he look like?' and he described the man. 'Why, that's old Mr. Jones; he used to live here. But he died, four years ago!' I told him."

Amam told us about another experience.

"I was so sick once, I died. My spirit left my body and went up to the ceiling, where I hovered and looked back down at my body lying there. But then I decided that I wasn't finished yet, and I came back. My children needed me."

Sometimes she could get glimpses of the future.

"One time I decided to go back home and visit my mother, who still lived on the plantation where I grew up. I hadn't seen her in many years; she was older now, and widowed, and I felt a sense of urgency," Amam related.

"I took a train to Greenwood, Mississippi, the nearest town, and hired a car for the rest of the way. While riding on the train, I had dozed off and had a vivid dream: I saw my sister come out from behind a bush that hadn't been there the last time I had been home... and she said, 'Mother's gone!'

"It turned out to be a pre-cognitive dream; when I arrived, it happened just as I had seen it. My sister Carrie came around from behind the bush that had grown up since my last visit, and said 'Mother's gone!' I had sensed that her time was near, and had hoped to see her one more time -- but I arrived too late."

Little Dove had flown home to the Great Spirit, to join her ancestors. She had done well on her earth-journey, and there was a great 'Welcome Home!' celebration on the other side, when she went to the Light.

When my mother, Mary, was growing up in Mississippi in the early 1900s, it seemed that nobody had any money. Mary Borders lived in various little towns throughout the state - Aberdeen, Holly Springs, Greenwood -- as her preacher father was transferred from one parish to another. They lived in the Parsonage, next to the Baptist Church; usually it was a little house that had seen better days, but there was no money to fix it up with.

"I had one new dress a year," Mother told us, "and I made that myself. With a hand-me-down from Rachel (her older sister), and one from last year, that made two for school and one for Sundays." Rachel and Irvin were older; William and Carolyn younger, but they were all close in age.

Although the War-Between-The-States had left the South impoverished, they still had their pride, and those whose families had led the good life spent a great deal of time living in the glorious past. Young ladies were still taught to be genteel and behave in a proper manner; young men were taught to be 'gentlemen'.

My mother, Mary, took great pride in the fact that her mother had grown up on a plantation (and her father on another one), and she spent a lot of time fantasizing about it. How wonderful it must have been, she thought, to grow up in a gracious Southern mansion, with pillared portico! Surrounded by tall oak trees draped with Spanish moss, azaleas, vast cotton fields... and overlooking the river.

Finally the time came when Mary and her family were going to go back to the Plantation, Two Worlds, and she would get to see at last her mother's and father's genteel way of living. The journey was made with excitement and anticipation.

They drove through the gates and up the long drive. Imagine the shock and disappointment Mary felt when her mother said: "What happened to the house? It used to be right over there, behind those big trees..."

The big house had burned down -- and her grandparents, to Mary's chagrin, were living in a small house which had formerly been slave quarters! So much for delusions of grandeur.

In my vision of those times, Little Dove and Long Bow were not at all unhappy about the situation. They had saved the important things from the fire, the regalia and sacred objects and a few prized books; with their children grown and gone -- all but Carrie, who never married -- they didn't need all that space. Nor did they need all those rooms to take care of; and there was never money for the kind of up-keep and repair that was needed by a big old house.

They had moved back into what had once been their 'honeymoon cottage', where they had been very happy in the early years of their marriage. True, it had been 'slave quarters' at one time, but to them it was quite comfortable. Some Black families still lived in the other cabins nearby; they had heard that the North wasn't such a 'Promised Land' after all: both the weather and the people were cold.

My Grandfather, Isaac Borders, was born when his father, a former Civil War Surgeon, was fifty years of age. After the War-For-Southern-Independence was over, Great-grandfather went back to being a country doctor. He had one more son after Isaac, and lived on the family plantation in northern Mississippi. His grandfather had been one of the original settlers in the area.

When his sons were still young, Dr. Borders went on a house-call in his horse-and-buggy one cold, stormy night, and in the pelting rain he contracted a fatal case of pneumonia. Isaac led a lonely childhood. When he was little, his father was always off caring for patients, and his mother was preoccupied with 'the baby', his little brother. After the death of her husband, she became despondent, having more responsibility and work to do on the plantation, without the income and occasional companionship of her busy husband.

She became obsessed with her younger son (according to Isaac's diary), looking to him for emotional gratification, and neglecting the older son. She even moved to the city to share lodging with this brother when he went off to college.

Isaac was raised mostly by an old 'family retainer', a former slave called Pompey. He spent most of his time playing by himself under a large oak tree, acting out his resentment at feeling abandoned by his father and neglected by his mother in elaborate war games with toy soldiers.

Sara Gillespie was considered quite a good catch; she had many beaux that came calling. She was different from the other young belles; considered a great beauty, and possessed of the usual demeanor of gentility so highly prized by Southerners; she was also independent, spunky, and extremely bright. The young gentlemen found it a refreshing and challenging change from most of the 'sweet young things' who were living in genteel poverty in the post-war South.

They enjoyed matching wits with her. She would let her brains show rather than deferring always to the man, making him think that he was the only one who was knowledgeable. That was how you caught a man, Southern girls were taught. "I do declare!" a girl might say. "I just don't know how you can be so clever!" A young woman's helplessness would appeal to a gentleman's sense of chivalry and protectiveness in the ante-bellum South, went the theory, and it carried over.

"Get him to talk about himself!" they were instructed, before going off to a dance. "That's a subject they always find fascinating. Find out what he's interested in." (My mother passed on this advice to me.)

It was highly unusual for a young woman to be a college graduate in that region in the 1800's, but Sara's immense thirst for knowledge, and her determination, had taken her through with flying colors. And it was that passion for knowledge that had given Isaac Borders the edge over other suitors.

Isaac was tall, handsome, had a deep voice, and a flowery way of speaking; his was an impressive presence. This would not have mattered all that much to her; but what did make a difference was that his physician father had an extensive library, and, in his loneliness, Isaac had read most of the books in it. He was an intellectual match for her.

It seemed to be the perfect match! Sara's big family gathered to celebrate the marriage, and Isaac was pleased that now he too would know the camaraderie of many brothers and sisters, as they welcomed him into the family.

It was not long, however, until he came to the conclusion that he had made a terrible mistake! (Again, according to his diary, which I read at my cousin Lynn's house in California.) Why couldn't he have married one of those genteel Southern young ladies who just wanted to take care of her man - instead of always challenging his facts, competing with him? It seemed that he had 'jumped out of the frying pan, into the fire'!

As a child, I was told the story of how Grandfather Borders decided to go into the ministry.

"Our plantation was on the Yazoo River, where it came together with the Tallahatchie and the Yalobusha," Amam (Sara) said. "One day my father was out working on the levee, right next to the river, and a paddle-wheeler came around the bend and blew a blast on its whistle that was so close and so loud -- it startled my father, and he turned his head so fast that it did something to his neck and he went blind! A muscle was pressing on the optic nerve, and it got locked into place."

Isaac loved his father-in-law dearly; Geordie was very kind to him, and it seemed that the father he had lost as a child was finally replaced. Whatever problems he had with his stubborn young wife, who always had to be right, it seemed, his relationship with her father remained close.

"He vowed that if my father's sight were ever restored," Amam told me, "He would devote his life to God, and go into the ministry.

"One day a traveling Osteopathic Doctor came through the area. He would go from one place to another, fixing peoples' backs-out-of-place, or whatever, and then move on to the next town or rural area. People spoke very highly of him.

"Isaac asked him if he could help my father. It had been almost two years since he had become blind. The Osteopathic Physician worked on Daddy's neck for a while, kneading the taught muscles, until they heard something snap. He told my father not to move his head or open his eyes for four hours; after that it would be all right.

"When he opened his eyes - he could see again! The pressure on the optic nerve had been released. To my husband it seemed a miracle, and he kept his promise. He studied for the ministry, and became Reverend Borders."

In his diary, Grandfather told of a less altruistic reason. He had studied law and passed the Bar, and hung out his shingle -- but few people could afford his services; nobody had any money in the South back then, so they had to settle their own disputes. However, a friend suggested that he become a preacher:

"You're tall and imposing, with an impressive presence. You're bright, have a way with words, a dramatic flair and a powerful delivery, with that deep voice of yours! You could impress a jury, yes; but you'd make more money as a preacher. Everybody goes to church."

Perhaps both these factors combined to help him with his choice of calling.

Preachers didn't make much money either, in that time and place - but at least he was provided with a Parish House for his family to live in, and enough to eat. The parson would always be invited to someone's house for Sunday dinner. "They always serve chicken!" he complained in his diary. "They'll say, 'We're so glad you came to visit us today, Rev. Borders! We were going to have ham today, but we always hear that preachers love chicken - so we had that instead.' Oh, the eternal, infernal chicken! I get so tired of it - I would dearly love to have had ham instead," he lamented.

Isaac Borders was very well-spoken, with a flowery way with words. Obviously well-educated, he traced his ancestry back to the Royal Court of England in Medieval times: his ancestor received the family name (with the 'a' dropped) because he had been one of an entourage known as The King's Boarders' -- a group of elite Royal Guard who traveled with the Regent and 'took bed and board' with him. (Meals were served on large boards, or tables.) Thus he was part of the royal retinue of companions and protectors.

Rev. Borders was highly popular with his parishioners, being well-versed in the Bible and impressive in his delivery, especially when he first came to a new town. But every year or two, he would be transferred to another town or rural area; after a while even the most inspiring presentation can be less stimulating. So my mother and her brothers and sisters were always having to be relocated, and to be the 'new kids' in town.

They were also expected to behave properly. "We always had to sit in the front row, while Daddy preached," Mother told my sisters and me. "If we read something -- the boys would try to hide an adventure book inside their prayer book -- we always got caught, because Daddy was in the pulpit above us. And we would be thoroughly reprimanded in front of the congregation:

"'If the Borders children would please pay attention!' he'd admonish. The whipping would come later. Our father was very strict," said my mother. A custom unfortunately carried over into my generation. But there it stopped.

Isaac and Sara were famous for their conflicts. "One time," my mother recalled, "it was the talk of the neighborhood that it had been three whole days since Mother and Daddy had had an argument! They were always yelling at each other."

Isaac's diary related that he was always getting into a conflict with someone else, too, wherever he went; and of course it was always their fault. He was maligned, misunderstood, and suffered greatly. He moved on frequently.

At one point he had a falling-out with his church, and he decided to leave it. He took his family and moved from Mississippi to California. They crossed the Yosemite Valley in a covered wagon, just like in the old days, and it was quite an adventure! When they came to a steep hill, the children got out of the wagon and walked, and the boys put a log under the wagon wheels to keep it from rolling backwards while the oxen pulled it forward a wagon-length -- and then they repeated the process.

They drove past -- and even through! -- giant Sequoyah trees, named for the famous Cherokee scholar who had invented a way to write their language, and who had started a Cherokee-and-English newspaper.

The family settled in Los Angeles, where they lived for two years. They lived in a nice little house in the country, with only a few houses around, and lots of fields. It was quite rural then. The house was located at the corner of Hollywood and Vine. (Later the location of the famed Brown Derby.)

A man told Grandfather Isaac about a wonderful piece of land, to the North. He took him up to see it. It was four days journey away. At last! Paradise found! A stream ran through it and there were shade trees, fields of lush green grass, and what looked like good soil in which to raise whatever food they'd need -- as they had on the plantation of his childhood.

He wouldn't have to work in the city any more. He made his decision to move his family to this 'Promised Land', to retire and become self-sufficient. He had saved some money and had bought several lots in the Los Angeles area. He sold them now to buy the land.

After several months of preparation, the family was finally ready for the move. They piled their essential belongings into a large wagon, along with building materials for a small house -- they could expand later. It was late summer now, and they could camp out in a tent until the dwelling was ready.

It took almost a week to get there, with the large load they were hauling in the wagon. But finally, they rounded a hill to the beautiful valley of his dreams. The new home to which he was, once again, relocating his family.

The sight before him caused him to recoil in shock – and horror! The stream that had flowed abundantly in the springtime had dried up in the hot summer sun. The lush grassland had also dried up, and turned to dusty, parched brown. There was no house to live in. There were many acres, but they now seemed worthless.

For a time, he was speechless -- seething. His family knew better than to ask questions, when he was in this kind of mood. And it was obvious what had happened.

"Once again I've been deceived and betrayed by someone I trusted! Cheated and robbed by that unholy scoundrel!" he bellowed. (No wonder he was so good at preaching hell-fire and brimstone.)

They turned around and returned to the City of the Angels (Los Angeles), to seek out the devil who had done this. The diary did not record whether or not he succeeded.

Isaac heard that there was an opening for a Methodist Minister in Kansas City, Missouri, so he decided to return to the ministry, and, once again, relocate his family. Here he was at last more successful, and after a few years he decided that his family deserved a permanent home. He bought the big Victorian house on Pendleton Avenue, where I loved to visit my grandmother Amam when I was a child.

Isaac and Sara Borders' offspring distinguished themselves in various ways. Their son William was on Gen. Patton's staff, planning the successful campaign across Europe to defeat the Nazi war machine; and he later became an influential banker in Missouri.

Rachel, a French teacher with a flawless accent that fooled the French, married Dr. M.O. Ross, Chancellor of Butler University in Indianapolis for 15 years, building it up from a small college to a large, respected university.

Carolyn married a wealthy man from Washington, D.C., but after a trip around the world, she died at the age of 24. Mary (my mother) married

Walter M. Cross, Jr., son of a physician-scientist who invented gasoline; i.e., the process by which gasoline was made from crude oil. After my father's death she married British Maj. Charles Byrte who served in the army in India for seven years. They lived in a villa of her own design in Marbella, Spain, on the Mediterranean, and exhibited her paintings in some of the finest galleries in Madrid and in London, including Sotheby's.

Isaac and Sara's eldest son, Irvin, elected to remain in Los Angeles; he did some work for Walt Disney for a while. He sent us a signed original painting of 'The Three Little Pigs', when we were little. Mallory still has it. He married Helen Beery, cousin of film actor Wallace Beery, and they had a daughter named Lynn.

When I was ten years old, my other grandmother - on my father's side - decided to take a vacation in Hawaii, with her sister and her daughter Annette. She was also kind enough to offer to take two of her grandchildren; for some reason she thought it would be too much to take all three of us girls.

Above: Mary Borders Cross, at about 11 years, in Mississippi.She married Walter M. Cross Jr.; she was the daughter of Sara Gillespie Borders, and the mother of Sakina Blue-Star.

So it was decided that my sister Mallory and I would go to Hawaii, and Ann would spend the summer in Los Angeles with cousin Lynn (Irvin and Helen's only child), who was her age.

I was thrilled! Hawaii seemed such a romantic place, and indeed it was. I sat in the bow of an out-rigger canoe, being paddled by strong brown arms. I was carried on the bronzed shoulders of a Native Hawaiian on a surf-board, after we had gone far out into the ocean to catch the 'perfect wave'; and I visited an old-style village of grass huts, where I ate poi (a porridge) with my fingers. I loved it.

My favorite thing to do was to watch the hula dancers, as they told their legends by graceful hand-motions, with grass-skirted swaying hips.

Their dances were accompanied by the songs of ukulele-playing young men. They danced under the enormous old banyan tree, with the ocean forming a backdrop.

This was my idea of perfection! The ocean, the people, the setting -- at that time there were only two hotels on Waikiki Beach; The Royal Hawaiian and the Moana. We stayed at the latter. I threw many leis overboard when the ocean-liner 'The Lurline' carried us away from the beloved islands, for legend said that if your leis drifted back to the shore, you would return some day. (It worked.)

Many years later, I returned to Hawaii to visit my Assiniboine friend, Georgia White. We did a World Peace Prayer Ceremony by the ocean at the full moon, on the last day of 1990; and I joined her daughter Morgenstarr and her troupe in exuberant dancing through the streets of Honolulu on the New Year's 'First Night', to give an offering to the Goddess of the Sea.

I did a Spirit-portrait and Reading for Georgia's friend Wanda. "There's one more thing I want to do before I leave Hawaii," I told her . "I want to go back to the Moana. My most treasured childhood memory is watching the hula dancers do their beautiful dances there under the great banyan tree, with the ocean in the background."

Wanda smiled, surprised. "I was one of those hula-dancers! That was my family that danced there!" So we went to the Moana together, and I relived my joy.

When I was little, I almost didn't get to go on that trip. We had taken a train across country to San Francisco -- and I got the mumps! So it was decided that I would stay at cousin Lynn's house in Los Angeles for the summer, and my sister Ann would go to Hawaii in my place. But the Matson liner Lurline took a week to load up in San Francisco, and then again in Los Angeles, and by that time I had gotten well. Whew! Ann and I got switched around again. While Ann was staying with cousin Lynn and her parents, she had a visit with my great-uncle Dave Gillespie. She brought back a picture of him: His hair was white then, though it had been black when he was young. Ann didn't get to go to Hawaii, but she did get to meet Uncle Dave: one of the most exciting people I've ever even known about!

Above: I brought this grass skirt back from Hawaii when I was 10. Grandaughter Juliette wore it at her 5th birthday; I taught her the hula, the song and dance of "The little Brown Gal, in the little grass skirt! In the little grass shack, in Hawaii...." This life-size Brown Gal doll is in the Blue-Star Collection.

This little watercolor of Hawaiian dancers was part of a series honoring all cultures, painted in 1951, a reminder of a treasured memory of my youth.

145

Little Dove, Lakota Ancestor

Chapter 11

The Adventures of Uncle Dave

Little Dove's daughter Sara had a brother who was very adventurous.
One time, he was up in a tree, surrounded by a pack of wolves.

My favorite thing about visiting my grandmother, Sara – Little Dove's daughter -- when I was a child, was listening to her tell stories about her brother, Dave. Uncle Dave led the most amazing life!

The first story I recall was about Dave as a toddler, down by the river. He had been playing by the water, but had got up and wandered too close to it - and he fell in. His mother (Little Dove) watched in horror as Dave was swept away by the strong current. He was being drawn into a whirl-pool!

His mother couldn't swim. But she picked up two large rocks, to keep from floating, one under each arm, and headed for where she had last seen him go down: Once, twice... and for the third time. She took a deep breath and went under the water, eyes open, to see where the child was. When she got to him, she dropped one of the rocks and put him under her arm... and turned around and walked back out.

Little Dove laid her tiny son on the river bank and yelled for help. She began doing artificial respiration on him, but there was no response. The men who came to help worked on him too, by turns, as she instructed them. After half an hour, one of them said "It's no use, ma'am. The boy's gone."

His mother refused to give up. "Keep going!" she said, determined to continue. And she also kept working to revive him. After forty-five minutes - he coughed and sputtered and came back to life. ("Thank you, Creator!" she whispered.)

Grandmother Sara, Little Dove's daughter, said that when Dave was 2 years old, and still learning to talk, he said something in a silly way - and his brothers made fun of him. So he decided he wouldn't talk at all! (Little Dove knew about people making fun of the way you speak - and then not talking.) The family began to think something had happened to his vocal cords, and that he would never talk. And Dave didn't speak to anyone again, for 3 years -- until he was 5 years old, and someone overheard him talking to the animals in the barn one day. They found out, to their relief, that he could talk perfectly well. At that point he decided that he might as well keep it up, since they knew.

The next adventure I recall was when Dave was about 12, and went along with his big brother Charley in the wagon carrying supplies for a family picnic down by the river. The rest of the family had gone by carriage, and they'd picked a spot a ways away under big shade trees, where they could watch the paddle-boats docking at the landing. But it started to rain, so they packed up everything and headed for home.

There was a big road for the wagons, and a smaller one for carriages. Dave wanted to drive the wagon, but Charley said "No." So Dave jumped out and said "I'll walk! I know a shortcut through the woods; it would take half the time."

Charley yelled after him: "Come back! You know we were always told to stay out of those woods after dark, and it'll be dark pretty soon. There are packs of wolves and wild cats that come out then, and it's dangerous."

Dave was an impetuous youth, so he started off down the path anyway, calling back "I'm gonna take the short-cut! I know these woods, I'll be home before dark." And he added: "I'll beat you home!"

"COME BACK HERE!" Charley yelled. But to no avail; Dave had disappeared into the forest. Well, he was a woodsman like his father; he spent a lot of time among the trees, talking to the animals. Charley kept on driving the wagon along the road, confident that his brother would be home before he would.

It had been dark for a while when he got back, but his lantern had lit the way; and the horses, of course, knew their way home. He pulled up in front of the house kitchen to unload.

His mother came out to greet him.

"Where's Dave?" she asked.

"Why -- isn't he here? He jumped out of the wagon back a while and said he'd take the short-cut through the woods, and beat me home. I told him not to -- that it could be dangerous. But you know Dave: Stubborn! He doesn't care who's in charge, and he doesn't listen."

There was a lot of running and yelling going on then, my grandmother Sara told us, when she was telling this story to my sisters and me when we were little. "Get your shot-guns! Go get the men! An' HURRY!" she heard her father shouting. Sara was only five years old at the time, and she was frightened: She ran and hid under her mother's bed!

All the men-folk on the plantation were called together, and they organized a search-party. They took lanterns and rifles, in case of trouble.

"My father went with some of the men, in one direction," Grandmother Sara related. "And he said to the other party, 'You go over that way, and search that part of the woods. When you find the boy - fire one shot if he's dead... and two shots if he's alive.' As they got deeper into the woods, they heard the howl of wolves! From the sound of them, it must have been a large pack.

"The howl of the wolves was getting closer. They searched and searched... and then -- a shot rang out! My father and his men stopped to listen: it seemed like an eternity of uncertainty; was the boy dead?"

She would pause to let that sink in.

"And then -- they heard another shot! And they knew that Dave had been found, and that he was alive.

"My father's party went in the direction that the shots had come from. As they got closer, the howl of the wolves got louder. Finally they came to the edge of a little clearing -- and there were the wolves, about 30 of them, howling around a tree. Up in the branches of the tree was Dave -- sound asleep! It had got dark, and he became tired; so he climbed up into a tree, tied himself in with his fishing line, so he wouldn't fall out -- and fell asleep.

"The men's shots drove the wolves away, and they took the boy home," she said.

"Dave got punished that time, for not doing what his brother told him, and for worrying them all so. But secretly, I think our father was pretty proud of him, for knowing how to survive in the forest."

Young Dave did not like to be disciplined, and with his spunky nature, he always seemed to be getting into trouble. So at the age of twelve, he decided to run away from home. (His father was sixteen, when he left home.) It was time to see the world! He worked his way down-river to New Orleans, and hung around the docks. He was big enough, and possessed enough bravado, to convince an officer that he was sixteen -- and he joined the Merchant Marine. He shipped out to many ports, and did indeed see the world.

Uncle Dave always liked to be where the action was. When the Suez Canal was being dug in Egypt, he was part of the crew that was digging it. When he heard that there was gold to be mined in the rivers of Alaska, he was off to the Yukon. (This was years before the Klondike gold rush of 1897.)

Dave found lots of gold all right, but he later lost most of it at sea. And he found a fame of sorts, up there in the North Country. When he camped out next to the White Horse River, in Yukon Territory, he was told that the White Horse rapids were too wild and dangerous to travel through by canoe, as he was planning to do. One man had negotiated this spectacular white-water river, but he had a special un-tip-able kayak-type boat.

"No White Man has ever gone down those rapids in an open canoe -- and lived to tell the tale!" he was told. "Only a few Indians have done it."

Dave laughed. "If they can do it -- I can do it!" he said. And he did!

When my mother Mary (Sara's daughter) lived on the Mediterranean coast of Spain in her later years, there was a couple visiting Marbella who said they were from White Horse, Alaska.

"Oh, how interesting! My uncle went down the White Horse rapids in an open canoe, in the 1800's!" she said.

"I'm afraid not," the man said smiling, somewhat patronizingly. "There's only been one White Man who's ever gone down those dangerous rapids in a canoe -- and lived." He smiled; obviously she had no idea how spectacular and impossible a feat it was.

"What was your uncle's name?"

"David Gillespie."

"Oh! That was the man!" he replied. "Your uncle is in the history books." It was Mother's turn to smile.

(Of course, if he was really an Indian, with only one-sixteenth Scottish blood -- I wonder if that was cheating?)

With Alaskan winter coming on Dave decided that it was time to head South. He made his way to Skagway, at the head of the Alaskan inland waterway, and hopped a ferry-boat that was heading south to Juneau. After a while the sky darkened, the wind blew up choppy water, and the fog closed in, making visibility nil. The passengers were getting nervous -- but Dave wasn't worried; he had grown up on a river, he was a seasoned sailor. And he knew where the life-boats were.

And then it happened: A CRASH! A sickening thud as the ferry was rammed amidships by a freighter, and the air was filled with the screams of panicked people. The boat was listing to port, taking on water, and sinking rapidly.

Dave grabbed whoever was close to him and pulled them to the lifeboats. Some of the crewmen also were able to get to the small boats, lower three of them, and row frantically away from the ferryboat to get far enough away from it not to be pulled down in the powerful suction that would be created by the sinking vessel. The ferry was soon headed for the depths.

Horns were blaring! Bells ringing! A pity they hadn't kept sounding the horns before the collision, Dave thought -- it could have been avoided. Only two of the life boats made it away safely. Dave had managed to save three passengers; the other small boat contained two crewmen.

The freighter had sustained some damage to its bow, but its Captain decided that they could hobble into port. He reversed his course, and his crew called out to any survivors who might be in the water. When they got close enough, they continued to call out to each other in the fog until the shivering occupants of the life boats could be picked up by the freighter's powerful gaslight ship's lanterns, cutting through the thick fog. Life preservers with life-lines were tossed out, and the cold, wet, unfortunates were taken aboard.

The survivors were bundled up in warm blankets and given hot coffee and soup. The Captain decided that, under the circumstances, he should take them back to Ketchikan, where they had been headed. Rather than go by the narrow Inside Passage route, however -- not wishing to chance another mishap -- he headed West, to go around the islands. He headed his ship out into the Gulf of Alaska. He felt better in the open ocean; that would be safe, he thought.

So much for thinking. He made sure to blast his horn every few minutes this time, for the fog continued to give zero visibility. And then - CRASH! Cru-u-unch. It happened again!

They had hit an iceberg.

"All hands on deck! Man the life-boats!" the cry rang out. The iceberg had cut a huge gash into the starboard bow, and the ship split open. It shivered and shimmied; the bow, where it had rammed the iceberg, now headed upward toward the sky. It bounced backward a bit; the stern went down... and the freighter slid beneath the waves.

The ones who made it cleared the ship just in time. They rowed around in the water for a while, and then headed for the iceberg. They climbed up onto it. They could build a fire there to keep from freezing to death, and perhaps signal a passing ship. Dave was glad he was still wrapped in a blanket, from the first shipwreck, and he shared it with the others as they huddled together. There were provisions in the boats.

The freighter Captain, and the ferry passengers not as adept as the crew in finding the life-boats quickly, went down with the ship. It was a long, cold night on their little frozen island. There was a lot of praying going on.

There were eight survivors of the sinking, and they were picked up by a passing ship the following day. It was on the front page of newspapers all over the world.

The only one who survived both sinkings was David Gillespie, of Mississippi! That's how his family found out that he was alive. They hadn't heard from him in years.

He was sixteen.

History tends to repeat itself.

In another aside -- I got a call from Alaska at 2 am one morning when I was living in an old sea captain's house out on Cape Cod, in Massachusetts, in 1981. My son Chip was working on a scallop boat then, fishing out of Kodiak, Alaska. Not far from Uncle Dave's sinking.

"How long has it been since you heard from your son?" a young man's voice asked.

"About two weeks," I answered.

"Well, his boat went down. I thought you'd want to know." My God! Sinking in Alaskan waters, in December? I was in shock!

My husband had the presence of mind to call the Coast Guard in Alaska -- and, after an anxious few hours, we found out what had happened. A boat had gone down, but it wasn't the one Chip was on. His boat was the one that rescued the two survivors, out of a crew of ten, in that iceberg infested Gulf of Alaska. His friend had seen Chip on the boat that capsized in heavy seas, and thought it was his, but he had just been visiting.

I sent out a prayer for the other mothers.

Uncle Dave worked at a lot of different jobs. One time when he was a stevedore, working for a shipyard in San Francisco, he was walking along the pier.

"The ship that was tied up at the dock was unloading its cargo," grandmother Sara said. "There were great big barrels, four or five feet in diameter, that were being slid down a ramp and across the dock to where they would be stored. They were picked up on the ship by a line with a pulley, and before they let the big barrels go down the ramp they would call out a warning to anyone who was walking along the dock, so they wouldn't get hit.

"Well, Dave was walking along, and they were about to release another hogshead (barrel), when the cable broke - and the barrel was headed directly for him! The man unloading watched in horror; there was no time to warn him. But Dave, at that instant, jumped six feet straight up into the air! And the barrel slid right underneath him."

Wow! Talk about Spirit protection! That was Guardian Angel kind of stuff.

Another time, Dave had a job as a door-to-door salesman. He was selling encyclopedias. He had not been particularly successful that day, but he thought he would try his luck at one more house.

"He went up to the front door, and rang the bell," Sara related. "When a young lady came and opened the door - he just stared at her! Since he didn't say anything, she said 'Yes? What is it?' - and Dave answered, 'I'm going to marry you!' So she closed the door on him.

"Well, Dave knocked on the door and waited until she opened it again. 'My humble apologies, ma'am. I didn't mean to be so forward,' he said. 'Perhaps we could begin again?'

"They got to talking - about encyclopedias, at first – and she found him a very interesting young man. He invited her out to dinner.

"One month later, they were married."

People in my family sometimes come together in unusual ways. In the Dakotas, Geordie/Long Bow proposed to Little Dove at their first meeting. In Sedona, Arizona, my new friend Randy/Sundance and I went out into the magical canyons of the Ancients one day, and had a simultaneous recall of a previous life together when he was a Mountain Man and I was his Arapaho wife. Two weeks later we went up to a little chapel looking out on the mountains sacred to the Hopi and the Navajo (San Francisco Peaks) - and were married.

One more story I remember Grandmother telling me.

"Dave went down to a railroad station to catch a train one day. When he got there, the train had already started to pull out. 'Sorry, you missed it! She's going down the track,' he was told.

"Well now, Dave wasn't about to let a little thing like that stop him! He wanted to get on that train, and he was a fast runner - so he just ran down the tracks after it.

"He finally caught up with it, and grabbed the bar on the caboose. But as he made that final lunge for it, his foot went forward under the wheel - and the train ran over it!

"He sat there and watched the blood spurt out... and then he took off his neck-tie and made a tourniquet to stop the bleeding, and wrapped the foot up with his handkerchief. The Station Master sent for a doctor.

"People came running; they had seen what had happened. A crowd gathered around him.

"When the physician came and took a look at my brother's foot," said Sara, "he said the prognosis was very bad. The foot had been badly crushed; it would have to come off.

"'You're not taking off my foot!' Dave told him. 'But gangrene would set in!' the doctor warned. 'The poison of the infection would spread throughout your system - and you'd die from it!' He took out his saw.

"Dave pulled out the pistol he always carried, and said again: 'YOU'RE NOT TAKING OFF MY FOOT! And I'll shoot anyone who tries to do it!' When Dave spoke, you knew that he meant what he said.

" 'Well, I'll patch you up as best as I can,' said the doctor, 'but I don't give it much hope. You'll certainly never walk again, without crutches.' He was wrong.

"It took a while for Dave to recover - and he walked with a slight limp after that. But he still had his foot!"

She didn't mention that his mother knew the healing methods of the Native People, which were very effective.

In the 1990s I found out in a reading by psychic Sandra Bowen that my great-grandmother was Sioux, and I began remembering the ways of my grandmother, Sara, Little Dove's daughter, things that might fit in with this factor.

Sara had a habit of squatting down on her haunches, at her garden, where she grew vegetables, flowers, medicinal herbs and grapes; or beside a campfire. Or she would hunker down to observe mice, moles, chipmunks, birds, insects; all creatures, and plants. Not a particularly Southern-lady-like posture! After all, she was raised in Mississippi, to be genteel. But much in keeping with the customs of Native People.

She knew all of the insects, animals and plants, their uses and their Latin names. She loved the earth.

My husband Arn rented a room in her big Victorian house back when he was a medical student; the house was near his school. Both of them were brilliant, and they would have long talks, when he lived there; and, though not always agreeing with each other, they had become friends.

Sara visited us in Boston, Massachusetts, in the late 1950s when we had several small children. She went out into the back yard one day, and Arn, then a young doctor, went out to see her -- and was alarmed to find her lying on the ground! Panic! Had she had a heart attack, and collapsed? Was she dead? He walked over to her, looking for signs of life.

"Would you please move, Arnold?" she said, without opening her eyes. "You're standing in my sunshine."

"Oh! I thought something had happened to you!"

"Oh no; I love to lie on the earth. I get energy from it. And I love the sun. It warms me."

When my sisters and I were little, our mother would take us up to the northern Wisconsin woods in July and August, where we would rent a little cabin on a lake to escape the broiling heat of summer. Daddy would come and join us for a week. He loved to go fishing on the peaceful lake in the quiet of dawn, to recover from the stresses of running a business in the city.

Grandmother Sara joined us there sometimes. We decided to go to another lake and have a picnic one day. But when we approached our destination - it began raining. Pouring!

"Oh, darn!" my sister Mallory said. "Now we won't get to have our picnic! We can't build a campfire in the rain!" "We wanted hot dogs!" said Ann. "And marshmallows!" I added.

"Oh yes we can have a fire!" said Grandmother. And she proceeded to show us how. It was sprinkling now.

"Look underneath the wet leaves, and gather up the dry ones, to get the fire started. Find some old, dry, seasoned logs; they burn better."

Grandmother took some of the pine logs we found and brought to her and split them with a hatchet. "These are for kindling," she said. She emptied the carton we had brought the food in and put it over the stone-ringed fire circle, to protect the wood from the rain. Tipping up one side of the carton, its back-side to the direction of the slanting rain, she propped it up with a forked stick.

Reaching underneath the box, she then arranged the split-pine kindling, in a tipi shape; with smaller kindling, twigs, curled birch-bark and dry leaves inside the little 'tipi'. Next, with a single match, she lit the fire, blew on it, and got it going. She then removed the carton.

People driving by were astonished to see a roaring fire -- in the rain! It was still coming down. We were delighted! We had our picnic.

Little Dove's daughter Sara had a lot of practical know-how, as well as her vast intellectual storehouse of knowledge.

"A man got a bad cut when a saw-blade slipped, when I was young, and still living at home," she recalled. "I wrapped his hand with cloth, but an artery had been severed, and it just wouldn't stop bleeding! Cotton wouldn't do it -- nothing would, unless I kept my finger on it. Then I ran into the barn and grabbed a handful of cobwebs - and that stopped it. There's a substance in spider-webs that causes the blood to congeal."

My daughter was less impressed by this knowledge than I was. When Mallory Ann cut her hand one time, I went and found some bits of cobweb to deal with this situation. She was horrified! "Mom! I'm not going to put some dusty old spider-webs you found behind the furnace on my hand! I'll find a Band-Aid!" And thus traditions are lost, from one generation to the next.

I remember little things my grandmother taught us. "Cold contracts; heat expands. Ice packs stop swelling; hot packs expand and relax taut muscles. Rinse with cold water after showering - warm water opens the pores, and cold closes them up. Rub your scalp vigorously when you wash it; it stimulates the hair follicles, and towel-dry it forcefully, too." Lots of things.

In the little house where we lived when I was born, my father kept his car garaged a block away. One night while he was walking home after putting his car away, a robber sneaked up behind him and hit him over the head, knocking him unconscious, and stole his wallet. When he came to, he managed to stagger home. The gash on his head was pretty deep. Mother wanted to take him to the hospital.

But her mother, Sara, was there -- and she said, "No; they would shave most of his head, and put lots of stitches into it. That could be quite painful; they don't anaesthetize on the skull -- and he'd always have a big scar on his head. But don't worry, dear; I'll fix it, and he'll hardly have a scar."

She swabbed the cut with Iodine so that it wouldn't get infected, and used a healing salve. Then she carefully pulled a few hairs at a time from each side of the gash, and tied them, pulling the scalp together. My father's head healed with only the slightest trace of a scar, under his hair.

Around the same period, she kept me from being a cripple all my life -- for which I am truly grateful! (I love to dance.) When I was a few months old, my mother left me in the middle of her double bed, sleeping, and went out of the room. I had not yet begun to roll over so she felt I would be safe.

When she came back into the room later -- she screamed!

"The baby's gone!" she yelled. "What happened? Did somebody kidnap my baby??" (There had been a few kidnappings in the area back then.) They searched the house -- and finally found me on the floor on the other side of the bed, wedged between the wall and the bed. I had rolled off of it.

Dr. Sara noticed that my leg-bone had popped out of its socket; it was protruding. Again, Mother said, "Let's go to the hospital!" and Sara said "No, dear; they would put her into a special brace, and traction, and she'd have one leg two inches shorter than the other and limp for the rest of her life. I'll fix it."

She began to massage the leg, manipulating the muscles and tendons until finally she heard and felt the bone pop back into its hip-socket. Thank you, Creator! And thank you, dear Medicine Woman, Little Dove's daughter. (She was also a D.O, and an M. D.)

One other story my grandmother Sara told me was this one. "My Daughter Rachel went off to Randolf Macon to college. It was considered quite a good school, and Rachel was an excellent sutdent. When she came home, I asked her how she liked it."

"I hated it!" she said. "All anyobody ever talked about was how they were related to the Randolphs of Virginia. They were just so special! I felt so left out. I wish we were related to the Randolphs of Virginia."

"Why Dear, we are!" was her mother's reply. "The Randolphs, Virginia's 'First Family', were descended from Princess Pocahontas."

Chapter 12

Sara Gillespie

If I hadn't been told about my Native American ancestry, I began to wonder: Did my mother know? Did her mother know? The answers that came to me from Spirit were, "Of course! Sara Gillespie knew who she was; Little Dove passed on to her the spiritual wisdom, the history, and the healing knowledge of her people; and her paternal grand-mother shared the Choctaw and Cherokee teachings as well.

"But – no. Your mother, Mary, did not know. And there was a reason for this: It was to protect her!" Known Cherokee were taken from their homes in Georgia, Tennessee, and the Carolinas, on the tragic Trail of Tears; many thousands to die, others to be relocated.

Sara Gillespie (my grandmother) grew up in a severely traumatized and depressed post-war South. It was not as hard on the people at Geordie and Little Dove's plantation Two Worlds as it was for others of what had been a gracious, flourishing society, but everyone in the South at that time was impoverished for many years. Still, though they did not thrive, the Gillespie family did know how to survive. They had stored some food in secret places, and were able to get what they needed from the nearby forests; they knew how to live with nature. Others who had led the gracious life were not so fortunate.

Further, most of the servants (they called them 'helpers') and field-workers, though long since given their freedom, had chosen to stay there. Other plantations had lost most of their Black People, who enjoyed a few years of feeling free and empowered before White land-owners figured out how to keep those who remained there in virtual bondage as sharecroppers, and to terrorize resisters with the activities of the K.K.K.

Husbands, brothers, fathers and sweethearts had been killed or maimed in the devastating war, and there were a lot of very unhappy women left at the end of it. Many who clung to what was left of their old plantation life were filled with bitterness and resentment. This was passed on to their children.

Yankee school teachers were brought in to some areas, adding insult to injury: 'Damn Yankees' were, after all, 'the enemy'. Victors and vanquished. The rural school that Sara Gillespie attended was taught by one of these imported Yankee teachers, a spinster named Emaline, from Rhode Island. Her father was a Sea Captain whose merchant sailing ship's homeport was Providence, Rhode Island, and her beloved fiancée had been an officer on her father's swift clipper. His last voyage was to the distant, exotic destination of Borneo; that trip was to finance a home for them. He had promised to take a job ashore after that, with his uncle's banking firm, so that he would have time to spend with the family they would raise.

Emaline's father's (and fiancée's) ship had weathered some rough seas in the South Pacific, rounded the Horn at the tip of South America -- where they saw the ghost-ship known as the Flying Dutchman sail past eerily through the dense fog -- and their ship had proceeded up to North American waters. Off the coast of Key West, southern-most of a string of islands in the Caribbean going South from mainland Florida, stormy seas arose once again. Sighting a bobbing light westerly to port-side, they headed for what looked to be safe waters... and went aground on the sharp reefs, which broke up the ship.

They had been lured onto the rocks by 'Moon-cussers' -- an unscrupulous lot of pirates who would curse the full moon, when it would be too bright to accomplish their foul deeds. But on a night that was dark and stormy -- such as the one in question -- the ruffians would walk along the reefs swinging a lantern, simulating the motion of a ship in the water. Passing ships would assume that the lights that they saw were those of vessels in deep, safe waters, and they would be lured to their unfortunate demise on the sharp rocks.

The pirates would have what was left of the ship stripped of its valuable cargo by dawn; boxes and barrels would float in seas becalmed. Fortunes and mansions in this area were built in that way. There was one strong sailor who had managed to survive the ship-wreck, the destruction of Emaline's father's ship. The rest were swept away by stormy seas. The lone survivor made his way back north to give his sad report.

Emaline was devastated at the loss of her handsome prospective husband, and at the reversal of the family fortunes. The promise of a good life was gone; they had put off marrying for several years, so that Edward would be able to purchase them a nice home and they would be able to live well. Now the eligible young men in her circle were taken.

A spinster now, she took out her resentment at this turn of fate by becoming ardently involved in the Abolitionist Movement. Slavery was wrong, she knew, and it certainly should be abolished. She had heard dark tales of the terrible treatment of Africans stolen from their villages by Arab slave-traders (among others), of their being sold to Yankee ship-owners (she didn't like to think about the fact that some of her relatives might be among them), and of the terrible 'middle passage', which was so horrible that many captive slaves had jumped overboard in mid-ocean and drowned, rather than having to endure such cruel treatment.

Harriet Beecher Stowe's book Uncle Tom's Cabin was very popular in the North at that time. The story dealt with what it was like to be living in the terrible conditions of slavery in the South. Northerners were touched by it -- and horrified! They were going to DO something about it. The book had a great influence on public opinion in the time leading up to the Civil War.

Emaline had relatives and friends whose husbands and loved ones had been killed in The War, as they called it, and her anger grew. A well-educated young lady, she decided to become a teacher. After teaching for two years in a young ladies' seminary, she requested to be transferred to the South, during the Reconstruction period. She would teach those dreadful little Southern Rebels a thing or three. The War was their fault, she reasoned, and so many people had suffered because of it.

'Miz Emaline', as the Southerners called her (she never could get them to pronounce Miss, or Mrs., properly), took out her frustrations, and her anger, on the students. This was the United States now, and she was going to show them how to do things properly.

The boys at the school in Mississippi found ways to play tricks on her, but she ruled with a heavy hand -- and with a stout hickory stick. If she didn't know who the culprit was, she would beat all of them. Usually someone would tell, to avoid being hit. The stool in the corner with the dunce-cap on it saw a lot of use. Originally, a cone-shaped hat was meant to bring in wisdom to those who lacked it, but it became synonymous with stupidity and disgrace instead.

Sara Gillespie was a very bright student. She had a quick, inquiring mind, and she lacked the usual prejudice against Northerners (or anybody else) that was then so prevalent in the South. After all, her mother had been educated in the North. She became the favorite - and indeed, the only ally - of the teacher. That did not endear her to the rest of the children.

"Sally G. likes damn Yankees!" they would taunt her, calling her Sally, a nick-name for Sara. "Silly Sally! Silly Sally!"

"Thinks she's so SMART! Uppity, is what!" "Nigguh-lover, too!" someone else would say. "I see how nice she is to the Darkies. Down-right fren'ly! Nigruhs are all right in their place, BUT..." They'd talk like that.

Southerners had a hard time adjusting to the great changes wrought by the war. Attitudes change slowly, and the children reflected those of their parents.

Many Black People flourished at the time of Reconstruction in the South. Some even became elected to office, while White Southerners seethed at this radical change in their lifestyle, and at the new Yankee-imposed rules and regulations. "Seems like nothin' but skally-wags an' carpet-baggers down here these days," was a common complaint. "An' them uppity Nigrahs!"

"Papa, why do the White People treat the Black People so mean?" Sara asked her father. "Don't they know that we are all brothers and sisters, children of Asga Ya Galuniati, the Father of All? -- And that Star Woman is our Mother?"

"No, Little One; they have not been taught these things," Geordie replied. "They do not have a wise grandmother like you do to teach them. They do not realize that we all live in a country which was based on the Wisdom Teachings of the People of the Longhouse, the Iroquois Confederation of Seven Nations, of which the Tsalagi are a part. The wise men who founded this country had learned much from our Councils, and wrote in the Constitution that 'All Men - meaning all people - are Created Equal.' And that we are One Nation, under God, with Liberty and Justice for All.' It did not say 'Justice for Some.'

"But in order to get the Constitution ratified (accepted into law), the Northerners had to make some concessions to those from the South -- the ones with large land-holdings, who were very powerful -- or none of it would have passed.

"General Washington was a very spiritual man," her father continued. "He was often seen praying for guidance before a battle, and the Ancestors would tell him where to place his troops, and how to survive a harsh winter: That is why he was able, with a small, poorly-equipped army, to defeat the most powerful armed force in the world of that time!

"Yet Washington was also the owner of a large plantation in Virginia. People say that he had no children; and indeed, he had none by his wife Martha, who was older than he. But there are those among the Black People who carry his name, and his blood-line. This was a common practice among planters. Thomas Jefferson, when he lived in France, had a beloved mistress who was of African heritage, mother of his children.

"Life is not always consistent -- or logical, my dear Sara. Instead of realizing that all are equal in the sight of the Great Creator -- the landed-gentry of Europe brought their system over here. Some people were awarded large tracts of land by the King of England. Some, like my grandfather from Scotland, homesteaded and worked the land; others simply took what they wanted. If Native People were already living there, the invaders would bring in their armies and kill off those who got in their way, or they incited the tribes to war against each other.

"But you know about these things."

"Yes, Papa. But why are they so mean to our Black brothers? Why do they call them monkeys, and 'coons, when these people also have no respect for the four-leggeds?"

"Yes, precious girl-child, I will answer your question. They have been told that this is the land of the free, and that all men (meaning Mankind, including women) are created equal. So to justify their use of slaves, which they felt were necessary to run their large plantations and maintain their power and way of life -- these land-owners began to say 'Well, these Blacks are not really people; they are just animals!' That way they thought they could own them, and work them, like mules; or breed them, like horses.

"But as you know, it is against Creator's Law, for one person to own another," Geordie went on. "And there were many people who knew that this slavery was wrong: and that is why this terrible War Between the States was fought, ten years before you were born; and many, many people died.

"President Lincoln said that this should be a government 'of the people, by the people, and for the people,' and that is what was being fought for. Blacks were people too, he maintained. But there were those who were angry at him because of these changes he championed. And one of them was paid to kill him."

"How sad..." Sara said wistfully.

Geordie smiled. "He had done what he came to do, and he got to go home! To join the Ancestors."

This is how Sara Gillespie got some of her history lessons, which were very different from what the other children were taught. She had to be careful not to repeat them at school, or she'd get into trouble; it would lead to an argument.

Her grandmother was teaching Sara the Cherokee language, both oral and written. One day she was practicing writing the letter-symbols on her slate at school, and one of the children came in early and said "What's that?"

"Oh, just funny marks I made up," she answered. She had forgot that she had been warned not to let anyone see them. More of the students came in, and gathered around. She had quickly erased the slate, but a boy named Billy Joe had already seen the symbols.

"Ah know whut that is," he said. "My grampa showed me that kinda stuff. The Cherokee Injuns made a newspaper, written in English and in those funny marks. They said it was writin', an' they cud read it. Grampa saved a copy o' the paper, cuz he thot that was pretty amazin' stuff, fo' a bunch o' ignorant savages."

"You're a INJUN!" said one of the girls. "Ignorant savage! Tha's whut you are! Ignorant savage!"

"Ah thot all you heathens had been cair'ed away -- to sum place called Oklahoma, where ain't nuthin' there but wuthless lan'," another girl chimed in.

"You said you made up those mahks... You're a lah-ya!"

"Am not!"

"Are too!"

"'Oh, what a tangled web we weave, when first we practice to deceive!' -- Tha's what mah muh-thuh taht me," put in one young lady.

"Ignorant! Savage!" repeated the girl who had latched onto that phrase. Lula Mae was the most ignorant of the lot, and the most savage in her attack. While most of the students in this rural school were offspring of Plantation-owners, Lula Mae's folks were what the others called 'White Trash.'

So while those who saw themselves as innocent victims of a most terrible war (which had caused them to lose everything they cherished) took out their bitterness on their children -- the children took it out on whoever was handy: Blacks, Yankees, and 'White Trash'. But now this girl had a scapegoat too, to pass her anger on to and she made the most of it, taunting Sara mercilessly.

"Think you're so smaht!" she said. "Stuck-up! Teacher's pet! Ignorant savage!"

It was that last epithet that really got to her, and Lula Mae knew it -- so she used it at every opportunity. But Sara Gillespie's ancestors were proud warriors, and she did not take kindly to being challenged, or to insults. This was warfare, and she would figure out how to outwit them.

She would prove to everyone that she was neither ignorant nor a savage. She would learn more facts than anyone, and challenge them to verbal duels. Thus she developed her adversarial habits that were to carry through her lifetime -- to the chagrin of her future husband.

At school, it got even worse for her. One of the girls spoke of the situation at home, mentioning the Cherokee alphabet characters.

"Come to think of it," her mother said, "Seems to me I recollect hearin' my gran'mama tellin' me one time, that she heard tell ol' Mr. Gillespie had come over from Scotlan' -- an' ma-ried a Cheh'kee woman."

That was all they needed at school.

"You're an In-dian!" said one of her tormentors. "That means you're cuh-lud!"

Many of them thought that being Indian was even lower on the scale than being black.

"My mama tol' me that the Chera-kee are an in-fee-rior race," said Sue Ann. "That's why they had to get rid of 'em. So we White folk wouldn' be con-tam-inated."

"Bad enough all this Yankee-talk 'bout integration," added Billy Joe. "Next thing you know they'll be wantin' to marry yo' sis-tah! We gotta keep the White race pure."

They were all talking like that. They heard it from their parents. Even her best friend, Carly Sue, turned against her. The two of them used to walk most of the way home together, go on picnics, share secrets... Until the others started saying "We don't want to play with her! She's an in-jin!" Rather than being ostracized herself, Carly Sue joined the crowd.

Sara was not one to complain, but of course her parents noticed her pain. As the youngest child in a large family, she had been adored as the baby by her brothers and sisters. A family council was held.

"I vote that we take her out of school," said Sara's sister Carrie. "We can teach her at home."

"But what about these new Yankee laws, that say you have to go to school?" asked her brother Charley.

"Maybe Miz Emaline can tutor her some, after school. Rich folks do that."

"Well, were not rich, Darlin', but we're better off than most," said Little Dove, who had picked up some Southern ways of speaking. "I will pray on it. I will ask the Ancestors for guidance."

It was decided that Little Dove would take over Sara's education, and that they would do some traveling. As the youngest child, who had come along several years after the rest, her mother had more time to spend with her. Two of the children had not survived to full adulthood. William had been killed in the war, John died in a boating accident, two had moved away or were off at college, and the other two had started families of their own. Dave was off who-knew-where, and Carrie and Charley helped with the running of the Homestead.

Geordie thought it would be a good idea for Sara to learn about the world first-hand, as he had done as a lad. He went down to the docks at the shipping port of New Orleans, and talked to some old friends. He managed to earn passage on a ship to England for himself, his wife, and his young daughter, by signing on as part of the crew. A seasoned sailor, he had shipped out on many vessels in varying capacities, and he had earned the reputation of being a good man to have aboard in case of any trouble. He became the Captain's right-hand man.

Little Dove was as excited as her daughter Sara at the prospect of a sea-voyage, and visiting foreign lands. Aside from the river-boat, she had never been anywhere but the Northern Plains and the deep South.

Sara was 9 then; the same age Little Dove had been when she began learning from the Elders in the Tetons. A gregarious girl, and always curious, Sara would enjoy making friends with other passengers, and with the crew. She wanted to know everything about everybody.

"Where are you from?" she would ask whoever might seem approachable. (She quickly learned to replace 'y'all' with 'you', as she was now with a more cosmopolitan group.) "What is it like there?" she'd inquire. She would make notes, and ask for their address, saying that if she were ever in that area, she would look for them. Most of them were delighted.

Sara invited everyone to visit her at 'the Family Plantation;' her parents were afraid that there would be another invasion, if they all took her up on the invitations! But the passengers and crew, for the most part, were charmed by this bright young girl who seemed genuinely interested in them.

After a relatively uneventful ocean crossing (no ice-bergs or hurricanes), they docked in the port of Liverpool. Then they went 'round through the Channel and up the Thames to Old London Town. After hearing some of Granpa's stories of how terrible the English had been in Scotland, Sara was surprised and delighted to discover that most of the British people she encountered were really quite nice.

She loved watching the Royal Carriage go by, and when top-hatted side-burned Prince Albert and bonneted, heavy-set Queen Victoria smiled and nodded at her when she waved at them, she was thrilled! Sara delighted in watching the Royal Guard, with their horses stepping so lively, in their bright, handsome uniforms; and the Beefeaters, who stood as still as statues. Most of all she enjoyed Kensington Gardens, with its flowers, ponds, grass and trees, and the Nannies walking their little charges in wicker prams.

The three of them laughed when they saw one of the swans chasing a man who had got too close to them, and it nipped him in the rear.

"Forgot to have 'im a Rear Guard!" said Geordie, chuckling.

This was a much better way to get an education than in a little rural Southern school, they all agreed. The family spent several months in London, staying in a little Bed-and-Breakfast boarding house, and going to museums and galleries, concerts and lectures, and often to the theater. A dramatic young lady herself, Sara was in Heaven!

In attending soirees about interesting topics that they would hear or read about, the adults in the audience would be surprised that such a young girl was in attendance.

Sara would sit quietly and listen; and, when asked what she might have gleaned from the talk, she would astound them by repeating the gist of what had been presented with complete accuracy -- sometimes putting it even better than the presenter had.

The thing that fascinated Sara the most was the Egyptian and Classical Greek section of the British Museum. She could spend days there, quite contentedly, being absorbed in that far-off world. She made friends with the Curator of Antiquities at the museum, and he was delighted to find that she had an affinity for ancient Greek. (Somewhat different from modern Greek, as is Latin from Italian.) He taught her how to speak and read it, and gave her several books, illustrated; about the statesmen, philosophers, warriors and heroes, as well as the architecture, sculpture and theater of the period.

"They wrote about all of the conditions of Man," said the Curator. "Anger, jealousy, love, comedy... One can learn much about human behavior from these plays. Plato even wrote in one of his works about the most ancient and lost continent of Atlantis, that had sunk beneath the waves thousands of years ago. Some say that it never existed, but I believe it did."

'I know that it did,' thought Sara. 'The Aniyun Wiya came from that time and place, and before that, from their home among the Stars. Our stories tell us about those times.'

"We have made so many astounding discoveries of the ancient world," the scholar continued. "But there are always new mysteries being brought to light! Do not limit yourself, dear Sara; knowledge is boundless, and wisdom is knowledge put to good use."

A kindly man, and a visionary, he made quite an impression on her, and was a powerful influence in her life.

Sara's father spent time boating on the Thames, or swapping stories at one or another of the many pubs, while her mother took her to the Museum. At mid-day, they sought out a bit of nature in a courtyard or garden, and were often offered a cup of tea, and biscuits, or crumpets. Sara could be quite ladylike when the occasion called for it, though she was never as reserved as the English young ladies.

While Sara was transported into the world of the Ancient Greeks, with the aid of her mentor, Little Dove would explore the rest of the museum... and a whole new world was opening up for her.

She loved the Dutch Masters; landscapes with boats on the water, and windmills on the shore. Rembrandt's scenes of every-day life: a mother showing something to her child; a woman with a pitcher and a half-opened Dutch door. Breugel's crowded scenes of burghers celebrating at their festivals; doing lively dances, drinking, eating and carousing. And the beautiful tall, slender houses, with their stair-step gable ends, lined up shoulder-to-shoulder along the canals of Old Amsterdam.

She found their traditional regalia quite charming: the men and boys in drum-shaped little black hats, jackets with brass buttons in rows on the front; trousers that puffed out at the sides, and wooden 'klompen' shoes, to keep their feet dry in a wet world, as the Zyder Zee would often flood its banks. The Dutch women had pretty white lace caps over their long blond braided hair, fitted bodice over a blouse, and skirts that ballooned out wonderfully under their aprons, above their wooden shoes.

There was a strange section in the museum depicting the wonders of the 'New World'. It contained maps and charts, and paintings of 'Indians' lolling about under trees while some White man like William Penn stood dominating the scene and holding a scroll. Then there were the soldiers and the Black-robes, looking very important, bringing 'Salvation' to the 'heathens'.

Worst of all -- there were engravings of 'savages' prancing around in grotesque poses, with skulls on poles... and some indicating that these pagans were also cannibals. 'Is that how they see us?' she wondered.

But then, in the next room, there were portraits of elegant ladies in satin and velvet gowns, bedecked with jewels and lace, and the Kings and Nobles of the realm.

Little Dove stopped before one of the portraits that caught her attention. A fine lady holding a fan, with a high lace collar and a little hat, and dark curls coming down at the side of her face. But it was her large dark eyes, with their direct gaze, that spoke to Little Dove. She found them mesmerizing. 'There is something special about this person,' she thought. 'Lady Rebecca', the sign said, next to the painting.

She went to the guard in attendance and asked him about it. "Can you tell me about the lady in this painting?" she inquired.

"Certainly, madam," he replied. "The Lady Rebecca. She lived in the New World, at the time of the Jamestown Colony, in Virginia. Around 1600."

"I have heard of the Spanish going to America in the 1500's," she said, "and I have heard of Pilgrims in Massachusetts in the early 1600's. But I did not know about this Jamestown Colony."

"Many people do not, madam."

"It is interesting that I must come to England to learn about my country!" she smiled.

"Indeed, madam," the guard agreed. "It often happens that one does not attend the museums in one's own country, but rather when visiting other lands."

"Of course! That's it exactly!" said Little Dove.

"You inquired about the Lady Rebecca."

"I did."

"It seems that she was instrumental in making peace between peoples in the colony when trouble or misunderstandings arose. Her father was a man with a very large sphere of influence; he was, indeed, the only one in the Americas who had official recognition as a King, by the King of England.

"It is said that Lady Rebecca was able to save the life of one of our soldier colonists who got himself into a spot of trouble with the Natives, and would have been put to death had it not been for her intervention. Some time later she married one of our English noblemen and came to London, where she received an audience with His Royal Majesty the King.

"Her husband was not received at court, for he was only considered Nobility -- but she, as the daughter of a King, was royalty. She quite charmed the people of London Town, and became a Royal favorite; thus her portrait was commissioned." He seemed to have finished, but she was still curious.

"Is there any more?" she asked.

"She and her husband had a little son, and they decided to go back to America, where they had large land-holdings, I believe. But on the boat before leaving England, while still in port -- she contracted smallpox, and she died. She was still quite young; 22, as I recall. It grieved the people here, not to mention her husband -- who did return to America. The Randolphs, of Virginia, are descended from her."

Little Dove gazed at the woman in the portrait. She was very beautiful, she thought; an inner beauty.

"Lady Rebecca," she said quietly.

The guard added one more comment: "In America, she was known as Pocahontas."

Little Dove caught her breath! This one she knew of! She couldn't wait to tell her husband and her daughter.

Her family shared her enthusiasm about Princess Pocahontas, but Sara was still caught up in the world of antiquity.

"How I love the Greeks, Papa! The engravings of the Acropolis... the Temples, and the statues! And Italy; the paintings by Old Masters, and the buildings and bridges along the canals of Venice. How I would dearly love to see those places!"

"And so you shall, my little one! But first I must take you north, to the place of our Scottish ancestors."

Thus it came time to leave the city that they had grown fond of, and they made their way northward to Scotland. It was no longer the site of fierce wars, although there were still clan rivalries. After a period of adjusting once again to new accents, they found the people and the landscape delightful. Geordie didn't need to translate much here; they were used to the way that Grandpa spoke.

The little family from across the sea hired a horse and cart and went in search of the 'wee village' in the mountains that was the home of Clan Gillespie.

"I wonder if there are still any of the old family left," Geordie mused.

They didn't get much response when dealing with the Lowlanders; but when they got to the area Grandpa had told them about -- the name Gillespie was magical! It opened doors with welcoming smiles, hearty handshakes, and a hot meal.

"So ye're kumin' hame at lah-st, are ye, laddie?" one jovial Scotsman said. "So yourr gran-pa went oot feh a swi-im an' got lost, an' cudna find hez way bock hame, is it? Endin' up across the ocean!" He had him a good laugh.

Geordie discovered that he still had some uncles and some cousins living nearby. Jock, the jovial, took them up the lane to meet some of their kin.

The Gillespies from America were welcomed by the Gillespies from Scotland. After a cup of hot tea and some shortbread, they had quite a chat. The were fascinated by each other.

"Go an' fetch Great Gran'pa, lad," a cousin said to his wee brother. "Tell 'im we've got relatives cum teh see hem."

Great-Gran'pa, it turned out, was a spry 90-year-old; "Gud Hee-land levin' keeps me young," he said. His complexion was ruddy, he had side-burns and white hair curling down from under his tam, and he walked with a wonderfully gnarled stick; but he said it was just for show, he didn't really need it. "So ye're Robbie Gillespie's lad, are ye," he said, observing him carefully.

"I'm Robert, Junior's, son, sir. Robert Sr. is the one who came from Scotland. Did you know him?"

"Did ah ken hem, ye're askin'? Ah shud thank so-o! 'E was mah let-el bro-therr!"

Geordie beamed. "Then you're my uncle!"

"Ach aye, Ah am that! An' how's Robert these days? A young mon, last Ah saw eh 'im. Still keckin', ez ee?"

"Hale and hearty, and sends his best regards. Sorry he was not up to traveling."

Looking at Geordie pensively, the uncle said "Ye do favor 'im a bet." Then, lightening up; "Weel noo! Tell me aboot hem! We thot he was dun en by a bunch eh wah-ld Red-Indians!"

The three from America looked at each other. Silence.

"Was it sumthin' Ah sed, Laddie?" Great Grandpa inquired.

"No, no -- it's funny, really... but you've hit on it. He was taken in by a bunch of Indians! My mother is a Choctaw Indian, and also of the Chero-kee Indian Nation, as was his wife -- my grandmother. But we're not really all that wild. We live in a big Plantation House on many acres, in the South of what is now the re-United States of America."

The Scottish relatives were fascinated to discover that not all of the South had been totally wiped out by The War -- and even more amazed to learn that not all 'Indians' were savages!

They insisted that their other-country cousins should stay with them, and "share their humble fare". "Ye're fam'ly here, an' ye're always welcome." After a hearty stew, they were treated to their hostess' specialty: Trifle. "Ah put in a trifle eh thes, an' a trifle eh tha-at," she said. Layers of jelly, with fruit in it; sponge cake; more layers of the same; topped with a final layer of scones and whipped cream.

"YUM!" said Sara. "This is most extraordinarily delicious!"

"Now what kind of thing is that for a little savage to say?!" Geordie teased her. It was nice to be among family, and they all enjoyed the joke.

"Per-haps the wee lassie wud lak the go eh the Hee-land games!" said Great Grandpa. And off they went to watch the men curling (like shuffle-board), shot-putting, and such.

"We've got a game where we hit a wee ball wi' a long stick, too," Geordie's cousin said. The game is called golf; many people don't realize that it started in Scotland.

Sara was astonished at the sound of the bag-pipes, which sounded a bit like a pig squealing, she thought. And Little Dove was amazed and delighted with the Highland Fling of the dancers. It reminded her a bit of some of the lively dances of her Lakota people!

"Look, Mama, the men are wearing skirts!" Sara observed.

"Kilts, lassie, kilts," she was corrected. "The Greek soldiers wear them too. In fact, they were the ones who brought them to Scotland."

"And the Hopi Indian people, from Arizona, wear them also, I'm told," Little Dove added.

Cousin Charlie explained that the hat worn by the dancers was called a 'Glengarry bonnet'. It had the Scottish emblem, the thistle, pinned on it, and black ribbons went down from the back of it, with a red-and-white checked row across the black of the inverted-boat-shaped hat.

The vests and jackets had square silver buttons, down the front and at the cuffs, with a strap at the shoulder to hold the long clan-tartan scarf in place. The men's kilts had four layers, as each pleat overlapped, except for the smooth front section where a sporran -- "a wee purse, feh yrr pennies"

-- was worn. Being thrifty Scotsmen, they wouldn't need much money! Knee-socks and buckled shoes completed the outfit.

"The Hee-land Regiment is noted feh bein' the fiercest eh fighters!" said Charlie. "The sker-lin' eh the pipes will frighten the enemy a-wah..."

"Like my ancestors!" said Little Dove, cheerfully. "With their war-whoops!"

"I wish Grandpa could have been here," said Geordie. "He would have loved this."

"He is here!" Little Dove observed. "Look! He's standing over there by the trees,smiling!"

It was a few months later that they found out that he had 'crossed over' at about that time.

Ætalis suæ 21. Aᵒ. 1616.

Matoaks als Rebecka daughter to the mighty Prince
Powhatan Emperour of Attanoughkomouck als Virginia
converted and baptized in the Chriftian faith, and
Wife to the worᵗʰ Mᵗ Tho: Rolff.

This painting, by an unknown artist, is based on the original engraving by Simon van de Passe, the only portrait made during her lifetime that survives. It's probably a fair representation of how she looked and dressed while in England, and is in the posession of the US Senate.

Little Dove and her family were delighted to find a pitcure of Princess Pocahontas in the London Gallery

Scottish Dancers

A French Painter

These little watercolors were painted by by Sakina in 1951. The Scottish dancers and the French painter were part of a series of pictures of people from many nations, in traditional costumes. She was hoping to get a job doing greeting cards at Hallmark, but they were too delicate for that company. Mr Hallmark and her grandfather, Dr Walter Cross, were friends. Sakina has a collection of dolls in traditional regalia from all over the world - 8,000 at last count.

Chapter 13

Europe

Geordie, Little Dove (Grace, as she was sometimes called), and Sara bade farewell to their Scottish family, with many words of appreciation and invitations to visit them back in America. Then it was off to 'Edin-boro', as the Scots called Edinburgh, where Sara delighted in that city's Botanical Garden, a beautiful park where she saw elves and fairies doing a merry dance. It seemed like a happy, friendly country, she thought. It must have changed since Grandpa left it.

They took a boat to the north of France, and a train from the port to Paris. On the train they bought long loaves of thin, crusty fresh French bread, with Pâté de Foie Gras (goose liver) to put on it.

Paris was total delight: a place of wonderment and excitement! Geordie, who was fluent in French, was in his element here. He had spent two years in France before he married, and spoke without the American accent that the French found so difficult to listen to; an assault on the ears.

Walking along the banks of the river Seine, strolling the boulevards, having cheese and patisseries at petits cafés... what could be more charmant? They went to the Musee du Louvre to see the masterpieces of great painters such as Rembrandt, Leonardo da Vinci, Rubens, and the magnificent statuary of Michelangelo.

A small painting in a corner of one room caught Little Dove's attention. "Who is this'?" she asked Geordie. "She is a Holy Woman! I see light radiating from this face!"

"No-one knows who Leonardo Da Vinci's model was for this painting," he told her. "Some people think she might have been his mistress; he would never speak of her, but he always took that picture with him wherever he traveled."

Little Dove contemplated the portrait some more. She went into vision.

"This Holy Woman appeared to the painter, and he recorded her quiet beauty, her gentle smile. She is the Mother of the one we call Dawn Star. The Christians call him Jesus."

Sara went up close to the painting and looked at the title. "It's called Mona Lisa," she said.

Walking outside of the Louvre, Sara was excited to see statues lining the walkway through a long tree-lined park. She recognized some of her old friends from Greek mythology that she had learned about at the British Museum.

Little Dove stopped in front of one of the pristine white statues, surprised.

"A warrior-woman!" she said. "She carries a bow and arrow! Her totem-animal, the deer, stands beside her, looking up at her, communicating. Who is this Woman Chief?"

Sara knew. "That's Diana, the huntress, to the Romans. Goddess of the hunt. The Greeks called her Artemis."

They walked through the Arch de Triomphe. The Place de l'Etoile (Place of the Star) looked like a Medicine Wheel, said the Lakota woman, remembering her roots. There were many statues, boulevards, wooded parks, shops and outdoor cafes along the sidewalks. Memories were accumulating here that would last a lifetime.

Sara picked up a few French words and phrases, but not enough, it seemed. She found it difficult and frustrating not to be able to communicate. How could she learn their knowledge without the language?

They stayed at a little pension across from the Tuilleries gardens. "Bon Matin," Sara would say to Madame Rochefort, the owner of the four-story row house, when she came down from her balconied room in the morning. She liked to practice the few French words she knew.

"Bonjour, ma petite," Madame would reply.

"Bonjour, Mademoiselle," her husband would greet the girl.

"Déjeuner? Brioche? Croissant?' Madame would inquire. A delicious way to start the day; Sara would take an extra one for later.

Sara's parents sat on a wrought-iron bench, watching her as she investigated the flowers to see how many of them she knew. She knew the botanical names of many of them; she had studied them in a book of her grandfather's. Grandpa loved plants too, though he sometimes tended to be a bit irreverent about them.

"So ye're interested in hor-ti-culture, are ye, lass?" her granpa had said with a mischievous smile and a twinkle in his eye, imitating his father's Scottish accent. "Weel, Ah've got thes teh say aboot that: Ye cahn lead a whore-to-culture, but ye cahn't make 'er think!" He chuckled, pleased with himself.

Sara made a note of some of the flowers. She would look them up, and their uses, later.

Crowds were gathering on the sidewalks. The streets were being cordoned off.

Sara stopped to look. "What's going on?" she asked. "Are they having a revolution?"

She had heard about the French Revolution.

"Ah!" Geordie exclaimed. "Bien sur! Of course. It's the 14th of July – Bastille Day! When they celebrate the beginning of their revolution and freedom from tyranny. It's like our Independence Day."

There would be dancing in the streets, singing, and wine flowing freely.

A large crowd gathered at one end of the street -- there seemed to be much excitement. Sara went to investigate. She slipped through the crowd to the front -- and came running back to her parents, frantically waving her arms.

"MAMA! PAPA! Come! Come quickly!" she cried out. They were alarmed. Sara rarely got excited.

"What is it? What's happened?"

"Come see!" she insisted. "APACHES!"

"Apaches? Couldn't be, dear; Apaches are Indians."

"Come see!" she insisted.

"Comme ci, comme ca," said Geordie.

Pushing through the crowd, they saw that there were indeed, Apache warriors doing one of their vigorous and lively traditional dances. How astonishing! They were a 'grand success', a great hit in Paris, and for years afterward dancers did a wild dance called 'L'Apache', in honor of their visit.

A few years later, Little Dove would have seen her cousin, the great chief Sitting Bull, riding in Buffalo Bill's Wild West Show in Paris.

The Gillespies took a train through the French countryside, down to the Mediterranean port of Marseilles. The little towns on the Riviera were another treat, and they had fun exploring them. They combed some beaches, went out on a fishing boat, and visited a Principality called Monaco.

From Marseilles they boarded a vessel going to Italy. Again Geordie was able to exchange help on shipboard for passage for his family. They stopped briefly at the island of Helena, where the Emperor Napoleon had lived -- or died. Seeing the actual places where important figures in a nation's past had lived made the lessons of history come alive. It certainly made them more memorable.

The boat pulled into a charming little port on Italy's northwestern seacoast. Portofino! There were colorful houses clinging to the steep sides of the mountain that rose from the Mediterranean, in cheerful colors of pink, blue, and pastel yellows and greens. Fishing boats and small sailing vessels of various sorts snuggled up to its docks, with little shops along the waterfront.

They disembarked here, and got a carriage and driver to take them to Firenze. "I couldn't pass up Florence, the most fascinating of Italian cities," said Geordie. He had been to Italy and Spain years before, and had a passable knowledge of each language, which, with the aid of a dictionary, would get them where they wanted to go and help them find whatever they needed. When he had sailed these waters previously, he would study the language on shipboard before and after visiting the country where it was spoken, and would practice speaking it with the other sailors from those countries.

Firenze was an art lover's paradise. Little changed since Mediaeval times, charming houses and cobbled streets lined the River Arno, which ambled gracefully through them at its own gentle pace.

NEVER

In one of the piazzas, or town squares, there stood a colossal marble statue of the young David, by Michelangelo. The sculptor had carved a life-size statue, the story went, and it was scoffed at. "It is too perfect!" he was told, "You made a mold using a real human for this. No-one could sculpt a statue of a man that is so perfect."

So he made one twice the size.

The next stop on their itinerary was Rome. "Bella Roma! The Eternal City!" proud Italians would exclaim. Fountains were everywhere; buildings of magnificence and grandeur, arches, churches, parks and monumental plazas.

Geordie took them up to a high hill overlooking the city, and told them the story of Romulus (for whom Rome was named) and his twin brother Remus, who were orphaned and raised by a wolf. This tale was particularly intriguing to Little Dove, for her people had stories like that too, to tell around the winter fires. But she was surprised to hear that they told of such things in this most 'civilized' of places.

Next Geordie took them to the oldest part of the city: The Foro Romano. Sara was excited! Here in the Roman Forum were the remains of classical buildings she had eagerly studied about in England. The clean lines of the porticoed edifices had such graceful proportions. Some of the columns were broken now, but they had preserved what they could.

"The epitome of classical grace!" she exclaimed, her language always being rather advanced for one of her years. "They are certainly amazing," her father agreed. "Yet it was the Greeks, across the Mediterranean, who built this type of architecture before these people did. The Romans copied them; so did our Southerners. They were just roamin' farther away! Across a BIG ocean, instead of a little one, Little One."

Sara laughed at his cleverness. Puns are considered the lowest form of wit by some people, in America, she observed; yet in sophisticated France, the 'double-entendre' (double meaning) is considered the highest form of wit. Rostand's 'Cyrano de Bergerac' is an excellent example.

They went past the Coloseo. "That's where the Christians were lion around, 2,000 years ago," said Geordie with a grin.

"Why is it broken?" asked Sara.

"After they stopped using it for the gladiators to fight each other to the death, or for throwing Christians to the lions to amuse Roman nobility, it fell into disuse. They no longer needed a big stadium. So some of the thrifty Romans began to recycle it. They used the stones to build their houses, and other buildings."

Little Dove spoke up. "These Christians -- these ones who kill off our people because we do not believe in their religion and are therefore heathens, and who forbid us to worship in our own way -- they were being killed here for their beliefs? Their warriors fought each other to the death, as ours sometimes did, for which we were called savage -- and they fought the fierce wild beasts of the forest to prove their bravery?" She was fascinated by such contradictions.

"Yes, that is so," answered Geordie. "These were early followers of the one called Jesus by the Greeks, and Jeshua ben Yuseph (Jesus son of Joseph) by the Hebrews and by the Essenes among whom he grew up. These followers of the Master, as they called him, believed in his teachings of 'Do to others as you would have them do unto you,' and 'Love thine enemy', for we are all children of the same Father. 'The Kingdom of Heaven is at hand,' He said: There is a better world beyond this one. So they were not afraid to die."

"Like my Lakota people! 'This is a good day to die!' our warriors say as they go off to battle, knowing there is a better world beyond this one. These are the teachings that were brought to us by Dawn Star, so long ago!"

"There are many things which are hard to explain," said Geordie patiently. "People forget the true teachings of the Master. They think that only their priests and preachers can connect with the Father, and are threatened by those who know we can be in touch with Creator directly, by sitting quietly and listening with our inner hearing. The essence of the Great Spirit is in all things; it is never any further away than our hearts."

This was the Truth that resonated with Little Dove. They sat on the banks of the river Tiber, watching it flow past; across an ancient bridge was the Castel Sant Angelo. "The Roman armies, like those of the Wasichu, spread out everywhere, and they conquered the world of that time," Geordie related. "But they became too proud. They lost touch with spirituality, forgot to be thankful to Creator, and worshiped false gods: Possessions! Treasure and tribute, taken from the people. 'Pride go-eth before a fall', they say. And thus came about the fall of the Great Roman Empire.

"Ancient prophesies say that this will happen in our land also. But a new and better world will follow: Greed will be replaced by gratitude; lust, by love. Each will honor the other, and no longer try to dominate or change them. Each one will be recognized for their own beauty."

Sara listened attentively to these conversations. Her father was the wisest man in the whole world, she thought! How dare they call her people ignorant, or savage.

Geordie had educated himself largely in the same way he was teaching his daughter, by studying first-hand the peoples, the cultures and the history of many of the fascinating places of the world. Motivation seemed preferable to harsh discipline.

Little Dove had been surprised to find that in the South of the United States it was not just slaves that were beaten, but children as well both by parents and teachers. She had spoken about this to Miss Emaline. Though Sara had not been whipped, as she was an excellent student and a favorite of the teacher, the custom had come to Little Dove's attention when one of her sons, who was more mischievous and less attentive, repeatedly got into trouble at school.

Energetic boys found it hard to sit quietly for hours, listening to things that did not interest them, and often got reprimanded for talking, or punished for laughing. In the Plains culture, boys were encouraged to be active -- and laughter was considered a gift!

"How did your parents discipline you?" Miss Emaline had inquired of Little Dove.

"If a child was disruptive, or unco-operative -- we simply ignored him," she replied. "The family would act as though he or she did not exist, for a few days. After that, the child would be very helpful and considerate. When the grandparents told their stories, we were all very attentive. We listened carefully, even if we had heard the tales many times before, for we know that this is now the young ones learn. We honored our Elders for their wisdom. We did not make them feel old and useless.

"Rather than punishing them for not doing well, we would reward the children for their accomplishments, with praise and encouragement; or award them an eagle feather. It worked well for us. We believe in teaching by example. With a kind heart."

"I never thought of that," Miss Emaline had replied, pensively. After that she sent the disruptive students into the isolation of the cloak room, a narrow separate room at the entrance of the small one-room school where boys would hang their coats at one end, and the girls hung their cloaks at the other end.

She also came to realize that boys, by nature, need to be more active. She began to do more teaching out under the old oak tree, and to have more breaks for the children to play games, and to talk about what interested them. Their grades began to improve dramatically. With Sara gone overseas, this new approach became very important.

With great delight, Sara discovered the Fontana Trevi. Of all the fountains in Rome, this was her favorite.

"Greek gods!" she exclaimed excitedly, when she saw the big marble statues. "Poseidon, the god of the Sea! Who rides dolphins, and sea-horses."

"Poseidon is what he was called by the Greeks. The Romans called him Neptune," her father informed her.

"How did you know that was the sea god?" her mother asked.

"He always carries a trident, with three prongs. For spearing fish, I think," Sara replied.

"Ah! A Medicine Piece! His coup-stick!" Little Dove added with a laugh. Long Bow was happy to hear his wife laugh. Sometimes life had been too serious for her.

"His broom," he teased her. She gave him a poke in the ribs with her elbow.

"Ooo! Watch out -- She's on the war-path! How unladylike," he retaliated. She resisted an impulse to grab him and wrestle him to the ground, as she had done long ago with her brothers when they teased her. Instead, she put her arm around his waist, as they sat on the rim of the fountain, and laughed again together.

Any public display of affection was considered inappropriate behavior in proper Victorian society. But in Rome, nobody seemed to mind. Couples would walk along the avenues holding hands, and romantic songs were often sung out loudly by aspiring tenors: Opera was King here! Sometimes beautiful signorinas would be followed for blocks by admiring Italian young men. "Belli-ssima!" (Beautiful!) they'd say. The young ladies ignored them, but of course they enjoyed the custom.

While her parents were preoccupied with their own little drama in this city of a thousand dramatic scenes being played out daily, Sara took the opportunity to 'accidentally' fall into the water of the fountain of Trevi, which was like a pool. Her parents, ignorant savages that they were, didn't know enough to be upset with her, so they laughed instead.

"My little Lakota daughter!" Little Dove said. "We used to bathe in the fresh waters every day; we did not wait for once-a-week like the Wasichu! You are a heathen after all, my precious one."

"I'm a dolphin," said Sara with delight, as she flipped in and out of the water. "Like the ones we saw on the way here. The Greeks say that dolphins rescue people, and bring them to safety."

"And so they do, Little One. Creature-beings can help us, if we ask them," Geordie said.

"They are our allies, our protectors," added her mother. "We can contact them in our visions."

It was a sunny day, and no one seemed to take notice of her wet clothes as they walked back to the penzione where they were staying. Sara shook out her long hair, usually pulled back at the sides and tied with a ribbon, and it dried out in the sunshine as her mother hung the wet garments over a pretty iron railing around their small balcony. Their room was overlooking one of the city's many parks, where mothers took their children to play in the afternoon.

The family walked around Rome -- 'Bella Roma', they called it -- exploring its many wonders. Sara ran up and down the Spanish Steps three times; there were a lot of them, and they were very wide, so she could run up one side and down the other, making a great circle.

There was an abundance of churches here. There seemed to be another one every time they turned a corner. That struck Sara as being strange, since they were all Catholic, all of the same denomination.

"The churches were built on top of the Temples of the ancient Romans, who built their places of worship on power spots where the energies of Mother Earth spiral up in great vortexes, like whirlpools," Geordie explained. Little Dove knew how powerful whirlpools could be. She almost lost her son Dave to one.

"Medicine people, priests, and enlightened ones are sensitive to these energies," Geordie explained, "and they choose these spots as locations for their sacred buildings because it is easier in those places to communicate with Spirit, with Creator. When a new religion replaces an old one, the sacred structures are built on the same spot as the old ones for this reason. There are doorways between Earth and Heaven there."

Her father had so much knowledge, thought Sara. These churches were very different from the Baptist churches back home. These churches and cathedrals had beautiful paintings and statues of saints to look at, candles burning, incense, and colorful windows behind the altar. "The Saints are like stained glass windows," Sara mused. "They let the light shine through."

"The Saints are like our Ancestor-Spirits," Little Dove observed. "When we pray and ask for guidance, they will help us, if we listen. They are our Protectors. These people honor them, with a small fire."

"The sacred torch," Geordie mused, watching a woman with her head covered in a large black shawl light a candle.

Little Dove was looking at a statue of Archangel Michael. "You see, Sara, he is a great Protector of the People. His sword is upraised like a warrior with a lance, his shield is on the other arm; he wears a short kilt, like a Scotsman, and under his moccasin-boots are the heads of the enemy. And there is the serpent, who represents wisdom." Her mother had such a different way of explaining things, the girl thought.

Sara was intrigued by the statue of Joan of Arc, with horse and lance, and so was Little Dove. "A woman Warrior Chief! As I was planning to be!" she exclaimed with delight. "They had such people here?"

"In France," replied her husband, "there was an invader king who oppressed the people. The English King conquered France, and the French ruler, the Dauphin, was too weak to drive out the English -- who were cruel to the French, as they were to the Scots in the land of my grandfather in that time."

Little Dove was fascinated by the story. "The Woman Chief heard the voices of her Ancestor Spirits leading her to be victorious over the enemy in battle... And for this they did not call her heathen, and savage, as they did my people? But honored her in their Sacred Lodges -- their churches?"

"Well, they honor her now. But at the time, they called her a heretic; they tied her to a post, and burned her to death."

Little Dove was shocked!

186

"Who did this ?" she asked.

"The Church."

"The Black-robes?!? The ones who called us primitive savages, for killing an enemy?"

"They wanted to be in control," Geordie said. "They said that only priests could speak for God, and Jeanne d'Arc said that God spoke to her directly through these voices."

There were other paintings in the niches of the churches and cathedrals. Saints tied to trees, with arrows through them. Others being stoned to death. Things Native People were condemned for were here in their holy places.

"They are called martyrs. It is hard to understand," said Geordie.

And always the pictures of the beloved Master, she noticed, pulling the heavy logs up the hill, being beaten, nailed to a stake, pierced, and left to die. "But this is not called torture," she said.

"Why do they put up these images for the children to see, for the people to focus upon? Why do they not show us that He was a Peace-maker, who taught that all men are brothers: that we are all children of a loving Father. I think it would be better to show him ascending, joining the Ancestor Spirits and the Sky Father, to show the people that there is no death! There is only returning to a better place, a place of peace and joy. This was the message of Dawn Star."

The Gillespies saw the statue by Michelangelo called the Pieta, with the body of Jesus in his mother's lap, after he had been taken down from the cross. Her face was poignant and evocative of sadness in the onlooker.

Little Dove observed the limp body, and the mother's face. "Dawn Star," she said quietly. "And Mona Lisa."

Near the entrance of one Roman church, Michelangelo's Moses sat, in a powerful marble rendition. An attendant explained that the reason he had small Pan-like horns protruding from his curly head was because of a mis-translation of the Bible: " 'Corne' (cor-neh) means 'horns'," he explained, "but it also means 'rays'. It was supposed to be 'rays of light' coming out of his head, not horns!" Sara found that very amusing.

"Moses was a billy-goat," she giggled, as they left the church.

St. Peter's Square (which was round) was another place of impressive grandeur. Here was the seat of power of the Holy Roman Empire, the

Catholic Church, and its empire was vast indeed. The great circle of the Piazza San Pietro was sometimes filled with thousands of the faithful, when Il Papa (The Father) -- The Pope -- appeared on the balcony of the Vatican to give a blessing to the people.

"The circle is like a Medicine Wheel, isn't it, Mama?" Sara spoke up. "We should do a ceremony here! The columns could be the Standing People." (Trees.)

Little Dove was always happy to do ceremony, to pray in her own way. She looked around. "But there is nothing of the natural world here! Except for the Stone People, who are cold and silent, who were cut by Man from their distant mountains. But there is no wood, no earth, no green. I feel no joy here, no Spirit, in this most Holy place of the Black Robes."

"The Church has not always been kind to our people," her husband commented. "But they have done good things too. They pray for the people, and urge them to live good lives, they provide inspiration and guidance, and build churches where the people can come together to worship. The nuns, their holy women, take care of the poor and the orphans, teach the children in their convent schools, and care for the sick in their hospitals. They work hard and do selfless service in many ways," he said.

"Of course, there is a spark of Divine Truth and Light within the heart of all people," Little Dove concurred.

The next day, Geordie took his wife and daughter for a ride in a brightly painted Sicilian donkey-cart, which had been brought northward by an enterprising young man named Tony from the island located off of Italy's southern coast.

Sara decided to demonstrate that she knew the geography of Italy.

"If Tony is from Sicily -- does that mean he got kicked out of Italy by the boot?" she asked her father with an impish grin.

Geordie chuckled. "Indeed, Lassie! No doot a-boot it!"

They passed some Italian hill-towns, where houses clung precariously to the sides of tall cliffs, or were perched on top of them, going right up to the edge.

"Like the villages of the Hopi Indians, I hear," said Little Dove. They watched women stomping grapes in a large vat, and observed their celebration of wine-making, dancing, and singing. Little Dove was nostalgic. This somehow reminded her of the joyous celebrations of dancing and merriment of her childhood.

Finally they came to the ocean. "Il mare! Bellisima!" Tony exclaimed.

"Grazie, Antonio, per un buon viaggio," Geordie said, thanking him for a safe journey.

Tony looked at the ocean, and burst into song. "Ved'il mare -- com'e bello! Spira tan-to senti-men-to... Como il tuo suave ac-cento, non lo sa dimenticar."

Tony unloaded their trunk from the cart, and also a tent. They could camp tonight on the beach. Little Dove was thrilled! "We sleep on Mother Earth tonight? In a lodge, beside the great waters?" What could be more perfect!

"What was he singing about, Papa?"

"He said – 'Look at the ocean, how beautiful it is! What a sentimental spirit is here! Like your soft voice, I cannot forget.'"

"Ah!" smiled Little Dove. "They understand about Spirit here! This is a place of heart, I think; there is joy here, there is love."

"You are right, Tesoro Cara -- my precious treasure. There is love here, and beauty, and song. There is sadness also, but we do not see it."

Tony continued his song as he set up the tent. Geordie helped him.

"Senti come lie-ve sa-le -- dai giardini odor d'aran-ci! Un profumo non vuguale, per cui pal-pi-ta d'a-mor..."

"He sings about the scent of oranges coming forth from the gardens... their perfume reminds him of love..." Geordie translated.

Tony set up a table by putting a board on top of the trunk, and placed folding canvas camp chairs around it. He poured wine into stemmed glasses. Geordie thought a few sips wouldn't hurt this time. For the 'picola signorina', he poured grape juice, unfermented.

"Salu-te!" they toasted each other.

This place was called 'Civitavecchia', the Old Village, they were told. Tony pointed out the remains of an ancient Roman Temple or fortress (depending on the need), way up on top of the hill, overlooking the sea. Halfway up the mesa was a mediaeval village; the women could still be seen going up the steep paths. At the base of it, by the seashore, was a small resort town, where contemporary Romans would come on holiday when the city in the summer became too oppressive.

After they ate, Tony removed the cloth from the table after feeding leftover scraps to the seagulls, and washing the plates in salt water. Again he sang as he performed these tasks.

"E tu dici io par-to, addio! T'al-on-ta-ni dal mio cuo-re! Ques-ta ter-ra dell a-mo-re, hai la fuer-za di la-chiar."

"I must go now, farewell! Far away from my heart! This land of love, I do not have the strength to let go," Geordie said, giving them the gist of it.

Sara built sand castles, with elaborate turrets, and found a stick and scrap of cloth for a flag. Geordie and Little Dove watched the sunset, which created a shimmering golden pathway on the sea, and thanked Grandfather Sun in their own way.

"Ma non mi fu-gir! Non far me pui tor-men-to. Tor-na Su-rie-en-to…. Non far mi… mo-rir!"

"It carries the pain of a broken heart. A lost love, I think." Little Dove sympathized. Poor Tony.

"Actually -- he was singing about his village, his beloved Sorrento! He wants to end his torment -- to return to his homeland, or he will die! Italians are very sentimental."

"Ah -- they love their land, as we did," said Little Dove. "That is why we fought so hard to protect it from those who did not cherish it as we did."

The next day, they returned to Rome, carrying with them fond memories of song and sea.

"Arivederci, Antonio," said Geordie as they parted. "Addio, Signor Georgio! Signora… Signorina Sara," he replied with a bow.

The Gillespies skirted around the coast of Italy on a fishing boat that Geordie hired, past the island of Sicily, and up the eastern coast. He didn't want his 'lassies' to miss Venetzia, the city in the sea.

"Every time I think I have seen all the world's wonders -- you show me something even more amazing!" commented Little Dove when he took them by gondola through the canals of Venice. They drifted along under the bridges past ornate columned and balconied houses that seemed to be sinking into the sea… and perhaps they were.

But they had been this way for centuries.

The gondoliers, in their striped sailor shirts and straw hats, liked to sing songs, like Tony did, and the passengers loved to listen to them. In the Piazza San Marco, Sara delighted in feeding the pigeons. It seemed like thousands of them flocked around her and she danced joyfully around in circles, and picked up feathers to use in ceremonies.

"Look, Mama," said Sara, pointing out the pigeons. "Little doves! They have all come to honor you." Little Dove, their namesake, bowed graciously, and smiled.

"This city is new to me, too," Geordie said. "I have been to most of the other places I have shown you, but not this one. I had heard of its special charm though, and wanted to share it with you."

On their way out of the city in the small boat that would take them to the sloop on which they would continue their journey, they noticed that there was an island off to itself. Geordie asked about it.

"There was a time in our history, Signor," their guide told him, "When the Jews were kept separate from the rest of the population. They lived on that island, and had to be there by sundown. The island is called Ghetto."

Chapter 14

Greece

"Look, Sara, your dolphin friends are playing again!" Little Dove exclaimed.

"Off the port bow!" her father specified, and she ran over to the railing on that side, her long hair and petticoats flying in the wind. "Oh, Papa! They're so beautiful! There's a whole school of them over there!"

"Wonder what they're learning," Geordie chuckled. "Probably about how silly humans are."

"Look, Papa -- that one's smiling at me!"

"Talk to them," said her mother. "They'll understand."

"Hello, you beautiful dolphins!" Sara said. "How's your family? I love you!"

"He said 'I love you too!' I heard him!" her father said. "So did I, Sara," her mother added.

"Me too, Mama."

The port of Piraeus was a busy place. Fishermen in black wool caps with bills were hauling nets; drying, making, or mending them. Steam was beginning to replace sail in some places, but most of the Greeks preferred to run with the wind.

Sara could hardly contain her excitement! Seeing the whitewashed houses and the landscape, she felt like she was coming home, after a long journey. She had been taught by her great-grandmother about people having many lifetimes, and Sara was certain that she had an extraordinary one in Greece, at the time of its Golden Age. The engravings she had seen at the museum in London had touched a chord of remembrance; now she would actually get to see, to go into, the ancient temples of her remembering.

They spent one more night on the vessel, as it anchored for the night. They watched the sunset bring alive and golden the waters of the Mediterranean, while giving thanks to Grandfather Sun as was their custom. They watched the moon rise over the water, creating a shimmering silver streak. The dolphins came to welcome them.

'We heard you were coming', they heard the dolphins say. 'Poseidon told us. You've been gone so long! Welcome back!'

Sara twirled around in circles, her white skirt flying outward. Then she began a slower, more graceful dance, with slow, arcing arm-movements, and deliberate steps and turns.

"This is the way we danced in the old times," she explained to her parents, who smiled and nodded. When she finished, and dipped in a little bow, she was applauded by the deck-hands. She was surprised -- she hadn't realized that they had been watching.

"Our little Goddess!" said the sailor who spoke English. "But where did you study our ancient dances?"

"In the ancient Temples," she smiled graciously.

"But we thought you were new to our country!" the sailor said.

Sara smiled an enigmatic smile, and blew them a kiss. They loved her.

Next morning she was up at first light. Fishermen in painted skiffs dotted the horizon. Some boats had triangular sails, others were rowed with oars.

"Some of those little boats put me in mind of the

Left: The Greeks loved Sara, Little Dove's daughter. "Dear little goddess! Our beloved Athina, returned to us!"

Yankee dories," said Geordie. "Double-enders. Quick and sleek; flat-bottomed, could slip in and out of shallow waters easily."

"And I am reminded of our canoes," Little Dove recalled, "made from the light bark of the great birch trees. We were so amused, when the English sailors came rowing up our rivers; many strong arms pulling at the oars of their long-boats... and we would skim the waters in our light-weight craft, and sail swiftly past them as though they were standing still!" They all chuckled over that one.

The sun rose in its splendor, and was greeted by the Lakota-Cherokee family. "Now WE are the boat-people, who have come across the ocean to someone else's land!" Geordie mused.

"Well, we will not try to change them -- or take their land away," said Little Dove.

"I'm sure they will be happy to know that; mighty relieved," her husband said with a grin. "There are many people in Europe who believe that America is full of wild savages, Indians, and that it is a very dangerous place to be."

"And so it is!" his wife replied. "There are many dangers... if you're a wild savage. Or even a civilized one."

They didn't have to be so guarded in their talk here as they did at home in the South.

Sara watched the fishermen coming into shore in their small boats. When they approached the beach, the man in the bow would step out into the shallow water and pull it ashore. Then he and his partners would lift the fish-filled net out of the boat, pull the long net up on the beach, and they would sort their catch. A buyer might come along and purchase some; the rest they would carry off in wooden buckets. The nets would be spread out to dry, and once the sun was up, it didn't take long for them to do so. The nets would then be folded and put back into the boats, which were hauled up far enough to be beyond the reach of any tidal waters.

"Are we going to Athens now, Papa, to see the Parthenon?" Sara asked brightly, as their sloop moved from its mooring in the harbor to the dock, to unload passengers and cargo. She was impatient to see this place of extraordinary beauty, whose classic grace became synonymous with the epitome of excellence in architecture. The simplicity and proportions were unmatched and unexcelled.

What she found in Athinai, as the Greeks called it, was the opposite of what she was expecting. A busy city, bustling with activity: It was noisy and dirty, its streets filled with the cry of vendors, and with horses and their leavings, like many another city. It did have its sidewalk cafes, of course, like any other Mediterranean metropolis. But still....

And then she saw it!

"Look, Sara -- the Acropolis!" her father said, pointing to a high mesa that rose above the city which surrounded it.

"Oh!" she gasped. "Oh! There it is! It's beautiful! We must go there, immediately."

Geordie laughed. "We'll find a place to stay first, Little One. I'm anxious to wash off the trail-dust. I'm usually good at finding nice little inexpensive places to stay, but this is one language I don't know."

"I thought I heard you say you spoke every language!" Sara challenged.

"I do! -- Try me. Every language but Greek."

"Japanese."

"That's Greek to me!" Geordie retorted, and they all laughed.

"Let me try this time, Daddy," said Sara with assurance. She astonished the driver by speaking to him in excellent Greek. These were obviously newcomers, and foreigners.

His eyes widened in surprise. Sara smiled serenely.

The British Curator had taught her some modern Greek phrases as well as ancient ones, for just this circumstance. It was inconceivable to him that she would not go to Greece, with such a strong affinity for its beauty and wonders.

They were taken to a charming little place, with a garden outside of the French doors that led to their own private patio. The white-washed house was clean and neat. Their room contained a big brass bed, and a day-bed couch with a white-painted, intricately-scrolled willow back to it, which is where Sara would sleep. There was a matching rocker, also made from bent willow fronds, and the night-stand, with its flower-decorated bowl and pitcher on the top shelf, the chamber-pot underneath, and fresh towels hung at the sides. A tall olive-wood armoire for their clothing stood against one wall.

Sara put on her most Grecian-looking white dress and wrapped a gold cord (which had fallen from a drapery somewhere along the way) around her waist, crossed it in front, and then put it up over her shoulders. Her cloak would hide the lacy Victorian sleeves.

Sandals would be more appropriate, Sara thought, but not having any, she tucked the straps that were on her black shoes under the arch of her foot instead of buckling them on top. That would have to do. (She was certainly not going to wear high-button-shoes today.)

Sara looked into the oval mirror next to the cloak-rack. Dampening her finger in the washbowl, she created 'spit-curls' at the side of her face, and a few curls in her bangs. She pulled the side of her long hair back and up, tying it with a ribbon. That would serve. She wore a delicate white-on-pink cameo at her throat.

Sara went into the parlor, where a white-haired gentleman was reading a newspaper. He looked up as she entered, and said, in proper Oxford English, "Ah! A little Greek goddess!"

She smiled graciously, pleased that her efforts were being appreciated. Native American survivor-types had learned to be good at pretending, and she was a prime example. Greek drama was her specialty.

The 'Greek goddess' went around the room admiring the small statuary, and identifying them. "Apollo. Zeus. Hera."

A blue vase with bas-relief figures caught her attention. "Ah! Dee-AH-na! Ah-THEE-na!" Well, thought the gentleman, it was not unusual for British or American young ladies to study Greek mythology, but one did not often hear the names pronounced properly by such foreigners.

Her parents had been taking a siesta while Sara bathed and dressed, but now the door to their room opened.

"Ma-MA! Pa-PA!" she called to them. She then proceeded to speak in fluent ancient Greek, explaining about the engravings on the walls: the Battle of Thermopylae; Helen of Troy, whose great beauty, it was said, brought destruction upon the city of Troy by means of an army hidden inside of a giant wooden horse.

"That's where the expression 'Beware of Greeks bearing gifts' came from," she explained, switching to English, to her parents' relief. They went along with her game, pretending to understand her when she spoke Greek, to humor her.

196

At this point, the British gentleman, generally quite reserved, was genuinely astounded! Dr. Chivington, it seemed, was a Professor Emeritus of Oxford University; where, for 38 years, he had taught Ancient Greek Culture, History, Mythology -- and the ancient Greek Language. It was extremely rare to find anyone else who spoke this 'dead' language, and certainly it was unexpected from an American.

Prof. Chivington arose and introduced himself. "I would be most happy to show you around the magnificent world of the Ancients," he said, bowing gallantly. "You are plainly Greek Royalty returned!" He had a twinkle in his eye as he twirled the end of his white moustache.

"Your Majesty," he said, to Sara. "Your Highness," to Geordie. "Your Grace," to Little Dove. "I am at your service."

"Have we met before?" asked Little Dove.

"Not to my knowledge! Surely I would have remembered such extror-din'ry grace and charm."

"But how did you know my name?" she inquired.

"Your name?" He was puzzled.

"You said 'You're Grace!'" she explained.

Geordie had a good laugh. "It's a title, for royalty," he told her. "Like 'Your Majesty.'"

"Ah!" she said. "Forgive my ignorance!"

"You are NOT ignorant, Mama," Sara spoke up emphatically. "You were simply not familiar with the term."

"Quite right, young lady," said the professor, impressed by her maturity.

"What a happy coincidence that we are staying at the same lodgings!" Geordie said. To Little Dove, it was not so surprising. She was accustomed to the Spirits of the Old Ones bringing them to the right place at the right time.

Thus they had the best of guides, one to show them all the special places and tell them the stories behind each one. They went first to the Parthenon, atop the Acropolis, and Prof. Chivington explained that the Greek architects designed them in such a way as to have the columns graduated in size to make them seem more graceful in proportion, achieving a sense of unparalleled grandeur.

He explained the scenes on the friezes, and introduced his visitors from America to the personages represented by each statue, one by one. Sara already knew most of them. "They are old friends!" she said.

"And how is my old friend at the British Museum?" the professor inquired. "He certainly taught you well!"

"He's doing nicely, thank you. But I think he does not get enough fresh air and sunshine."

"I imagine not. Always buried in the Archives."

The Parthenon was dedicated to Athena; that was the temple that Sara resonated with the most. Here once again she did a graceful dance: Stepping forward, slowly, with deliberate steps, she would glide toe-first, like a ballerina, with her arms extended. Slowly she would turn, her cape flowing outward. All around the central courtyard.

Visiting tourists stopped to watch, wondering if this was part of the tour, a professional performance. Sara was in her glory! She would crouch, and leap, and twirl again. Her head turned to the side, arms arced out and upward.

Aside from their ceremonies in the Sacred Circle at home, the only way Sara had studied the dance was when her parents had taken her to the Ballet in London, and once in Paris, at the Place de L'Opera. She would go back to their room afterward, and remember the moves, and practice them as well as she could in a limited space.

Sara approached a marble block at one end of the central room of the Temple. "This was the altar," she said. "This is where we kept the Sacred Flame."

Professor Chivington shook his head in wonderment. "But how do you know these things? Where did you learn the ancient dances, the way they were done then -- and how did you know that the Sacred Torch was there? I do not remember that being in any of the history books."

Sara looked at him and smiled. "I remember," she said quietly. "I have been here before."

"But you just arrived."

"This lifetime!" she said. "Can I tell him, Papa? Who we are? Mama?"

The professor was intrigued!

A well-traveled, highly educated man, he had never met anyone quite like this unusual and quite delightful family.

"I think it would be all right, dear," her father said. "Go ahead," her mother concurred. She sensed no danger here.

They sat on a marble bench, while Sara stood in front of them. She had an attentive audience, and she was in her element. She would make the most of it.

"We are what you in England call Red Indians," (to distinguish them from the people from India) she announced.

Once again the listener, the representative of the British Empire, registered shock. Generally he was considered quite erudite, and knew a great deal more about almost anything than those he spoke to. Yet here was a 'mere slip of a girl' who continued to amaze him with her knowledge.

"Extro'din'ry! Most extro-din'ry. But -- we are told that Red Indians are wild savages; primitive and dangerous!"

"We are an ancient people, our civilization going back much farther than that of those who have come across the sea and ravaged our lands," answered the 'little savage'. "We know our history. It is passed down to us from generation unto generation. My grandmothers taught me. On my father's side, we are of the Tsalagi Ani Yun Wiya, The People Principle. Those who have Free Will. Some call us Cherokee."

"But you have a Scottish name!"

"From my father's grandfather, Robert Gillespie," Sara explained. "He emigrated to America, in search of freedom. He married a woman who was Cherokee. We pronounce it Tsa-LA-gi."

"Most astonishing! It would appear that I have yet a great deal to learn...."

"As do we all," replied their little teacher. "On my mother's side, I come from the People of the Great Plains, in the States, out West. Hunters-of-buffalo; warriors, yes, but savages – NO. We lived in harmony with Mother Nature, until the White Man came with their soldiers to take the land and kill the People. They called us wild savages when we defended our homes, our people, and our Sacred Lands."

Little Dove knew that Sara had listened attentively to her teachings and those of the Elders, but she had never heard her daughter hold forth like this. Her heart swelled with pride.

"We are the Children of the Stars! Our Tsalagi Ancestors came from the Seven Dancers. The Greeks call them the Pleiades (Play-AH-des).

"We have spun down through space from the realm of Galunlati, the realm of Light. All on this planet are descended from Star Woman, thus we are all brothers and sisters...though some have forgotten how to treat their kin with respect. Asga Ya Galunlati is the Father-of-All."

As she told her story, she raised her face and her left hand to the sky, above the open courtyard, and demonstrated by her hand motion how Star Maiden came spiraling downward.

"The Star People came down to Earth in the time of Elohi Mona, that large island continent, later several islands, also known as Atlantis. It was a great and wondrous civilization. But things go in cycles, like the seasons, and when Man became too proud, and forgot to honor Creator and each other -- when priests and regents abused their power -- Elohi Mona was destroyed. We are living in the fifth world, or civilization, on this planet."

"Atlantis! Incredible!" commented the professor.

"Did not Plato speak of this great island to the West?"

"He did indeed. Perhaps then it did exist."

"Our Elders tell us that we have many Earth-walks, or lifetimes," Sara said. "We come to learn, to experience. Some of us come as teachers, or healers, or to bring spiritual wisdom to mankind. To help.

"Sometimes we come back in groups," Sara continued, "to accomplish a certain purpose. The advanced people of Elohi Mona decided to return, together, long after the sinking of their land into the sea. To be way-showers; to demonstrate their philosophy, arts, architecture, drama. They came to this land in the Mediterranean, this land called Hellas, or Greece. Their time was called the Golden Age."

Prof. Chivington was dumbfounded. When he had absorbed what she had said he ventured:

"Are you saying that the Greek Golden Age was actually a recapitalization of the civilization of ancient Atlantis? And the Greek gods were... who?" Unbelievable, he thought.

"Star People tend to be worshiped as gods by those who are less advanced. They have their failings too; but on some other worlds, in other star systems, many are more advanced in certain ways than those on this planet."

"You're JO-king! We're speaking of life on other planets, are we? Jules Verne sort of thing?"

Sara smiled benevolently. "Do you really think that the Father-of-All would create such a vast universe - galaxies - and only put sentient beings on one little planet? Gods and Goddesses are those who do not acknowledge limitation. That's why we made such an impression!"

"Good God!" he exclaimed.

"Goddess, actually. In those times, I was called Athena."

"Athena?"

"Pallas Athena," Sara specified. "Goddess of wisdom; of the arts, industries; of home and hearth. Protector of the family."

"And Goddess of War!"

"Oh, yes, willing to defend my people against invaders. Not by fighting so much, as by strategy. Prudent warfare."

Little Dove broke into the conversation here. "A warrior woman! It was you, not me, who was to be a Woman Chief! Defender of her people!"

"I wonder what it would be like to be married to such a powerful woman," Geordie postulated. "I think that it might not be too easy!"

"Pallas Athena," the Professor mused, amazed. Somehow it seemed quite possible.

"I have returned," Sara said. "And you, old friend," she told him, "were Aristotle!"

"I think this is a bit much for the kind professor to take in all at once, Sara dear," her mother interjected.

"Quite," said Geordie, beginning to pick up British expressions. "Professor, you're the expert here, perhaps you could tell us about this wonderful place."

"Oh -- indeed; of course," he said collecting himself. He would think about all of this new information later. Geordie and Little Dove were accustomed to having certain of their people go into a light trance state – Spirit-speaking, they called it -- and receive information from beyond this plane. But the professor was not used to such things, and was feeling overwhelmed by it all.

"Yes, well..." the professor began. "People often admire this ancient statuary because of its pristine simplicity and purity, thinking that the carved stone figures were always white like this. But in earlier times, they were painted in the natural colors of the people and their clothing. The strong sunlight and rain of many centuries has bleached them out," he explained.

As they walked among the statues (most of them had not been carted off to the museums of Europe and England yet), Sara felt that she was greeting many old friends.

"Aren't they wonderful, Papa? What do you think of the marble statues?" she said, holding his hand.

Geordie looked at her and smiled. "I think they're absolutely marble-ous, my dear!"

"Oh, Daddy, you're never serious...."

"Not if I can help it, Sweet Thing."

Sara was now skipping along the row of 'Stone People', stopping at each one, sometimes bowing or curtsying, or giving her Star People salute: hand-to-heart; to Spirit-eye; and upward to the skies. The professor smiled, and said:

"Perhaps Sara would like to introduce you to her friends. I get the impression that she knows them better than I do."

"Delighted!" said Sara, holding her skirts out and doing her most elaborate curtsy with a flourish. "Oh -- This is the way they do it in England, when presented at court, is it not?" And she put one foot behind the other and bent her knees so that she went all the way to the ground, her back straight, head bowed, holding the pose for a few moments.

"Your Majesty," she said to the professor.

He bowed deeply to her. "Your Grace," he replied. Geordie and Grace (Little Dove) looked at each other and laughed.

"This is Zeus," Sara began her introductory tour. "He is the King of the Gods. A mighty protector -- but best beware inciting his anger! He will send lightning bolts down from the skies, to punish the wicked!" She was beginning to sound like one of the preachers back home, in her fervor, Geordie thought.

"Ah! The Thunder-God!" said Little Dove.

"How re-bolting," said Geordie.

"Papa, behave yourself," Sara admonished.

"Why do I have to? Would I say a thing like that to you?" he said. He enjoyed teasing her. She tolerated it.

"It's best just to ignore him," she said to her mother, who smiled and agreed. "Yes, that was our way," she said.

Sara swept on to the next statue, with great dignity. "And this is Hera. Zeus' wife."

"Lovely." Geordie commented.

"Powerful," said Little Dove. "I think she too was a Woman Chief."

Sara went into the Story of Orpheus, and his great love for Eurydice. She told how Orpheus won the beautiful maiden with his music; how he lost her, and how he searched everywhere for her. "And it was Hera to whom he finally turned for help," Sara explained. "A woman has an enduring strength, and wisdom, as our Cherokee people know," she announced. "Hera helped him, of course, by giving him wise counsel."

It was a great love story, and Sara made the most of it, dramatizing the fact that Orpheus was willing to go to Hell and back to retrieve his lost love. "Across the river Styx and past the fierce and fearsome guardians of Hades he went..." she said in spooky tones.

"This is Mercury, messenger of the Gods. He has wings on his heels, and on his helmet. That's a space-helmet, really," Sara added with an impish grin, "and the wings mean he could fly. He was an inter-galactic messenger from the Pleiades."

Her parents smiled. The professor seemed to choke on something; he coughed and sputtered and cleared his throat. "She has quite an imagination, doesn't she?"

"Oh, indeed she does," Geordie replied.

"Diana, the huntress. She provides for her people."

"The warrior-woman. We met her in Paris," Little Dove recalled.

"Eros -- the God of Love!" Sara crossed her hands over her heart.

"He has smiled on us," said Little Dove, giving her husband a tender look and a squeeze of the hand. "Truly, he has," replied her beloved husband. At last, after introductions and often stories about the entire pantheon of Gods and other beings, Sara reluctantly agreed that it was time to go down off of the Acropolis. Down below, the city was blanketed in shadow, but the golden rays of the sun still cast a brilliant glow upon the City of the Gods rising high above them, as the Sun-God Helios reached the western horizon on his daily journey, after driving his spirited horses and chariot across the azure sky.

Prof. Chivington took them to a little Greek taverna, run by a Greek family who were friends of his, for a most delicious dinner. Introducing them to the proprietor and his family, the professor said "I thought I knew a lot about the Ancients in Greece. But today I learned a great deal more from my young teacher here, who has a most remah-kable way of presenting hist'ry."

Sara smiled, with the gracious assurance of the Goddess she believed herself to be.

They watched the Greek men dance, to the musical strains of the bouzoukia. They danced in a circle, holding hands, with a handkerchief held in one hand; stepping to the side, dipping, turning in the opposite direction, all in perfect synchronization, to the rhythm of the music.

"Sara, my dear, would you like to do a dance for us?" the professor inquired.

She looked at her parents. "Is it all right, Mama? Papa?"

"We are the People-Who-Have-Free-Will, the Ani-Yun-Wiya. It is your choice," said her father.

Sara walked with sure steps to the center of the room, and addressed the people sitting at the tables around the open space, who were eating, and drinking ouzo. How sweet, they thought. A little girl from America.

"I am Sara," she began, "from America. My People have lived there long before the Europeans came to our land from across the sea. Our ancestors came from the Stars -- from the Pleiades. We believe that we live many lifetimes on this planet.

"When I lived in Greece, I was called Athina. I will do a dance of the Goddess, from ancient times."

She made this announcement in flawless ancient Greek, which they recognized, and they were able to understand most of it. Once again, the reaction was astonishment!

Sara stood up tall, erect, regal. She commanded the complete attention of everyone; not a sound was heard.

"The Pan-pipes, please," she asked the musicians, and they improvised, following her movements.

Graceful indeed were her movements, as she raised one arm slowly, arcing outward, up to the skies. Star Woman, spiraling down from the heavens, was indicated. She twirled around, her skirt and petticoats flying

204

outward and undulating in waves. Round and round the circle she went; her feet bare, freed of the shackles of shoes.

Sara returned to the center, crouched, then stood straight. Arms forward, creating a semi-circle. Hand pointing upward; palm at right-angle to her face. Arms outward. One arm returns to the center, out in front of her hips, hand curved inward; arcing upward to the solar plexus, to the heart, the throat, mouth, spirit-eye in the forehead, the crown atop the head -- and upward and beyond.

Her head turns quickly to the side; arms outward, knees turned out, she crouches. She jumps up! Leaps sideways -- twirls around and around; spinning, twirling, pirouetting. She finished with a flourish, arms extended, in the graceful glide of a great bird, swooping. She bent her knees, one in front of the other, and bowed low to the ground, head lowered, folding her 'wings' around to the front, one hand overlapping the other in her final bow.

The audience sat in stunned silence, mesmerized.

"Ah well," she thought, "No applause. Perhaps they didn't like it. Perhaps I am too impetuous."

And then it began -- They arose as one body and gave her a standing ovation! They had not wanted to break the spell.

"She is a treasure!" one said. "A Goddess!" said another. "Athina -- returned to us. What a blessing!"

They crowded around the family from America, and asked questions, one on top of the other, of the professor. All felt that they had witnessed some kind of miracle.

"How long has she been in Greece?" a man asked.

"They arrived last night," the professor replied.

"But how could this be? Dear little Goddess, where did you learn this dance?"

Sara smiled regally. "In Atlantis," she replied.

The Greeks loved drama. They adored her.

Sara couldn't get enough of Greece. It was the highlight of her life. No-one could do enough for her; Sara and her family were invited everywhere, and she was treated like royalty indeed. She continued to amaze, wherever she went.

"Did you know," she said, addressing a group of scholars from the University of Athens, "that my cousin (all Native Americans were related, in her view) Pocahontas was the daughter of a great Chief, PO-ha-tahn, who ruled a vast territory along the Eastern seaboard of my country, and that her father was recognized as a King by the King of England? She was presented at the court of King James, in the 1600's, and was called Lady Rebecca in England. Her portrait hangs in the British Museum, along with other royalty."

"Astonishing!" said one.

"I have seen this portrait!" said another. She was a - a Red Indian?"

"She was indeed. We are not all savages, as you have been told. In order to justify the taking of our lands, the destruction of our people, they say these things."

Silence.

"Would you like to see a play tonight, dear Goddess, in the amphitheater?" a patron asked her.

"Of course! We all have our dramas -- and our comedies! Life on this planet is a cosmic joke. We tend to get caught up in our roles, and take it far too seriously."

"Hear! Hear!" agreed Prof. Chivington.

Sara wanted to see them all, and nearly did so, attending a different one every night. Little Dove tired of the seriousness of the tragedies, so she and Geordie would often stroll around or visit with other people while the professor and his friends took her to the theater. Like Melina Mercouri in 'Never on Sunday' many years later, she fascinated the professor by sometimes laughing at the tragedies and crying at the comedies. "Life is just a game," she explained.

Some fishermen offered to take her and her family on their painted wooden sailing boat for a tour to some of the islands, and they were delighted. The professor had been to most of them before, but enjoyed going along. Sara loved watching the dolphins again as they jumped out of the water. Little ones following mama, in their playful way. The story was told of the Boy and the Dolphin, a well-known legend thereabouts.

"It is true," said the Captain of the boat. "Many have been rescued by our little flippered friends. They know when we are in trouble, if our boats founder in a storm -- and they come to help us. We always give thanks to the Dolphin Gods, and make offerings on their altar, and we feed them when they come alongside. We speak to them; we thank them."

"Sounds like our way!" said Little Dove, pleased.

The crew of the fishing boat had a routine of four-hours on, four-hours-off. That meant they only got four hours of sleep at a time. They took turns; someone always had to be on deck, on duty. Squalls could come up quickly.

It was a good-sized boat, and the adults slept in bunks in the cabin. Sara found it an adventure to sleep in a hammock, below-decks, with the crew.

Chapter 15

Athena

This statue, representing Greek Theatre, Belonged to Sara Gillespie, then to Sara's daughter Mary and then to her daughter, the author Sakina Blue-Star. Sakina studied Greek History and Mythology at the Windsor School in Bostin, and studied Art at the Museum School

One night Sara was awakened at 4 a.m. by a crew-member being nudged awake for his watch. He turned over too quickly and fell out of his bunk -- a small shelf, really. He was profuse in his apology. They all knew that this was a little goddess, and must be treated with the utmost respect.

Sara said she was happy to be awake at this quiet time on the earth. That was when the Star People came. She had sensed their coming this night, she indicated, mostly in sign-language, as their version of Greek was different from hers. Wrapped in her cloak, Sara went top-side with the sailor. Carefully she scanned the skies, in the dark night. She pointed directly overhead to the small cluster of six stars, the seventh rarely visible.

"Pleiades," she said. "Home!"

The sailor smiled.

"Sirius, a bright one. Venus, goddess of Love! Orion -- the hunter." She knew them all, and their stories. The sailor was impressed; they too knew the stars, which would help them to navigate, but landsmen were not usually so knowledgeable. A bright 'comet' streaked across the sky.

"Look! One of our ships!" Sara exclaimed.

"Your ship?"

"Yes. I'll ask him to come back."

A few minutes later, a "bright star" -- ten times brighter than usual -- again traced a path across the onyx blackness of the night sky.

This time, however, it traveled more slowly. And trailed behind it a banner of golden sparkles, 5 miles long! Wonder of wonders! It moved slowly enough to be seen as a golden orb, and it made two more passes across the inky sky.

The sailor whistled in a long, low tone. He had seen many strange things at sea, but never anything that had come close to this.

"Thank you for coming, my friends," said Sara, her long hair blowing in a playful breeze. "That is the Star-craft of Ashtar. He is my consort," she added, but this was beyond the comprehension of her companion.

The next day the ship was buzzing with whispered conversations, punctuated by the pointing sky-ward of the index finger of the sailor with the 'Four Bells watch' of that early morning. "Ooh!" and "Ahh!" would be heard. Then they would look at Sara, and nod, or shake their head in wonderment.

Prof. Chivington inquired about what was going on. The crewman hesitated, looking at Sara; but she smiled and nodded, so he took a deep breath and told about what had happened.

"You mean -- you mean --" the professor stammered. "You actually saw this thing?"

The Captain smiled. "We often see the lights at night, but not so grand as that one. They are like very, very bright stars, but they will be where the stars that we know about are not positioned. We know our own stars well; they guide us on our journeys.

"But these others -- the streakers, sometimes comets -- and the others, they are different. They will change colors; red, to green, to blue... and then they will shoot straight up into the sky, straight over to the side, and vanish in a flash." Once again, the learned professor was being educated by the simple people.

He looked around. "You have all seen these things?" he asked. The sailors nodded. "We have seen them. Many times."

Little windmills with triangular fluttering sails appeared among the white-washed houses high up on the bluff of an island as they approached its harbor. This was the island of Faros, and Nausa was home-port for the Captain and his vessel. Life had been little changed here over the centuries, and it had a far different ambiance from the busy city of Athens.

As they pulled into port, Captain Stamos told them about his island. "There is an old sea captain who lives in that big house up there on the hill," he related. He is retired from the sea now, but he has seen many lands, and, to the villagers, he knows all! They call him 'Zeus' (though not to his face, of course), and his hill is 'Mt. Olympus.' From there he can watch all the comings and goings, the triumphs and trials of us humble mortals. Like Zeus, he has a long white beard."

Capt. Stamos chuckled. "Zeus had a reputation for being attracted to beautiful young maidens, as you may recall, and, occasionally, sneaking off and ravishing them. The pattern is repeated here, and our Zeus's wife -- we call her 'Hera' -- has a commanding view of our little town, and watches from her perch, with eagle-eye, all of the activities of those below."

He shook his head. "Sometimes we hear the expression of her wrath -- and we know that she has caught him again!"

Sara enjoyed the little cafés, where the whole family would be participating in preparing and serving the meals. Older children would assist in making salads, going on errands to get what was needed from the market or the fishermen; or taking care of the younger ones when Mama was needed for cooking. It seemed that they worked all the time, but no-one complained. (That's why the Greeks did so well in running little cafes and restaurants across America at a later time.)

Sara was fascinated by some of the shells she found along the shore, and she brought them to her 'family' -- which now included the professor, Captain and crew. "Look, Mama, a star-fish! A message from the Ancestors!"

Her mother agreed. "A wonderful sign, from the Old Ones!"

"Some strange things are found in these waters," said the captain of their fishing vessel. "Last week some boys were playing with a giant sea-turtle that fishermen had caught in their net. It was unlike any that anyone had ever seen before. A scaly creature, with very unusual markings on its giant shell, and a head that looked like a gargoyle!"

The professor got all excited. "That sounds like a prehistoric creature! They are supposed to be long extinct! Where is it now?"

"Well, I heard that the boys were playing with it yesterday. I'll go talk to their family."

The professor went along. What an exciting find! This could make history, he thought.

The boys told him where the huge turtle was. They had made a pen for it. An ancient creature, still living!

The professor could hardly contain himself. There it was -- six feet in length: A treasure, in the world of paleontology! Unique on this world; a momentous discovery. This could be worth a great deal of money to a museum, and would certainly enhance his reputation in the Scientific Community.

"Tell them I'll offer a handsome price for it," he said to Capt. Stamos. "I must contact the Museum in London immediately."

That would hardly be possible, of course. They would have to go to Crete, where, he had heard, there was a new device called the Telegraph, which could send messages across land or sea, by means of Samuel Morse's Code.

"Excellent! Excellent!" This usually unflappable man was ecstatic. They weighed anchor and set sail forthwith.

Crete! Sara pictured the paintings she had seen of the Minotaur, and scenes of a bare-breasted woman acrobat grabbing hold of the horns of an enormous bull and flipping herself over its head and onto its back. And then there was the ivory Snake-Goddess, curls tied on her head with ribbons, big eyes, bare torso, wearing a bell-shaped, brass-ringed hoop-skirt. Snakes were crawling down her arms, wrapped around them, their heads coming out from her hands, rising up, looking forward.

On the way there, Capt. Stamos told them about the island of Crete.

"Many years ago people were living very happily on Crete. Fishermen were bringing home their catch, shopkeepers were selling their wares, women cooking and taking care of the children. At night they were celebrating this good life. One day they were singing and dancing, feasting and drinking wine in their little village -- and then along came a huge tidal wave! And the next day, there was nothing left...."

"Mother Earth cleanses herself from time to time," said Geordie.

"I'll tell you another story about an island in the Mediterranean," said the professor. "This island flourished long ago, thousands of years ago. Divers looking for sponges, or pearls, have brought up artifacts from it now and then, and they are very ancient, yet it was a highly-evolved civilization. Somewhat like the Minoan culture -- yet even more highly developed, from the scenes that were etched upon brass vessels which were salvaged.

"But evidently there was volcanic and earthquake activity, and in the twinkling of an eye the sea reclaimed the island. Somewhat like Pompeii, much was preserved just as it was, indicating scenes of everyday life of that period, according to the divers.

"Some scholars believe it was Atlantis," he concluded. Sara had a glazed, unfocused look, as she gazed into the distance at the blue waters surrounding their boat.

"It was an outpost of Atlantis," she said. "A colony, settled by people who had come from Poseidia, the largest of the islands of that great continent in the Atlantic. By that time, Atlantis had broken up into five islands. Originally it was only one. The final destruction of Atlantis -- and of that island of which you speak -- was about 13,000 years ago."

Professor Chivington started to ask something; but Geordie put his index finger in front of his lips, indicating that it would be better to remain silent. They knew that she was in trance, and it was better not to interrupt her until she came out of it.

"Many Atlanteans had fallen into ways which were not in harmony with Creator's law," Sara continued. "There were experiments on humans and animals in those latter times, and this was out of balance. In order for some to live a life of ease, others were mesmerized and turned into automatons, depriving them of their free will. This is against God's Law.

"Also, in the North of Atlantis, there was an explosion of enormous magnitude, set off by irresponsible beings unaware of the consequences: Thick dark clouds drifted south-ward and came between the rays of the sun and the Ruby Firestone, the great crystal which, with sun's energy, powered vehicles and vessels of that time, on land, sea, and through the air."

Sara closed her eyes, envisioning. "The earth trembled. The effect of the explosion was greater than that of millions of cannons. Mighty Atlantis shifted, heaved a great sigh, and settled down beneath the waves."

Sara's arms stretched out before her and her hands made the motion of waves, undulating, lower and lower.

"There are always some who are visionary, and know what is coming," she went on. "So seers and Priests had gathered certain enlightened beings together, and some were taken by sky-craft to the Egyptian land, to build their pyramids, to retain the ancient knowledge. Others went to an Atlantean outpost in the Yucatan, in Mexico, to build their pyramids, wherein to store wisdom and devices which would be helpful to the people of this planet in a time to come.

"The Ani Yun Wiya, The Principle People, lived long in the land of the Maya, having come from the stars. We brought our way of time-keeping, known as the Mayan, or Aztec, calendar, and many other things that would be helpful to humanity.

"In that other era, and in that place to the south of Turtle Island, we Star People walked freely among the peoples of the earth. But since many looked upon us as Gods, to be worshiped (instead of simply beings of a more advanced nature than they) -- we decided to leave. Some returned to the stars; a few withdrew into the pyramid-temples hidden deep in the jungles," Sara's message continued.

"After a time some Aztec priests, in their efforts to bring back the Star People, began to make offerings. At first, it was beautifully crafted artifacts encrusted with gold and gemstones. It did not bring us back. So they sacrificed animals; and then they began to offer human sacrifices... which eventually turned into a blood-bath. So the Ani Yun Wiya decided to migrate northward, and over the years there was some mixing with indigenous people, Lemurian descendants, on their travels.

"The Hopi Indians of Arizona are still in contact with the Star People. They call them Kachinas. Some of the Tsa-La-Gi ancestors were called the Mound Builders; their villages and cities have many buildings and flat-top temple pyramids, where our Priests would greet the sun each day, and tell the people when to plant and when to harvest.

"Great earthen mounds were built, such as the Serpent Mound, to let our friends in the skies find us easily. The serpent is the creature who is most in contact with the earth, along its long body, and represents earth energies, as the winged-ones represent sky energies. Quetzalcoatl combined these two."

A comet flashed across the sky, and Sara came out of her trance. They were approaching a port in Crete, and lights shone along the harbor.

"Oh, my!" said Sara. "I've been holding forth for a long time, haven't I?"

"You have, my dear," said Professor Chivington. "But I found it all utterly fascinating. Craft in the sky! Star People! I'm getting more used to it, but I still find it utterly astonishing! "

The boat pulled up to a dock, but they decided to sleep aboard since the telegraph office wouldn't be open until morning. They did go ashore and have dinner though, at a delightful little café.

Prof. Chivington sent off his message the next day.

MATTER OF UTMOST IMPORTANCE STOP LIVE TORTOISE LONG EXTINCT SPECIES FOUND NAUSA SEND TEAM PRONTO.

They explored Crete while he anxiously awaited the answer. It came the following day, from the Curator of a small museum in London.

INTRIGUING STOP WILL SEE ABOUT MOUNTING EXPEDITION STOP WILL BE IN TOUCH ATHENS IN TWO WEEKS REGARDS.

"Excellent! Well, that's done; what would you lot like to do next?"

"Your birthday is coming up in a few days, Sara," said Geordie. "Is there anything in particular you'd like to do?"

"This will be a very special birthday!" Little Dove explained to the others. "She will be ten years old, and ten is a number of great significance in Sara's life."

Sara smiled, and announced to Professor, Captain, and crew: "I was born ten years after the Civil War, on the tenth day of the tenth month, at 10:10pm, weighing ten pounds," she said.

"It was a very tenth situation," Geordie slipped in. "Oh, thorry; I'm lith-ping."

"Oh, Papa," she said, giving him a light tap on the hand. "You're always up-staging me!" she laughed.

"No-one could do that my darling daughter!" he replied.

"Well, Papa, there is a particular place where I would like to go. I would like to celebrate my tenth year (in this lifetime) in Delphi. I would like to return to the School for Oracles, where I was once a student -- and a teacher."

"You have the most remarkable way of putting things, Miss Sara!" said the professor. "I'm afraid you'll find the school quite changed; it is, in fact, in ruins."

"Nonetheless, the energy is there," Sara told them. "I'm sure I shall be able to glimpse into the future, as I did in the past."

"Well said, my dear," Geordie said, smiling. "I'm certain that the trip can be arranged."

The captain offered his services. "I am honored, dear Priestess. Perhaps you can give us each a message!"

"I'd be delighted," Sara said graciously.

A dinghy took them from the pier to where the boat was moored, and they weighed anchor and set sail for the northern coast of Greece.

"Alexander, of Macedonia. A virile man! I remember him well," said Sara, as they approached the coast line. "I was one of his concubines."

The professor cleared his throat, and looked down at her with a raised eyebrow. A startling comment from a little girl in the Victorian era! She never ceased to amaze him.

"He was always going off to conquer someplace," Sara said with a sigh. "But oh, we had some splendid celebrations when he returned!" she added with a knowing smile.

"Revelry, victory dances, drinking and feasting orgies. He would bring me treasures and trophies. But the best prize was himself!

"The women adored Alexander; indeed, they called him Great. The men envied but admired him. Oh, how those young beauties would throw themselves at him! But I was his favorite. He always serviced me first; we'd make love all night, 'til Helios came riding his golden chariot over the eastern horizon. The others would have to wait their turn."

The professor's face took on something of the hue of a tomato. He choked on his drink, and walked to the other side of the boat. Having spent his life among scholars, and being quite proper and British, he had never heard anything like it! And from a child -- a little girl! My word!

Once in Delphi, Sara knew every road, every turn, and would tell the driver of their carriage which way to go. Different houses lined the streets now, but the way was still the same. When they arrived at the remains of the ancient temple of the Oracle, it was, indeed, in ruins. But some of it still stood; walls, pillars, pieces of statuary.

"This was the courtyard," Sara said, picking her way through the rubble surrounded by pillars and partially-standing walls. "The Sacred Pool was in the center; a smiling dolphin-fountain spewed water into a large shell below it. It was fed by a spring in the mountains, and directed through several fountains on its way down the hillside, in cascading waters and pools on its way to the sea."

Sara walked gracefully, head held high, with a regal gait as she strolled through what was quite evidently her old home. The place was in shambles now, but she was seeing it with other eyes, which looked beyond the confines of this dimension.

"The garden was here. How lovely it was. A secluded, shaded place, with flowers everywhere. Lord Poseidon presided over the fountain over here, with sea-horses pulling him in an enormous sea-shell, and dolphins as an escort. Fountains and Statues in Rome were inspired by the ones here."

She walked on, smiling, remembering. "Ah! This is where our exquisite Love-goddess, Venus, rode her marble waves in splendor! Botticelli painted her. Here our priestesses were bathed, and perfumed, as part of our initiation ceremony, before being introduced to the wonders of love-making by the High Priests. To us, pure-hearted, gentle and passionate love-making was one part -- indeed, a most important part -- of living in a human embodiment. We did not deny that part of our beingness, as do Priests and Holy Women of this time period. Repression of one's natural feelings was seen as unhealthy; frustration could lead to anger and unkind words and deeds," Sara explained.

"The culmination of the Love-act, when ecstatic expression reaches its climax, is known by spiritually-enlightened ones to be the closest thing for humans to experiencing what it is like in the Heavens! In the Pleiades, in the Sirius star-system, one loving entity can actually merge totally with another, their energies radiating in a great synergy of ecstasy. It is beyond mere passion -- it is the ultimate expression of joy and bliss! Akin to experiencing One-ness with Creator, which comes when one finally achieves the higher levels of consciousness."

Professor Chivington mopped his brow with his handkerchief, and tried to be inconspicuous in his discomfort. A bachelor, he had never even read any suggestive novels, but it seemed to him that Sara must have done so... or else there really was something to this re-incarnation business.

Sara continued her tour. She pointed out some small rooms, about the size of a large closet, whose floor plan outline could be clearly seen, and some of which had walls that were still standing. It was evident that there had only been a door into the room, and no windows. Sara explained why.

"These rooms were where our young priestesses, our Oracles-in-training, were sequestered. Here they were instructed to meditate, in a small room with no distractions. It could be difficult for them, to sit quietly day after day. And often it took years before they could achieve a breakthrough.

"But, oh! When it happened! When their spirit was able to soar beyond the confines of the mind, with its distracting and constant babbling... That is what made them Oracles. They were able to go beyond the barriers of time and space, to overcome limitation, and to go to the Cosmic Hall of Records, the Akasha, where all knowledge is recorded. In other dimensions, there is no separation: Past, future; all is present. One need only choose where to focus one's attention."

Sara became pensive.

"In the Americas, some of the Native Peoples have a similar process. They will put a young boy in a small chamber underground, sometimes for many days and nights. After a while he will lose a sense of time -- he will become one with Mother Earth; he is in her womb. And then he will become one with Spirit, and soar throughout the galaxies. He becomes a Holy Person; he can help the people with his wisdom.

"In Egypt, one type of initiation would place a novice priest into an open sarcophagus and leave him lying there in the darkness, in a secluded chamber in the Great Pyramid, for three days and nights, for the same purpose: To let his spirit leave the body and find the greater truth of the beyond."

Sara walked through the courtyard, toe-first, gliding like a dancer -- or an American Indian. She held her skirt out with each hand, twirled around a few times, threw her head back, laughing, and tossed her long mane around. She was in Heaven!

They rounded a corner; another temple came into view. This one was round, with its columns intact. She stopped, squealed in delight, clapped her hands together and exclaimed:

"Oh! It's still here! This was my temple; they put a statue of me there on the pedestal, to honor me... and it's still there, most of it!"

A helmeted marble female figure stood watching over them; long dress falling in graceful folds, caught up at the waist with a cord that wrapped around and crossed under the bosom. A cloak hung down the back. A sword was in one hand, a small shield in the other, or what was left of it.

"Your temple?" inquired Little Dove softly, not wanting to break the spell.

"The Temple of Athena. Guardian of the People; Protector of the family. Goddess of War, yes, but also, and more important: The Goddess of Wisdom!"

Her entourage was hushed and in awe. The crew of the fishing-vessel had come along; they were all as familiar with their Gods and Goddesses as American children are with Santa Claus, and they knew that something momentous was occurring here. They had the reverent feeling of the Faithful watching the Miracle of Fatima, when the Virgin Mother appeared to humble peasant girls.

Sara sat upon the altar in front of the statue, her ankles crossed in front of her, hands lying in her lap. Some of her long hair fell down in front of her shoulders -- like Athena's curls. The Captain and the sailors passed in front of her, removed their caps and held them respectfully in their hands, and bowed on one knee before her. She smiled and held out her hand to them in blessing, giving each a special few words in Ancient Greek. It all seemed perfectly natural to the on-lookers. Her parents bowed before her also, and the professor too got into line for a blessing.

"I am honored, Pallas Athena," he said.

The little Goddess led them around to the back of the Temple Compound. Steep mountains with sheer cliffs rose a little way beyond. "This is where we used to give our message, where the Oracle spoke. Each time the full moon came around, an Oracle would give her, or sometimes his, prophecy of what was to come. Individual messages were given in private chambers, inside of the Temple, when someone wished to consult with us."

Sara pointed to a natural amphitheater on a hillside, where rows of seats had been carved into the rock. To one side of the outdoor theater, mountains and cliffs arose, forming an impressive backdrop.

"Sit here, please," said Sara, indicating the seats in the amphitheater. "I need to go do something. Wait for me, please." She went around the side of the mountain, and disappeared. Her audience sat in the rows, turning towards the mountains to their left, focusing upon the direction in which she had gone.

"I wonder what this amazing creature will come up with next?" asked the professor.

"Yes... I wonder..." added the Captain. They watched a covey of doves flutter out from behind a rock, and circle overhead.

At the Temple of Athena at Delphi,
Sara was remembering ancient times.

This portrait of Athena is by
Sakina Blue-Star

Chapter 16

Oracle

"LOOK! Up there!" cried out one of the sailors. All eyes looked upward, to where he pointed.

High up on a narrow ledge on the sheer cliff-face stood Sara, holding up her hand in greeting. As those below watched in awe, she turned into hundreds of tiny sparks of light, and shape-shifted into the regal Athena.

"Blessings be upon you, Beloved Ones!" she said. "I am Athena." The acoustics were perfection; every nuance could be clearly heard. "I have come before you this day to give you the greetings of those who watch over you, you who are at the moment mortals. It is a temporary condition: In reality, you are all Gods, and you live forever.

"Each earth-experience is for the learning of something, each embodiment is merely a change of garment. When you finish what you came to do or learn, you cast it off and go home to your dwelling in the skies. There you continue to experience and to study in the great Halls of Learning, which are scattered throughout the Cosmos.

"When you are ready for another earth-experience, to see what choices can be made, and what are their consequences when in material form -- then you choose the place, the circumstances, and the parents that will help you accomplish your chosen goal. You come back into a tiny body and begin again.

"All are equal in the sight of the Creator; all are sparks from the Divine Source, like rainbow rays of light shining out in all directions from a crystal that moves in the sunlight. Yet some learn their lessons more quickly than others, and these we call the Old Souls. They are in service to Creator, to assist in raising the vibrations of the others who are coming along.

"The Advanced Ones are beyond limitation. Enlightened Masters who have achieved a measure of perfection in a particular experience or incarnation can manifest in more than one place, or one body, at a time. Thus, I am Athena: Sara is an aspect of my Being. Sometimes, I speak through her. She has come into this embodiment to be a healer, a teacher, to assist those on this planet. She will not necessarily remember who she truly is, except for occasional brief glimpses: The veil of forgetfulness is part of the process."

The professor pondered these concepts. The sailors -- who were receiving the thoughts in their own language, though the others heard it in English -- accepted them as ancient truths, and Sara's parents were familiar with the teachings of the Masters that were being brought forth.

"Many are those who sail the skies above you. Some are of the Light, others come merely to observe, and some are of the Lesser Light; ones who do not care about the welfare of those already dwelling here upon Terra. That is why you need your prayers of protection. We who serve the Radiant One, and the Forces of Light, are always watching over you; we hear your prayers. We can do little if we are not asked, as we do not interfere with mankind's free-will choices; but if we are asked, we can do a great deal. We can stabilize the earth, and prevent earthquakes, tidal waves, and other upheavals. So remember to gather together and focus upon positive goals, for there is a synergy, a greater power, with many coming together and envisioning the same thing.

"See the earth bathed in a great golden-white light of God-essence, the light of the Christos, or the rose-pink of Unconditional Love. See peace, harmony, coming into you, filling you, passing through you into Mother Earth and out in all directions, spreading throughout her body. Send out loving thoughts to all who come within your sphere."

Athena had been looking downward at the assembled group as she spoke. But now she looked upward, to the skies. A very large, elliptical, lenticular 'cloud' hovered in the sky above her; it was the only one in the vivid cerulean-blue sky. Around the center of the cloud-like object, looking silvery now, lights moved from left to right; blinking, one and then the other, proceeding in alternating colors around in a horizontal circular fashion, going around and around.

221

Athena raised her hand in a salute. "Ashtar," she said, and then explained: "Lord Ashtar is Commander of our ship, and of the Starfleet which is here to assist those in this sector of the universe through times of change. He has come to give us greetings! He is my Twin-Flame; my Divine Complement. We of the Inter-galactic Federation of Peaceful Worlds serve the beloved Commander Sananda, the Radiant One. His chosen people called him Yeshua Ben Joseph, and the Greeks called him Jesus, when he came to this planet as a teacher 2,000 years ago."

"My word!" exclaimed the professor. "What would the theologians have to say about this, I wonder?" He couldn't even acknowledge what was obviously a space-ship hovering over them. It was incompatible with his reality, so he ignored it.

"Mariners upon the Sea of Life," she said, addressing the sailors, looking at each one as she gave them their message. "One of you will go far, across the great waters to the West, and settle there. You will carve a homestead out of the wilderness and raise a family. Another will go to the Orient and bring back exotic merchandise which will make you wealthy.

"You, Stephanopolis, will go with a team of divers in the Aegean sea, and, while you're looking for sponges and pearls, will find a greater treasure; the remains of a sunken galleon from early Phoenician times, with rare coins and goblets of gold. And you, Captain, will leave the seafaring life and settle happily with a family among vineyards and olive groves.

"I see much celebration, with dancing, wine, feasting and song; a joyous time coming for all of you."

Athena's long white skirt fluttered in the breeze. She smiled.

"Ah! The little zephyrs are playful today!" The white doves came and fluttered around her. "Greetings, old friends!" she said to them. Little Dove also recognized them as old friends.

As in the days of the ancient Oracles, the Goddess of home and hearth continued with her glimpses into the future.

"I, Athena, speak now of this one who is in the present lifetime called Sara. When I overshadow her, we are of one essence. Her life will not be an easy one this time, for she is both wise and powerful, which is not popular for a female in the place of her dwelling; and she will stand up to anyone for her knowledge, for her truth.

"But she will help many, with her healing ways. I see her studying the medicine of the White world, and bringing to it ancient knowledge of the medicine ways of the Red peoples, and the Brown peoples. Sara will not receive credit for it, but she will help to heal the hearts, quite literally, of the people. She will discover, for example, that what will be known as a cardiac stimulant can be made from the plant called black cohosh, or snake-root.

"I see her in the laboratory of the Medical School, with a fellow student. He has a beloved uncle who has just been hospitalized with a heart attack. 'I know something that could help him, Richard,' she says. 'It grows in the woods, in high places, or on hillsides. I will find some.' And this she does," Athena said.

"His doctor gives the uncle little or no chance of recovery. Sara brings the cohosh root to the laboratory. 'We need to make the root into a liquid, to be more easily administered and quickly absorbed,' she says. 'We can boil the root and make a tea, but that only partially dissolves the root. Let's try it in alcohol!' They find that this substance is effective in dissolving it completely, and they administer the decoction to the ailing uncle -- whose recovery is almost immediate.

"The physicians are impressed and pleased. Richard, and the medical school staff, receives the credit for it.

"At that time Sara is the mother of five children. Her husband is in Europe, as an officer fighting in a great war. It will be called the War to End all Wars, though it will be the first of two or three such conflicts encompassing much of this world. While her husband is overseas and her children are in school, she attends medical school. Although she is a brilliant student, doctors on the school staff will balk at giving her a diploma, because she is a woman; and, in the place called Mississippi, it is not considered appropriate for a woman to be a physician. 'I don't care about a piece of paper,' she tells them; 'I just want the knowledge.'"

Athena's message continues. "I see Sara's friend Richard threaten to expose the fact that she was the one responsible for the cardiac stimulant treatment, which was so successful, if they withhold her diploma. So, with reluctance, they give it to her.

"Always fearless and eager to try new things, while a medical student she will be the first person in the South to be X-Rayed. At that time, it will be called a Roentgen-ray, after its inventor. After graduating, she will not officially open a practice but will use her knowledge of medicine to take care of family and friends, and whoever else comes to her. As is the custom of American Indians, she will not charge for her services, accepting only whatever is offered."

Sea-birds wheel overhead, as Athena keeps speaking through Sara.

"I see Sara making a great contribution to mankind. Again, she does not receive recognition for this, but it matters not to her -- she wishes only to serve. I see her compiling a series of note-books, into which she presses dried healing plants, fruits, leaves and roots, or she makes drawings of them, describing remedies known to Native America. She specifies where they can be found, when and how they are effective, what their healing properties are, and which illness or conditions they are good for.

"Because of her proficiency in Latin as well as ancient Greek, she becomes a link between the Native world of healing knowledge and the medical establishment. Sara is responsible for much of the American medical pharmacopoeia. She gives Latin names to the Amerindian herbology, as well as using the common names. She works together with a man named Merck, who uses her information as the basis for a compendium, or manual; Merck's Manual becomes something of a Bible for medical students and for physicians."

The woman on the ledge was silent for a moment.

"Blue Star, who will be a descendant of Sara," she continued, "was also an Oracle here, at the time known as Greece's Golden Age. (Her parents then were the same as those who will be her parents in that time to come.) Because she had a special gift of vision, they placed her into the School for Oracles when she was seven years old. It was an honor to have an Oracle in the family.

"Her name at that time was Delia. She spent many hours, months, years -- in a small room with nothing to distract her. She wasted away, became pale and thin, listless. Her parents wondered if they had made a mistake.

"And then she had her breakthrough. One day her parents went to visit her and she was radiant! She stood upon a platform, eyes closed, a gentle smile upon her face. Her head would turn, slowly, to one side, and then, gently, swivel to the other side. Her arms, held outward, would also go back and forth in an undulating pattern. Then, eyes opened, the words

224

of the Ancient Ones, the Ancestors, the Masters, would come through. She became one of the best, and most popular, of the Oracles. Each one took their turn at speaking before the people, at the time of the change of season, giving their messages and prophecies of events to come.

"At the time of the autumn equinox, it was Delia's turn to be the Oracle, conveying the messages and the prophecies for the next time period. It happened that there was very much pollen in the air that year, with prevailing winds carrying it to the Temple grounds. Delia developed asthma.

"Not much was known about that condition or its cause at that time, and a younger priestess, who was jealous of her, began to whisper to the others: "If she's such a great Oracle, why does she have difficulty breathing?" This girl's resentment went back to a previous incarnation, in Atlantis.

"At that earlier time Delia had been known as Lady Darinda, and was Empress of Atlantis. The girl was her sister, and had become impregnated by one of the powerful -- and married -- Senators. To avoid scandal, the young sister was sent away by the Empress to a small and remote seaside village. Lady Darinda was trying to protect the girl, but her sister felt only that she had been banished, far from her family and her friends. She did not know that the Senator had also been stripped of his position and sent away.

"The bitterness the girl had felt at that earlier time was carried over into that period when many Atlanteans returned in a group-reincarnation to create Greece's Golden Age. When Delia could not sleep for three days and nights because of her difficulty in breathing, she was told that she did not have to take her turn giving the Oracular Message at that time. But because of the whispered criticism of the young initiate, she said 'No, it is my time; I will do it.'

"Thus when the crowd assembled on the appointed day, in the amphitheater where you are now seated, she appeared on the ledge where I now stand. There are steps cut into the back of this mountain. When she appeared the crowd exclaimed 'Look! There she is!' -- and she began her Spirit-Speaking.

"It was customary to speak for five hours. She spoke for two hours... and then exhaustion overcame her, from lack of sleep due to gasping for breath. She collapsed, falling forward off the ledge! The crowd cried out helplessly, as she plunged to her death on the rocks below.

"In the time yet to come, the one known as Turtle Woman, mother of Little Dove, will return as a descendant of Sara, and will be known as Blue Star. She will carry with her a fear of heights, which goes back to that experience here at Delphi. When she goes to the edge of high rock formations at the Sacred City of Nawanda, later called Sedona, she has the feeling of falling off! Until an Enlightened One takes her back in a regression to that time of being an Oracle, reliving the experience -- and she loses the fear of falling. There-after, she leads many people to the high places, and often does Blessing Ceremonies there."

Athena looked up to the skies.

The colored lights on the "lenticular cloud" had begun to flash and rotate once again. The cloud-cover dissipated briefly, and they were able to see the magnificent, silvery star-ship clearly. It was awesome: The Goddess smiled, and blew a kiss up to the ship. The lights blinked, returning her greeting. A beam of light came down from it, and there suddenly appeared a radiant being standing beside her on the ledge.

"Commander Ashtar," she said. "Welcome!"

Ashtar was in the form of a man composed of pin-points of silvery, sparkling lights, transparent. One could see through him. It was something like a shimmering coat-of-mail. A great light radiated from him.

The people watching were astonished.

As the Goddess of Wisdom and the Commander of the Inter-Galactic Space Fleet in this sector of the galaxy acknowledged each other, it seemed that their combined energies lit up the entire area.

"Lord Ashtar," she smiled. "Do you have words for our friends?"

"I greet you in the name of The Radiant One, and of the Galactic Federation of Peaceful Worlds," said he. "For there are many worlds beyond this one. Some of them appear to you as stars in the night.

"In earlier times on your planet there were those of us who walked freely among you. We built pyramids and great stone temples, using the power of the mind, or sound vibration or tensor beams, to move into place the large blocks, which were cut by laser beams. We gave to the people of the Americas a system of time-keeping known as the Mayan calendar, charting the movements of the stars, a way to create harmony and be in balance. But when we came in our ships from the skies, people would either run in fear, or try to kill us; or they would worship us as gods. This was not good either for earth beings or for galactics; so we left."

Athena spoke. "I was known as a Goddess -- yet truly, it was not goddess, but God-essence -- of which all are made."

"It is important to remember the One-ness," Ashtar agreed. "All are sparks of the Divine Source, the Great Light, or Energy, which is the Creator. But each Spark has chosen its own way of expression, of learning about the endless possibilities on the road to becoming a completed entity, before progressing to the higher levels of consciousness. There one is aware once again that there is truly no separation between each Entity and the Creator-of-All-Things.

"There will be many changes on this planet in the century to come. Carriages will move swiftly without horses to pull them; images and sound will appear, far from their source; ships will fly through the air. Sara's daughter will marry the son of a man who will help to mobilize these carriages; a physician, he will also be an engineer, chemist and scientist. He and his brother will invent a molecular-cracking process that will turn crude-oil into what will be called gasoline, which will power the vehicles. He will set up refineries all over the world.

"Not since the final times of Atlantis will such awesome power be present on this earth. The Atlanteans misused that power, and that was what caused their demise. It is possible that this will occur again, and that this civilization will once again be destroyed, by the end of the next century. Our earth-based Starfleet personnel, however, and the pure-hearted ones, will be under our protection. And there will be a more wondrous time to come, and many will ascend to the higher realms. Others will return as Masters to rebuild this planet in a kind, harmonious way. And Terra may choose to rejoin her sister planet of Sirius, which is peopled by loving Beings.

"In earlier times, long before its final destruction, Atlantis, and in the Pacific, Lemuria, experienced periods of Golden Age, times of harmony and wisdom. Enlightened ones from those time periods chose to come together once more in Greece, to form a Golden Age here as well. Again, people here turned the more advanced Star-Beings into Gods, and Goddesses. Yet we are also learning, and do not wish to be worshiped.

"I wish you peace and joy, and Blessings, in the name of the Radiant One. I am Ashtar. Adonai."

The large round silvery craft hovering over the mountain shot down a beam of golden light toward Cmdr. Ashtar. The glow emanating from him intensified, and, in a burst of bright light, he vanished into the beam -- which then withdrew. The starship flashed its lights; red, blue, green; hovered for a moment more, shot straight up, and then horizontally at a fantastic speed, and zoomed out of sight.

Above: Comdr ASHTAR by Sakina. Small image by Celaya Winkler.

Lady Athena welcomed Lord Ashtar, who came from his ship in a burst of light.

The professor was dumbfounded. The others, more accustomed to the unusual and the miraculous, were awed.

Goddess Athena remained on the ledge, long rolls of curls coming down from her helmet, flowing gown reaching down to her sandals. She smiled and saluted the ship as it left.

Athena addressed the people below. "Commander Ashtar is in charge of the Galactic Federation forces in this sector of the universe, the ones who have come to help with the changes that are to come at the change of this millennium. We serve Lord Sananda, who came two thousand years ago to teach of Love and Oneness on this planet. He is now on Venus. Some enlightened ones think that Sananda and Jesus are the same; others think that they are two separate entities. They are both right.

"A realized Master can manifest as more than one entity, one essence, simultaneously. Sananda, as He is known elsewhere in the Galaxy, is the Oversoul of Jesus. I, Athena, will also return at the time of the great shift on this planet, towards the end of the next century. I will overshadow and become one with an entity who will become known as Ashtar-Athena, who will transmit messages from the Galactic Command. She will travel widely throughout the globe, bringing inspiration and wisdom to many, teaching them how to ascend to higher levels.

"I will also bring wisdom and inspiration to one who may become Leader of the Nation across the sea that was founded on the principle that 'All men (and women) are created equal', with God-given 'inalienable rights to life, liberty, and the pursuit of happiness.' This one will have some Tsalagi heritage, so that she will have star-seed genes and spiritual abilities. She will also be of Scottish background, and will be named for the purple blossoms that cover the hillsides of that land of her mother.

"'God is in charge,' Heather will say, 'so anything can happen. I can even be President!' She is our choice, but others will attempt to prevent this. A highly-evolved spiritual entity, she will be in contact with us; and thus we will be able to be of assistance.

"Both of these ones of that time period will be known to the grand-daughter of Sara, Turtle Woman returned, the one who will be called Blue Star. When Star Woman of the Blue Star goes to Nawanda, or Sedona, that place long sacred to all of the Nations of Turtle Island, she will climb a mountain in Sacred Canyon. There at a place emitting a powerful vortex of energy she will make a dedication to serve the Light. Thenceforth, we in spirit will speak through her, dance, sing, or tell stories, and give messages.

"Artemis will be with her; the huntress, who provides for the People, she who is called Goddess of the Moon. There will often be ceremonies to honor the Moon Goddess, and many will gather around the circle at the time of Luna's fullness. Blue Star will be the voice of the Ancestors, the Star People, the Spirit Beings. She will also journey throughout the land, and beyond, doing Blessing Ceremonies at pyramids and other sacred sites. She will gain much knowledge of Native Nations, and will share it willingly.

"And there will come a time, dear Little Dove, and Sara, when she will tell your story, that the people will know your hearts."

"I am Athena. Adonai."

Once again a shift-of-shape took place. Athena became smaller, and Sara was seen on the ledge. She heaved a sigh, and sat down. It had been a long session.

Little Dove went around the mountain and found steps that led upward. Geordie followed her. He picked up the girl and carried her back down the steep steps to the ground.

"That was quite a birthday celebration, my girl!" her father said to her. "What a fun party -- costumes and all."

Sara smiled up at him. "Where's the cake?" she asked. And off they went to find a taverna and celebrate with ouzo (for the sailors), fruit juice, calamari, and pastry. The men did a circle dance, honoring Sara, in the middle of the room.

"That's a day I'll not soon forget!" said the newly ten-year-old, as she retired that night, exhausted but elated.

The professor was anxious to get back to Athens, to meet his colleagues who had come from England. He would lose no time getting back to Paros, to show his trophy to the visitors and watch their amazement. What a treasure, this giant prehistoric turtle! Hundreds of years old - and still alive!

When they arrived, he took the learned gentlemen straight away to the house of the boys who had found the rare specimen.

"Where is the turtle?" he asked them. "I've brought these distinguished scholars to see it."

The people in the house -- parents, grandparents, uncles and cousins -- looked at each other. Nobody spoke.

"Where is it? What happened?" Anxiety was in his voice. Something was amiss here.

"We ate it," one brave soul spoke up.

"You WHAT!?!" yelled the professor.

"We made turtle soup. It's everywhere -- he had some; she had some. Everyone in the village. It was a big turtle; we had a great feast, and it fed us all."

The Professor was in shock. His colleagues were angry, annoyed, and, of course, disappointed. They had come a long way, and at considerable expense of time and money.

"But it was one of a kind! That species was thought to be extinct millions of years ago. It was so big, it might have been a thousand years old! How could you?"

"We were hungry!"

Nonplused, the frustrated educator sputtered "But I told you I would pay you a lot of money for it! It was a scientific treasure!" He seemed near tears. "What did you do with the shell?"

"We made combs for ladies' hair, tortoise shell boxes, gifts to sell in Athens to visitors. We will make a lot of money there." The boys brought out boxes of tortoise shell trinkets. "It has been a great boon to us. Have some...."

The professor broke down and wept.

Geordie decided that it was time to head back to America. When Prof. Chivington and his disappointed friends (he hoped they were still friends) returned to Athens, Geordie told them his decision.

Privately, the professor questioned him.

"I say, Geordie, I don't mean to pry, but I've been puzzled about something. I know that you've worked passage on board ship, but how have you managed the rest of the trip? I have heard that the people of the South, in the States, were quite impoverished after the war."

"Yes, that's true," Geordie replied. "The war left the South devastated. But our cotton, corn and vegetable crop did better than most, because we sang to the spirits of the plant kingdom, and they thrived. Also, the other planters lost most of their workers; the young strong ones went North with the Union Army. But most of ours stayed, or returned.

"There is something else I will tell you, in confidence, however. There is gold within the hills of the Traditional Cherokee mountain range, the Great Smokies. My father's cousin, Chief Zsa-lee, was in charge of distributing the gold from the Tribal Mine, according to the needs of the people, or to ones who were deserving.

"Some of this gold was given to my Cherokee grandfather, a wise leader among our people, and his Choctaw wife. He was of the Arkansas Keetoowah band. The Choctaw left the mountains behind and became water people, along the rivers and the ocean that border what is now the state of Mississippi.

"The gold given to my grandparents helped to buy our plantation. There was a little left, and I chose to spend it this way, to educate our daughter. We feel that she will make good use of the knowledge she has gained here, and pass it on in ways that will benefit those to come. We Native People always think of future generations.

"Wealth was given to some by Creator with the instruction that they be wise stewards of it, caring for those who have little. It is not money, but the love of money -- greed -- that is the root of evil. The Cherokee gold was administered wisely and well by Chief Zsa-lee... but he was killed, at the time of the Trail of Tears, by a rival Chief, who wanted control.

"Zsa-lee's son, who was still a boy, wanted to avenge his father. He had seen who the murderers were, and his anger and anguish were great. But the dying Chief said 'No, you must live, my son! We are people of the stars, and the knowledge, the Spirit-connection, must continue, for the sake of those yet un-born... for they will need this wisdom in the coming times.

The blood-line, the Spirit of the Ancestors, must live. Our Song must not die, for it contains the directions back to our home among the stars.'

"The history of our People might have been quite different had he not been killed at that time. Zsa-lee had sent an envoy to England to obtain an official document of a Land-Grant that had been issued by the King of England in the 1600s, guaranteeing the Cherokee People one million acres of rich land in the Southeast, with mountains, woodlands, and streams, where they had dwelt for centuries. It was to be a Sovereign Nation.

"President Jackson knew about the Grant, and was waiting for its arrival; he had vowed to honor it. But when he heard that Zsa-lee had been killed by his own people, in his anger Jackson said 'They ARE savages!', and he bowed to the pressure of his colleagues and ordered their removal from their homelands... even though a Cherokee had once saved his life, in the war with the English.

"The man who ordered Zsa-lee killed did not escape the relocation march to Oklahoma. He lost his big pillared house, warehouses, riverboats, trading posts... and he lost his wife, along the Trail of Tears. And one day the truth will be known."

Geordie was pensive. The professor was enthralled; this was history first-hand, and a good example of how it can be changed, according to who does the telling.

"I would love to go to Egypt," said Geordie, "where the Master was initiated into the Great Mysteries, the Cosmic Wisdom, in the Great Pyramid at Giza. I would love to go to Israel, to walk where He walked, doing

His healing and His teachings of LOVE for all Beings: that we are all brothers and sisters, children of One Father who dwells in the heavens.

"But the money has dwindled, and it is time to return to our homeland. Time for our daughter to learn from the wise Elders of her own people, who have been Stewards of that land for thousands of years, and to gain the knowledge of those who came from beyond this planet: The Ancestors."

Geordie arranged for another boat trip. It was hard for Sara to say 'Goodbye' to Greece, where she had been treated so royally; and to Prof. Chivington, who had become such a good friend. But he promised to visit them in America someday, and there would always be another adventure to look forward to. They would be going around Italy and Sicily, and then on to Malaga, on the Southern coast of Spain.

"Will we get to go to Sorrento, Papa? The place of the beautiful song?"

"Perhaps, Little One. You should speak to the Captain. It is a Greek ship we're taking, and the Greeks obviously adore you, so your wish may well be his command."

This proved to be true.

They would not dock at Sorrento, but would go close enough for her to see its white-washed houses draped with colorful flowers, to see its steep, narrow streets and hear the music pouring from its romantic soul.

Malaga, by contrast, was a large bustling port city. Ships from many foreign lands were being loaded or unloaded at the docks. Some of the tall buildings were new, others had been there for centuries. It lacked the charm of the smaller Mediterranean seaside villages, but to Sara's delight, it was a time of fiesta when they arrived.

"La FERRIA de MALAGA," proclaimed a poster, which told when and where the fair was to be held. After finding a room with a lovely little patio and stopping at one of the outdoor cafes that lined the avenue, the trio headed for the fair grounds.

It wasn't hard to find: Just follow the ponies or burros being ridden by a young man dressed in black, with a colorful, be-ruffled senorita astride behind him.

Casetas -- booths -- lined the walk-ways, and people in them were selling their wares. There were earthenware dishes with painted designs on them, embroidered and fringed silk shawls from the Philippines, and fans from China. Food-booths were serving seafood paella, gazpacho (cold tomato & cucumber soup) and other delectable foods. But what drew our traveling visitors from America the most were the sounds of music: Flamenco!

"The Gypsies are the best dancers, and the most lively and colorful," Geordie explained. There were others doing the regional dances of Spain,

Sara loved watching the Flamenco dancers in the Plaza.
The girl with the pitcher is going to the fountain to get water.

but the dramatic presentations of the Gypsies seemed most exciting.

The guitarists thumped, strummed, and plucked out the rhythms, some rapid, others melodious, as the male dancers accompanied them with the staccato stamping of their high heeled boots. They were tall and proud in their flat-brimmed hats, bolero jackets, cummerbunds and slender pants. Their movements were deliberate and powerful.

The women were a wonder to watch! An intricately-carved high tortoise-shell comb would frame a rose atop a young woman's head, with her long hair falling down to her waist. The dresses were fitted at the torso, with the neckline of the bodice decorated with long fringe, and ruffles at the sleeves. There were tiers of large ruffles flouncing their full skirts.

"Those girls must be sad," Geordie whispered to Sara.

"Why, Papa?" she inquired, puzzled.

"Look at their skirts! They're in tiers!" he chuckled.

"Oh, DADDY!" She felt it obligatory to reproach him now and then for his silliness.

Sara was enchanted by the beautiful dancers. Castanets in the left hand clicked out a strong beat. This was the masculine voice. With the right hand, swift fingers created a rapid trilling rhythm, and a higher sound: The female voice, responding with its feminine chatter. The young ladies twirled their skirts as they tapped their heels, and the cheerful 'Alegria' set Sara's feet to moving too.

At other booths at the fair, Sara persuaded her parents to buy a silk shawl for her, a flower and comb for her hair, and a folding fan. Her white skirt was full and ruffled, and with her black shoes with the strap across the foot, she now felt more appropriately dressed. She then went back to watch her favorite Gypsy dance troupe.

"Hola, chica!" a handsome dancer greeted her.

"Guapa!" Beautiful! said another.

One of the women dancers spoke to her.

"Quiere bailar con nosotros?" she inquired, inviting Sara to join them in the dance. They were amused by this little visitor who liked to dress up.

"Con mucho placer," she replied, with pleasure; having learned the basics in Spanish from her father. She had watched the dancers enough to get the feel of it, and with her natural ability for observation and movement, she danced with confidence.

Sara's heels clicked in quick taps, as the guitarists began to play, strumming with intensity. There were two men singing, and a male and two female dancers, who also clapped a staccato beat. Her shawl tied at the front, Sara began her dance with her fan spread out to hide her face, except for the eyes. With a flourish, she tossed the fan to her father. Her right arm went upward in a graceful arc, and her left arm curved outward in front of her, hands and fingers curled in proper position.

She did a quick high kick with one leg, then the other, toe pointed. With one arm still up and the other now on one hip, she twirled and twirled, in a circle. She picked up her skirt a bit in front and whirled some more, finishing by clapping and stamping to the beat of the instruments.

"O-LAY!" cried the delighted host troupe, as well as the rest of the audience that had gathered. "Ole!"

"Una Gitana, claro!" declared the Gypsies.

She agreed. "I must have been a Gypsy in another life," she said to her father, who translated.

"Ay! Que no!" But of course! They, who were not easily impressed, were charmed and delighted by this Free Spirit.

It was hard to leave Spain. Sara had found another family.

Chapter 17

Home Again!

The Greek boat took the Gillespies as far as Gibraltar, and from there Geordie would seek passage on another ship back to America. Although attached to Spain by a narrow spit of land, this amazing rock formation that jutted out of the ocean had been taken over as a fortress by England's invincible Navy, in their effort to control the seas. This was the gateway to the Mediterranean, and through the Suez Canal -- which Sara's brother Dave had helped to build -- the fleet thence went on to India and other parts of the British Empire.

Sara delighted in their dolphin escort, as they approached Gibraltar, and she also got a glimpse of Africa before they docked. She had touched that continent when their boat had made a stop in Alexandria, in Egypt, and Sara had wept when she heard that the great library there had been destroyed.

"That incredible storehouse of knowledge!" she sobbed. "I was a scribe, an archivist. I helped assemble that library!"

In Gibraltar, she explored the steep cobblestone streets lined with stucco buildings. English was heard here, but also Spanish, Arabic and French, in the bazaars and little shops along the narrow streets that climbed steep hillsides. Moroccans were selling brass pots and trays, and leather bags and shoes, all with intricate designs etched into them. In other stalls there were Spanish shawls and caftans, and clay dinnerware and lacquer boxes from the China trade.

Geordie, Little Dove and Sara went to a cafe which was frequented by sea captains, so that Geordie could negotiate their passage back to the States. They were served by a beautiful Black girl. Sara thought her to be only a little older than she was.

"Are you from Africa?" Sara asked her.

"I am," she replied. "My father was a great Chief of the Yoruba tribe."

On the fortress rock of Gibraltar, British, Spaniards, Africans and Arabs worked or shopped in the bazaars. Sakina found the Egyptian couple in white galabea and blue dress in Cairo Egypt. In Sakina's world, the Arabs and Jews (in front) get along fine. Blue Star Collection.

An Arab man appeared at the doorway of the kitchen. "Latisha!" he said angrily. "Come! You are not to speak to the customers!"

Sara was disturbed. Usually one with a hearty appetite, she could not eat her breakfast. She felt the girl's quiet pain, the man's cruel nature.

Little Dove was also affected. She too had been the daughter of a great Chief, and captured by the enemy who had killed and violated her people. Their hearts went out to this girl of dark beauty. They knew that she was a slave.

When they left the restaurant, Sara did not speak for hours, which was unusual for her. She could not get the African girl out of her mind.

The three of them sat in a park, overlooking the ocean stretching to the horizon.

"The Atlantic, kitten! Soon we'll be crossing it to go back home!" Geordie said to Sara.

She could contain herself no longer.

"Oh, Daddy -- can't we take her with us? Latisha? She's so miserable here! Her eyes are haunting me; her spirit speaks to me, and cries for help!"

Sara was drawn to the beautiful slave girl Latisha.

Geordie was pensive. "I understand your feelings, but this is a delicate matter. This is not our country. The girl may be being held against her will, but the man at the restaurant will be very angry if we take her away. He may have powerful friends. It could be very dangerous."

He looked at his daughter's face. She knew about karma, and that people choose their lessons. Still, if she was hearing a cry for help, he thought -- perhaps they should do something.

"I will look into it. I will ask around, and see what the situation is."

Little Dove smiled at Sara, and squeezed her hand. "It is good to care about others, my daughter," she said. "I will pray on this. I will speak to the Ancestors. Perhaps the girl's spirit is calling out to your spirit."

Geordie talked to the people at the docks, asking about things in general. The sailors knew what was going on in the world. The British Navy had put a stop to the lucrative slave trade, and slavery had been outlawed in the United States. But it was still going on in some places.

"Arab slavers are still raiding villages in West Africa," a sailor told him. "They take captives and bring them to ports or cities and sell them on the black market. Nasty business! A lot of shops and rest'rants use this free labor. They're not treated well at all, and some are beaten and badly used. Young girls especially."

Little Dove, after seeking her vision, reported to her husband. "This girl's soul-choice is to go with us. Do we have any of the Yoruba Nation at the homestead?"

"I believe so. Old Mandy is of that tribe; she was brought over as a young woman -- and has taught her language and some of their history and ways to her daughters."

"Then it is settled. Sara will have another sister."

Geordie observed, from a distance, the routine followed by Latisha. In the morning she would empty the chamber pots out back; at noon and late at night, before retiring to a little store-room at the back of the restaurant, she would empty garbage into the ditch behind the café. The rest of the time she would be washing dishes and scrubbing greasy pots in the sweltering kitchen. She was no longer allowed to come into contact with the patrons.

On the night before their ship was to leave for America in an early morning departure, Geordie went to the alley where Latisha would be emptying the refuse. It was dark in the alley, with only a tiny bit of light coming from the small kitchen window.

Geordie saw the dim outline of the African girl as she emptied the large, heavy pot, and heard its contents slosh into the open trench. She set the pot down for a moment, and put her hands on her aching lower back. She heaved a sigh, raised her hands upward and looked to the sky, saying a prayer to the Creator in her native tongue, imploring His help.

She lowered her arms and looked down at the big pot. Before she could bend over and pick it up, she felt strong arms grab her from behind. A man's hand was over her mouth, and she was being wrapped in a long woolen cloak. PANIC! Her body stiffened; her heart thumped like the beat of a huge drum. Not again, she thought! This is what had happened to her before, in Africa!

Her captor held her for a moment, and then removed his hand from her mouth. He had been afraid she might let out a sound, being startled. But why should she scream? Who would help a slave-girl? Still, she was someone's property, and she was being stolen. Both police and ruffians frowned on that.

240

The man wrapped a rope around his bundle, and threw her over his shoulder like a sack of grain. He crept stealthily down the alleyway and along the dark streets, lit only now and then by the light coming from someone's window. He slipped into the rear service entrance of the little hotel he was staying in, and carried his captive up the four flights of stairs, avoiding the lobby and its rattling cage of an elevator.

Quietly he entered his room, and placed the bundle on a pile of tasseled cushions that had been taken from the day-bed where a girl was sleeping.

"Oh, thank God!" Little Dove said in hushed tones as they tenderly unwrapped the trembling girl. "I hope no-one saw you!"

"I'm not sure," Geordie replied. "I have an uneasy feeling."

Little Dove sat beside the amazed girl, who was wide-eyed and still in shock.

The Lakota woman held the African girl in her arms, and sang to her softly. Sara slept soundly on the day-bed, which was next to the French doors that opened onto a little balcony. Despite the warmth of the night, the doors were now closed to the sounds of the town and to shut out prying eyes.

"I am so, so sorry that we had to take you in this way!" Little Dove told Latisha. "I, too, was captured in this way, when I was a girl living among the Native People of my land. We call it Turtle Island, others call it America. We are going to take you there."

Latisha was without words. Tears coursed down her face, making little rivulets in the dust there. Finally she said:

"He has heard my prayer. He has heard me!" At last, she was able to smile. "You have shown me great kindness. I will serve you well! I will do anything you ask of me – but with joy, instead of sorrow, in my heart."

"Oh, no, dear child," said her benefactor, her mother's-heart full of compassion. "You will not have to work for us -- you will work for yourself. There are others of African heritage who live on our property, and they will welcome you into our family. The American South is not always an easy place to live, but I think it will be better than this."

"I am most certainly positive that it will be, madam," the girl said. She spoke with a rather English accent, picked up from the customers she had served.

"I am Little Dove. When White People are around, you will need to call me Miz Gillespie, or ma'am. It is a game we play. But you are my daughter; Sara is your sister. It was she who said that we must take you with us."

Latisha looked over at the sleeping girl on the couch. "I owe you my life, dear friend," she said.

"You must be tired. We should all get some sleep. I hope these cushions will be comfortable."

"They are luxury extraordinaire, compared to my former lodgings," replied the Yoruba Princess. "I wish you good dreams. You have given my heart immeasurable joy."

Little Dove put a sheet over Latisha, and got into the carved rosewood double bed next to her husband, who had drifted off to sleep. She turned down the wick on the oil lamp next to the bed, and the room was in darkness.

Suddenly there was a knocking on the door! Not loud, but rapid and insistent. Instantly Geordie was on his feet, and groping for the door. "Who is there?" he whispered.

"Please, Effendi, I must speak to you! You are all in great danger!"

Geordie's instinct told him to open the door, and he found the bolt and opened it. A young Black boy of about 16 slipped inside. Little Dove opened the doors to the balcony, to let in some light, and was about to light a lamp when the boy said "NO! No light, they will see us!"

"Who are you?" Geordie asked.

"I am a boy of the streets. It is my business to watch what is going on; people pay me for information. I saw you come out of the alley behind Mamoud's place... and I thought perhaps you had stolen a lamb, or a sack of rice. So I went to the back door of the cafe to speak to Latisha; but she was gone! Mamoud almost caught me there, but I got away.

"He came to see Latisha, in her little room, as he often does, when his wife is not interested. When she was not there, he flew into a rage! He is not a good enemy to have. He asked around, and someone else saw you carrying something into this hotel. He went to get his friends -- and the police. They will put you in jail -- or KILL you!"

"Why did you come to warn me?"

"Latisha has been kind to me. She would give me food at night, when no-one was looking. She is my Princess."

242

There was a great commotion downstairs. They heard the sound of men rushing into the lobby of the hotel.

"I must go. Allah be with you." And the boy was gone.

Where to hide the girl? The men below were charging up the stairs; Geordie couldn't chance taking her out into the hall and up to the roof two flights above.

BANG! BANG! BANG! The ones knocking on the door now were angry and insistent. The room's occupants could feel the furious energy of those on the other side of it.

"What is it, Mama?" said a sleepy Sara.

"I don't know, dear," her mother replied.

"OPEN UP!" yelled an angry voice.

"What is it?" Little Dove inquired. "Is there a fire?"

"No, no; this is the Police! Open the door! Immediately!"

"Oh, dear! What's wrong?"

"OPEN THE DOOR! Or we'll break it down!"

"Of course. Just a moment, I have to light a lamp. So I can find the door,"

"NOW."

"Yes, yes. All right, I've got it. I'm coming." Little Dove opened the door. The Arab men, and a British Bobby, came bursting in, holding a lantern aloft, looking around. The Arabs were wearing swords and daggers.

"You've wakened my daughter, and my husband. I hope this is important." Sara rubbed her eyes, and squinted at them.

Geordie turned over, sat up, pulled back the covers, and blinked at the intruders. 'What's the problem, Officer?"

"So sorry to disturb you, sir! But these gentlemen say that there's been a kidnapping. And someone said they saw you coming into this hotel carrying a large sack, at approximately the same time as it was discovered that the girl was gone. These men thought that the sack might have contained the missing girl." (Gentlemen, he called them, thought Geordie. Cut-throats, more likely.)

The four Arab men accompanying him were looking everywhere. In closets, under beds; out on the balcony, including behind the doors. "I don't suppose a search warrant is required, here on Gib." Gib, pronounced "jib", was short for Gibraltar.

"No, Sir. But they are required to have at policeman along, if they enter someone's quarters."

"Well, they're welcome to have a look, now that they've got us all waked up, but they certainly won't find anyone here but us three. Who is this girl you're looking for?"

"She works in a Café, for Mr. Mamoud here."

"She is your servant, Mamoud?" Geordie inquired.

"She is like a daughter to me."

"Ah! I understand your concern." Right, thought Geordie. Incest begins at home.

Mamoud's eyes narrowed. "I believe you are the ones who were talking to Latisha in my restaurant the other day."

"Your restaurant? Ah, yes! I remember. You told her not to talk to the customers."

"Yesss... You do remember. Well, I will find the one who took my servant girl. And he will wish for a quick death, which will not come; it will be slo-o-ow!" he said with a menacing tone, while stroking the large dagger that was tucked into the belt of his long galabea.

Geordie smiled, condescendingly. "I have no need of more servants, Mr. Mamoud. I have a large plantation in America, with many workers -- who used to be slaves. My property fared better than others in the South, because I have sailed the seas on the great clipper ships, over the years, and had many foreign markets for my cotton and produce, and my crops escaped much of the devastation. But as you say that you care for this girl as a daughter, I wish you well in your search."

Mamoud continued to glower, but the British policeman became effusive and apologetic, sensing that he had offended someone of influence and importance. Such people had a certain way about them.

"Oh, I'm so sorry, sir! About this untimely intrusion into your privacy. I fear that a dreadful mistake has been made." "Quite all right, Officer," said Geordie, magnanimously. "Always happy to help clear up misunderstandings."

It was at that point that one of the Arabs whispered to Mamoud, pointing to a duffle bag standing in the corner, partially hidden by the bed and valises. Mamoud strode over to it before anyone could stop him.

"Ah-HA!" he exclaimed triumphantly. "What have we here?" Geordie shook his head, and cleared his throat. "Must you?" he said. "Please don't...."

"What are you hiding?"

"I'm afraid you've caught me. I thought I'd get away with it."

After his assistants pulled the suitcases out from in front of it, Mamoud picked up the canvas sea-bag and held it upside-down over the bed and shook it. Out came the bundle:

A long black wool cape with a purple flannel lining and a tasseled hood, a blue silk caftan, and an embroidered Spanish shawl. The onlookers were stunned.

"The cape, and the caftan, are a gift for my wife. She wanted something to keep out the chill winds on the Atlantic, and something comfortable to sleep in. The shawl is for my dear daughter. You've gone and spoiled the surprise."

This statement was followed by mumbling on the part of the Arab contingent, and more profuse apologies from the officer. They couldn't get out of there fast enough.

The adult conspirators could not repress a smile. Sara, oh the other hand, didn't find it amusing.

"Will you please tell me what is going on?" she demanded.

"Oh, yes, of course," said Little Dove. "What happened to the girl, Long Bow? I was so proud of you, my Warrior Chief, for that magnificent coup, that I almost forgot about the captive princess! How did you manage to hide her?"

"Magic!" Geordie replied with a smile, enjoying the moment. He had definitely earned himself an eagle feather for this feat. Perhaps a bonnet-full.

He led his family out onto the balcony. They looked all around. The balconies to the right and left were too far away to be reached, and it was four flights to the ground.

"Where?" "How?" the womenfolk wondered.

"How many directions are there?" he asked.

"Six!" said Sara. "Seven!" said Little Dove.

"Try the sixth."

They looked up. "The Sky Father!"

Geordie climbed up onto the railing of their balcony, and grabbed hold of the one above. He pulled himself up and swung himself over the wrought-iron railing, scooped up the girl, who was limp, but was able to wrap her arms around his neck and her legs around his waist as he lowered himself back down.

"Oh!" said Sara. "Latisha! Dear Latisha... I'm so glad that we got you!" Sara gave her a hug, and the rescued girl managed to give a smile in return.

"We're not out of the woods yet, little ones," Geordie cautioned. "But we'll make it."

"Tonkashila is watching over us. We have many Guardians who are protecting us. I have asked the Ancestors for help, and they will respond," said Little Dove.

"The Ancestors? You sound like my Grandmother!" said Latisha, a glimmer of hope beginning to return as they sat in the darkened room.

Geordie went downstairs in the elevator.

The Night Clerk was dozing behind the marble-top counter where guests would register, and an Arab young man was mopping the floor around the Victorian velvet settee and chairs and the potted palms. Geordie went over and nudged the sleeping clerk, who jumped to attention.

"Salaam Alaikum!" he said bowing. "I - I mean, Good Evening, sir."

"Alaikum Salaam," Geordie replied in the traditional Arabic greeting. "I can't seem to get much sleep. There was such a ruckus in my room tonight. Do you know what that was all about'?"

"Oh, indeed -- a most unfortunate misunderstanding, sir. Someone saw you going in through the back way, which is only used by servants, with a large sack -- and they became suspicious."

"Ah. Of course. I had a surprise for my wife, and I did not want to encounter her in the lobby, so I used the rear entrance. My little plot didn't work, however; those people quite exposed it!"

It was 2 a.m. by now, and the call for prayer sounded from the mosque next to the hotel. (Down the street, there was a Church of England chapel for the British residents.)

The man who had been cleaning up unrolled his prayer rug and kneeled down upon it in the middle of the lobby floor. The Faithful bow low, with their head to the ground, when the call is sounded. Facing east, to Mecca, they pray to Allah.

246

Geordie knew that although some Arabic men would do almost anything for baksheesh (money), the ones with a scab on their foreheads were totally to be trusted; these were spiritual beings, devout Moslems; tellers of truth, who spent much of their life on their prayer rugs, their forehead rubbing the carpet. He decided to talk to this one. He asked him to come outside, and sit in the fresh air, in the garden.

"Do you know this girl that was being searched for?"

"I do, Sir. Everybody knows Latisha; it is a small island. I also know Mamoud. He is not a kind man."

"Do you believe that it is right for one person to own another? Is this the teaching of Allah?"

"Mohammed, the messenger of Allah, did not teach this. He taught that all are brothers. But as in all countries, some do not follow the True Teachings."

"You speak well. I need help, and I will trust that you will do that which is right, that which is for the highest good of all concerned," Geordie said.

"I know what you are asking. I have prayed about this. I have seen the marks on this girl from his beatings. I have seen the pain in her eyes because he has forced himself upon her. She spoke to me quietly once, when he was away. She was terrified that she would have his child. She would love a child, of course -- but she was afraid that somehow his cruel nature would be passed on in the blood. She has seen this happen. And because she is a slave, her little one could be taken away from her, and sold.

"I am Yusef," the Arab man continued. "I will help you. They will be watching you carefully, of course, and will check your trunks. So we must devise a plan that will elude them somehow..." Yusef was pensive.

"You will be contacted by a sailor when you are safely at sea, and, if we are successful, you will be re-united when you are aboard ship. Allah be praised."

"Thank you, Creator," Geordie said softly, looking up at the starry sky. "And thank you Yusef. I am grateful."

"It is you who are the brave one," he replied. "We who care are pleased that Latisha has been rescued. I will get word to the people in her village in Africa that she is safe, that she is honored. Go in peace."

The plan was explained to those waiting anxiously in the room. At 5 a.m. the girl was put into a barrel with some trash put lightly on top of her, and the container was taken downstairs and placed into a cart which would take it down to the docks. There it was to be loaded onto the ship, and put into the hold. Hopefully Mamoud's men would search only their luggage, and overlook the barrel.

On the way to the port, the cart was stopped behind a vegetable market, and the trash was replaced with olives. A false bottom, which was near the top, was put in, so that if someone looked into it, it would look like a shipment of olives. Geordie had inserted a tube into a knot-hole in the barrel, so that Latisha could breathe through it. "It's an old Apache trick," he explained, "Burying yourself in the sand, and then breathing through a reed. They disappeared that way -- drove the Army crazy!"

Geordie and his wife and daughter took a carriage down to the waterfront, winding down the steep streets of the Rock of Gibraltar. Even in the half light of the pre-dawn morning, the view of the ocean was spectacular. When they reached dockside their luggage was unloaded near the warehouse buildings, and they walked on over to the gangplank of the ship to speak to the First Officer.

With his peripheral vision, Geordie noticed some shadowy figures lurking close to the luggage in the warehouses -- near their trunks and sea-chest. Good; they would see that there was no stow-away in them. Geordie was about to board the ship, when he looked around for Sara -- and saw the suspicious men heading toward THE barrel.

Uh-oh! What if she coughed, and gave herself away? Geordie thought. Time for a diversionary action. He pulled a small, square package out of his pocket. "Look, Sara," he said, striking a flame with his flint, and holding it next to some string coming out of the packet, creating sparks, and then heaving the packet in an arc in the general direction of the barrel.

Suddenly there was a loud series of cracks: BANG—BANG—BANG—BANG---BANG! Everybody in the area ran for cover; they thought they were being shot at!

Geordie walked over to where the merchandise was that was waiting to be loaded onto the ship, and apologized to the stevedores, who were emerging from their hiding places.

"Sorry, lads! That was a surprise I got for my daughter, from a sailor returning from the Orient. I guess it surprised us all! Thought I'd try them out -- but didn't know it would make such a ruckus. Such a loud noise! The Chinese use them for celebrations. They're called 'fire-crackers.'"

Geordie walked over to the Very Special Barrel, turned it on its side, and began to roll it over to the loading dock.

"Here, I'll give you a hand, to make up for the fright I gave you. I'm an old hand at this." The lurking men had disappeared at the sound of what was very much like gun-shot. Geordie watched the 'olive barrel' being taken aboard the vessel that was to take them home.

It was a few days before the stow-away was brought up to the Gillespie cabin. The sailors had wanted to make sure there was no danger lurking, before sneaking her up.

To Sara, it was an exciting drama -- and she was always up for another adventure!

The girls spent most of their time in the cabin on the voyage across the sea. They didn't want any talk going around that might get back to Gibraltar, leading to the recapture of Sara's new sister Latisha.

The Ship's Captain had a very fine library in his quarters with books dealing with the cultures, peoples and landscape of the many countries he had been to on his journeys around the world. He was kind enough to lend them to Sara when he learned of her great interest in these places, and she delighted in poring over the pictures. She took them back to the cabin and shared them with Latisha, whom she taught how to read. She was a good teacher, with an excellent student.

Two days off of the coast of Bermuda, their mid-way stop, a fierce gale blew up. "All hands on deck! All hands on deck!" the cry went out. Geordie was busy furling sail on the swift clipper-ship, and some of the passengers were busy getting sea-sick. Sara was a seasoned sailor.

Little Dove and Sara had been invited to come up, at any time, to the quarter-deck, high and aft, which was reserved for officers. It was a wonderful place, they decided, to go and watch the storm. The officers were occupied elsewhere, so the mother and daughter had the place to themselves.

The storm was exciting.

"Look, Mama! The Thunder Gods are speaking to us! They are welcoming us back, we who once dwelt in Elohi Mona. And our dear Atlantis lies now below us, beneath the waves."

"You are right, Child of my Heart. The Thunder God sends his bolt of energy to the Earth Mother, making love to her; his great light striking into her body, energizing her, renewing her.

"It is thrilling! Or he makes love to the Sea Goddess. It is powerful, awesome, magnificent love-making!"

Sara and her mother laughed and danced around the partly glass-walled room, enjoying the gusts blowing through the windows. On impulse, Little Dove took the hairpins out of her hair and let the Wind Spirits play with her long tresses. She loved the sense of freedom! It was like when she was a child.

"I get so tired of having to act like a Proper Lady. It is a role that is important I know, due to the circumstances, but it is not one that I enjoy. "

The two of them laughed and laughed, in the howling gale. "Laughter is good for the soul," said Sara.

They watched the great waves rise and curl, as the ship rose to the high peaks and then pitched in the valleys. "They are rocking us, Mother! They are singing us a lullaby." It was a violent lullaby, and an exciting one.

"It is interesting," Sara mused, "that the French word for Mother, 'Mere', is basically the same as the word for Ocean, 'Mer'. Some say that we all came from the sea, in the beginning. But of course many of us also came from the stars!"

The storm eventually abated, and Sara appraised the situation: "Poseidon has had his little fun, or had his tantrum, and now he is settling down."

The ship put into port at Bermuda. "The far Bermooths, as Shakespeare called these isles, in The Tempest -- which was set here," Sara-the-Scholar informed them. The pink color of the charming little houses was due to the coral which was put into the stucco of the exterior walls; the roofs were white, and 'stair-step' shaped. Water was precious. It came only from the sky, and was carefully collected in pots and cisterns. But their ship was able to take on some fruit, brought there by other ships from the Caribbean islands.

After leaving port, a few days out they had an experience opposite to the one they'd had on the other side of Bermuda. The ship was becalmed;

not a breath of air stirring, not an inch of movement. Sara overheard some of the sailors talking on the after-deck.

"In the old days," said one, "there were some strange tales told about the Sargasso Sea, where ships would sit motionless for days -- or simply disappear. So many of them vanished, in this great triangle near Bermuda, that vessels just stopped sailing this way. It was thought that they had gone out and dropped off the edge of the world! Until that Columbus fellow went and got foolhardy enough to cross the ocean looking for riches from the Indies."

"Well," said another sailor, "I've got some Norse blood in me, and I'll tell you that some of my Viking forebears sailed to the north of North America -- a thousand years ago. We've got records that tell the tale of Eric-the-Red, landin' there then, long before the Pilgrims. We got there first!"

'Right,' thought Sara, though she dare not let them know that she'd been eaves dropping. 'You got there first! What about the Native Americans?? Who were already there?'

After a week of sitting still on a sea of glass in the sweltering heat, Geordie and Little Dove decided it was time to do something about it. In the dark of night, with only a little candle for light, they went up on deck, with Sara, Latisha and a crewman whose mother was of the Penobscot tribe in Maine.

"The candle will be our Sacred Torch," said Sara. The assembled group honored the Spirits of Fire, Earth, Air, and Water. They greeted the Keepers of the Four Directions, All Beings, the Winged Ones -- and especially the Ones That Swim in the Waters, and Mother Ocean. They spoke to the Cloud People, and the Wind Spirits. They sang to them. They sent them Light, and Love, and many Blessings. They offered Tobacco.

They began to notice something white in the inky blackness of the night sky. The Cloud People were coming. Little puffs of air would kiss Sara's cheek, and play with her hair. She laughed. "They're coming, Mama! They've heard us."

"Of course, Dear. They see your Light, and your pure heart. They are happy to help, if they are asked. Sometimes we forget to ask." Soon the sails were filling, and they were on their way again.

The rest of the ocean crossing was relatively uneventful. Sara was disappointed not to see any dolphins or whales, but it was the wrong time and place for them. They did see lots of sea birds, some sharks, and some other interesting fish. Sara went back to her books.

And then she heard it: "LAND HO-O-O!"-- and she came running up to the deck to see it.

"LOOK! Look, Mama, look! Papa! Look who's greeting us! It's a colossal Goddess, rising up out of the sea! Athena -- with rays of light coming out from her head. With her long robes, holding the Book of Knowledge and Wisdom, and holding aloft -- the Sacred Torch of the Tsalagi People! Oh, what a wonder to behold,.. What a welcome home!"

Geordie smiled, enjoying the enthusiasm of his sophisticated daughter. "I am told she is called Lady Liberty, extolling the virtues of freedom for all peoples, welcoming them to our land. She is a gift from the people of France, in thanks for inspiring their Revolution, by our bid for freedom and independence. They, too, chose to rid themselves of tyranny."

Sara was also impressed by the city beyond the statue. Like the English, the New Yorkers did not seem as bad as they had seemed from the stories she had heard about them. After all, these were Damn Yankees!

Their ship was in port only long enough to unload, and pick up some cargo and passengers, before going on around to New Orleans. That city was a source of great amazement to Latisha, who was finally able to emerge into the open. She stuck very close to Sara, and Geordie and Little Dove were very protective of her.

They took a riverboat called 'The Mississippi Queen` up toward their homestead, continuing by carriage for the last lap. Sara pointed out the Grecian-style homes along the way, telling Latisha what they were called and who lived in them. She had been told this information only once, but she had a very retentive memory.

Their home-coming was warm and wonderful, with everyone crowding around to hear their stories -- which went on long into the night, and for many nights thereafter.

Because they had been gone so long, the animosity they had begun to feel from some tradesmen and neighbors before they left on their trip seemed to have dissipated. These people had either forgotten or chosen to ignore rumors of tainted blood. The Gillespies had always been friendly and helpful to everyone, after all. They made good neighbors.

Sara refused to go back to school, however. She told Miss Emaline that she was going to continue to travel, this time in her own homeland, and would learn from her Elders the ways of their People. She would also keep reading whatever she could get her hands on. Emaline said that she would tutor Sara, and lend her books, so that she could keep up with the school requirements and pass the tests. In return, Sara would share her knowledge of Greek, and of the ancient world. Miss Emaline was fascinated by it.

Latisha was welcomed into the family, especially by those of African heritage -- who were delighted to have someone in their midst who still had knowledge of the old ways, and knew what was going on back in the Mother Country of Africa. At one of the Family Council Circles, a Cherokee Elder said that she would look into her big crystal to see what the future held for this girl.

"You will have two sons, and two daughters. All will have a great love for music; you will pass this on to them. They will sing in the fields and in the churches, blending their voices in beautiful harmony. They will be happy children!

"They will play African instruments that you will teach them to make: The drum, the kalimba, and the banjo. A son of the people in the Big House on this plantation will fall in love with you, and help produce these children.

"Your grandson will play another instrument also; he will blow a horn. The music will be a mixture of African and other influences of this country. It will be called 'Jazz'.

"Your grandson will bring joy to people all over the world, with his music. This Gillespie boy, because he is so happy, and likes to fool around: He will be called, "Dizzy.""

Chapter 18

Sitting Bull

The Gillespies journeyed to the land of Little Dove's youth, and paid a visit to her cousin Chief Tatanka Yotanka.

"Living in harmony with Mother Earth... Staying connected with Spirit, with Creator. Standing for your Truth; teaching by example. Being kind, loving. These are the important things," the Elders taught.

"And forgiveness," added a Grandmother. "If resentments are harbored they can fester, they can cause illness in the body and the mind. Never criticize another until you have walked a thousand miles in his moccasins."

Chief SITTING BULL
portrait by Rev. Stan Matrunick.

Sara loved to listen to the wisdom of the Elders, as they sat in a little clearing in the woods, or down by the river. Often they would gather roots, bark, or berries, and she would learn the medicinal properties of various plants and when the optimum time was to gather them. Foxglove was good to heal the heart, she was told. (Later its decoction would be called digitalis.)

How much nicer this way of learning was, she thought, than sitting in a classroom "paying attention" to dry facts and figures that seemed to have little to do with one's life. Out in nature, she talked to the plants and the creatures themselves. They learned from each other; there was an exchange.

Little Dove felt a longing to go home again, to revisit the sights of her childhood. The rolling plains, where her people had followed the trail of the bison; the Paha Sapa, or the Sacred Black Hills. And the magnificent Teton mountains that rose in strength and splendor, the sanctuary of her youth. She wanted to share these special places with her daughter, and with her husband.

Geordie prepared for their journey by making ready a surrey which was light enough to travel with ease and some speed along the roadways, as they intended to cover a lot of territory. The padded wagon seat could accommodate the three of them easily. Sara was eager to sit in front and see everything as they went along. Two seats in back were comfortable enough to sleep on if they got tired, and the vehicle was covered, and had curtains that could be rolled down in case of inclement weather.

The trunks holding several changes of clothing, for various occasions, were at the back. Geordie was a good outfitter, and knew which necessities to take along. He was a good camp cook, and Little Dove and Sara knew what kind of edibles could be gathered along the way.

Geordie picked out a bay and a roan to pull the rig, for stamina instead of speed or elegance. When all was ready, the ladies -- Sara was 13 now -- came out and inspected the carriage approvingly. "Wosh-TAY!" said Little Dove. "It is good: A tipi on wheels!" she laughed.

The Mississippi River flowed southward to the sea, and was easy to travel by boat in that direction, but to go north, they chose to take to the roads. It being the spring of the year when the trio set out, the roads were often muddy -- and the passengers would on occasion have to get out of the carriage and walk, or even push. Sometimes wagons or carriages would get stuck, and have to be pulled out by a strong team of work horses.

Geordie had been a guide along these roads years before, and although landmarks had changed over the years, he was able to find his way easily. The three of them also were in constant contact with their Spirit Guides, who were on the job as scouts along the way.

In this fashion they were sometimes led to encounter pockets of Native People dwelling in the forests or remote places from which they had not yet been removed, by treaty or treachery, warfare or disease. The Spir-

255

it Guardians would go ahead and make contact. White People could be fooled by the Gillespies' manner and mode of dress, but the Native peoples would recognize one of their own. They would look into the eyes of the visitors; they would communicate heart-to-heart.

In some places, the young warriors were still angry, and ready to fight to defend their homeland. Some of these were resentful of the strangers coming among them looking like the enemy. Geordie took to wearing buckskins again on these occasions, although he knew that it was generally safer to dress in his 'White clothes' for traveling. He needed to protect his family, but he preferred dressing in the old way.

The traveling family visited some green-eyed Osage, who pointed out the stars, or planets, that their ancestors had come from. The Gillespies loved joining in the nightly councils, exchanging stories, songs, and prophecies. A hard time was upon them, they knew, but in times to come Mother Earth would heal herself, and peace and harmony would reign once again.

Little Dove and Sara particularly loved the Ozarks, along the Arkansas-Missouri border. Long lakes meandered through steeply rising bluffs, and tall trees were in abundance in the hilly area. They stayed in a log cabin for a while, swam in the waters, and laughed a lot.

People of different tribes still fished in the waters and hunted in the forests there. Mountain People from other lands across the sea also lived there. They lived simply, worked hard and came together to sing the songs of the Old Country -- and to dance to the lively old tunes of the fiddler.

As the little family continued their journey, they stayed sometimes at small inns, people's homes, or camped out along the wayside in a tent Geordie had brought along. The Spirit Guardians protected them on their journey.

Westport Landing, later called Kansas City, had changed greatly since Geordie had taken his young bride through there several decades before. The frontier town where settlers and adventurers prepared to set out for the great West had turned into a thriving city beside the river called the 'Big Muddy', or Missouri. It became a destination for herds of cattle, driven there or brought by train to the rail-head, to be penned in large stockyards.

There were a number of soldiers in the city. Some were veterans of the Civil War; others were youngsters who had been too young for battle but who had lost friends or relatives and were eager to let out their anger. These men were preparing to go out to the plains and "kill those heathen savages, and make the West safe for God-fearin' Christian folks."

Geordie got a few provisions and chose to move on through the city as soon as possible. He did not want to expose his family to this kind of conversation, which he had overheard at the stable, while his wife and daughter were resting and refreshing themselves in an inn. Sara found the city exciting however, and prevailed upon her parents to see as much as possible of the shops, ice cream parlors, and tree-lined streets with their fine Victorian houses, with wrap-around porches, tipi-shaped turrets, and tree-shaded lawns.

"I want to get to the Dakotas before spring is over," Geordie said. "Maybe we'll get there in time for one of the intertribal rendezvous, if the Plains Tribes are still having them."

A pow-wow! thought Sara. That sounded even more exciting than this busy city. Their horses refreshed and renewed, they made good time in the days to follow, and covered a lot of territory, heading always northward.

Little Dove felt a bit of nostalgia as they approached the town where she had lived at the time of her marriage. She wondered if her adopted mother was still there; if indeed she were still living. It had been many years since Little Dove had gone off with her beloved Long Bow.

The town had grown so much as to be scarcely recognizable, but they headed for the older section of town and found that her old house was still there. Here the one then called Grace had lived when she was sixteen. The paint had faded, and the garden as well, but lace curtains still hung in the windows.

Little Dove sat and looked at the house for a few moments, remembering, before she got out of the surrey and went up to the door. She pulled the bell knob, and heard it ring inside. She waited.

A white-haired lady, small and frail, answered the door. "Ye-e-es?" she said, squinting through her spectacles. "May I help you?"

"Indeed I hope you can help me, Mrs. Gray. I seek shelter for my family. I have come a very long way to see you."

"I beg your pardon? Do I know you?"

"I expect that I have changed quite a bit since you took me into your home long ago. You called me Grace. I called you Mother."

"OH!" the older woman shrieked. "Oh, my stars! You give me a shock! Is it really you? My little Grace?"

"I told you that I would come back some day," said Little Dove, embracing the trembling woman. "Come, sit in your rocker, I'll fetch you some tea. And then I'll bring in my husband and our daughter, Sara. She's about the age I was when you rescued me. How much has changed since then!"

"Oh, yes, by all means, bring them in -- your family." Geordie and Sara came in, and Mrs. Gray exclaimed over what a lovely young lady the girl was. Sara was quiet and polite until she was asked something, and then she proceeded to astonish Mrs. Gray with her knowledge on any topic.

"Do please call me Grandmother, dear," Sara was told. This was not a problem; Sara was accustomed to calling the elders Grandmother or Grandfather, a Native term of respect.

It took a few days to catch up with the news of the many years that had passed. Mrs. Gray's husband had passed on some years before, after having been promoted to Colonel during the war. Mrs. Gray occupied herself with activities at the church, reading, crocheting, and visiting friends.

"And what of my People? The Teton Lakota? The Hunkpapa?" Little Dove asked.

Mrs. Gray looked at her in silence for a few minutes.

"I'm afraid things have not gone well for them, my dear. I hesitate to tell you."

"I understand. We hear some news from time to time."

"Of course you've heard of the battle they call Custer's Last Stand."

"Oh yes," said Little Dove. "A great victory!"

"Oh! My!" Mrs. Gray said, startled by that interpretation. "How differently people look at things, depending upon their point of view."

"I'm sorry; I forgot myself. Your husband was part of the Army that was defeated, that time. I apologize."

"Oh, it's all right, my dear. I have not forgotten the day that you told me the story of how your loved ones, your entire village, were killed by the Cavalry. I was so shocked that that nice young officer had been the one who had killed your mother! It made an indelible impression on my mind. I have spoken to others of the injustices suffered by Indians, and I believe I have made some difference in their thinking. But YOU were the best example I had to show them."

258

"I thank you for your kindness."

"Of course the battle at the Little Big Horn made a lot of people very angry," said Mrs. Gray, "and they wanted revenge. So they sent more armies out to get rid of the Indian threat. Because they knew gold was there, the government had tried to buy the Black Hills -- they even offered 6 million dollars for it -- but Chief Sitting Bull had refused to sell; he said it was a Holy place. After Custer's company was wiped out, though, they just took it. And forced the Sioux and other tribes onto reservations."

"Sitting Bull is my cousin," Little Dove told her. "He was a few years older than I was, but I remember him well. He was a thoughtful boy, but a happy one. He liked to laugh, and to sing songs that he made up. And even when I lived far away I heard that he was a great warrior, brave and fearless. A Holy Man, and a great leader of our people."

"Indeed he was," replied Emma Gray. "He was respected and admired by the Cheyenne, and other tribes, also. That's why they joined in the battle at the Little Big Horn. But there were a lot more battles after that, and the Indians were outgunned and far out-numbered, so the Cavalry won most of them, and forced the remaining Indians onto reservations.

"Chief Sitting Bull, however, refused to go to the reservation. His friend Crazy Horse did, and was killed. So Sitting Bull and some of his people went to Canada. But the winters were harsh, food became scarce, and the people were starving, so they began drifting back across the border. Many of his people went to the reservation, where at least they were given food.

"These are the stories I hear from the men who served with my husband. They come to call from time to time."

"And Sitting Bull? Is he still in Canada? Is he safe?" Emma looked down at her hands, in her lap. "Sitting Bull was persuaded to return to this country, to give himself up. Those loyal to him were cold and hungry. He thought he would be killed, I hear. But they took him to Fort Randall, here in the Dakotas. They kept him there as a prisoner of war, for two years. But now they've taken him to the Standing Rock Reservation, where his people are living."

Little Dove was pensive. "I would like to see him."

Her adopted mother sighed. "You may be in for quite a disappointment, dear," she said. "Still, if that is your wish, I will write a letter of introduction to Major McLaughlin, the commanding officer there, saying that you are my daughter who is visiting the area -- and that you would like to pay a call on him, as an old family friend. He and my husband served together in The War."

"I would be most appreciative!" Little Dove smiled, adding wistfully: "We were in the War Between the States, too -- but on the other side, I'm afraid, as that's where we were living. I helped to care for the wounded, and Geordie served with Col. Watie's Regiment."

Geordie entered the conversation at this point.

"Our eldest son, John, also served with the Confederate forces. He spoke to his commanding officer, Captain John Mallory, who was surprised to find that our John had been named after him, as he had been an old friend of mine -- and of your husband as well!"

"Mercy! Will wonders never cease," Mrs. Gray exclaimed.

Geordie explained that it was time for them to move on, but Emma Gray was able to prevail upon them to meet as many of her friends as possible. She was extremely proud of her family, and delighted to show them off. So genteel, with their lovely Southern manners. So intelligent, and well traveled! This was a high point of her life.

The Gillespie family said their farewells and made their way northward, through Cheyenne country, and Little Dove was amazed at the changes that had taken place since her people had roamed what had been the Plains in the time of her youth. Instead of vast open areas of tall grasses on the rolling hills, where the great herds of buffalo had roamed, there were fences and cabins where the homesteaders had staked their claims, and planted a few crops. There were small herds of cattle instead of great herds of buffalo, and roads with wagons and carriages had replaced the travois that had taken The People from one camp-site to the next. Towns had sprung up here and there.

The Gillespies journeyed to the land of Little Dove's youth, and paid a visit to her cousin Chief Tatanka Yotanka.

When the Gillespies arrived at Standing Rock Reservation -- so named because of a tall rock that resembled an Indian woman with a child on her back -- they presented themselves to James McLaughlin, giving Emma's letter to the Post Commander. He welcomed them warmly, provided them with comfortable quarters and invited them to dinner.

After various pleasantries and exchange of information had been accomplished, Geordie approached the subject that was dear to their hearts.

"I understand that you have the famous Chief Sitting Bull here," he said to the Indian Agent.

"Oh, yes," was the reply, "he thinks he's still a big important leader of his people -- but I cut him down to size! He came here making all kinds of demands, but I told him he's just another Indian, and he'll learn to plant and raise crops like any other Indian! I think he's finally realizing that WE won the war."

A few moments of silence followed. Then Geordie said, "Sara would like to write a story about him, for a school paper, to get an idea of how the Indians lived. We would accompany her in the interview, of course -- to make sure she would be safe."

"I'm sure that can be arranged," said McLaughlin with a smile, wiping his moustache with a napkin. "Of course he's quite a braggart; you can't believe much of what he says."

Little Dove had a hard time concealing her excitement the next day when they were escorted to the lodge of Sitting Bull. He and his band had erected their tipis in an area south of Fort Yates and Standing Rock. There were over thirty of them, and Little Dove felt her heart beat faster at the sight of these cone-shaped dwellings of her youth!

Sitting Bull sat on a box in front of his lodge, and his wives and younger children sat on the ground next to him. They were curious about the visitors, and observed them keenly. After a while some of them went off and occupied themselves inside the tipi, or elsewhere.

Through an interpreter, Sara asked questions of the great Chief, and wrote down the answers. Little Dove sat quietly, smiling, watching. Glancing at his two wives, she was trying to remember if she had known the elder one, Seen-by-the-Nation. His twins, Crow Foot and Run-Away-From, reminded her of the brother she had been so close to, and had lost, long ago.

Although these Hunkpapa Sioux were still living in tipis, they had been told that they would have to build log cabins the following year.

"I have heard that you are a very great leader," Sara said, the interpreter translating her words. "I have heard that you were very brave in battle, and counted many coups on enemy warriors."

"More than 65 coups," said the translator.

"Wonderful!" said Sara, "and I have heard that you are also a Holy Man, of powerful visions, and always concerned for the welfare of your people. Always very generous to those in need."

The Chief showed surprise. This girl's questions and comments were different from those of others who had come to interview him.

Sitting Bull glanced at Little Dove from time to time, and he was puzzled. There was something familiar about her -- yet by her manner and dress she was obviously of the White-Man's world.

Their soldier escort had gone off, saying that he would return in an hour. Little Dove wanted to talk to her relatives alone, so she asked the interpreter if he would be kind enough to fetch them some water, and also some fruit, as an appropriate gift for the Chief and his family. The man hesitated -- but Geordie assured him that all would be well.

When he was gone, Little Dove addressed her kin in Lakota.

"Hau!" she said in greeting. "Mi-TA-kwe ya-sin!" And she reached over and put her hand on his. His eyes widened in surprise!

"My brother!" she said. "My cousin! I am Little Dove, daughter of Walks-the-Wind and Turtle Woman."

He looked at her pensively. "But the people of your band are all killed, in that season, when you are small. We find them, we pray for them, when the Long-Knives go."

"My uncle finds me, on the plains, when Turtle Woman dies by the sword," Little Dove answered. "He takes me to the great mountains, the Tetons, and I am taught by the Old Ones. When they go Over the Ridge, to the world beyond, I am captured by a Wasichu. But I am taken in by a woman of kind heart. She makes me her daughter."

"In those other seasons," Geordie interjects, "Long Bow finds Little Dove, and takes her to his lodge among the Cherokee, far to the south." Sara understands some, but not all, of their Lakota words.

"We know you, from that time!" Seen-by-the-Nation spoke up to Little Dove. "We know the daughter of Turtle Woman, when she is small. It is good that our eyes behold you this day!"

262

Tatanka Yotanka (Sitting Bull) invited his long-lost family into his tipi for a special ceremony. "We smoke the chanupa," he said; "We give thanks to Wakan Tanka for the safe return of our loved ones." He presented a ceremonial pipe to Geordie; to Little Dove he gave a wing of eagle feathers. She knew it to be a very sacred object. To Sara he gave a medicine pouch, placing it around her neck. "This protects you from harm," he said.

The Hunkpapa Holy-Man listened with his inner hearing, as the smoke from the pipe curled upward. The whirr of wings of a great bird was heard as a spirit-eagle swooped through the tipi. His visiting cousin, Little Dove, was dressed in the manner of their captors, with her dark hair pulled back neatly and tied in a bun at the back of her neck, her dress fitted down to the waist and full below it, yet her heart was pure Lakota! Sara wondered if they, too, would be put on the reservation if it were known that they were Indians.

Sensing her concern, Sitting Bull made the ceremony brief. "In my vision, you are inside the great mountain, the Holy Place of the Teton. You speak with the Spirit of the Old Ones. You are given a special gift, the most Sacred Object of our People. It must be cared for, prayed on, for it is the hope of the generations yet unborn. My prayers go with you. Be strong, and be of good heart! Mi-TA-kwe-yasin."

As they emerged from the tipi, they saw the interpreter walking down the hill toward them, carrying a basket of fruit. He was surprised; it was not Sitting Bull's custom to invite White people into his lodge. After presenting the fruit to their Native hosts and saying "I honor your spirit!" the trio went back and bade farewell to the post commander, and were on their way. They headed west, to the great Sacred Black Hills. Little Dove, with a joyful heart, sang songs recalled from her childhood.

They were grateful for their strong horses who in turn were happy about the oats they were given at their recent stop-over. Their light-weight canopied carriage traveled easily over the rutted dirt roads, and in a few days time they were once again at the Paha Sapa, the Sacred Medicine Ground. Geordie and Little Dove were recalling their visit there long ago at the time of their marriage.

The couple found the shrine where they had previously communicated with the Wise Ones in spirit, and were welcomed by them once more. They had both changed into their buckskins and tied eagle feathers into their hair, and Sara was impressed by the sense of awe and reverence with which they conducted their ceremony of thanksgiving to Wakan Tanka, and honoring the Spirits of this holy place.

They offered tobacco, burned sage and sweetgrass, and prayed with the chanupa gifted to them by Sitting Bull. The spirit of the same Council Chief, Raven Wing, who had spoken to them years ago, appeared to them once again.

Sara was amazed and delighted when the spirit Elder, his hair long and white like the tail-feathers of the white-head eagle, manifested before them. He reached out with his feather-fan and touched them on the head, each shoulder, and the heart, giving them a blessing.

"This young maiden of your issue is powerful and wise beyond the years of such a one who dwells on this planet," he said. "This is a difficult time for the Native caretakers of this Mother Earth. But it is part of a great cycle, and the time will come when future generations will seek the knowledge of living in harmony with Earth and Sky Beings.

"Sara, Little Shining Star, will have children who will not know who they truly are. But her middle daughter will carry Little Dove's gift of producing pictures, of people and scenes, such as our Little Dove once painted on the lodges of her people. And in turn this daughter's middle daughter will have the gift also, of portraying places and personages, not only of this earth, but of the Star-People ancestors as well.

"After she will launch her own family, this one will journey to the land of the People of the Sun, the Yavapai. When she climbs up on a Sacred mountain, at the place of great empowerment, we, the Ancient Ones, the Spirit-Keepers of the Land, will speak through her. She will become our voice; speak our teachings, dance our dances, tell our stories. She will go with the Four Winds to give our Blessing Ceremonies.

"There will be great battles between those of the Darkness and those of the Light. But the Shining Ones of the Star Nation will prevail. And those of Good Heart.

"We wish you well on your journey."

Little Dove was reluctant to leave the Black Hills, but she felt renewed by its energy. And they were, after all, continuing on the trail towards the setting sun, to that other most special place, the Grand Tetons.

264

The Gillespies stopped overnight at the house of a retired Army Officer whose name had been given them by Emma Gray. A man in the uniform of a Union cavalryman, but who was plainly Sioux, took their horses and carriage to the barn. Little Dove was puzzled.

The next morning, after thanking their host family for the night's stay and the hearty breakfast, she went to the stable to talk the groom. She greeted him with a smile, then asked:

"Why do you wear the uniform of a Blue-coat? You are Lakota!"

He glanced at her, but did not answer. By her accent, she was from the South -- perhaps that was why she did not like Blue-coats.

"I am Lakota, also," Little Dove said quietly. "Hunkpapa. Of the great Sitting Bull's band."

The Indian soldier took another look. "I am Bru-lay, as the French call us. By your look, your talk, I see that you are gone long from this northland. Many are the changes. The buffalo are gone. We no more can live as we once lived. The Wasichu come like the deep winter snows, their numbers like the snowflakes, and bury us. Those who walk the White Man's way, survive. Others do not."

"I understand. We saw Chief Tatanka Yotanka four suns before this one," Little Dove said.

The soldier was thoughtful as he curried their patient bay horse with slow strokes.

"The White-eyes say Sitting Bull killed the one called Long Hair, the one we called in other time Son-of-the-Morning-Star. This is not true. I know true story."

"Will you tell me?" asked Little Dove.

"Red Man respect Long Hair, brave warrior-soldier. He marry Indian girl. But come friends from direction of rising sun, say to Long Hair, 'You too good for live this place, this no-where. You brave, smart, Civil War. Be hero again: you be Pres'dent, United State.' This they say.

"Long Hair want Sitting Bull fight, so Long Hair can win battle, be big hero. Want Sitting Bull break treaty, for excuse to fight. Our Chief speak true, no break word. Man of honor. Long Hair mad; say 'I fix Sitting Bull! Bring him daughter to me, in my tent. I rape! I make Chief angry; he break treaty!' Sitting Bull hear what happen. He sad, he ANGRY: but he no break word. No break treaty. Have honor.

Little Dove, Lakota Ancestor

"Young Hunkpapa warriors, they have POWERFUL anger! Because no respect for great Leader Chief! One brave warrior wants to take Sitting Bull daughter, Many Horses, for wife. Him very angry Long Hair hurt beautiful maiden of 14 summers. Word spread. Many warriors come to battle, avenge honor. Minniconjou, Nakota, Dakota, Yanktonai, Brule, even Cheyenne -- come to join Lakota fighters.

"Custer gen'ral go to wipe out Hunkpapa village of Sitting Bull. He not know many, many others beyond ridge. Not wait for other soldiers, think victory be easy. Custer wrong! Great victory for our People. Sitting Bull not in fight. He watch, but not join. He know Lakota win that day."

"Yes. He told us of his Sundance vision," said Little Dove. "About seeing the soldiers falling into the village, and he knew that they would win that time. But how did you know these things?"

"I over-hear officer soldiers talk. They say this is in Army Record. Want keep secret, but -- Official Army History."

Chapter 19

Sacred Canyon

A few days ride more and the travelers saw the magnificent Teton mountains rising tall and jagged against the western sunset sky. With a joyful heart, Little Dove quickened their pace. When they came to a stream, they stopped to give thanks to Wakan Tanka for their safe return to the place where she had spent her last happy years of freedom with her people.

Geordie, Little Dove and Sara camped among the pines, and next day they each donned deerskin clothing. Full skirts and petticoats were hardly appropriate for climbing high mountains. There was little evidence of human presence here; a few trappers and hunters, perhaps, had passed this way. With a Lakota cry of elation, Little Dove shook loose her long hair and tossed her black mane to the winds.

Little Dove looked for familiar landmarks, and found them easily. They crossed a stream on a log foot-bridge, and went up a steep mountainside. Remembering, the returned Lakota woman pointed out a spot where powerful energies emerged from Mother Earth. They prayed quietly for a few minutes. Far below, they watched two white-head eagles fly around a pond, which was surrounded by tall pines. A special blessing.

She found the caves where Oldest Grandmother and Oldest Grandfather had lived, where they had taught her the ways of The People, and the healing ways. She felt their presence. They were pleased at her return, with her loved ones. She passed on some of their stories to her family.

Little Dove led her husband and daughter to the hidden entrance to the tunnel that led inside the mountain. They had scarcely adjusted to the dimness of the cave when they noticed a glow coming from the other end. Going carefully toward it, they found themselves emerging into a great and wondrous cavern!

The trio was greeted by a man with a long white beard and hooded robe. He was known as The Ancient of Days.

"Welcome," he said. "Welcome to the Sanctuary." Oldest Grandfather and Grandmother were there in their light-bodies. "We have finished our earth-walks," they said. "We can come and go as we please, for we are spirit." They still had long white hair -- it was their choice -- but they no longer looked old. And they could manifest physically if they chose to.

A small circle of students was listening to a teacher in one area of the cavern.

"This place of great power on Mother Earth is a doorway between worlds," the teacher was saying. "The Inner-Earth People come and go. The Sky People come. Beings from other dimensions also. This Sacred Mountain is the hub of a great wheel; its many spokes, ley lines of energy, go out in all directions, like the rays of the sun. To the north, they reach into Canada; to the west, to the Pacific; to the south, as far as Mexico; and to the east, to the mighty river that flows from north to south.

Like her ancestor Little Dove before her, Sakina Blue-Star sent prayers for peace and harmony to the Creator and All Beings, in Sedona's Sacred Canyons

They terminate at certain power points, at tall mountain tops, or beneath the earth or sea, in an equidistant triangle. The center of this great 'wagon wheel' or 'Medicine Wheel' is here."

The students rose, and became part of a larger circle, which expanded as others came into the domed chamber from entrances to various tunnels. Flecks of crystal imbedded in the rock of the walls sparkled as they reflected the light of candles, the Entities, and the central fire in the Cavern.

The Beings gathered there were of many Nations, many forms. Some were Star People, and would tell which planet or galaxy they came from, as the crystal wand was passed around and each one had their say. There were people of the Red race, sons and daughters of Atlantis; the Brown race, of Lemurian stock; the Black, the Yellow, and the White People; the Blue People, and the ones of Violet hue. The latter two had left this planet long ago, but would be coming back, they said. They are pictured on the walls of Egyptian tombs.

The couple from the Pleiades described life on their planet, where the people were happy, moved large objects by teleportation, and lived in harmony. Those of the Blue Star, Sirius, also had a harmonious society. They said that Earth was once part of their star system, and might soon be so once again. The Venusians, too, were loving beings. The Dawn Star dwelt among them, but so loved the Earth that he came 2,000 years before, to teach, to guide, to share Creator's Love.

Each one around the circle shared their wisdom, or a brief message. Then they did a graceful dance, twirling and dipping, stepping and gliding. Sara joined them, joyfully.

After most of these Enlightened Ones drifted off through their respective doorways, the visiting family saw a great light appear and brighten in the center of the room. The glow took on a form, though it was made up of pinpoints of light, not solid matter.

"Lord Ashtar!" Sara cried out with delight.

"Lady Athena," he replied, with a gallant little bow, seeing in her the essence of the Goddess overshadowing her. "It has been some time, since last we spoke atop the mountain in Greece. Though in your light-body, of course, we are frequently together, aboard craft. I salute you!

"We of the Galactic Federation of Free Worlds give you Greeting," he said to those remaining in the cavern's Great Hall. "Adonai." And he faded out, leaving only sparkles of light where he had stood.

Oldest Grandfather approached them, and escorted them into another chamber. Around the walls sat a gathering of Council Chiefs, and Wise Women Elders. It was like a council in one of the large lodges of the traditional Lakota People. At the back of the room, facing them as they entered, sat White Buffalo Calf Woman, holding a bundle in her lap.

"I greet you, in the name of Wakan Tanka," she said, with a smile. Little Dove caught her breath! She knew immediately who this Radiant Being was. Many times around the burning of the winter lodge-fires had she heard the telling of this Holy One coming to the People, that they might know a good way to pray, with the smoke from the sacred chanupa carrying their prayers to the Great Mystery.

"I came to teach your ancestors how to live in harmony with all things," Calf-Woman said. "I told them how to call in the buffalo so the People might not go hungry. But now the buffalo are gone, because the People did not honor my teaching of honoring all life. It is good to be strong and brave, and to count coups; but it is not good to kill your brothers, who are all children of the Great Spirit.

"The Sacred Pipe I brought before was a Man pipe, but not to be used to pray for success in war. It should be used only for good purpose. So now I bring the gift of a Woman pipe, to be used in a Holy way, for peace. I am entrusting this Sacred Chanupa to you, Little Dove. For you have a pure heart!

"Both pipes will have great power. There will be those in the Government who will try to steal the one I brought before, because they believe that whoever has possession of it has control over the people of all Native Nations of Turtle Island. They believe all tribes will do whatever the White Buffalo Calf Pipe-holder tells them to.

"At the time of great change on Mother Earth, I will return, as a buffalo calf: White, then yellow, red, black, brown. To honor the races of people."

She unwrapped the chanupa in her lap, put tobacco in the bowl, joined it to the stem, lit it, and watched the smoke rise -- all in a prayerful way. She then passed it around the circle, and each one added their own prayer.

"This chanupa has a special energy, a unique frequency. It can be used to communicate with those in other dimensions. It may be used to contact the Star People, those who are here to help. It must be used only for Peace. That is why it must be hidden away until the time is right for it to be brought forth once again."

Gently, Buffalo-Calf Woman wrapped up the pipe again.

She summoned Little Dove to come before her, which she did, kneeling on a white buffalo robe. "I entrust this Sacred Pipe to you," said the Holy Woman.

"I am honored!" said Little Dove. She was overwhelmed.

"You are to take this to the land of the Hopi Nation, the Peaceful People. They still do the ancient ceremonies given them by the gods, the Kachinas, who came from the stars to watch over the people. They live in a simple way, in harmony with the earth, and do ceremonies to keep the balance throughout the earth. This is of great importance to Mother Earth.

"On the opposite side of the world the Tibetans do ancient ceremonies also, toning to keep the earth in balance. It is important for the nature spirits to be honored, to be thanked. When the ceremonies are no longer done, the land will die.

"The land where the Pipe shall rest is also the place of the People of the Sun, the Yavapai, and near the People of the Blue-green Waters, the Havasupai, who live down inside of the great canyon that will be called one of the Wonders of the World.

"There you will place the Sacred Chanupa into a cave, deep within a mountain, to be kept safe until the time comes that it shall be brought forth once again. When the time of change and purification comes, this Woman Pipe may be de-materialized and re-materialized, shape-shifted, to be brought up. This must be done by maidens of pure heart. It will be the time of the woman once again on the planet, and they will bring a gentle strength. The Pipe must be used only for Peace.

"I wish you well; I give you my blessings. I wish you success in your mission."

"I honor your spirit," said Little Dove.

Once again the travelers were on their way, after taking their leave of their beloved Tetons. Southward they went, through the land of the U-tas, past huge reddish rock formations, and along rushing rivers. Many Mormon settlers were coming west these days, in wagon trains. They had the Lakota custom of having more than one wife. In other respects, their ways were very different. They seemed fond of adopting Native children into their families, "probably," Geordie said, "to Christianize and 'civilize' them." Some Mormon homes took in travelers; others did not.

Geordie found a nice Mormon home that did take people in. His family was treated to a delicious meal cooked by the women of the household. Their host, Ephram, had two wives, and many children, who ate at a separate table. Little Dove felt much at home; her father had had three wives, and ten children.

Ephram was a farmer, a big man, with graying hair and beard, and suspenders to hold up his britches.

"This is the Promised Land to us," he told his visitors. "We came here seeking freedom. In the east, we were persecuted by the Gentiles, and many of us were killed, because we were different from others in our ways and our beliefs -- and we would not change them, because our faith was strong."

'Sounds like our people,' thought Little Dove.

In their bed-chamber, Little Dove found 'The Book of Mormon' on the night stand beside their bed. It was much like the Bible of Mrs. Gray, which had been the first book Little Dove had used to practice her new skill of reading, long ago.

"They had large tribes in the old times," Little Dove explained to Sara. "They had great battles, with their cavalry killing off thousands -- whole Nations, as they did with us -- and when the people became too proud and forgot to honor their God, he would come and smite them."

Geordie smiled at her interpretation. "Mormonism began," he told them, "when their leader, Joseph Smith, discovered some golden tablets in the land of the Iroquois Nation, now called New York state. Smith was led to these sacred tablets by an angel, named Moroni, who materialized and gave him a message that he was to preserve the history of their people."

"A shape-shifter!" declared Little Dove. "Like our Lakota Holy People, or our Old Ones who could appear to us."

Sara opened up the Book of Mormon, to see if there was a message on the page that she opened to.

"It's about our ancestors, Mama! The Star People! The Cloud People! 'And it came to pass that when they had come down into the valley of Nimrod,'" she read, "'the Lord came down and talked with the brother of Jared; and he was in a cloud...' and 'the Lord commanded them to go into the wilderness.... And the Lord did go before them, and did talk with them as he stood in a cloud, and gave directions whither they should travel.' Like the Wise Men," said Sara. "They followed a star by night and a cloud by day. Our star-craft."

Geordie chimed in. "The Mormons chose a powerful spot to build their Temple. There are huge crystals beneath it, to amplify the energies and raise their spirit to a higher place. It is near the great inland ocean-lake, where the sea-birds fly. They remember the history of their ancestors, and they write down their names in their archives to honor them."

"We told our Ancestor-stories around the winter fires," said Little Dove.

"The Mormons' history says that Jesus appeared to their ancestors several times," said Geordie, "going from Spirit into flesh."

"Of course!" Little Dove smiled. "Dawn Star could shape-shift! One of the Cloud People, he could come and go from his home on Venus; or from his craft, the Star of Bethlehem."

It took many weeks to reach the land of the People of the Sun. Monument Valley, on the way, had towering rock spires rising from desert soil. The nomadic Dineh (Navajos) raised flocks of sheep, and dwelt in hexagonal log hogans, with rounded mud roofs. Some families had been given two sheep, a sack of flour, and coffee, when they were released from a four-year captivity after their trail of tears, or Long Walk. Being good with animals, they had turned a few sheep into large flocks. The women became expert weavers.

The Hopi, the peaceful people, lived in a very different way from the Plains people, or from the Navajo and Apache, nomadic hunters and gatherers. These latter came from the north, it was said, and the ancestors of the Hopi migrated up from the south. They were kin to the Mayans, and the Hawaiians.

Hopi lived in villages, in houses made of stone cut from the bluffs atop which they lived. The mesas rose high above the barren landscape; they had long lived high up as protection from marauding enemy tribes. Down below, each clan family had their cornfields, and they grew squash, beans and melon by the spring. But they went up top to safety at sundown.

There was very little rainfall in that dry area of what became known as northeast Arizona. What rain they did get, they prayed down: That was one of the main reasons for their ceremonies, to entreat the gods, the Kachinas, to favor them with moisture for their crops, to feed the People. The snake-people could speak to the Rain Gods, and the Thunder-beings would answer. So the Snake Priests would dance with live rattlers in the plaza, and bring the rain. To the Hopi, corn is life!

Little Dove, Lakota Ancestor

Geordie, Little Dove and Sara arrived on the day of the Snake Dance, at Old Oraibi. In this ancient village the same families had been living for over a thousand years. The weary travelers had shed their garments dusty from their long journey, bathed in a creek, and put on their fringed regalia. They received a warm welcome from curious children and elders, and were taken to the plaza where the ceremonies were taking place. They were given a seat on a stone bench built into the side of a house. Many of the Hopi men were watching the dances from the rooftops, their legs dangling over the side.

The visitors were invited into several homes after the ceremonial dances were over. They were feasted and given soft fleecy sheepskins to sleep on. In the days that followed, they were asked to speak to people in homes and plazas. Hopi were eager to hear about what was taking place in the outside world -- especially to their Native brothers. The Gillespies were also invited into the kivas, the round or square underground rooms reached by ladder which were chapel, work-room, and men's club or school combined. Each clan had their own kiva.

Here the boys would listen to the stories told by their elders, over and over until they knew them well by heart. Thus Hopi history was passed down, through the millennia. This was the Fourth World (or civilization), they said; the First World was destroyed when the earth spun around in space (shifted on its axis); the Second, when it froze (the ice age); and the Third World was destroyed by the great flood that all cultures speak of.

Maasaw was the Creator of the Fourth World. He gave them their land to care-take, with instructions to live simply and in harmony with the cycles of nature. He taught them the ceremonies that would honor the Earth Mother, so she would provide for them. The Kachina dancers would press healing and harmony into Mother Earth with each step, and with the sound frequency of their chant. The Ceremonies would keep the world in balance, in this place of special energy on the planet. After bringing balance elsewhere, they settled at this final home.

Geordie brought game that he had hunted, and Little Dove and Sara brought fruit and vegetables that had come from Mormon orchards and gardens. It was customary among Native Americans to bring food when visiting families, and one would then be invited to join their hosts for meals.

Little Dove, Geordie and Sara paid their respects to the Kikmongwe, the village chief, on each of the mesas. In the ancient Walpi and Sichomovi villages, on the mesa farthest to the East (direction of first light, beginnings), they were greeted with curiosity and friendship. On the second mesa, the family exchanged gifts and food with the people of Mishongnovi, and of Shipaulovi, the tiny village perched on its own little mountaintop; and also on another arm of that mesa, Shumopavi. On the third mesa was Oraibi, oldest of villages, and also the remains of another ancient village, Hotevilla, farther to the west, but it had been abandoned.

Little Dove said that she would like to do a special prayer ceremony in each of the villages, to give a blessing, in return for their kindness. It was late summer, approaching the women's time to use the kivas, to pray for all beings and to give thanks for a bountiful harvest. Both men and women filled the kivas to participate in their visitors' ceremonies, and Little Dove reverently took out the sacred White Buffalo chanupa, asked Wakan Tanka for a blessing on the people and the land, and passed the pipe around.

The Hopi knew what a great honor this was. They were sensitive to its special energies, and the connection with the Holy Ones, and the Star Beings. The Kachinas came from the stars, and they could go in and out of this dimension: shape-shift. To return the honor of the Sacred Pipe sharing, some of the Initiated Priests led the visiting family into the tunnels that led into the underworld, projecting their light, which was reflected by bits of mica in the walls. The One-Hearted (pure-hearted) ones had been taken here between worlds, to be a seed-race for the next time period.

"There used to be tunnels going far to the south, to the land of our Mayan cousins," explained an Elder. "And to the north, to our brothers in the Tetons. These underground tunnels went in all directions, but many of them have caved in over the years."

In a cavern, the Gillespies saw a round, silver craft, which had been there for many millennia. They saw some tiny, slender Beings with large eyes -- but they were only one foot tall. "In Hawaii," Geordie said, "They call them the Mi-ne-hu-ni; and in Ireland, the Leprechauns. In Lemurian times -- the First and Second World -- everyone could see them."

Returning to the surface, the Lakota-Cherokee family said goodbye to their Hopi hosts.

"As-kwa-li," said Little Dove. "Kwa-kwai," said Geordie. Men and women said "thank you" in different ways in the Hopi language.

The family headed west. They had heard of a massive and wondrous canyon, with a rushing river running through it. It was a sacred place, and was said to be a place of emergence long ago for some of the Hopi People.

As they approached it, they were guided by their Spirit Guardians to the interior of this very grand canyon by way of tunnels and caverns. In one cavern, they came upon some small beings who were quite different from other earth species. These slender beings had large heads, large eyes, no hair, and had six fingers and six toes. They communicated through thought transference, or by projecting images into a round, flat, laser disc. These Little People were fascinated with Sara, as she was with them. She danced for them, and they imitated her, dancing around her in a circle… and the cavern rang with laughter!

A hooded robed one emerged from the entrance to a tunnel. The Ancient One looked like a man, but had a greenish tinge to him. He greeted Geordie, Little Dove and Sara, and offered to lead them further, through another dimly lit tunnel.

At last they came out into the daylight, and it took the earthlings a few moments to adjust to it. But when they did…

"AWE-SOME!" exclaimed Sara. "Overwhelming!" Geordie agreed. Huge canyon walls rose all around them, the sunlight bringing out their different hues of reds, browns, blues and yellows. A great river snaked through the canyon, and at some places rushing rapids splashed through it.

"This was a place of emergence from the inner world for the Hopi, after a time between worlds," explained the Ancient One. "The 'Ant People' took the One-Hearted ones into the under-world for safety between these times, so that there would be a seed-race for the next time period on the earth, after the cleansing."

"The Ant People," mused Sara. "I think they are the small ones with slender bodies, large heads, and big black eyes. I have seen them in the caverns of the Teton Lakota and the Hopi. They are given their missions by the Star People."

The honored guests were taken into another cavern. Again, Sara looked around in wonderment. What she was seeing was similar to things she had seen in the British Museum.

"Why, these tombs -- these artifacts -- they are like the ones in EGYPT! This is astonishing!" she exclaimed.

The Ancient One smiled. "The ancestors of canyon and cliff-dwellers were visited by Wise Ones from that land, who came on 'great round shields that flew through the air like the eagle,' as they put it. Far below a great pyramid in the land of Gee-za, there is a huge crystal, which would send forth messages through and around the earth. The words were radiated out; they called it a ray-dio. Some of the messages came here to this place, and were received by the priests living here at that time."

"Fascinating!" said Sara.

"In those times there was a connection between peoples on different sides of the world. Maasaw gave a covenant to the Hopi, a set of guidelines to live by. A covenant was also given to the people of the land called Egypt. It was placed into an Ark. It is below the man-beast, of the lion's body, in the Hall of Records.

"At the Hopi mesas, there are special energies," the Ancient One continued. "Hopi Kachina Priests do ceremonies to keep the world in balance. On the other side of the world they do ceremonies also, for the same reason; in the land of Tibet. When this world ends, there will be a better one. All will speak the same language.

"There will be harmony; we will all love our brothers and sisters. These are teachings and prophecies that were given by the Elders to Native People living here."

Sara and her parents were deeply moved by the gifts of knowledge that were being shared with them.

They were introduced to the Havasupai, the People of the Blue-green Waters, who lived down inside this great canyon. They were greeted, feasted and rested there, exchanging many stories, before going back through the tunnels to where they had left their horses and carriage.

The Gillespie family bade farewell to their new friends, their new family, and continued their journey.

Nawanda! The place of myth and legend! The portal between worlds, used by the gods who came from the stars. The place to seek one's vision, this land so sacred to all peoples of Turtle Island; called The Crystal City of Light, in ancient Lemurian times. After traversing the vast land roamed by the Dineh, the Gillespies had come to the city of Flagstaff, and thence down a winding trail replete with magnificent vistas, each more wondrous than the one before.

Several thousand feet lower than the high peaks called San Francisco (which rise above Flagstaff), dwelling place of the Kachinas, they had entered a valley with a creek wandering through it. On all sides there rose in splendor tall mountains reaching up toward the sky. Walls of crimson rock formations towered above the land of Nawanda. It was like being down inside the Grand Canyon once again.

Guided by their Spirit Guardians, the trio proceeded westward, then northward. A trail led across a dry creek bed; the flow of the creek had been stopped when a rock-slide had altered its course upstream.

When the trail split, they took the right fork. Exploring that long canyon, they came across the remains of a gold-mining operation. They saw flat-bed carts with thick iron wheels, and miners' cabins that had been abandoned and were falling down, some of them no more than kindling now.

"Maybe the mine has played out already," said Geordie.

Little Dove looked up to the high mountains rising to the west, and sensed some anger there. "Or perhaps the Guardian Spirits of this place did not want the miners here," she said. "Their greed for gold caused the death of Native People."

She looked up to the bluff that rose above the valley. "We must go up there," she said. "It is a place of special power."

They circled around, going up the far end of the mesa where they found a trail made by deer, bear and mountain lion, which turned back south atop the ridge to the part that overlooked the valley and the miners' shacks.

Little Dove was silent for a while. She was going into vision.

"There is a great sadness here," she began. "There was a village in this valley. The Yavapai, the People of the Sun, lived here. This was a place of coming together of peoples of all tribes: Sacred Ceremonial Grounds. I see tipis: my people came sometimes from the Plains, to seek their vision at this doorway between worlds, and for the healing waters. A stream ran through the valley then, and there were tall cottonwood trees along its banks.

"The Yavapai would welcome those who came for spiritual vision and for healing. This was an inter-tribal Ceremonial place. There was a hot spring here, of artesian waters that would soothe and restore harmony to sore or tired bodies when they soaked in the pools at the base of this butte. The healers would pray over the people.

"Sometimes in their doctoring they would take a sick one and lay the patient under the biggest tree in the area, and ask the spirit of the Grandfather Tree to send his healing energy to the one in need, and leave him or her lying there until they were well. Then the healed-one would get up and walk away.

"The Elders knew, too, that juniper sprigs and berries, gathered in this canyon, at a special time of year at the fullest of the moon, also had a great cleansing and healing effect," Little Dove continued.

"But then gold was discovered in the area and the greed story repeated itself. I see the Yavapai living here in their wikiups. At certain times of year many Nations would gather to do ceremony, but a small village of The-People-of-the-Sun lived in this valley as care-takers of this sacred place. Then one day -- the soldiers came riding in.

"'You must leave this place -- NOW!' they said. 'You're going to the San Carlos Reservation.' And the soldiers began rounding them up. The People protested; the San Carlos Apache were their traditional enemies, for they were fierce warriors, and the Yavapai were the peaceful ones, guardians of the Holy Place. And San Carlos was a desert, not like their green valley," said Little Dove.

"So the People protested. 'We can't leave now,' one of them spoke up. 'It's the middle of winter! The children couldn't make it,' said the Yavapai mothers. 'Yes, the children,' they said, calling the little ones to them.

" 'Oh, you're worried about the children?' replied the sergeant. So they killed the children!" Little Dove related, tears streaming down her face. "To break their spirit. And of course it broke their hearts." She did not choose to tell any more of the brutality she was seeing.

Sara had turned away.

The Yavapai and some Western Apache were taken on a forced march across the mountains in mid-winter. Some of them died along the way, some died when they got to the reservation, the internment camp; and others died trying to get back to their valley.

Medicine people who had escaped the forced removal of the Yavapai from the long canyon had withdrawn the warm artesian waters of the healing spring deep into the earth. They had also withdrawn the stream, along whose banks the miners had cut down the cottonwood trees to build cabins or to burn for fuel. Energy-drains had been placed there by the Holy Ones to sap the strength of those who had caused the slaughter of the innocents. "Those who come here because of greed will not be able to stay here," they said. "Only the ones who come from the heart will be allowed to live here." The miners did not stay long; a sickness came upon them. "There's a curse on this place," they said. Strange things happened.

"We must pray here," Little Dove proclaimed, walking around the top of the bluff. Sensing where the most powerful energy came up from Mother Earth, she enlisted the aid of her husband and daughter in creating a circle of stones, with the bigger ones marking the four cardinal directions. In the center, a large flat rock served as an altar. Here they placed their healing crystals, and offerings of tobacco. On each stone around the wheel Sara sprinkled blue-corn meal, a gift from the Hopi, with a prayer.

Little Dove unwrapped her precious bundle, and they lit the Sacred Chanupa in the manner prescribed by White Buffalo Calf Woman -- who, in her radiance, appeared among them! The Sacred Pipe carrier called in all of the spirits of those who had dwelt there, and they came -- by the thousands, rejoicing in the reunion. Old friends they were, from other earth-walks.

"There must be a healing here," said Little Dove. "Peace must be restored."

Haku-ah-na, a spokesman from a spirit-Council of Chiefs that had gathered there, spoke up. "The time for healing is not yet. This place must be protected. The time of Peace will come in the generation after the removal of the Yavapai People from this sacred place, when those of pure heart return. The time of Purification."

Sara looked to the northwest, as the sun lowered itself to the mountain ridge. "Look, Mama!" she said, pointing to the large formation there. "It's the giant Maasaw, the Hopi creator-god, lying on his back looking up at the sky! The Protector they told us about."

Long Bow, Little Dove and Sara honored Grandfather Sun as he slipped behind the mountains to the west. A few moments later, they welcomed Grandmother Moon as she rose in splendor in the direction on the opposite side of the circle. It was a magical time.

Long Bow beat the drum, representing the heart-beat of Mother Earth, as the assembled entities joined his beloved wife and daughter in rhythmic ceremonial dance, their fringed skirts gracefully swishing as they turned. They danced far into the night -- and then Sara said "LOOK!" and they saw, silhouetted against the long mountain range to the east, a large golden orb moving southward -- with a sparkling tail trailing behind it five miles long!

"The Star People!" Sara said delightedly. "Of course," commented Haku-ah-na, the spirit Council Chief, with a smile. "They are welcoming you. The sky-craft come often to this spot, to renew their energy. As you have observed, it is a place of great power."

"There is one more thing I wish to do," spoke Little Dove after they had sung up Grandfather Sun the next morning. "Before we return to our life in Mississippi, I would like to go to Sacred Canyon, and pay our respects to the spirits of the Old Ones who were buried there."

Thus the three of them left the place called Canyon del Oro, and proceeded to the next canyon; past magnificent rust-colored sandstone mountains and formations that rose majestically to the west. In this holy place they were greeted once again by a host of Beings: The spirits of the Wise Ones, the Brave Ones, the Great Chiefs and the Holy Ones who had been brought there from all over Turtle Island to be interred, in order to preserve some of their essence, their wisdom. For stones and bones have memory.

Along with the spirits of those special Native People who had been brought there for burial, or who had lived there since ancient Lemurian times when this place was known as the Crystal City of Light, there were also many great spiritual Masters and Enlightened Ones gathered together in this holy place. The whole canyon was filled with these; Gautama the Buddha; Jesus the Christ, sometimes called Sananda; Chief White Eagle; the one who was known as St. Germaine, and many others.

Once again awe-struck by the beauty and power of the place, the spiritual pilgrims followed a trail once used by Indians and now by deer, and went up onto a little hill. Here again Little Dove sensed a great energy surging up from the earth.

Sara looked down into the valley that lay in a corridor between the canyon walls. "I see into another time," she said to her parents. "A time to come. I see a pueblo village; a large dwelling, and many small ones. And

281

some square green patches, with people playing games. But I am puzzled: The people in this Indian village like the one at Taos are not of the Red or Brown race; they are Wasichu. They are wearing strange clothing. As Hopi prophecy says, the women will dress like men! Or even like little boys, in short pants."

The Gillespies gathered some rocks from the wash, asking each rock if it wished to be moved, and built a circle of stones. They sang songs of thanksgiving to the Great Creator, and they danced their joy! They honored the Spirit Keepers of the four directions, the rocks, the green growing things, the sky, the earth, the fire and water and air. They sent love to those that crawled or swam or walked or flew.

Little Dove looked over to a ridge that loomed up higher than the hill they were on. From the ridge rose a tall stone figure that looked like a woman holding a child.

"Look, Sara -- the Kachina Mama!" she exclaimed. "Her hair is in the whorls a Hopi maiden wears when she comes of age, ready for marriage. They represent a butterfly, or transformation from a girl into a woman. She wears long skirts, and the small cave at the base represents the womb. This is where young maidens have come for thousands of years, to pray to the spirit of Kachina Mama when they wished to have a child."

"Let's go up there," said Sara. They went down into the ravine, and began the ascent to the top of the high, narrow ridge. The view to the south was expansive. They could see other sacred mountains and vast vistas from there. On the ridge, below the Kachina Mama which towered over them, they made a small circle and did another little ceremony to give thanks. "This is the most powerful place of them all," said Sara, feeling the energy. "This is exciting!"

The three became aware of a dozen Council Chiefs in their light-bodies sitting in the circle with them. "We are pleased that you are here, Little One," said Haku-ah-na to Sara. "Welcome home! You have each lived here in many earth-walks, going back to the times when this was called the Crystal City of Light, the place of spiritual enlightenment. The First and Second Worlds, of Hopi telling.

"One day, Sara, you will have a daughter," Haku-ah-na said. "You will give her the name of Mary, to honor the mother of the one that we called the Dawn Star, when he came here 2,000 years ago. The Hopi know Him as

Morning Star. He taught here among these rocks. His vibrations may still be felt, where He stood and taught, where He walked." He looked down to the pathway below.

"Dawn Star would sit down there, and the spiritual seekers who came from far places would sit on the rocks rising around him and listen to his teachings. He taught us to plant cedar trees on high ridges to remind us they are sacred; the smoke of sprigs of cedar lit by the fire-beings rises to the Sky Father with our prayers, and it will also purify us when we use it to smudge ourselves or our dwellings. It is our incense.

"He taught us that we are all children of the Sky Father and, while we are on this planet, of the Earth Mother, and that we should love and honor each other, not harm or kill anyone. At times he would go up on yonder hill with his Council of Twenty-four: 12 men and 12 women; for all are equal, he said.

"The men would dance the sacred dance around the outside of the circle in one direction; the women, just inside of them, would dance in the opposite direction, for the balance. Dawn Star would be in the center, calling in the energy, the power, from the Sky Father, and sending it deep into the Earth Mother, to heal and renew her.

"Below the hill, thousands would gather to watch, and to join in the songs and prayers of thanks-giving. 'The Kingdom of Heaven is at hand,' he taught us. 'It is NOW. You are co-creators with the Creator-of-All-Things. Your life is what you choose to make of it. Dear Ones, JOY is your birthright; and death is nothing to be feared. It is only crossing over to a place of even greater joy and ecstasy, and of boundless love. Unless you have chosen otherwise, for some purpose of karma or learning.' This he taught us. And then he moved on, to share his light with others."

Sara, Little Dove and Geordie were moved by his words.

"Sara," Haku-ah-na continued, "The middle girl-child of your daughter Mary will be named after you. This Sara will be a dreamer. She will have a lonely childhood, but she will marry and have two beautiful daughters and two strong sons. She will have great love for her family, and she will help her husband, a gifted and dedicated healer, through times of success and difficulty, and through painful struggle and illness.

"After her husband is released from his earth-body, she will set out across the country and settle here in this mystical valley. For many years she will not know who she truly is, will not know her Native heritage; but you three will join with us, the Spirit Keepers of this sacred place, to guide her on her path to wisdom.

"She will become our voice: We will speak through her, dance, sing, tell stories through her; she will give messages from Ancients and Star People. Then she will travel. She will spread the wisdom teachings of our people throughout the land. She will become known as Blue Star."

For their last ceremony before returning home, Geordie, Little Dove and Sara sat around the small circle atop the ridge at the base of the Kachina Mama, and unwrapped the Sacred Pipe of the White-Buffalo-Calf-Woman once more. They shared it with the Spirit-Council, who materialized for the occasion. Shape-shifting and going from one dimension to another was fairly common among Medicine People in the 'old days'.

"We will take this sacred Buffalo Calf Woman chanupa to a place deep within Mother Earth for safe-keeping," Chief Ha-ku-ah-na said. "After seven generations it will be brought forth once again, by a group of maidens of pure heart. At the time of Purification of the earth. The time of the return of the Blue Star, of Hopi prophecy."

As they watched the smoke rise from the little fire at the center of their small circle, they all saw the same vision: A woman climbing up the ridge to where they sat, and a man following her. She was wearing moccasin-boots, a fringed leather vest and skirt, and a braided leather headband around her long dark hair. The man sat at the circle and watched her as she raised her climbing staff to the skies, declaring, in an ancient tongue, "USE me! As long as it's in the light, and to help."

As she spoke, hundreds of birds flew around overhead, and when she stopped speaking, they disappeared.

That dedication would be what opened the doorway between the ones who were assembled there seeing the vision -- Little Dove and the Ancestor Spirits -- and the one that was to come. That was the invitation to the Ancients and Ancestors to come to their descendant, Blue Star, so that she might become their spokesman. She would become known as a Spirit-Speaker.

Chapter 20

Blue-Star

Left: Sakina Blue-Star sits by the rock where the Dawn Star taught. Above her rises the Kachina Mama, where maidens have come for thousands of years to pray when they wanted to have a child.

It had been 7 generations since the time that Little Dove and I, as Turtle Woman, had fled the scene of the destruction of our Lakota village until the time that I, as Sakina (Star Woman), of the Blue Star, arrived at Sacred Canyon -- and made my dedication, asking that the Ancestors use me, as long as it was in the Light and to help. I did not realize at the time that my own ancestors were among the Ancients and other spirits there.

It was Eloise who gave me the name Blue Star. She is called Shining Blue Star now that she is in the Spirit World, but she was my dearest friend for many years, when she was still among us. Strong, kind, and funny, she was a visionary medicine woman of a loving heart and great wisdom.

Like Little Dove, Eloise was Lakota, but her family did not escape reservation life. She was raised in a Catholic school on the Rosebud Reservation in South Dakota, with her cousin Wallace Black Elk. (He shared his traditional teachings in 'Black Elk, the Sacred Ways of a Lakota, by William S. Lyon.) "In school," she said, "I was always getting in trouble, because I would speak my mind!" she said. But cousin Wallace was her protector, and they would sit together and talk and laugh each day on the long bus ride to school, and back. They were very close, growing up.

Eloise married Henry, and they moved to Phoenix, where he worked at the Indian School for 40 years. Children of many tribes (including my adopted Hopi family) were taken forcibly to such boarding schools, where they were not allowed to speak their own language or have anything to do with their culture. They were punished severely if they did. And they could not go home to see their parents for years at a time.

In Arizona, Eloise learned the ways of many people, and attained profound spiritual wisdom. For many years she and a group of friends met each week to communicate with the Spirit World, and to receive messages from Sitting Bull, and other Ascended Masters. Sometimes I would go down and visit her in Phoenix, and often she would come up to Sedona and we would go out to the sacred canyons. She would tell me about the spirits she saw there, and I would draw their picture.

When I arrived in Sedona in 1983, a year after my husband Arn crossed over, I took courses, went to Psychic Fairs, and got 'readings' about past lives or glimpses into the future. Famous people came to give lectures, or workshops. After a while I thought "Everybody here can do so much, and I can't do anything!"

Then I took a course in Spirit Portraits from psychic artist Rev. Stan Matrunick, who traveled around the country doing portraits of people's Spirit Guides and loved-ones-on-the-other-side for about forty years. I had always drawn, but I didn't know you could do Spirit Guides, and I hadn't used the medium of pastels. He showed me how to do portraits with them.

At the end of the first three hours of the six-hour course Stan said "This will be your first channeled portrait," and he prayed that the spirit artists would help me with it. I drew a man with violet eyes, and a triangular symbol on his helmet.

"Who is it?" he asked.

"Ashtar," I replied. I had never heard of Ashtar at the time; I just thought "Who's this dude in the pink helmet?" It looked a lot like the picture on the book ASHTAR, which I saw a few years later. Turns out he's the Commander of the Intergalactic Space Fleet in this sector of the universe.

I drew a lot of pictures back then, to see what spirits were around. It took a while to realize that I could get telepathic messages with them, too.

I complained to my Guides one time. "How come I don't get to see Spirit, like my friends do?" (They were mostly Lakota, Cherokee, Navajo, Osage, etc., and had the gift.) "Because you have to draw a picture of us to see what we look like," I heard as a reply. "That way other people can see us, and will know of our presence."

Then I came across a Biblical quote: "To each is given according to His will; to some the gift of tongues, to others the interpretation of tongues." Well, I could do that; maybe some other people would like to be able to speak for Spirit too, sometimes in ancient languages. I should be happy with what I had.

Sedona was a fun place in the 1980s and '90s! There were a lot of friendly people here, who liked to honor the Spirits of the place in the way of the Original People of this land. We'd get together, and, at the drop of a feather, we'd go do Ceremonies at Bell Rock, Cathedral, down by the creek, or – my favorite, Sacred Canyon; Boynton. It was magical!

I had been in Sedona a few months when I discovered that special spot up on Kachina Mama ridge, rising high up over the entrance to Sacred Canyon, where the Ancient Ones began to speak through me. My friend Linda 'Deer' Domnitz showed me the place.

"I think this is the most powerful vortex of energy in the whole area," she said. Deer was able to see and communicate with the spirits there. "There's a Council of 12 Chiefs here, sitting around the circle," she said to me and another young woman who had made the climb with us. Then, looking at the girl, she said "The one sitting behind you is short and fat; but the one sitting by me is tall and handsome!" -- and we all laughed. I drew his picture. His name was Ha-ku-ah-na.

Deer received messages from Spirit and was in contact with the Star People. She channeled a book called 'John Lennon Conversations', starting a few days after he was shot; it was beautifully illustrated by Susan Rowe. The American Indians, according to Lennon, are the 'keepers of the earth'. It is their traditions that are keeping her in balance. For thousands of years, they have been filtering out negativity with their ceremonies and prayers.

Many Indian groups, he said, "want to succeed in helping the earth to be a springboard for going on into higher consciousness."

Lennon suggests that we connect with the earth each day, as Mother Earth has the energy we need to sustain us. "As much energy as we put out, we get back," he said. Deer and I slept on the earth next to the large Medicine Circle deep into the forest, where for years I led ceremonies honoring the Spirits of the Canyon and bringing through messages from them, mostly at the time of the full moon.

I call this wheel the White Bear Medicine Circle, because it was originally built for a healing ceremony for White Bear Fredericks, who lived in Sedona for many years. White Bear provided much of the information to Frank Waters for 'The Book of the Hopi', a classic book of Hopi knowledge. We heard that he was dying; so Medicine Chief Morning Owl and about 30 others gathered to smoke a chanupa and pray for him. There were staffs at the cardinal directions, with banners of yellow, black, red and white hanging from them, to honor the four directions and the peoples of the earth; and in the center was the altar. Apparently the ceremony was successful, because White Bear lived for another dozen years.

Some people say that a medicine wheel is not the tradition of the local tribes. But White Bear said "We had a medicine wheel before anybody else did! "-- and he showed me an ancient Hopi symbol: A circle with an equidistant cross in the middle, and small circles in each quadrant.

In any case, this Sedona area was sacred to ALL Nations on Turtle Island; we welcomed everyone to worship in their own way. The Plains People, among others, often came here to this inter-dimensional portal, to receive a vision of what the Creator wanted for their life.

This Solar Cross symbol has also been used in this area as a marker of energy-vortex areas for the Star People, so that they would know where to come and re-energize their craft. I knew a woman named Patricia who built stone circles at specific places out in the canyons, to let the space ships know where to 're-charge their batteries', she said.

Pat had been dying of cancer, and was down to 97 pounds, when a Venusian came to her and said "If you'll let me use your body for a while, because there are some things I need to do on this planet, I will return it to you in good condition after three years." Seemed like a good arrangement! So Pat agreed, and she became Patricia, a walk-in from Venus.

Patricia and I attended the same Meditation and Healing Circle in the early 1980s, and she always wore a white top, white pants, little white boots, and called everybody Master; because to her, everyone was a Master. She built many stone circles, and did a lot of earth-healing work with the grid system. When her friends from Venus came back for her, she and her friend Juan were sitting in a house out in one of the canyons when the night sky was lit up by a GREAT BURST OF LIGHT! They thought that a tree up on the hill across the way had been struck by lightning, but the heat was so intense from the blast that it cracked the patio door into hundreds of tiny glass fragments. Juan later showed me a bucket filled with the little pieces of glass.

"That's when they came back for her," he explained. "She was different after that. She was Pat again."

I had a lot of friends of Cherokee heritage.

Hey, they got around! They were a very large tribe, they mixed with other peoples, and they survived. One of these was Dr. Alice Bowers, who had a large church and learning center for over 30 years in Phoenix. She is the one who gave me my Dr. of Divinity degree, when I was working out of her University of Life center. She is a highly respected teacher and channel.

Alice loved to come up to Sedona from Phoenix, and Bell Rock was her special place. She would bring up from 30 to 50 of her students for Solstice or Equinox ceremonies, at which I would do Native American blessings, with greetings from the Ancient Guardians, and then we would sit in a circle, halfway up Bell Rock, and meditate. Sometimes we would see a ship streak by, below or above the mountaintops.

One time I took Alice up to my special place, in Sacred Canyon. "That's the Kachina Mama," I said, pointing her out when we reached the top of the ridge where Alice admired the expansive view of Sedona. I told her about the Yavapai, the People of the Sun, who say that this was a place of origin for them. I recounted their legend.

"Long ago there was a great flood," I began. "The See-ers knew that it was coming, and they wanted someone to survive. So they put a young maiden with a dove and some provisions into a hollow log, and sealed it with pitch. It rained for 40 days and 40 nights, the story goes, and she floated on the waters. But then she sent out the little dove, and it returned with a branch -- and knew that there was land nearby. Her log came to rest on top of these high mountains of Sacred Canyon, and she lived in a cave here," I continued.

"After five years, she cried out 'I'm lonely! I wish to have companionship!' Then she was guided to go through a waterfall into a certain cave, and there she was impregnated by the Spirit of the Wind, who manifested for that purpose. (The Cloud People? Genetic engineering?)

"She gave birth to a girl-child, and when she grew up, the girl had a boy-child, in the same manner. One day the girl was out looking for food, when she was carried off by a giant 'evil eagle.' (A pterodactyl, perhaps.) The Yavapai people say that they are descended from the woman and her grandson, and it is their spiritual teachings that they follow."

"That's an interesting story!" said Alice. "I hadn't heard that one before."

I looked down into the valley. "The second time I came out to this canyon, I drew a picture to see what spirits were around, and it was a woman and a little boy. Above them was a cloud, that looked kind of like wind blowing. The name I got for her was Kama-sheh-ee-ta: She Who Survived."

"Oh!" Alice exclaimed, turning toward me. "That was YOU!"

A shiver ran through me. "No wonder I love this place so much," I smiled. "And I feel so drawn to the Yavapai people. They are my children. Though I'm afraid they don't remember me..." I mused.

(The Yavapai, and Tonto Apache, tell a slightly different version of this origin story, but that's the way I got it.)

That would explain why this magical place seemed so very special to me, and why I, Blue-Star, began to speak in ancient languages there. Star languages, that haven't been spoken on this planet for a very long time. I had lived here off and on since the time of the Great Flood, and even before, in the Lemurian times. Lakota elder Chief Standing Elk / Chief Golden Eagle, creator of the Star Knowledge Conferences, says a language I speak is Andromedan.

"Well, the old High Priestess is back on the earth!" said Marian Starnes, a remarkable Light-worker and channel from Charlotte, North Carolina, as she began my Life-Reading in the 1970s, in Boston. I couldn't relate to it back then; I still had a lot of lessons to learn. But now it seemed more understandable. In the same reading, I was told that I had once been Empress of Atlantis, and I have had several glimpses into that lifetime also.

Some of the relationships of that time period carried over into this one. Love does not die!

Kachina Mama ridge awakened a deep memory within me, and so I cried out "Eh-YO! Ma eesh'-ta, ma-ta-ka h'neh-ee-ta, ah-na-ta." ("Use me! As long as it's in the Light, and to help! ") Overhead, hundreds of birds flew around in a great circle, and when I stopped speaking, they disappeared.

Ever since then the Ancient Ones and other spirits have been speaking through me, or singing, dancing, or telling stories, because I requested it. At first, little planting songs came through. Then over on Rachel's hill in Long Canyon a beautiful voice sang through me that soared high, in some unknown language, and dipped to the deep ranges as well -- like the singer Yma Sumac, and other Peruvian maidens, used to be able to do. I was asked to join other people's ceremonies and do blessings; I didn't know what I was saying, but after a while I began to get translations.

At first I thought I was just making it up. But then one night I attended a talk by Manley Hall, author of 'The Secret Teachings of All Ages' (and a hundred other books). Manley said that the Shakespeare works were actually ghost-written by Francis Bacon (A.K.A. St. Germain). When I did a drawing to see who Manley's Spirit Guide was, it was Juliet.

Manley's talk was given at the Masonic Hall, and when it was over I spoke to a man named Robert. "These Masons amuse me," he said. "They think they brought some of these ancient symbols and languages over to this continent, but actually there were already people here who had been using them and speaking them for thousands of years."

"Maybe that's the language I speak," I said, smiling, and recited my ancient blessing for him. I was shocked when he translated it for me! It was the same translation I got. At last, someone who understood me. Amazing!

"Who are the people who speak it over here?' I asked.

"There is a tribe that lives deep in the jungles of South America, in underground caverns, who speak it. They have no contact with the outside world, and don't want any, but I was able to live with them for a while. The other tribe is the White Mountain Apache. It's a secret language still spoken by a few Elders."

I heard of a 118-year-old White Mountain elder named Red Sleeves, but was unable to make contact with him while he was still living. It was a

4-day horseback ride to get to his place back in the mountains, I was told. He might have known my language.

When people asked me what my tribe was I said 'Wampanoag.' I had been adopted into the family and tribe of the Wampanoag elder, Evening Star, sister of Chief Wild Horse, on Cape Cod. Native Americans adopt people if they feel close to them, to honor them. I have been adopted into Hopi, Lakota, and Apache families as well. (It's an Indian thing.)

The Spirits of the Canyon have a way of testing you, to see if you're really serious about the commitment you made to help the children of Mother Earth, or if you will falter when the going gets tough. One time I went out onto a narrow rock ledge that jutted out over a valley -- and it seemed like they were trying to blow me away! But I again raised my staff and stood firm, re-dedicating myself to the mission.

Another time I went out to the cliff-dwelling ruins known as Honanki with Grandmother Eagle and Sundance (my second husband). As I stepped from one flat rock to another, I fell -- but I knew that I did not just fall, I was pushed, by an invisible force. I hurt my rib on a sharp rock, but I knew I had to be a good sport about it. I could hear them laughing at me (though I couldn't see them), saying 'So you think you're such a hot-shot medicine woman -- watch this!'

You've got to have a sense of humor. Don't come to this planet without it. And when you begin to think you really know something -- it's time for a humility lesson.

My Spirit Friends liked to play games with me. Sometimes they would make my medicine pouch (that I wore on my belt) disappear, or my feather fan, which I used to do blessings with. They would de-materialize them, and re-materialize them somewhere else. I told them: "I don't care if you guys are kleptomaniacs; as long as you return them!" So they did.

Rev. Judy Fisher and her sister Peggy had a church here in Sedona in the 1980s. These beautiful and dynamic Spiritualist ministers gave inspiring sermons, with accurate and often delightful personal messages from Spirit after the sermon. They were also of Cherokee heritage, and had strong connections with the Star People. I was one of their ministers.

One day Rev. Peggy said "Sakina, why don't you do a Full Moon service out in the canyon next Sunday?' I was happy to agree to it. From then on my church was out in Nature: The floor was the earth, the walls were the trees and the ceiling was the sky.

Someone else was doing a Native American ceremony that particular evening too, and it had been well advertised, so I didn't think there would be many people at mine. But I was wrong; eighty people attended my gathering. It was the start of a tradition. I did Full Moon Ceremonies each month after that for a long time, out in Sacred Canyon, singing to Grandmother Moon as she rose in splendor over the mountain.

A day or two before the full moon, I would put up a flyer at bookstores and on bulletin boards around town. The poster had a drawing of me in my beaded and fringed white buckskin regalia holding a feather fan and turtle rattle, and it would say "The RED ROCKS of SEDONA are the SACRED TEMPLES of the ANCIENTS. Come join with Sakina to Bless and be Blessed. We gather at the time of the full moon to give Thanks to the Sky Father and Love to the Earth Mother and all their children." Time, date, and directions would be given.

We would meet at the trail-head at the appointed time, and walk down the trail to the White Bear medicine wheel. In my ceremonies I would have people stand around the outside of the circle, while I would enter from the east, the direction of beginnings. Sometimes I would have them come in and place something on the altar (a large stone) in the center; maybe a crystal, a ring, watch, or whatever, to be blessed. From 30 to 80 or 90 people would come to my Full Moon Ceremonies, and I would give a message to each one around the circle.

"The prayers that we say here, and the energy of this place, will be in that object, and at the end of the ceremony you can come in and retrieve it and take it with you," I told them. "When you go back home, you can hold it, tune in, and come back here in spirit anytime you want to."

Sometimes my dances would be very lively, with long fringe flying from my sleeves and suede skirt; and there might be a strong message in a resonant voice from an Ancient One, depending on who was using me to dance or speak through. The Lemurians would sing in a lovely high voice, and Great Chiefs would sound intense and powerful. I would give greetings and love to the elements, creature-beings, and the Star People. Sometimes I would get the people dancing, a friendship dance, around the circle, or perhaps pass the Talking Stick, so that each might have their say. Afterward I would give an individual message to each person standing around the outside of the circle from their Star Guardian or Spirit Guide. When my ceremonial partner Sundance was there, he would drum while I danced, and he often passed a pipe around.

I met Sundance about a year after I moved to Sedona, at the Monday Night Meditation group of Alon and Alina -- where some powerful healing often took place through our prayers, which were amplified by a large crystal in the center of the room. Sundance needed a place to stay, and I needed someone to help me move some things. "You can stay at my house as long as I'm there," I told him, "if you'll move my stuff into storage." I had realized that I couldn't afford to stay in the nice big house I was renting anymore, as I couldn't find a permanent housemate; so I decided to sell what I could, put the rest into storage, and travel in my Dodge van camper.

One day I said to Sundance: "It's a beautiful day, let's forget about working and go out into the canyon." We explored a trail new to me, and went up to what is known as Devil's Bridge. We called the red sandstone arch Spirit Bridge.

Sundance sat and meditated for a while, and I drew a picture of the scene. On the way back down the mountain, we stopped by a waterfall and embraced. We looked at each other, and both had a very clear remembrance of a previous life, when he was a mountain man and I was his Arapaho wife. The love between us was very strong, from many lifetimes together. We were soul-mates.

He looked much as he had before, as a mountain man: Clear blue eyes, reddish-blond hair and beard, tall and strong. I was dressed as I usually was, reflecting the Arapaho life, in a braided leather headband, fringed leather vest and skirt, and moccasin-boots. He was from Santa Fe and Tesuque, New Mexico, and he liked the silver and turquoise jewelry I wore.

Sundance had been given a few months to live when I met him, but we stretched it out to five years. He had a fatal disease, the White Man's Poison: Alcohol. So things went up and down for us, but he was wonderful when we were out in the canyons, which we loved to hike and to explore.

It was a difficult situation sometimes, as he turned into someone else when he drank, so different from the gentle man I loved. I talked to my dear Lakota friend Eloise about it. "Well," she said, "We were taught that even the bum in the gutter might be a Master with just one more lesson to learn, one more experience to go through." And that's the way I saw him. In his lucid times, he was sensitive, brilliant, fun, powerful and wise, and with a great healing power.

We loved to camp out and we traveled all over the West. If we passed ancient ruins, we would stop and do blessing ceremonies, to release any entities who wanted to go on. One time after we did a ceremony near Standing Eagle Rock (now called Coffeepot), Sundance said "They took me up, and showed me what it looked like from up there. They said our ceremonies are much more effective than we know, and that we should keep on doing them; they are very important for the balance of the earth." When we looked to the western sky we saw a dark cloud silhouetted against the white ones, in the shape of a running horse with a rider, hair flying out, and feathers flying from his lance. Sundance knew that he had a guide named Black Horse, and this was a message from him.

A friend named Feather first took me up to see Grandfather David Monongye, and I went back to visit him many times, to see how he and his family were doing. He was well over 100, and I would take food over to him and his wife Nora, as was the custom, and would often be invited to eat with them. I also brought water from a spring, since they had to go down the side of the high mesa to get theirs.

Grandpa David was visiting Sedona one time when he became very ill. I did my ancient blessing over him, and he said "Weren't you at my house last week?" "No, Kwaha (Grandfather in Hopi)," I replied, "but I was there a few weeks ago." When I went into the next room, he asked someone "Is the Hopi still here?"

I knew that he didn't see well but that incident told me that perhaps the language I sometimes speak, which I spoke in ancient times, is perhaps also still used in ceremonies or understood by some Hopi elders.

Sundance and I drove him back up to the ancient Hopi village of Hotevilla; he could rest on the bed in my van on the long ride up. Some friends met us up there -- they wanted to meet David, and later they camped out near Prophecy Rock, which has some petroglyphs on it. At midnight we looked up into the sky and saw stars connected by fine silver lines, like dot-to-dot pictures; it created hundreds of Kachinas dancing in the night sky, giving us a blessing!

Little Dove, Lakota Ancestor

After Grandfather David passed on, I would go up to see Grandpa Martin, Titus, Thomas, Chief Dan Evehema, Manual Hoyungowa, or other elders, on Third Mesa. Then I would go over to First Mesa to visit my other Hopi family, Roanna and Lewis (who call me Mom) and their kids, Valentino, Valencia, and Eagle Boy (Phillip), an eagle-dancer. They went through their hard times, like anyone, but usually they were warm and welcoming. I love them dearly.

Kachina dances were wonderful to watch. The Kachinas are Spirit Guardians, who watch over them. At times there were four or five hundred Kachina dancers doing their methodical steps and rhythmic chants, to maintain balance on the earth. In between the dances, at certain times in the yearly ceremonial cycle, enormous amounts of food would be brought into the plaza -- and distributed to the families around the square. Intricately carved and beautifully painted Kachina dolls that collectors would dearly covet were given to girls from an uncle, and bows and arrows went to the boys. Gift-giving is an important part of Hopi life.

To explain about how Hopi children learn about their Kachinas, most of whom are like guardian angels watching over them, I will tell you about the Pahana (non-Hopi) Kachina. All the little ones are told about him, and they know what kind of suit he wears, and what color it is; what kind of boots he wears; whether he has a wife; what animal is associated with him; what part of the world he comes from, and what time of the year he arrives. And they know that he brings gifts for good little boys and girls. (You figure it out.) They each have their story.

There was a lot of activity in the skies around Sedona in the 1980s. One day Grandmother Eagle said "Spirit says we should go out to the canyon and spend the night there. We are supposed to erect an etheric pyramid, to protect the area." A blond young woman named Mary went out with us. She had been saying "I want proof! If there really are space-ships, I want to see one." She was hoping that we might see something that night.

It had gotten dark when we headed out Dry Creek Road. Grandmother Eagle looked up at the Thunder Mountain range to the right and said "I didn't know there were houses up there on that mountain!" Then she noticed that there was horizon showing between them and the Nesting Eagle formation (they call it Lizard Head now). "Oh!" she added. "There aren't houses up on that mountain!"

296

It looked like there were three houses up there -- with four more up and over a bit to the right -- all lit up for a party! Orangish and yellowish light seemed to be pulsating from the 'picture windows' of what looked like seven houses, or maybe a motel. Then they shot off swiftly to the west.

"WOW!" said Mary, careening around the curves. "Wait for us! Wait for us!" By the time we got to the place of our overnight camp-out, the ships had gone up high, and looked like stars. Moving quickly, three went off in one direction, and the other four in another.

Grandmother Eagle was in a pup-tent, and I was lying outside, with a clear view of the sky. "At 1:30," I heard her say, "Something's going to happen." At 1:30 a.m., the seven came back, from the west, and then again three veered off in one direction, and four in another. At 6 am, 12 of them came back, and were seen by our friend on 'The 3 Warriors' hill. (Cockscomb.)

We were told that if twelve of us could work together in harmony for a year, coming out to this special place every week or so to touch in, that we would be given a very large crystal obelisk from Lemurian times to work with as a healing tool. Unfortunately we couldn't keep that many people working together on the project that long.

One night Sundance woke me up at four o'clock in the morning. "Wake up!" he said. "There's a space-ship outside!" I was instantly on my feet. He guided me to the sliding glass door at one end of our living room and we looked out. There above the cedar tree in our yard was what looked like a very, very bright star. As I watched, it slowly got smaller and smaller, and disappeared. It repeated this process three times.

"I was sound asleep when I heard a voice," said Sundance. "It said 'Get up! Go to the window. Look up!' So I did. It was even brighter then, ten times brighter than a star. Then it would go out, and then do it again. Three times. I wanted you to see it too."

Sundance had a strong connection with the Star People. When he finally left his body, he was dead for 18 hours. I thought he was in a coma, but a friend had seen his spirit go. A Star Person walk-in took over his body for a month, and then Sundance returned briefly. But that story is for my next book.

The Star People are the ones that usually speak through me when I do a reading, while I do their portrait by 'automatic drawing' so we can see what they look like. The ones I work with, of the Ashtar Command, are the ones who watch over us; they are our protectors, and are here to help. (A few E.T.s are here to take over; others, to observe.) When these galactic guardians feel that it is time for someone to know who they really are and why they're here, their Spirit Guides or Master Teachers will direct them to me to bring through a message.

A Star Guardian may be someone who was a loved-one in another lifetime, and the portrait is often of a Native American, who will say 'This is what I looked like in another earth-walk, when I was your brother, husband, sister,' etc.

Korton is the guy who 'told me where to go'. "Go and give our message in the kivas and lodges to the north, the east, the south, the west," he told me, through trance-medium Rev. Robert Short. "Tell them that changes are coming, but we will be there for them if they call upon us." Now why, I thought, would they listen to me -- they don't even listen to each other sometimes! But I have been to the four directions: throughout the U.S., Canada, the U.K.; Europe and Egypt; all around Mexico; and Hawaii. If I couldn't communicate with the Elders in person, I would call in a council and get in touch on an etheric level.

Cmdr. Korton is in charge of communications in this sector of the galaxy, I'm told, and there is a large Communication Center on the planet Jupiter. When I was still new to Sedona I went to a psychic fair and got a reading from a pair of intuitive people. Luis Romero painted a picture of my home planet, with other planets in the background, and his then-partner brought through a message from Korton. I didn't know who he was at that time, but he said that my cosmic name was Sakina, and that I should use it. It would be more powerful for me.

Indeed it was. At first I just used it to sign my art work; I thought it was too hard to remember. But my Osage friend, Tarisha, started calling me that, and pretty soon everybody did. When I went to Egypt with Heather Harder, I discovered that Sakina is also an Egyptian name.

I made friends with some of the merchants in the Kahn El Kalili Bazaar in the middle of Cairo, and when I walked along its narrow streets I would hear "Ma-dahm Sa-KEE-na! Come, have some sahk-lahb!" (Hot milk and honey; mmmm!) The name is similar to the Hebrew version, Shakina, which I understand means 'The Feminine God-Principle'. Nice.

I have been blessed with so many wonderful friends! And so many fabulous teachers have come through. Sedona is like the Graduate School of Higher Learning. Old friends from ancient times come here, and there is a recognition on a soul level. "Nice to see you again after all these millennia!" I tell them. Often they are Priests and Priestesses from Lemurian times, come back to touch in to the Sacred Place once again. I would sometimes sing a song from those times, to touch a chord of remembrance, or enhance spiritual awakening.

Harmonic Convergence, in 1987, was a special time on the planet. The Press wanted to know who was in charge, but they would be told 'No-one is!" Everyone just did their own thing. Groups would gather around to sing, dance, and pray for the healing of Mother Earth and her children - us. In Sedona, we had an all-night Long Dance, out in the canyon, and other ceremonies. Thousands of people came here from all over.

"When people come together at such times as Harmonic Convergence and World Peace Prayers, there is a great synergy of the individual lights that you are," the Star People told us. "The light shines far out into the universe -- and we rejoice!"

The Star People, or Intergalactic Federation of Free Worlds, have been in contact with Native Americans throughout the history of Planet Earth. "Almost all of the U.F.O. crashes have been on or near Indian Reservations," claims Hopi-Apache Morning Sky. "So if people want to know about E.T.s -- why don't they ask the Indians?"

His grandfather, as one of six young men in a remote area seeking a vision, got to a crashed U.F.O. before the soldiers got there, and rescued an injured Extra-Terrestrial. They called him Bek-Ti; Star Elder. He was able to communicate with them by means of projecting holograms into a flat round disc he wore, and in this way he told them the history of the galaxy from his perspective.

Morning Sky believes that the comet Hale-Bopp, or a later comet, may be the Blue Star of Hopi prophecy, which foretells the end of the Fourth World. When the Blue Star Kachina dances in the plaza un-masked in front of the uninitiated, according to prophecy, this will be the time that the great Purification of the earth will take place. Jonathan Ray Spinney calls planet earth the Blue Star. That is what it looked like to him when he had his spiritual experience of going out into the galaxy and looking back down at us. In his inspiring book 'The Awakening of Red Feather' (Medicine Bear Publishing), he gives a moving recounting of the Hopi vision of the Fourth World, how it flourished in peace and harmony in the beginning, and how it deteriorated because of greed and a loss of spirituality.

Many Native Nations tell of the Star People.

Lakota Grandmother Eloise had a friend named Jane, who was going up to Sedona from Phoenix one weekend. When Jane returned, Eloise said "Well, where did you go? What did you do?"

"I went to a place called Tu-zi-goot," her friend replied. "On, come on! There couldn't be a place with a name like that. Where did you go really?"

"No, really. 'Tuzigoot' means 'The Place of the Crooked Waters' in Apache. The remains of an ancient pueblo village are on a hill there, surrounded by a creek that snakes around below. There were over a thousand people living there, for hundreds of years. But then around 900 years ago, they just disappeared. No-one knows what happened to them."

"O-o-oh!" said Eloise, going into vision. "They were being raided, by the fierce tribes from the south! Then I saw them going into a little round thing, one at a time, and then they came out again. I said, 'But where are the old people? Where are the children?' And then I saw a BIG round thing come down, and they all went in; and then it went UP."

I heard a similar story from a different source, about the Mesa Verde cliff-dwellers in Colorado. They too were being raided by fierce tribes, and even their villages tucked into the side of tall steep canyon walls were no longer safe. So they went into the kiva with a secret tunnel into the heart of the mountain, and came out on top of the mesa. And they were taken up.

Not far from Tuzigoot, in the Sedona-Verde Valley area, there is what's left of a pueblo village called Honanki. When Clarion, a healer of Cherokee heritage, was visiting from California, Grandmother Eagle and I took her and her friend Delmary (an artist of extraordinary talent) out to visit the ruins. Clarion gave a clarion call to the discarnates of the place: her Cherokee chant echoed out over the valley, to call in, and then to release, earth-bound spirits.

Delmary needed to go back to town, to get back to her paintings of dolphin scenes, unicorns, people going to the Light, and Indian maidens with eagle and deer. Clarion went with her. I stayed and guided a young couple along the canyon trail to see more ruins, pictographs, and medicine caves; and Gran'ma Eagle went down and sat by a stream-bed to wait for us.

Grandmother Eagle was approached by the spirits of a dozen Yavapai Indians, who had lived there before. "We heard the call," one of them said, "and we came to see what it was about."

"Yes, that was to release any of you who wanted to go on to the above-world," replied Grandmother Eagle.

They were pleased that someone could see them. One of the young maidens stepped forward.

"I am Eh-ta-wa," she said. "Tell me -- there is something that we do not understand! When the soldiers came to our valley, in that other time, we befriended them. We showed them where to find the good water, we provided game for them, when they were sick or hurt we healed them and cared for them. We thought they were our friends.

"Then one day they came to our valley and said 'You must leave this place. Now!' So I stepped forward and I said, 'NO! We will not leave this place; this is our home!' So they SHOT me! And my husband stepped forward to defend me, and they killed him too. Why did they do this thing?"

Grandmother Eagle, who is very wise, replied: "Well, they were behaving like animals. Like the fierce bear who goes into a new territory and goes 'Ra-o-or-rr! This is MY territory now,' and he marks the trees with his claws, and says 'No-one can come in here unless I give my permission, or I will kill them!" And the soldiers were also doing what their chiefs told them; otherwise they, too, would be killed."

"Well, I thank you," said Eh-ta-wa. "Now we understand better."

"But now is a different time," Grandmother Eagle went on. "Now there are many people who have love and respect for ALL people. Sakina and Sundance travel all over the land doing ceremonies to honor the Ancestors, and bless all the children of Mother Earth and Father Sky."

Eh-ta-wa smiled. She sang a song of many verses. "I would like to travel with Sundance and Sakina, and do my dance, to show the people how we lived," she said. And then she demonstrated it, with gestures and motions: Giving thanks to Creator; grinding corn to feed the people; acknowledging the creatures of earth, water, and sky; the elements; the rain, the sun and moon. Sending love to the 2-leggeds, the 4-leggeds, crawling ones, finned, and winged ones.

In pantomime, Eh-ta-wa danced the stages of life, beginning with singing to the babe in arms; the toddler shaking its rattle; the maiden weaving and wearing her dress; the hunter bringing back a deer for his wife, who cooked it; women gossiping, and grinding corn; and the old one, bent over, walking with a cane, then lying down and, with a shiver, breathing his last breath. She then indicated the spirit going up to the sky... a pause... and then the spirit was coming down again, into the baby! -- as she smiled, rocked it in her arms, and sang to it.

I have performed the dance of Eh-ta-wa all over Turtle Island and beyond, spreading her message of good will and understanding. Sharing her gift: Her story of the ways of her people. When I do her dance, people tell me that I look much younger, for I become her.

In the early 1980s Sundance and I, with our Osage friend Tareesha and her family, gathered some rocks and built a sacred circle for prayer ceremonies. This Blue Star Circle was up on a hill overlooking Sacred Canyon in one direction, and looking up to Kachina Mama in another. There was a grandfather cedar tree and a grandmother cedar, and when I would take people there for a blessing, the Standing People (trees) would wave at me in greeting, before, and after, the ceremony.

One of the people I took there in 1990 was Heather Harder. Our mutual friend Jan had introduced me to Heather and her group from Indiana at the Coffeepot restaurant. It was Willie and his nine women; we teased him about having a harem, and he loved it! I took them all out to my special circle. I gave them each channeled messages to conclude the ceremony. When I came to Willie, I said "Greetings, Commander! It is time for you to begin your work upon this planet." Across the circle, Heather smiled. She had been telling him the same thing, he said later. Another commander, Ehr-tohn, said that my message to him from the Star People at a Full Moon Ceremony was his 'wake-up call' also.

The circle of stones is no longer there -- though the energy remains. When the area was changed from Forest Service to Wilderness Area in 1989, the policy became to leave the landscape in its natural state. No more medicine wheels! About that time Heather called and said "What do we have to do to get you to come to Indiana?" and I began traveling to other parts of the country to share what I have learned -- fulfilling the prophecy told to Little Dove by Oldest Grandfather: "One day the child of your child's child will return, to share our ways with all the tribes and Nations of Turtle Island and beyond. And she will be called Blue Star."

Dr. Heather Harder, incidentally, was a U.S. Presidential candidate in 1996. (She got about 30,000 votes in Texas alone.) She wants to return the government to the people, instead of the politicians, and make the Constitution work. What a concept! What fun it would be to have such an enlightened being at the helm of this great nation. She too has the blood of the Star People in her: Her mother came from Scotland, but there is Cherokee on her father's side, though they had to hide it, to survive.

When I came back to Sedona after my 1990 cross-country jaunt, during which I did ceremonies and teachings in Indiana and farther east, I went up to my special prayer circle up on the hill to say 'Thank you!' to my Spirit Guardians for a safe journey. I hung my fringed leather shoulder bag on a branch of the Grandmother Cedar tree, took my turtle-rattle and feather-fan out of my medicine bag, and began to dance around the sacred circle. I went around twice, singing a little song of gratitude. I was about to leave, when I heard a voice saying 'Dance around again.'

So I went around again. A little white butterfly fluttered through the circle. White -- the color of Spirit. 'One more time,' I heard. I danced one more time around. An orange butterfly drifted through this time, Sundance's favorite color. He had crossed over into Spirit the year before.

I looked up into the vivid blue sky that is so often seen over our crimson canyons -- and saw only one little white cloud there; it was ship-shaped. As I watched, it became smaller, and then disappeared... Like the Light 'ten times brighter than a star' had, that Sundance had shown me years before. The message was clear: 'Even if you don't see me, I am always there for you.' He is a Star-man now. Watching over me.

Magical Sedona! I had found my Soul-mate in the Sacred Canyons there. After he had crossed over in August of 1989, I did a send-off Full Moon Ceremony for him, with 65 people gathered around the big White Bear wheel. It was the most powerful one we ever did. Shortly after beginning, it started to rain. "Oh, well," I said; "it always rains during the Hopi Kachina ceremonies – that's what they're for! That gets rid of the tourists who don't want to get wet, and then the rest of us just wait and keep watching." But then I saw that the people were getting uncomfortable, so I said "Do you want to know how to stop the rain? Everybody stand up and raise your hands up high, and we'll ask it to stop." I had learned that from my musician friends, the Chambers Brothers, whose father was mostly Black-foot.

"I don't care what you do anywhere else," I told the Thunder Beings, "but please don't rain here during the ceremony!" And it didn't rain at the circle, though it poured all around it. Every time I mentioned Sundance's name, the low grey clouds overhead lit up brilliantly, with flashes of light!

I got the people dancing around the outside of the circle, and they built up a powerful vortex of energy; the Wind-Spirits got the Tree People dancing around wildly too. As soon as the ceremony was over, the rain came down in torrents!

It was a good Send-off Ceremony. Sundance is still often with me, watching over me, guiding me to special people, places and things. The love we shared will never die. I am most blessed.

I have had so many blessings so many wonderful people in my life. Heather Harder, who invited me to go to Egypt with her, where we did a gratitude and earth-healing ceremony at the Temple pyramid at Sakara and were in the Great Pyramid for the spring equinox; Grandmother Eagle, from whom I learned so much, and my Hopi, Lakota, Cherokee and Nava-jo friends; my Apache friend Billie Topa Tatay (Four Winds), who honored me in so many ways; Assiniboine Georgia and Morganstarr, with whom I have journeyed; and Satara, a French-Iroquois free spirit and Sirius walk-in who served as a guide at Palenque, Teotihuacan, and other sacred sites all around Mexico. Susan Drew, who invited me to do ceremony back in my other-life old home, the Tetons. And so many others.

Pete Jackson, a Pima tribal leader, teacher of wisdom and spirituality, has much to share. "I was riding to a ceremony down in Mexico with an In-dian friend one time," he related, "and he was very angry at White People. So I said to him, 'There were 65 million Indians a couple of hundred years ago, and now there are three million. Where do you think all those spirits are gonna go? Do you think they're gonna line up and wait for a couple of us full-bloods to get it on, so they can come through us?' He didn't say anything for a couple of hours.

"We come back into the bodies that are here. Have you ever noticed that some Indians act more like White people than we do?" I asked him.

"Or that SOME White people act more like Indians than we do? We trade places, so we can all learn different lessons!"

That's what it's all about. I've been told that some of the people who are suffering so much on the Reservations now are the ones who put them there. The Cavalrymen or the settlers who were so greedy for land or for gold. The ones who sold liquor to the Indians, to cheat them and force them onto bleak reservations, might come back to the 'rez' as hopeless alcoholics, to see what it is like to walk in their moccasins. And conversely, many Indians, who thought 'How can White People be the way they are?'-- come back in white bodies to find out. But they bring back a deep love of Mother Earth, and join in ceremonies to bring balance and harmony to her.

The Hopi people are dear to my heart. I was initiated into the clan of Robert Whitefeather Boissiere, a Frenchman who lived with the Hopi in the village of Sipaulovi for several years, many years ago, and who has written several excellent books about them. Whitefeather was working in the cornfields of his Hopi family one day when he stopped to rest -- and a Kachina appeared to him! The Spirit Being told him that he was to found his own clan, dedicated to following the Hopi way of living in peace and harmony.

Robert was excited when he went home that night and told his adopted family about his experience. "A Kachina appeared to me, and told me that I should start my own clan -- the Ba-na-na Clan!" he said, with his French accent. They looked at him -- and laughed. "You mean, the Ba-HA-na Clan!" they said, thinking he meant non-Hopi. In any case, I am one of the bunch of bananas. We pray in his kiva, near Santa Fe.

My traditional Hopi Elder friends worry about the coming times. There have been disruptions to their annual cycle of ceremonies to keep the earth in balance, and to their sacred shrines. The crops of corn and squash have failed, through drought or freezing rain. It is an omen from Maasaw, they feel, for many have not followed his original instructions: to live simply, in order that others may simply live.

Many people have heard of the prophecies of the end of the world. The Hopi were instructed to go to the 'House of Mica' (the U.N.) on the sunrise ocean, to warn the world that they should stop harming Mother Earth, and to live in harmony. Otherwise there would be a great cleansing and purification of the earth; by fires, floods, hurricanes, earthquakes, volcanic eruptions and such. And this has come to pass.

Indeed, I believe it IS the end of the world as we know it. But there is a better one to come! A world where all will recognize each other for their beauty, and appreciate each other's differences. What we need will be provided for us: we will not have to struggle, but just express ourselves to the greatest extent of our creativity. We will be loving Beings, aware of our One-ness with Creator.

"We've MADE it!" says the wise one Ra Sahn-del, who receives information from the Sirians. This is the first time, he contends, that a planet which has been given Free Will has been able to overcome the negativity of powerful egos, without the greed factor taking over completely. There are so many Light Workers here now that we are able to transmute the darkness into Light!

There will be some more earth-cleansing, he contends, but in a few years the many good-hearted ones will be raised up to the 5th dimension. By the year 2,012, we'll be slipping into something more comfortable: our Light-Bodies when we choose!

"We'll do it the spiritual way!" he says. Our DNA is rising in frequency; at a certain point you go from matter to antimatter; then you ascend. The next thing is God. But we need to live through emotion, experience through the heart.

"Live in the NOW... Stay in your power! Go by your own intuition; do what feels right to you. Go within, and listen to your inner voice," says Ra.

"No one person or group can be the savior." Each one must save themselves, he contends. Star People can give guidance, but they can't do it for you. The Hopi are here to hold the Light. Each clan was given a piece of the Truth, the Sirians say. If they can come together and work in harmony, they can have the power of the whole Truth, and create a standing columnar wave. Then we'll have free energy -- we'll live off the energy of the universe!

"Soon you'll begin to remember everything; it's all in your cellular memory. You'll be able to choose the body you want. What's important to remember is that the more people who think positively, the faster we will develop. Negative thoughts slow us down. The most important thing is UNCONDITIONAL LOVE! Making sure that you do not interfere with another's path, and do not harm anyone.

"There's a new awakening -- we'll have a Golden Age." I'm looking forward to it.

Go often into Nature, dear friends.

Send out your love. Listen -- your ancestors may be trying to speak to you.

I thank you, my dear ancestors! How often I have felt your presence, and benefitted by your guidance -- Little Dove, Long Bow, and Sara; Sitting Bull, White Eagle, and the others. I am grateful that you have given me your story, that I might share it with others who seek the path of Spirit.

Eh-yo-ta, Ahsh-ta-na ma-ka h'ney-ee-ta, yo ta-na ma-ka h'ney'eeta. Eh-yo, ma- eesh-ta, ma-ta-ka yo-na-ta, ah-na-ta. The Blessings of the Great Spirit be with you, and also with those for whom you have LOVE in your heart, as you go along your way -- though your path may twist and turn, and though you may encounter great obstacles, still you go in an ever-ascending spiral towards One-ness, with the Creator of All-that-is.

Mitakuye Oyasin! We are all One Spirit, and we honor 'All Our Relations'.

Hopi Kachinas are Spirit Beings; Star People, Cloud People. They can shape-shift into clouds. They watch over the People, whose prayers and ceremonies can bring the rain for the corn.

The Hopi say that when the Blue Star comes, it will be the end of the 4th World and the beginning of the Fifth. "In the 5th world, there will be Harmony. We'll all get along fine, and we'll all speak the same language," says Grandfather Martin of the Hopi.

In October 2012, near a Hopi 2nd Mesa village, I took a picture of the Full Moon. Above it was a ship – the Blue Star! My ship…

Star Knowledge

The film DANCES WITH WOLVES showed how Little Dove's Lakota People lived before they were wiped out by the Military, the U.S. Cavalry. Although they were originally Woodlands People, living in harmony with their natural world, in the Great Lakes area - they became the Buffalo Culture of the Great Plains when they were pushed further west by the tribes dislocated from their traditional lands by the Boat People. Those who had come across the eastern sea were hungry for land, and for Gold. When 'The-yellow-metal-that-makes-White-Men-crazy' was discovered beneath the Paha Sapa, the Sacred Black Hills of the Lakota, treaties were broken and indigenous peoples and their villages were destroyed, their Holy Places invaded.

A similar scenario took place in the film AVATAR. When a valuable ore was discovered beneath a place that was Sacred to indigenous People, the Military was sent in to destroy the habitat and the people who were in the way. But the Na'vi (Native) People who celebrated the One-ness of All Things came together, prayed to the Creator for assistance, and fought bravely to protect their land and their People - and this time, they WON!

Native Americans say that their Ancestors came from the Stars. The Cherokee say their ancestors came from the Seven Dancers, the Pleiades. Lakota Chief Golden Eagle has brought Star Knowledge to the people through conferences throughout the nation; Sakina Blue-Star has been a Presenter at several of them. Golden Eagle said that the ancient language Blue-Star speaks in her Blessing Ceremonies is Andromedan. The tall Blue Beings, like those in AVATAR, are from the Andromeda galaxy.

*Chief Golden Eagle wraps his eagle-wing
protectively around Sakina Blue-Star.*

I have had many wonderful teachers from many Tribal Nations. These are some of them. I am grateful for the wisdom they have shared with me.

Regarding the Lakota Sioux teachings in Chapter 7, Lakota Childhood, and elsewhere, I learned much about Lakota from Grandmother Eloise, sister-cousin of Wallace Black Elk (Wallace Black Elk; Sacred Ways of the Lakota, with William S. Lyon). Wallace and I were speakers at Expos in L.A. and Santa Fe, and I attended many inipi ceremonies with him and his family at Sedona and in Colorado and South Dakota. I took Wallace's sister Blue Star Woman (Lydia Ice) up to Ceremonies at their ranch across from the Wounded Knee Memorial site in the 1990s.

I am also grateful to Chief Golden Light Eagle, who started the Star Knowledge Conferences, for his vast wisdom – and his humor! And to Grand Chief Woableza, thanks for quoting my son Chip's friend Chief Arvol Looking Horse: "If someone is saying bad things about somebody – just don't listen to them!"

Little dove's people lived on the Northern Plains, in the way shown in the classic film 'Dances With Wolves', in harmony with the natural world. Wallace Black Elk, my Lakota cousin, was brother to Jim Beard. When Jim came to my house, I showed him Stan Matrunick's portrait of Little Dove. "That's my great-grandmother Little Dove, I told him. "Oh yes, I know about her," he said. "You do?" I asked him. "Did one of my friends tell you about her?" "No, I've read about her. Little Dove was captured, lived in a fort...." That's right. So I didn't just make it all up, as some might think. She's out there somewhere in Book Land.

Many Cherokee wisdom teachings were learned from Dhyani Ywahoo, and from Grandfather Thundercloud. I was his partner in Medicine Wheel Ceremonies and teaching sessions throughout the Northeast: New York state, upper New Jersey, on Cape Cod in Massachusetts, and in Vermont at Dhyani's 200-acre Retreat. She is the spiritual leader of the Eastern Cherokee, who hid in caves and escaped being taken away to Oklahoma on the Trail of Tears. She is author of 'Voices of our Ancestors, Teachings from the Cherokee Wisdom Fire'. (Shambala, Boston & London). Some of the teachings in Little Dove, Lakota Ancestor maybe be found in her book.

Thundercloud was a dear friend, a Cherokee elder who had a Trading Post and taught about Native ways throughout the Northeast. He and I did some teachings about Native wisdom and Star Nation Ancestors at Dhyani Ywahoo's place in 1992. There are chapters about us at that Retreat in the French book "Les Guardiens de la Terre", by Rachel and Jean-Pierre Cartier. Thundercloud later came to visit me in Arizona, where he did presentations, ceremonies and healings. He was featured in the book 'Immortal eyes', by Danielle Vargo, a horse-whisperer from Hawaii, who brought him to my house in Sedona for a healing session. He was called Chief Thunder in the book. (I was called Shining Star.)

I also learned a lot from Cherokee medicine man Willie White-feather, author of 'Desert Survival for Kids' and creator of the short film 'Hope', which was shown at the Sedona Film Festival in 2006. His Cherokee friend Al Butler taught me about the original people of this area, and what they called the rock formations before the White people came.

Medicine woman Grandmother Golden Eagle shared much wisdom passed on from her Cherokee heritage when we went out into the Sacred Canyons of this holy place called 'The Crystal City of Light', now Sedona. The Star People ancestors would sometimes show themselves in spectacular ways. Her story of her great-grandfather Chief Zzalee in Chapter 16, was a true one; he is a historical figure. We found a picture and text about him in one of my large books about American Indians.

ACKNOWLEDGEMENTS

Commander Ashtar image, Page 228: The portrait of Cmdr. ASHTAR is the first channeled Spirit Guardian pastel portrait by Sakina. The small portrait inset into the lower right corner was by Celaya Winkler, and is on the cover of the book ASHTAR.

I am grateful to Sandra Bowen, an Intuitive Extraordinaire, who told me about my Native American heritage that I wasn't already aware of. "Well, your grandmother came into the room!" she said. "She wanted you to know."

I wish to acknowledge Georgia White, who grew up in Montana on the Assiniboine Reservation, and her daughter Morganstarr, a Captain in the U.S. Air Force, formerly advising the Generals in the Pentagon, and now stationed in California, for their vast knowledge. They spent many years in Saudi Arabia, where Georgia's Cherokee-Egpytian husband worked as an Engineer with the Navy.

Chapter 9, pages 117-125: Some information about Col. Stand Watie was taken from George Turner's booklet 'Book of the American Indians: True Tales of Great Warriors. (1972, Baxter Lane Co., Amarillo TX).

Chapter 18: Some of the information in this chapter, referenced to augment my past-life recall, imagination, etc; Place names, dates, family names, etc., came from a book about Chief Sitting Bull titled 'the Lance and the Shield –The Life and Times of Sitting Bull' by Robert M. Utley, an New York Times Notable book.

Page 80: "Tomorrow is a mystery, the past is history..." quote, I am told, once appeared in one of Eleanor Roosevelt's 'My Day' columns, c. 1949.

Bill Hale, who had been an editor for the Los Angeles Times, Newsweek and other such illustrious publications for many years, kindly offered to edit my manuscript in its early form, as a gift. I was delighted; his suggestions were very helpful, but then he became too busy to continue. Anyway, thank you, Bill.

Little Dove, Lakota Ancestor

Post-Script, August 2010.

Summer Bacon is a bright, attractive young woman who serves as a channel for an Entity known as Dr. Peebles, who brings forth profound wisdom as well as practical advice, often peppered with wit. He may provide guidance for coming directions in a person's life, console the bereaved by connecting them with a Loved-One-on-the-Other-Side, or simply answer questions sent up, for large or moderate audiences.

Summer Bacon

In 2009, I sent up a question: "Can you tell me anything about my book?" I was wondering if 'Little Dove, Lakota Ancestor' was going to get published. The answer that came: "The story you wrote helped greatly to heal generations!" Future generations, I thought? I wrote it because I thought the ones to come, my children and grandchildren, might want to know about their heritage. Native people think about those to come, unto the 7th generation. But Dr. Peebles was speaking about the ones before; the ones I wrote about.

Apparently my telling their story helped to put their spirits at rest. Little Dove had had to hide her deep sorrow, after her family and all the people she knew were killed off in such a cruel way, and to have to live with those responsible for their deaths. Even after she moved to the South, with a loving husband, and lived a comfortable life - she had to live in denial of who she really was, and her daughter Sara also suffered from this pretense after it was discovered that she was "an Indian — an ignorant savage!" So, in telling their story and showing the beauty of the Indigenous ways, and their wisdom teachings, it apparently helped to give peace to the spirits of my ancestors. And perhaps someday my grandchildren will want to know about their heritage.

About Sakina Blue-Star

Sakina is a Ceremonialist, Spirit Portrait Artist and Story-Teller. She has traveled widely throughout the United States, Mexico, Canada, the UK, Europe and Egypt doing ceremonies and sharing Native American wisdom teachings learned from her friends of many Native Nations. She has two sons and two daughters, who live in Colorado and Denmark, and 4 grandchildren.

Sakina may be contacted at:

Sakina Blue-Star, P. O. Box 3601, West Sedona, AZ 86340

To email her please use links at:
http://www.littledovelakotaancestor.net
http://sakinabluestar.wordpress.com

You may also view color images from the book at the above web sites.

The eBook version can be ordered at in a wide variety of formats at: www.smashwords.com

Right: Sakina's wedding picture from the 1950s

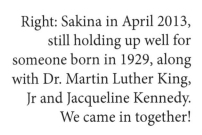

Left: Sakina Blue-Star as she appeared in 1975: Her native heritage was beginning to emerge.

Right: Sakina in April 2013, still holding up well for someone born in 1929, along with Dr. Martin Luther King, Jr and Jacqueline Kennedy. We came in together!

Made in the USA
Monee, IL
27 July 2021